The
Snow Angel

Dilly Court is a No. 1 *Sunday Times* bestselling author of fifty novels. She grew up in North-East London and began her career in television, writing scripts for commercials. She is married with two grown-up children, four grandchildren and three beautiful great-grandchildren. Dilly now lives in Dorset on the Jurassic Coast with her husband.

To find out more about Dilly, please visit her website and her Facebook page:

www.dillycourt.com
f /DillyCourtAuthor

Also by Dilly Court

Dilly Court

The Snow Angel

HarperCollins*Publishers*

HarperCollins*Publishers* Ltd
1 London Bridge Street
London SE1 9GF

www.harpercollins.co.uk

HarperCollins*Publishers*
Macken House, 39/40 Mayor Street Upper
Dublin 1, D01 C9W8, Ireland

First published by HarperCollins*Publishers* 2024
1

A catalogue record for this book is available from the British Library

ISBN: 978-0-00-858079-7 (HB)
ISBN: 978-0-00-858080-3 (PB)

This novel is entirely a work of fiction.
The names, characters and incidents portrayed in it are
the work of the author's imagination. Any resemblance to
actual persons, living or dead, events or localities is
entirely coincidental.

Typeset in Sabon Lt Std by HarperCollins*Publishers* India

Printed and bound in the UK using
100% renewable electricity at CPI Group (UK) Ltd

This book contains FSC™ certified paper and other controlled
sources to ensure responsible forest management.

For more information visit: www.harpercollins.co.uk/green

In loving memory of
Irene Elizabeth Dornan Cox

Chapter One

Although it was still mid-afternoon it was getting dark and the heavy cumulus clouds threatened snow. After she had done the rounds of the sick, the poor and the needy, it was the biting east wind, together with the thought of tea and freshly made crumpets laced with butter that made Rose race on ahead. She glanced over her shoulder to see her elder sister, Marianne, following at a more sedate pace. Rose smiled to herself. Always calm and proper, Marianne would not run even if the Devil himself was after her. As the eldest of the vicar's three daughters, she considered it her responsibility to set a good example. Rose was quietly rebellious, and their younger sister, Emily, managed to get her own way in more or less everything.

1

The square, castellated tower of St Michael's church came into view, with flickering candlelight shining a welcome from the tall windows, and bell practice at full strength. However, it was not the familiar place of worship, nor the sprawling Georgian vicarage where Rose and Marianne had been born and raised, that had attracted Rose's attention. She stood in front of the carefully constructed wooden replica of a stable with the well-used plaster figures of Joseph and Mary leaning over the manger. There were a couple of bedraggled-looking sheep huddled in the background, but what had caught Rose's attention was the fact that baby Jesus had been ousted from his bed of straw, and a skinny youth had somehow managed to fit his lanky body into the crib.

Rose waited until Marianne caught up with her. She held her finger to her lips. 'Look, he's asleep,' she said in a low voice.

Marianne picked up the oil lamp that illuminated the scene and held it higher in order to get a better view. 'He's barefoot, Rose,' she said in disgust. 'He must be freezing in those rags.'

'We can't leave him here.'

'I don't think we should wake him. He might be violent or a runaway criminal. Perhaps we should get Mr Huggins to wake him up and advise the fellow to move on.'

'He obviously can't walk any further, Marianne. Look at the blisters on the soles of his feet. I expect they're why he chose to sleep here.'

'What would Papa say if he saw such desecration of a holy tableau?'

'That's the point. It is just a representation, but the poor boy looks half-starved. We can't leave him here, Marianne.'

'If you're so concerned you'd better cover him with some straw. I'm cold and it's started to snow. I'm going home.'

'I'll go and fetch Mr Huggins. I expect he's in the church, setting up for Midnight Mass.'

'Do what you wish, Rose. As always.' Marianne walked on, clutching her cloak even more tightly around her as the snow began to fall in swirling white clouds.

Rose opened the lych gate and made her way between the towering yew trees, which were said to have been planted when the church was first built. She had trodden this path so many times in her twenty years of life that she could walk it blindfold. The heavy oak door, banded with iron, creaked and groaned as she thrust it open and Ron Huggins, the verger, looked up from tidying the hymnals.

'Is anything wrong, Miss Rose? You look a bit flustered.'

'Is my pa here, Mr Huggins?'

'He's in the vestry, or he was a few minutes ago. He was having a chat with the bell-ringers. Miss Jones has fallen out with Mr Finch.'

'Again?' Rose shook her head. 'Don't worry, Mr

Huggins. You know they'll patch it up – they always do.'

'We can but hope. Did you want anything special, miss?'

'You'd better come with me, Mr Huggins. I'll fetch Pa when he's sorted out his quarrelling bell-ringers.' Rose did not wait for his answer and she hurried out into the snowstorm, her feet crunching on the icy flakes already settling on the dry ground.

Huggins followed her, grumbling about the weather and the prospect of a wild-goose chase, but he came to a halt in front of the Nativity scene and his jaw dropped.

'The cheek of it,' he said angrily. He poked the sleeping youth with the toe of his boot. 'Oy, you, get up. You're on Church property. Have you no respect?'

Rose leaned over the boy. 'His breathing is ragged, Mr Huggins. I think he's sick.'

'We don't want no foreigners bringing disease to the village. I'll call the constable. He'll know what to do.'

'No, please don't do that. First of all, we need to get him somewhere warm and dry.'

'If you're thinking of my cottage, I can tell you that Mrs Huggins wouldn't stand for it, miss. You know how she can be when she gets into one of her moods.'

The whole village knew when Martha Huggins was in one of her rages, and wise people took cover.

Rose thought quickly. 'Pa would want us to look after him. Could you pick him up and carry him to the vicarage, Mr Huggins?' She could see that he was not convinced. 'It's Christmas Eve and it's snowing. He'll die if he's left here all night.'

'He might be a Frenchie, come to spy on us, miss. I don't want to have anything to do with the likes of him.'

Rose shrugged off her cloak and laid it over the inert figure in the crib. 'Stay here then, and I'll run and fetch my pa. He will know what to do.' She could see the wheels of Ron Huggins' mind turning slowly. The Reverend Matthew Bottomley Northwood was the noblest of men, but he could be impatient at times. Rose was only too aware of this and she knew that Huggins had witnessed several such outbursts over the years and would not want to be the target of one himself.

'You're right, Miss Rose. Seeing as how you've sacrificed your warm garment to the boy, you'd best run and fetch the vicar. I'll stay here and make sure the young felon doesn't suddenly rise up and cause mayhem.'

Rose ran back to the church and found her father and the bell-ringers about to disband.

'What's wrong, Rose?' Matthew Northwood asked, frowning. 'You're wet through. Where's your cloak?'

'You must come, Papa. There is a young fellow asleep in the manger, but he's obviously unwell.'

'Is he a village boy?' Miss Jones demanded suspiciously. 'If he comes from the town, he might be a criminal.'

'Not all city dwellers are villains, Miss Jones.' George Finch, ringing master, occasional organist and local solicitor, glared at Miss Jones as if daring her to argue.

'I say we go and take a look.' Ned Guppy, the village baker, turned to Mr Northwood. 'What do you say, Vicar?'

'Of course we must help this poor soul in need.' Matthew Northwood took his black cloak from a wall hook and wrapped it around his shoulders. 'You had better stay here, Rose. You can't go without the proper attire for such weather.'

But Rose was already out of the door. She picked up her skirts and ran into the blinding snow. Huggins was waiting for them, but she could tell by his expression that he was not happy.

'I wanted to call Constable Dent, Vicar. But Miss Rose said you would want to take this fellow into your home, whoever he is.'

Mr Northwood bent over the inert figure. 'Wake up. Tell me your name.' He straightened up. 'Mr Finch, if you would kindly take the boy's feet, and you, Huggins, take his head and shoulders, we can get him into the vicarage.' He shot a warning look at Huggins, who had opened his mouth as if to protest. 'I will then consider what must be done.'

Miss Jones and Ned Guppy had followed them and were watching on with interest.

'He was obviously up to no good,' Miss Jones said gloomily.

'You can't know that for certain.' Rose faced her angrily. 'He needs help and it's Christmas Eve. Perhaps we should all be more generous to each other.' She walked on behind the oddly assorted procession.

'Vicar! Are you going to allow your child to speak to me in that tone?' Miss Jones hurried after them.

'Rose is right, Miss Jones. We should all be more charitable, whether it's Christmas or any other time in the year.' Mr Northwood marched towards the vicarage, leaving Miss Jones to stomp off in the direction of the small cottage where she lived with her aged mother and a large, ferocious tom cat called Spike.

Minutes later, the unfortunate youth lay on the slightly threadbare sofa in the morning parlour. Ron Huggins and George Finch had returned to their respective homes, leaving the problem squarely with the vicar and his family. Marianne hovered in the doorway with Emily, while Rose rushed around fetching pillows and blankets to cover the still-unconscious youth.

'He looks very dirty,' Emily said in a loud whisper. 'Mama won't like it if he makes the upholstery filthy. He might even have fleas.'

7

Mr Northwood was standing with his back to the fire, stroking his grey beard as he always did when perplexed. 'If you can't say anything sensible, I suggest you go and sit with your mama, Emily. You, too, Marianne, and please say nothing of this. I don't want her upset any more than she is already at this time of the year.'

'Very well, Papa.' Marianne shooed Emily away from the door. 'Should I tell Cook there will be one more for supper?'

'I don't think this fellow will be dining with us.' Rose looked up from arranging the pillows beneath the boy's head. 'But you could ask Cook to warm some milk. Maybe that, with a tot of brandy, will help bring him round.'

'I'll be as quick as I can. I just hope that Emily doesn't say too much in front of Mama.' Marianne left the room closing the door behind her.

'Your mama's nerves always get the better of her at this time of year,' Mr Northwood said, sighing. 'She has never been able to accept the fact that your brother is no longer with us, which is why I do not want her to see this boy. Felix would have been about this age, had he lived.'

Rose could feel his pain, but her father was not a demonstrative man and he would disapprove of any physical show of emotion. Felix had drowned while trying to save a young friend who had fallen through the ice on the boating lake at The Manor. Rose would never forget that Christmas Eve six years ago, nor the ensuing grief that had left their mother prone to fits of megrims and bouts of illness that kept her confined to her bed for weeks at a time, particularly in the festive season.

'Perhaps we should send for Dr Buckingham?' Rose suggested tentatively.

'Excellent idea, Rose.' Mr Northwood reached for the bell pull by the fireplace. 'I'll tell Winnie to fetch him. He might have an inkling as to this fellow's identity.'

Rose laid another blanket over the boy. 'He's still very cold, Papa.'

'I don't see what else we can do. Anyway, I have a few notes to write for my sermon tonight. Stay with him, Rose. I'll speak to Winnie myself.' Mr Northwood opened the door just as a young maidservant was about to enter.

'Winnie, I want you to go to The Manor and ask Dr Buckingham to visit. Tell him it's a matter of some urgency.'

Winnie craned her neck to see round Mr Northwood's corpulent figure. 'Is he the one what was in the crib, Vicar?'

'That's none of your business, Winnie. Now do as I say, please.'

'Yes, Vicar.'

Rose found herself alone with the patient and she stoked up the fire before pulling up a stool to sit beside the sofa. 'Who are you?' she asked in a low voice. 'What brought you to Abbotsford in the first place?' She looked up at the sound of footsteps and Marianne entered the room with a glass in her hand.

'How is he? Has he said anything yet?'

'No. He's still the same.'

'Cook warmed some milk for him, but Papa keeps the brandy locked in a cupboard. I can't get to it.'

'He's afraid that Mama might find it again. You know what happened last time she had an attack of nerves. And it's Christmas Eve – we should expect the worst anyway.'

'I won't forget last year in a hurry. Thank goodness for Dr Buckingham.'

'Winnie has gone to fetch him. He should be here any minute.'

Rose smiled. She knew that Marianne had a soft spot for Dr Buckingham, although she would not admit it. Rose also suspected that Dr Buckingham was rather fond of Marianne. He was always very prompt when it came to calling on anyone poorly at the vicarage, and today would be no exception, even if it was Christmas Eve.

Marianne placed the glass of milk on a side table and went over to the window, pulling back the curtain. 'It's still snowing. I doubt if many people will make it to Midnight Mass. At least the doctor hasn't far to come.'

'That's if Lady Buckingham allows him to come out in such bad weather,' Rose said, giggling. 'That woman is such an old dragon. I wonder that her son chooses to live at home.'

'He's duty bound to look after his mama, with his father away on government business. You know that, Rose. You just like to tease me.'

'I pity any woman who marries into that family. Lady Buckingham is a termagant. She'll make a terrible mother-in-law.'

Marianne tossed her head. 'She's always been perfectly sweet to me, Rose. It's your imagination, or perhaps you offended her in some way. You do sometimes speak before you think.'

'Yes, I admit it's one of my faults, although I do try to curb my tongue most of the time.'

'Not often enough, obviously.' Marianne peered out of the window. 'I see lantern light – that must be him coming now. He must have walked.'

'He must have run to get here so fast. Better check your appearance in the mirror, Marianne.'

'Why? What's wrong? Have I a smut on my nose or something?' Marianne rushed to look in the wall mirror, smoothing her glossy dark blond hair into place, her hazel eyes bright with anxiety.

'No, I was just teasing. You look beautiful, as always,' Rose said, smiling.

Both her sisters had similar colouring and Emily would no doubt grow into a beauty. If pressed, Rose would describe her own hair as 'fair', although someone had once likened it to the colour of ripe corn, and he had said her blue eyes were like the sky on a summer's day. She had laughed and told him not to be silly.

'Go and let him in,' she added hastily. 'Don't keep the poor doctor standing outside in the snow, or Winnie, either.'

Marianne hurried from the room and Rose waited anxiously. It would be so sad if the young man died without regaining consciousness. She stood up as the doctor entered the room.

'Well, this is a to-do, isn't it, Rose? Finding an unconscious boy in the middle of the Nativity scene must have been a shock for you.' Tom Buckingham came to a halt by the sofa. Even though she had known him for most of her life, Rose could still appreciate his classic handsomeness, and his innate good nature. Tom pushed a lock of dark brown hair back from his forehead and leaned over the patient. 'So this is the poor fellow, Rose? I'd only just come home from doing my rounds when Winnie came to fetch me, but I passed Miss Jones in the street and she told me you'd found a French spy in the crib.'

Rose laughed. 'That is silly. He's just a young man who has obviously fallen on hard times, for whatever reason. I'm worried because he is still very cold and he hasn't opened his eyes once since I found him.'

'Since *we* found him,' Marianne said hastily. 'I was there, too, Rose.'

It was on the tip of Rose's tongue to correct her, but she did not want to embarrass her sister in front of Tom Buckingham. 'Yes, you were there, too. That's what I meant.'

Tom pulled the blankets back and checked the boy's pulse. 'Yes, he is very cold, but I'll give him a full examination, if you ladies would like to leave the room?'

'Of course.' Rose hustled Marianne out into the hall and closed the door.

'It will be awful if he dies,' Marianne said in a low voice. 'Another death so close to Christmas seems like an ill omen.'

'I'm sure that Dr Buckingham will bring him round, and then we'll find out who he is and reunite him with his family, if indeed he has one.'

'If anyone can save him it's Tom.' Marianne clasped her hands, her eyes shining. 'He is wonderful, isn't he, Rose?'

'Yes, he's handsome and a good doctor. Added to those qualities, he's a nice man. What more could you wish for in a husband, Marianne?'

'Stop teasing me. You'll make me blush when I see him and then I'll feel foolish.'

'Forget what I said.' Rose gave her a hug. 'We have more important things to think about at the moment. For instance, how are we going to keep this young man's presence a secret from Mama? At least until the New Year, if he makes it that far.'

Marianne sighed. 'I don't know, Rose. Christmas is difficult enough without having any extra worries. We'll have to hide our presents and open them in secret, unless Mama takes to her room, which looks very likely this year. So how are we going to stop Mama from finding out about this fellow?'

'It won't be easy, but we could put him in the bedroom above the coach house. We can look after him there until he is well again.'

'I swore Cook to secrecy, but Winnie is a chatterbox.'

'Luckily she can't go very far while the weather is like this, so hopefully the gossip won't spread around the village.'

'You're forgetting that Ron Huggins knows, as well as George Finch and Fanny Jones. I doubt if the men will talk, but Miss Jones will tell everyone she sees at church in the morning.'

Rose sighed. 'Then we simply have to keep it from Mama for as long as possible.' She turned as the parlour door opened and Dr Buckingham beckoned to them.

'The young chap has a fever and he shows signs of having been severely beaten. I also suspect that there might be a couple of fractures, but I will have to examine him more thoroughly. We need to get his temperature down first.'

'Do you know him, Tom?' Rose asked eagerly.

'No. I've never seen him before, although I'd say by the state of his shirt and breeches that he's recently been in the sea. He might have come from a wrecked ship or maybe he fell overboard from a vessel and managed to swim ashore. There are grazes on his legs that could have come from being washed up against rocks.'

'A shipwrecked mariner,' Marianne said dreamily. 'How romantic.'

Tom smiled indulgently. 'Maybe, but you need to take care, all the same. We know nothing about him or how he might behave when he regains consciousness. My main concern is that he could develop pneumonia.'

'We can take care of him,' Rose said stoutly. 'Just tell me what to do.'

'First of all, he needs to be put to bed and sponged down with cool water.' Tom lowered his voice. 'Does Mrs Northwood know about this, Rose?'

'No, and we have to keep the boy a secret from her. This is a bad time of year, if you understand what I'm saying.'

'Of course. That's what I thought. I would suggest taking the fellow to the nearest hospital, but the journey would be virtually impossible in this weather. The snowstorm is turning into a blizzard.'

'I was thinking of putting him in the room above the coach house,' Rose said, frowning. 'But it hasn't been used for years and we'll need to light a fire and air the bed.'

'There's a spare room in the servants' quarters.' Marianne moved to the doorway. 'I could get Winnie to make it ready, if you wouldn't mind carrying the patient upstairs, Tom?'

He nodded. 'Of course. Maybe someone could sit with him until he regains consciousness. He might be in some distress.'

'I'll do it,' Rose said firmly.

'What shall I tell Winnie?' Marianne asked anxiously.

'You stay here with Tom,' Rose said, smiling. 'I'll deal with Winnie and Cook.' She turned to Tom. 'Will you stay for dinner?'

He shook his head. 'I would love to, but Christmas Eve is something of a tradition in the Buckingham household and my mother is very strict about keeping that. I'll stay long enough to see the young fellow tucked up in bed, and you may send for me at any time, day or night, if you need me.'

'You are so kind.' Marianne sank down onto a chair by the fire. 'I wonder who he is,' she added, gazing at the inert figure on the sofa. 'He might have a family desperate to know his whereabouts.'

'We'll find out when he wakes up,' Rose said, firmly. 'Let's hope he hasn't escaped from prison or something of the sort.'

She left the room and was crossing the entrance hall when she saw their mother descending the staircase, looking ethereal in a voluminous white wrap trimmed with lace.

'Mama, are you all right?'

'My head is pounding, Rose. And I have terrible palpitations. I need to see Dr Buckingham or I fear I will die from anxiety.'

Rose hurried to her mother's side. 'I understand, Mama. Let me take you back to your room and I'll send for the doctor. He will give you something to make you feel better.'

16

'Nothing will heal a broken heart, Rose. You don't know how I suffer.'

'Of course not, Mama. I wish I could do something to ease your pain.'

'You are a good girl, Rose. I rely on you to look after your sisters. I just want to sleep until the festive season is at an end.'

Rose guided her mother upstairs and along the landing to her room. She settled her back in the large four-poster bed with its tapestry tester and faded brocade curtains.

'I'll send Winnie up with a cup of warm milk, Mama.'

'I need to see the doctor, Rose. My poor heart is beating so fast I can scarcely breathe.'

'Yes, Mama. Please try to sleep.'

'A few drops of laudanum in the milk will help.'

'I will see what the doctor says, Mama.'

'Hurry, Rose. Please hurry.'

Chapter Two

Rose sat up all night with the unfortunate youth. The room at the top of the house, next to the one where Winnie slept, was cold despite the fact that a fire had been burning in the grate for several hours. Outside the blizzard seemed, if anything, worse, judging by the amount of snow on the windowsill. Rose had taken time to attend Midnight Mass, but she had hurried back to the patient, who was still deeply unconscious. His temperature continued to be high and he had begun to babble incoherently. Rose bathed his forehead with a wet flannel, but there was little else she could do for him. She toyed with the idea of sending for the doctor a second time, but that would entail asking Winnie to brave the terrible weather. Although it was only half a mile or so to The Manor, the roads would be treacherous, and too dangerous for anyone even to think of going out until daylight.

Rose found herself drifting off to sleep and she awakened with a start to discover that the fire had burned low. She added more lumps of coal and returned to her chair, but a low moan from the bed made her jump to her feet and hurry to the patient's side. His eyes were closed but he was babbling again, although she could not make out the words. She took hold of his hand, stroking it in an attempt to share some of her warmth with the boy. He was burning up with fever and yet his hands were icy.

'I don't know who you are,' Rose said in a low voice. 'But you are safe here. You are with friends. I just wish I could help you.' She did not expect an answer and the boy remained unconscious. All Rose could think about was losing her much-loved younger brother on Christmas Eve. She could still recall the terrible shock and disbelief that she and all the family had felt then. Even now it was hard to accept that Felix was gone from them forever. He had been such a lively, fun-loving boy, full of mischief and afraid of nothing, which had been his downfall. He had saved a life but had lost his own in doing so. Rose leaned closer to the unconscious youth, wondering if there was a family somewhere longing to hear from him.

Almost as if he sensed her distress, his eyelids flickered and opened. He stared up at her.

'Who are you? Where am I?'

Rose pulled the coverlet up to his chin. 'I'm Rose.

Don't be scared. You are safe now. We'll look after you.'

'Sadie?'

'No, I'm Rose. Is Sadie your sister?'

'Sadie likes roses.' The boy closed his eyes and drifted back to unconsciousness.

Rose sighed. He had seemed almost reasonable, yet it was obvious that the fever had overtaken his malnourished body and it was impossible to know what he had gone through before he took shelter in the crib. However, the fact that he had briefly regained consciousness must be a good sign. Rose could not wait to tell Tom Buckingham, although whether he would be able to get away from his domineering mother on Christmas morning was another matter. She resumed her seat but the silence was broken by sounds coming from Winnie's room. Rose realised that it must be six o'clock, the time when Winnie went downstairs to the kitchen to riddle the embers of the fire in the range and put the kettle on to boil for early morning tea. Cook was very particular about routine and getting things done on time.

Rose was tired, hungry and thirsty, and she decided to go down to the kitchen. She must remind Winnie that the boy's presence was to be kept secret from Mrs Northwood at all costs. Rose liked Winnie and appreciated the fact that she worked hard, but Winnie had very little common sense, a very bad memory and a tendency to gossip. Rose went downstairs to the kitchen and found Winnie trying desperately to coax the banked-up embers of the fire into flames.

'Oh, Miss Rose. I'm sorry I can't get this blooming thing to light.'

Rose smiled tiredly. 'Let me try. Fill the kettle and we'll make tea.'

'I'm supposed to do that, miss.'

'There's no law that says I can't help you.' Rose walked over to the range and rolled up her sleeves. She glared at the cold stove. 'I don't want any argument from you, you lump of black-leaded cast iron. We need hot water for tea and we need it now.' Rose set to work riddling the embers and adding small nuggets of coal until the flames leaped into action. She straightened up. 'There, Winnie. It just took a little bit of persuasion.'

Winnie grinned. 'I never saw the like, but please don't tell Cook that you had to help me. I'll get a clip round the ear for sure.'

'It's our secret. And that reminds me, Winnie. You must not tell anyone about the young man we found asleep in the Nativity scene, especially my mama. You know how she gets at Christmas each year, and why that is.'

'Yes, Miss Rose. I knows and I won't say a word.' Winnie solemnly crossed her heart.

'I know I can trust you. I'll wait for my tea and then I'll return to the patient, although I might have to send you for Dr Buckingham again. I'll see how the boy is progressing before I decide.'

Winnie glanced out of the window. 'I think it's stopped snowing, miss. I don't mind the walk to The Manor, but we all have to go to morning service.'

'Yes, of course. We'll arrange it somehow, and the boy might be better after a night's sleep.'

'Yes, miss. I hope so.' Winnie made the tea and filled a cup for Rose. 'Here you are, Miss Rose. I don't mind going to The Manor, really I don't. They have a huge Christmas tree in the entrance hall, covered in glass balls and tinsel. We never have one here, do we?'

'Anything that reminds Mama of the festive season is too painful for her to bear. It's a small sacrifice, but a necessary one.'

'They have roast turkey and plum pudding, even in the servants' hall. My friend Betsy is a scullery maid there. She says—'

Rose picked up her cup and saucer. 'I'm sure that Lady Buckingham is an excellent employer in her husband's absence abroad. She is a very capable woman.'

'Will you be down for breakfast, Miss Rose?'

'I expect so. Maybe one of my sisters will take over at the patient's bedside for a while so that I can have something to eat. Anyway, I'd better go upstairs and check on the boy with no name. I'll take my tea with me.'

Back in the attic bedroom Rose found that nothing had changed. The young fellow was still feverish, and he lay on the bed, tossing and turning. She made up the fire and sat sipping her tea as she wondered what to do next. The boy needed to see the doctor again and she tried to work out the best way to get Tom Buckingham to the house without causing undue comment. Despite the weather, there would be many people making their way to church for the Christmas morning service, and news of the boy's mysterious arrival and illness was probably already in the public domain. Miss Jones would almost certainly have broadcast it to whoever would stop to listen.

Rose looked up as the door opened and Emily peered into the room. 'May I come in?'

'Yes, of course. He hasn't got anything contagious, as far as I know. What is it, Em?'

'Marianne and I are just about to have our breakfast and exchange our gifts. Please come down and join us. It won't be the same without you.'

Rose sighed. This had been their Christmas morning routine ever since the tragedy. Cook made them a special breakfast, which included porridge laced with sugar and plenty of rich cream, crisp bacon and a mountain of scrambled eggs, together with warm muffins, butter and a choice of honey, marmalade or apricot jam. Such a meal was only served on special occasions as the girls normally breakfasted on porridge and toast with a scraping of butter. It was not that their father was mean, but a vicar's stipend was not overly generous and he had no other form of income.

'I'm starving, Em, but I don't think I should leave him in case he regains consciousness and finds himself alone in a strange place.'

Emily moved a little closer to the bed. 'He spoke to you?'

'He seemed to want someone called Sadie. He said that she liked roses and then he drifted away again.'

Emily shrugged. 'That doesn't make sense. Anyway, please come down for a little while, Rose. I have a special present for you. I can't wait to see your face when you open it. We could take turns in coming up here to check on him, if you are so worried.'

Rose needed very little persuasion. Hunger was getting the better of her and she doubted if she could remain awake if she were to stay by the boy's bedside any longer.

Marianne was waiting for them in the dining room. The table was laid with the best silver and Marianne had done her utmost to make it festive with tinsel and glass baubles, which would normally adorn a Christmas tree. Candles had been lit in the silver candelabra, regardless of expense, and small gifts wrapped in brown paper and tied with coloured ribbons were set at each place.

Rose clapped her hands. 'This looks wonderful, Marianne. You must have been up very early to do this.'

'To tell the truth I did it last evening when I was

sure that Mama had retired for the night. Anyway, how is the patient?'

'He spoke to Rose,' Emily said eagerly. 'He knows someone called Sadie, who likes roses.'

'How odd.' Marianne went to the sideboard and helped herself to porridge, cream and sugar.

Rose followed suit. 'He wasn't conscious for very long. We do need to get Tom to have a look at him as soon as possible.'

Marianne took her place at table. 'I'd go for him myself, but you know how delicate my constitution is, Rose. I don't want to come down with a chill, especially now.'

Emily filled a bowl with porridge and emptied the cream jug over the contents, adding a generous amount of sugar. 'I'll go. I love the snow, and anything is better than staying in this dreadfully dull house on Christmas Day.'

'Don't say things like that, Em.' Marianne paused with a spoonful of porridge close to her lips. 'Have some respect for Mama's feelings, please.'

'I'm sure she didn't mean it that way.' Rose motioned her younger sister to sit down. 'I think it's a good idea, Em. After breakfast you must wrap up warm and walk to The Manor. No one will think anything of it as it's Christmas morning.'

They settled down to eat their porridge and had only just finished when Winnie sashayed into the room carrying a platter of bacon and scrambled eggs with a rack of toast balanced carefully on the side.

Rose jumped to her feet and went to the sideboard where she opened one of the cupboards and took out a handful of gifts, one of which she handed to Winnie.

'Merry Christmas, Winnie. It's just a little present, but I hope you will find it useful.'

Winnie's eyes filled with tears as she deposited the food on the table and took the present from Rose's hand.

'Open it,' Emily said, laughing. 'If you could see your face, Winnie . . . You look so shocked.'

'I weren't expecting nothing,' Winnie said, sniffing. She opened the package and took out a small white cotton handkerchief. 'Thank you, Miss Rose.' She stared at it in amazement. 'It's got my initials on it.'

'It's just a small gift, Winnie. I embroidered the letters myself. If you've seen my other attempts at needlework you will understand that it's a small miracle they are legible.'

'I dunno what to say, miss.'

'There's a present from me, too, Winnie.' Marianne held out another small parcel and Winnie took it, this time unable to stop the flow of tears as she unwrapped a length of blue satin ribbon. 'It matches your eyes, Winnie,' Marianne added, smiling.

'I haven't got you anything,' Emily confessed, shamefaced. 'But if I should get some toffees or peppermint creams from anyone, I will share them with you.'

'Ta, miss. I love toffee.' Winnie clasped her gifts to

her flat chest and backed out of the room. 'Ta, again. I'm ever so obliged.'

'Just remember not to say anything to anyone about our guest,' Rose called after her. She sighed. 'News of him will be all round the village by midday. That girl means well but she cannot keep her mouth shut for more than a couple of minutes.'

'Never mind her, let's open our gifts.' Emily tore the wrapping off her presents. 'Thank you, Rose. It's beautiful.' She held up a string of green glass beads. 'I love them.'

'Now open mine,' Marianne said, smiling indulgently.

Emily unwrapped her other present with a cry of delight. 'Thank you, Marianne. It's so pretty.'

'Let me see.' Rose leaned over to examine the brightly painted wooden box lined with pink satin. 'That really is lovely. You will be able to keep all your jewellery in there.'

'Now you, Rose,' Marianne said firmly. 'Then me.'

Rose exclaimed over a small painting of a red rose that Emily had executed in watercolour. 'I will have to find a nice frame for this, Em. You are very talented.'

Emily blushed and smiled modestly. 'Yes, I know I am, but I'm glad you approve.'

Marianne's present was a pair of silk stockings. Rose gazed at her sister in amazement. 'This is too much, Marianne. These must have cost you most of your allowance.'

It was Marianne's turn to blush. 'Actually, they were a gift from Great-aunt Margaret and they are too small for me. I only tried one on, Rose. I never wore them.'

'It doesn't matter. They are a welcome gift. I have only thick cotton stockings, but these will be for best. Thank you, Marianne. But I'm afraid my present to you pales in comparison.'

Marianne carefully unwrapped her gift, taking care not to tear the paper. 'A book of poems. Thank you, Rose. You know I love poetry.'

'And mine now,' Emily added eagerly.

'Another of your beautiful paintings. Am I a pink rose, Em?' Marianne held the painting up for Rose to admire.

'Yes, I suppose so. Although you and Rose are so alike, except for your eyes, you could be twins. I'm the plain one in the family.' Emily reached for the platter and helped herself to bacon and scrambled eggs.

'Nonsense, Em,' Rose said firmly. 'You will eclipse both of us one day. You take after Grandmama Northwood. If you look at the painting of her in Papa's study you will see the likeness.'

'Yes,' Marianne added hastily. 'She was reckoned to be a great beauty. You will grow into your looks.'

Emily stabbed the bacon with her fork. 'You're just saying that to please me.'

'Don't be grumpy, Em.' Rose smiled. 'You are beautiful and I am starving. Let's enjoy our special

Christmas breakfast.' She tucked into her food, momentarily forgetting about her patient, but suddenly the door opened and the half-naked youth stumbled into the dining room. He came to a halt, leaning heavily on a walking stick he must have picked up from the hall stand. He stared dazedly at each of them in turn.

'Where's Sadie?' he demanded as he collapsed onto the floor.

Rose pushed back her chair and leaped to her feet, as did Marianne and Emily. They crowded round the boy, but he was unresponsive to their attempts to rouse him again.

'Oh heavens! What will we do now?' Marianne stared down at him aghast. 'We'll never get him back upstairs unaided.'

'His right ankle is very swollen. I don't know how he managed to walk on it.' Rose could see that someone needed to take control of the situation. 'Emily, you said you'd go to The Manor.'

'Yes, but I haven't finished my breakfast.'

'Never mind that. You can eat it later. Put your outdoor things on and go as quickly as you are able. Tell Tom what has happened.'

Emily gazed longingly at the food on her plate, but she nodded. 'All right. No one runs faster than I do. I'll be back before you know it.' She raced from the room, leaving the door to swing shut after her.

'What do we do in the meantime?' Marianne clasped her hands as if in prayer.

'I'll fetch a blanket and a pillow. We will just have to make him comfortable on the floor until Tom arrives, and we'd better hope that Mama stays in her room all morning.' Rose did not wait for an answer, but headed upstairs to her own bedroom, where she stripped a blanket off the bed and took one of her pillows. She returned to the dining room to find the boy motionless and in the same position on the floor.

Marianne was standing by the window, looking out into the snow-covered front garden. She turned her head to give Rose a worried glance.

'I wish they would hurry.'

'You know Tom. He'll come as soon as he can.'

'That dreadful mother of his might stop him. You know what she's like, Rose.'

'Yes, I do. But Tom would always put his patient first.'

Marianne sighed. 'Yes, of course. He's a good doctor, but I'm worried as to what Papa will say if he comes home between services and discovers that we've kept the boy here.'

'He will think we've done the right thing.'

'But not if Mama gets to hear of it, especially at this time of the year.' Marianne paced the floor agitatedly.

'Calm down. You won't do any good by fretting, Marianne. We'll make the room above the coach house ready for the boy, and then it will be much easier. Maybe he'll regain consciousness and be able to tell us who he is and where he comes from.'

Marianne came to a halt as the door opened and Tom Buckingham strode in, bringing with him a gust of cold air. Emily followed him and went straight to the table to finish her breakfast.

Tom went down on his knees beside the boy. After a brief examination he stood up again. 'It's likely that he has a broken ankle, although I can't be sure. It could be a very bad sprain. And he's still feverish. Emily told me that he came round for long enough to speak to you, Rose.'

'Just a few words, Tom. He wanted someone called Sadie and he said she liked roses. That was all.'

'That doesn't help us,' Tom said, frowning. 'Where do you want me to take him, Rose?'

'I think he'd best stay in the room on the top floor until the weather improves. Then we'll put him in the old coachman's accommodation.'

Tom smiled. 'It sounds as if you're expecting to have him here for quite a while.'

'You're the doctor, but even I can see that he's weak and poorly nourished.' Rose took the blanket and Tom lifted the boy in his arms.

'You don't think his fever is contagious, do you, Tom?' Marianne asked anxiously.

He shook his head. 'As far as I can tell, he's half-starved and suffering from exposure. He's obviously been very ill-treated. However, if he doesn't respond to treatment I will take him to the hospital as soon as the roads are passable.'

'We'd better get him upstairs before Mama awakens. If she realises it's Christmas Day I think she will keep to her room, but you never know.' Rose opened the door and checked to make sure that no one was coming. 'All clear, Tom.'

When the boy was safely tucked up in bed, Rose went back downstairs and said goodbye to Tom, who had another call to make in the village. He promised to return later in the day, or sooner if the boy's condition changed or if Rose was worried about him. Then it was time to go to morning service, but Rose decided she should stay with the patient in case he came to again and started to wander. Marianne and Emily agreed with her so quickly that their relief was obvious. Cook and Winnie were also to attend the service and that left Rose to see to her mother's needs, if required, as well as taking care of the boy. She waved everyone off and checked on her mother, who was resting in an armchair by the fire in the large, comfortable but shabby bedroom.

'Dr Buckingham has given me laudanum for my nerves, Rose. Will you measure out a couple of drops and add water, please?' Grace Northwood fixed her daughter with a pleading look that would have been hard to resist even in normal times.

'Yes, of course, Mama.' Rose took the small medicine bottle from the mantelshelf and poured the required dose into a glass of water, which she passed to her mother.

'It's stopped snowing, Mama, but the roads are very treacherous, so I am told.' Rose tried to sound conversational but she knew that her mother was not really listening.

'Yes, dear.' Grace sipped the laudanum mixture. 'I will be glad when spring comes.'

'Yes, Mama. Perhaps you might feel like going out when the weather is warmer.'

'Maybe, but now I am drowsy. You may go, Rose. I think I will take a nap.'

'Ring your bell if you need anything, Mama.' Rose left the room and went up to the top floor to check on the boy, who was still lying with his eyes closed as before. She was unable to settle and she put on her cloak before going out of the house through the kitchen. She crossed the snow-covered yard and made her way to the coach house. The trap had not been in use for a couple of years as their horse was too old to work and had been put out to pasture in a field belonging to the neighbouring farm. These days the Reverend Matthew Northwood did his rounds on foot, or if he was called to an outlying farm he would borrow a horse from The Manor stables. Lady Buckingham was very generous when it suited her, especially if it could be known she was the one doing the lending.

Rose made her way upstairs and found the room cold, dusty and with cobwebs hanging from the rafters. However, it was nothing that an energetic and thorough cleaning would not make right. The single bed needed only a mattress and clean bedding to be quite suitable for the patient. The grate was clean and it only required Winnie to bring coal and kindling and to light a fire, although it would probably take a couple of days to bring the room up to temperature and chase away the dampness caused by disuse.

Rose made her way downstairs and was about to leave when a shadow fell across the doorway. She froze, wondering who could be wandering around in this weather and when most of the local people would either be in church or at home, cooking the festive food.

She stepped back into the shadow of the trap and held her breath, hoping that the stranger would go away, but a tall male figure filled the doorway. He was clad in a dark cloak and a wide-brimmed hat. The lower part of his face was covered in a neatly trimmed beard and moustache, but the rest of his face was in deep shadow.

For a moment Rose thought he had not seen her, but he took a step closer and seized her by the arm.

Chapter Three

'Don't be afraid. I won't hurt you.'

Rose snatched her arm free. 'Who are you? This is private property.'

'You're very bold for someone at a disadvantage, young lady.' The man took a step backwards, looking her up and down. 'Are you a servant here?'

'What business is that of yours?' Rose demanded angrily. 'What do you want with us?'

'Nothing, miss. I'm looking for my young brother.'

Rose eyed him suspiciously. 'It's Christmas Day and the roads are virtually impassable. Why would your brother be here?'

'That, I think, is my business. Have you seen a stranger in these parts recently? It's not a difficult question.'

'The real question is why are you looking for your brother in an old coach house?' Rose eyed him suspiciously. 'That's very odd behaviour. People usually knock at the front door and announce themselves or make enquiries within. They don't go skulking around like criminals.'

There was a tense moment when Rose feared she had gone too far, but she faced him squarely, which, to her annoyance, seemed to amuse him.

'You are no housemaid. Who are you and why were *you* skulking around in a deserted building on Christmas morning?'

'I have every right to be here, which is more than I can say for you, sir. I don't wish to speak to you.' Rose went to walk past him but he barred her way.

'Not until you answer my question, Miss Whoever-you-are.'

Rose held her ground. 'I'll respond to you when you tell me what I want to know. Perhaps the village constable is a more suitable person for you to question.' She waited for what seemed to be a long time and then he nodded.

'Very well.' He took off his hat with a flourish and his startlingly blue eyes twinkled. 'My name if Benedict Rivers, and I am here to look for my errant brother, Jago.'

Despite her initial anger, Rose felt herself weakening. Benedict Rivers was undoubtedly the most attractive man she had ever met, but that did not excuse his behaviour. His boat cloak was stained with salt and his weathered complexion suggested that he might spend as much time at sea as on shore.

She was not entirely convinced by his story, but they could be going round in circles for ever if she did not answer him. She took a deep breath.

'I'm Rose Northwood. My father is the vicar here, which is why everyone is at morning service.'

'Everyone except you, Miss Northwood. Might I enquire why that is?'

'My mother is an invalid, sir. I stayed behind to look after her.'

'And yet you are out here in the bitter cold.'

'If you think your brother might be hiding here, I suggest you look for yourself. When you are done perhaps you should try elsewhere.' Rose sidestepped him and walked away with a measured gait, resisting the temptation to run.

She entered the house through the kitchen and closed the door. She would have bolted it but for the fact that Cook and Winnie would be returning from church very soon and they would be locked out.

Rose went straight to the boy's room on the top floor. He was asleep but his breathing seemed a little easier, or perhaps she was simply desperate to see an improvement in his health. His face was deathly pale but with bright spots of feverish colour on his cheekbones. His hair was so fair it was almost white, but his long, thick lashes formed dark crescents on his pale cheeks. If this boy was Benedict Rivers' lost brother there seemed to be no family resemblance to confirm his claim, and no explanation from Rivers as to why his brother might be in such a poor state of health. Rose decided that she had done the right thing by refusing to reveal the patient's whereabouts. When the fever abated and the boy was able to speak for himself, he would confirm or deny that they were related. Something was not right, and Rose was determined to find out why Jago Rivers – if that really was his name – had been found semi-naked, injured and feverish in the crib on Christmas Eve.

The sound of doors opening and shutting and subdued voices announced the return of the family, and Rose went downstairs to greet them. She was surprised and pleased to see that Tom had accompanied them.

'Tom escorted us home,' Emily announced proudly. 'It was a lovely service, Rose. Such a pity you missed it.'

'How is the patient?' Tom asked in a low voice. 'Has there been any change, Rose?'

'Come into the morning parlour,' Rose said urgently. 'I have something very odd to tell you all.'

Marianne slipped off her cloak and untied her bonnet strings. 'What is it, Rose? You look quite flushed. Are you feeling well? I mean, you haven't caught anything from you know who, have you?'

Rose shook her head, but she refused to speak until they were in the parlour with the door firmly closed. 'I don't want Winnie to hear me,' she said hurriedly. 'I was in the coach house, having checked the room to see what needed doing, when a stranger walked in.'

'No!' Marianne clasped her hands to her mouth. 'On Christmas Day and in such awful weather.'

'The roads are virtually impassable for vehicles,' Tom added. 'He must have walked a long way.'

'Or maybe he came by boat and landed on the beach.' Emily looked from one to the other. 'It's possible. He could be a smuggler or a Frenchman.'

'He wasn't French but, for all I know, he might be a smuggler,' Rose said hastily. 'He was quite rude and abrupt, but I stood up to him.'

'Weren't you afraid?' Marianne asked anxiously. 'I would have been.'

'Did he threaten you in any way?' Tom frowned. 'We should let Constable Dent know straight away.'

'No, not really. He was a bit aggressive at first but I didn't let him see that I was scared. He said he was called Benedict Rivers and he was looking for his younger brother, Jago. I didn't tell him about our boy.'

'Why not?' Marianne demanded, frowning. 'They might have been reunited and the boy taken to his real home.'

'If it was true.' Tom met Rose's concerned look with a frown. 'You obviously didn't believe him, Rose.'

'I didn't know what to think and I still don't. It's possible he was telling the truth, or maybe he was the person that the poor boy upstairs was running from.'

'And only he can tell us.' Tom made a move

towards the doorway. 'I'll go and check on him. But I think you were right, Rose. There is something very odd going on here.'

Rose sank down on a chair by the fire as the door closed on him. 'Thank goodness for that. I was really afraid that I had done the wrong thing, but somehow I knew he wasn't telling me the truth.'

'How exciting.' Emily's eyes sparkled with pleasure. 'It's brightened up a dull Christmas Day. We have a real-life mystery to solve, just like in books.'

'I don't know about that,' Rose said slowly. 'The poor boy was obviously terrified of something, and someone has treated him badly. If Benedict Rivers is his brother, he should be ashamed of himself.'

'Whether or not that is true, it doesn't help us in our situation.' Marianne sank down on the sofa. 'Do we continue to hide the boy? We might be in the wrong by doing so.'

Rose patted her on the shoulder. 'Don't upset yourself, Minnie. Let's wait until Tom has examined him.'

'Don't call me Minnie. I hate that silly nickname.' Marianne managed a weary smile. 'As if it isn't bad enough having to creep around on Christmas Day so that we don't upset Mama, and now we have a sick boy in our house, who might be related to a man who terrified you, Rose.'

'I wasn't terrified, Marianne, just a bit scared at first.'

Emily slumped down in a chair by the fire. 'Don't start arguing. If you ask me, I think we should send for Constable Dent. I don't like the sound of that man you saw this morning, Rose. He might still be lurking outside, waiting for one of us to go out and then he'll do his worst.'

Rose laughed. 'That's ridiculous, Em. Even for you and your fertile imagination. Save such things for your journal.'

'I will, thank you, Rose. One day I'll be a famous author and then you'll wish you had been nicer to me.'

'Don't be so touchy, Emily.' Marianne shook her head. 'It is Christmas Day. We should all be nice to each other.' She turned to Rose. 'But I do think that Em has a point. We don't know anything about Mr Rivers, and we certainly don't know where he is at present.'

'He might be dangerous,' Emily protested. 'He might break into the vicarage and take the boy by force.'

Rose and Marianne exchanged worried glances. At fourteen Emily was still very young for her age, although Rose blamed their mother for mollycoddling her, especially after the devastating loss of their brother. Their father, although still loving in his own way, had seemed to withdraw from family life after Felix died. He was devoted to his parishioners and endlessly patient with his wife, but Rose sensed a deep and enduring grief in her father that even his strong faith could not quite overcome. She still mourned for her brother and she tried hard to be strong for her sisters. It was never easy, and today, so soon after the anniversary of their brother's death, they were faced with what might turn out to be yet another tragedy if their patient failed to recover.

'I can't wait for Tom to come down,' Rose said impatiently. 'I'm going up to the boy's room to find out how he is doing.'

Marianne opened her mouth to protest, but Rose left the room and headed for the stairs. Inactivity was not in her nature and the meeting with Benedict Rivers had unsettled her even more than she cared to admit, even to herself. She crept past her mother's room and made her way to the top floor. The door was ajar and she opened it further, peeping inside.

Tom turned his head as if sensing her presence. His expression was serious. 'Come in, Rose. You won't disturb him.'

Rose's hand flew to her mouth. 'Oh, no! He's not . . .'

'No, he's not worse. I'm sorry, I didn't mean to alarm you, but he's no better. I will take him to the hospital when the weather improves. However, as it is, we will have to care for him here. Do you think you will be able to do so?'

'Yes, of course. He must stay here in the warm until he recovers. I don't think it would be a good idea to make up the bed in the coach house at the moment.'

'I agree, especially with a strange man lurking around. I'll see if I can find out anything about the person you described. Someone in the village might have knowledge of him.'

'Rivers is not a name I recall,' Rose said thoughtfully. 'Do you think he really could be this boy's brother?'

'It's possible, but the poor young fellow must have had a reason to run away. Looking at the state of him, I think he hasn't been well cared for, and there is considerable bruising on his back. It appears that he's been whipped at some point.'

Rose shuddered. 'That's awful. Poor boy.'

'I've strapped up his ankle and he must keep his weight off it for quite a while.'

'He won't be able to run away, then.'

'I agree, but we must keep open minds about him. It could be that he is a criminal and was escaping justice. Until he recovers consciousness we won't know.'

'I choose to think the best of him, Tom. He doesn't look like a villain.'

'Whether he is or not is immaterial at the moment. He has a high fever so I suggest you get one of the servants to sit with him. He should be bathed at regular intervals with cool water.'

Rose laughed. 'I don't think Winnie would be any use there. She would probably drown him.'

'Will you do it then? I can't imagine Marianne tending to such personal matters.'

'I will take care of him, Tom. But I'd be grateful if you would look in again tonight, just to make sure I am doing all I can.'

'Of course I will. In the meantime, I suggest that you keep an eye on him and try to get him to drink a little as soon as he is able.' Tom was about to leave the room but he hesitated. 'He will need some fresh clothes. I doubt if I have anything suitable.'

Rose frowned. 'There are Felix's old garments stored in a trunk in one of the attic rooms. He seems to be about the same age as Felix was when we lost him, so I dare say they would fit. It's better to find a use for them rather than allow the moths to feast on the material.'

'If you're sure?'

'Yes, I'll see to it. Please don't worry. Go home and enjoy the rest of Christmas.'

'My mother did suggest that you and your sisters might care to join us for luncheon, Rose. But I didn't like to ask in case it upset Marianne.'

'I'm sure both Marianne and Emily would love to go home with you, Tom. It's very hard on them to see everyone celebrating the festive season except us. It would do them good.'

'But what about you?'

'I'll be here for Papa when he comes home from church. He'll understand, and I'm sure he will be very grateful to Lady Buckingham for her kindness. Please give her my apologies.' Rose hoped she sounded positive and not a little envious. The thought of

44

forgoing roast turkey and all the trimmings followed by a rich plum pudding flamed in brandy was almost too much to bear, but she could not leave Jago or her father. She managed a smile. 'Go home, Tom. Take my sisters with you.'

He nodded and stepped out onto the landing, closing the door behind him.

Rose turned back to the boy, who was mumbling feverishly. 'Don't worry, Jago. I'm here to look after you.' She plumped up the pillows and, having made sure that he was not in danger of falling out of bed, she went downstairs to see that her sisters had accepted Tom's invitation to luncheon. It would be just like Marianne to refuse out of a sense of duty, and Emily would follow suit, albeit reluctantly. However, it was a relief to glance through the window in the entrance hall and see them arm in arm with Tom as they made their way down the front path to the road. Wrapped in their warm cloaks, and with fur-lined bonnets to keep the cold wind off their faces, they looked happy, and although she could not hear them, Rose was certain they were laughing and chatting as they slipped and slid on the frozen snow. At least they would enjoy a break from the solemnity and sadness in the vicarage for a while. It was hard not to envy them, but Rose was determined to crush any such feelings as she made her way to the kitchen.

Winnie was in the scullery crashing pots and pans about, and Cook was sitting by the range sipping a cup of tea. She stood up guiltily.

'Miss Rose. Is there anything I can do for you?'

'No, Cook. Please sit down. I just came to tell you that it will be just myself and Papa for luncheon, and Mama, of course, but she will take her food in her room.'

'Miss Marianne and Miss Emily are not here?'

'Lady Buckingham invited them to The Manor for luncheon.'

Cook sighed. 'I remember the days when we had the largest goose you've ever seen and apple sauce as well as Cumberland sauce, followed by Christmas pudding and custard.'

'Well, I'm sure you have something very tasty for all of us, but what I came to say also was that the young man upstairs might need something like soup or gruel when he regains consciousness. I didn't want to spring it on you, when you have quite enough to do as it is Christmas Day.'

'I appreciate the thought, Miss Rose. I have some chicken stock that would make a good broth, or I could make some beef tea. How is the poor fellow?'

Rose pulled up a chair and sat down at the square pine table, which was laid out with military precision, ready to serve the family meal.

'He is quite unwell, Cook. I will be sitting with him when I have taken my meal with Papa.' Rose bit her lip, wondering whether or not to warn the servants about Benedict Rivers. He had probably gone on his way, but she could not be certain.

46

'There's something I need to tell you, Cook, but I don't want you to be alarmed.'

'It takes a lot to upset me, Miss Rose.'

'I went to the coach house to see if the room would be suitable for our guest. I was about to leave when a strange man walked in and said he was looking for his younger brother. I didn't trust him enough to tell him about the boy upstairs. I think he's gone, but tell Winnie to be careful if she goes outside for any reason.'

'Lord help us! Whatever next, and in this weather, too!'

'The man said his name is Benedict Rivers and his younger brother is called Jago. It might be true, but if so, why didn't he simply knock on the front door and ask?'

'You didn't like the look of him, miss?'

'No, although I'm not sure why. Anyway, I think I did the right thing by keeping quiet about the sick boy. Had Mr Rivers come knocking on the front door and announcing himself properly I might have given him a different answer.'

'You think he was the one the boy was running away from?'

'I don't know, but it's possible. I don't think Rivers is actually dangerous, but if you see him, please say nothing.'

'You can trust me, Miss Rose.'

'I've asked Winnie to keep his presence here a secret, but I don't know how long she will hold to that.'

'She's not very bright at times, miss. I'll have a word with her.'

Rose pushed back her chair and stood up. 'Thank you, Cook. I knew I could rely on you. This is a difficult time for all of us and always will be. Anyway, Papa will be home soon and I'll take luncheon with him. What have you got for us today?'

'Roast beef and vegetables, miss. Followed by treacle tart and custard, your papa's favourite.'

'Excellent as always. Thank you.' Rose left the kitchen and was on her way to the dining room when her father entered the house, his hat and overcoat laced with snow. He took them off, shaking the flakes onto the polished wooden floor.

'It's started again, Rose. We'll be snowed in if it goes on for much longer.'

'Let's hope for a miracle then, Papa.' Rose took his damp coat and hat from him and laid them over a carved oak chair. 'Come into the morning parlour. It's nice and warm in there. Would you like a glass of sherry wine before luncheon?'

'That would be more than welcome, my dear.' Matthew gave her a tired smile. 'I shouldn't say so, but I am always glad when Twelfth Night arrives and we are already into the New Year.'

He wandered across the hall and entered the morning parlour, leaving Rose to go to the dining room and pour two glasses of sherry from a decanter on the sideboard. She took a sip from one of them and felt the warmth of the sweet wine running through her veins. It was unlike her to drink at any time, least of all at noon, but this was not just any day. She would have to explain why her sisters had accompanied Dr Buckingham into the dragon's den at The Manor. Rose smiled to herself: if Marianne followed her heart and married Tom, she would have a mother-in-law if not from hell then from a very similar place.

Fortunately for Rose her father was too preoccupied to question her further when they sat down to luncheon and she explained why Marianne and Emily were not present. He smiled vaguely and ate his meal in silence. Rose was glad when the last crumb of treacle tart had been eaten and her father left the table.

'I had better go upstairs and make sure that your mama is all right, Rose. This is a very bad day for her.'

'Yes, Papa. It's a difficult time for all of us.'

He came to a halt in the doorway. 'How is the young fellow? What have you done with him?'

A vision of the boy being left out for the dustcart flashed into Rose's mind. However, she managed to keep a straight face. 'He's feverish, Pa. Dr Buckingham is taking care of him.'

'I'll pray for the boy. When the weather permits we must make an effort to find his family.'

'Yes, Pa. That's what I was thinking.'

'Precisely.' Matthew wandered out into the passage that led to the entrance hall and his footsteps echoed off the high ceiling as he made his way to the staircase.

Rose waited until she heard her mother's door open and close before she went upstairs to the room on the top floor. She found that the boy's condition had changed little although his fever did not seem to be any worse. She settled down to sit at his bedside and moistened his lips with water when he became too restless.

It was early evening when Marianne and Emily returned from The Manor, accompanied by Tom, who went upstairs to examine the boy, leaving the sisters seated around the fire in the drawing room.

'So how was luncheon?' Rose asked, trying not to laugh. She could tell by their set expressions that it had not gone easily.

'Lady Buckingham talked and talked,' Emily said, yawning. 'I feel tired just thinking about it. I have no idea what she was saying, but it went on and on.'

'Lady Buckingham is a very clever woman.' Marianne folded her hands primly in her lap. 'She was speaking about the current state of political affairs and it was very interesting.'

'You don't mean that, Minnie,' Emily said, pouting. 'It was so very boring. You would have agreed with me, Rose.'

'Probably, but I am not enamoured of Lady Buckingham's son.' Rose shot a sideways glance at Marianne. 'You are very fond of Tom, are you not?'

Marianne tossed her head. 'There's nothing wrong in that. We've known each other since childhood. And don't call me Minnie, Em. You know I hate it.'

'And I don't like being called Em.'

Rose raised her hands. 'Stop it. You sound as if you are still in the schoolroom. I'm sorry, Marianne. I should not have said that. Of course you are fond of Tom, as are we all, and it's very good of him to care for the boy. You didn't tell Lady Buckingham about him, did you?'

'Of course not,' Marianne said hastily. 'As a matter of fact, I think we know where the poor fellow came from, and possibly your strange man, too.'

'Yes,' Emily added excitedly. 'There's a ship anchored offshore. We saw it as we walked to The Manor, and we could see the lights bobbing about and reflecting off the water on the way home.'

Rose was suddenly alert. 'That would explain the sudden arrival of Benedict Rivers. His cloak was salt-stained and he had the look of a man who spends time at sea.'

'What does that look like?' Marianne rolled her eyes. 'You have such a vivid imagination, Rose. I never know when you are telling the truth.'

'Well, I am now, and the poor boy had been beaten. That's the sort of thing they do on ships, or so I read in books.'

'You mean the cat-o'-nine-tails,' Emily said eagerly. 'I think I read that story, too. Perhaps he's a cabin boy.'

Rose laughed. 'Now your imagination is running away with you, Em. We'll just have to wait until he regains consciousness to know the truth of the matter.' She looked round as the door opened and Tom strode into the room. 'Is he any better, Tom?'

'I think the crisis is coming, Rose. He needs someone to sit with him all night, if necessary. I hope his fever will abate but I can't be sure. Would you be willing to keep watch?'

'Yes, of course. I've hardly left his side since we brought him back here. If I can do anything to save him, then I will. I was too young to do anything for Felix but perhaps I can help this boy back to health.'

Tom nodded. 'I knew I could rely on you, Rose. I will return first thing in the morning.'

'Can you stay awhile, Tom?' Marianne asked casually. 'We could have a game of bezique.'

'I would love to, but I should return home. Mama is on her own.'

'Apart from an army of servants,' Emily said, grinning.

'That's enough of your cheek, young miss.' Tom opened the door. 'I have to go now, but I will see if any of the servants know something of the ship in the bay.'

'So you think that, too.' Rose walked over to him. 'I'll see you out, Tom, and then I'll go upstairs and sit with the boy. We'll get him through this, I know we will.'

Chapter Four

Rose sat up all night with the patient. She dozed in the rocking chair by the fire, but she awakened at the slightest movement or stifled moan from the bed. When the boy was restless she gave him sips of cold water and bathed his forehead, which seemed to calm him. Sometimes he mumbled deliriously or else he fell into a comatose state, which was more alarming, and Rose had to lean closer to make sure he was breathing.

Eventually, overcome by exhaustion, she fell into a deep sleep but was awakened by the boy calling out once again for Sadie. She jumped to her feet and went to kneel at his bedside.

'Sadie isn't here, Jago. You are Jago, aren't you?'

He opened his eyes and she was struck by their blueness, the colour of forget-me-nots, fringed by thick black lashes. 'Who are you?'

Rose brushed away tears of relief. He was conscious, although he seemed to be confused, which was natural considering the circumstances. She laid her hand on his brow and he felt much cooler. His fever, it seemed, had abated.

'My name is Rose,' she said gently. 'We found you asleep in the crib outside my pa's church. You've been very poorly.'

He attempted to rise on one elbow but fell back against the pillows with a sigh. 'Where am I?'

'You're in the vicarage adjacent to St Michael's church. I'm Rose Northwood and my pa is the vicar. I have been looking after you with some help from my two sisters and our maid, Winnie.' Rose eyed him curiously. 'Who is Sadie?'

'I don't know who she is, but I must find her.'

Rose could see that he was getting upset and she laid her hand on his shoulder. 'Don't worry now. You've been very unwell, but I'm sure your memory will come back when you get stronger.'

He turned his head away. 'I don't remember anything, except for the name Sadie.'

'Don't worry about that now. Our friend Tom is a doctor and I'm sure he'll be able to help, but I'll have to call you something in the meantime,' Rose said thoughtfully. 'What about Jago? Does that sound familiar?'

He shook his head. 'Not really.'

Rose was about to ask him if he knew anyone by the name of Benedict, but she thought better of it. There was no point in upsetting him further. She managed a smile. 'Will you promise to lie here quietly while I go downstairs to get you some food and a drink?'

He nodded wearily. 'I ache all over. I don't think I could get up, even if I wanted to.'

Rose stood up. 'I'll be as quick as I can.' She did not wait for an answer as she left the room and hurried downstairs to the kitchen.

Winnie was going about her morning routine but she stopped, staring at Rose in surprise.

'You're up early, Miss Rose. Is the boy all right?'

'He's awake and the fever has broken, but he's still very poorly. He needs some thin gruel, or if there's porridge in the pan I could dilute it with milk.'

Winnie took a large pan off the range and set it down on the table. 'Cook made this last evening.' She spooned warm porridge into a bowl, adding a trickle of creamy milk.

'Thank you, Winnie. I'll take this up to him, and if you make some tea you could bring me a cup and one for the boy, only make his very weak. I don't know when he last ate or drank anything other than sips of water.'

'You can rely on me, Miss Rose.' Winnie puffed out her chest. 'Cook said I can go home this afternoon to spend the rest of the day with me ma and pa and the little 'uns.'

Rose smiled. 'Of course you must. You've been a great help, as always, but please remember not to tell anyone about the boy, not yet anyway.'

'Not even Ma and Pa?'

'No, Winnie. I need to find out who he is before we tell anyone he's here.'

'What if I meet the stranger on my way home, Miss Rose? What should I do then?'

'Walk on, Winnie. He doesn't know who you are and he's probably far away by now, or maybe he's back on that ship anchored in the bay.' Rose picked up the bowl and took a spoon from the cutlery drawer. She could see that Winnie was mulling the last piece of information over and was about to question her further. Rose made her escape.

The boy looked up as she entered the room and gave her the ghost of a smile. 'I think my name is Jago,' he said breathlessly. 'It does seem familiar.'

Rose placed the bowl of porridge on the chest of drawers while she helped him to sit, propping him up with pillows and a couple of old cushions. 'That's very good. If you can remember your name then I'm sure the rest will follow in time. I've brought you something to eat and Winnie will bring up some tea in a minute.' She sat on a stool at his bedside, holding the bowl, but he was too weak to feed himself and she spooned the thin porridge into his mouth. He managed a little but then he waved the food away, shaking his head.

'I'm sorry. Can't eat any more.'

'That doesn't matter, Jago. It's a good start.' Rose looked round as the door opened and Winnie entered with a tray of tea. 'Thank you, Winnie.'

'Dr Buckingham is downstairs, miss. He apologised for being so early.'

'Ask him to come up, please. I'm sure he'll see a great improvement.'

Winnie closed the door and moments later it opened to admit Tom.

Rose stood up and moved away from the bed. 'I think he's over the worst, Tom. He's even managed a few mouthfuls of porridge.'

'Excellent.' Tom smiled and nodded. 'Good morning, young man. How are you feeling today?'

'He thinks his name is Jago,' Rose said in an undertone. 'He's still asking for Sadie.'

'If you would give me a few minutes, Rose? I'll examine him and we can chat then.'

'Of course. I'll wait downstairs in the morning parlour.' Rose left them, closing the door behind her. She went first to Marianne's room and found her sister sitting up in bed, sipping a cup of tea.

'You're up early, Rose,' Marianne said, suppressing a yawn.

'I haven't been to bed. I did sleep a little in the chair, but I didn't dare leave the boy when he was so ill.'

'How is he this morning?'

'He is quite a lot better. The fever has lessened and he remembers his name – it is Jago, or so he thinks. That seems to be the extent of his recall, except for Sadie, whoever she might be.'

'Oh, well. I suppose that's good news. Has the

thaw set in? I really want to go for a long walk today. I hate being stuck indoors for days on end.'

'I haven't had a chance to go outside, but you can ask Tom. He's with Jago now. I'm on my way downstairs. We'll be in the morning parlour.' Rose had the satisfaction of seeing her sister's bored expression replaced by one of alertness.

Marianne put her cup and saucer on a side table and threw back the coverlet. 'Why didn't you say that in the beginning? Keep him talking until I've made myself presentable.'

Rose smiled and left Marianne to make herself pretty for Tom, not that she needed to do anything other than dress and brush her hair. Marianne was naturally lovely no matter how she presented herself.

Downstairs in the morning parlour, Rose added more coal to the fire and warmed her hands in front of the blaze. She did not have to wait long before Tom joined her.

'Is he on the road to recovery, Tom?' Rose asked anxiously.

'Yes, I think I can safely say he's over the worst, although he must be kept in bed for another couple of days at least. Good food and rest should do the trick, but as to his memory, I think that might take time.'

'Benedict Rivers said his brother was called Jago, if we can believe him.'

'As far as I know, that fellow hasn't been seen since he startled you in the coach house. I'm almost certain he must have come from the vessel moored in the bay, but that's not all, Rose.'

She was suddenly alert, all tiredness and aching limbs forgotten. 'You've found out something?'

'I was speaking to our butler this morning. He managed to get down to the village last night to make sure that his elderly mother was all right. He told me that the ship is called *Sadie Lee*. Not only that, but the owner is a man called Benedict Rivers, and he's staying at the Crown Inn.'

'Who is he, Tom? Do you know any more about him?'

'No, but I intend to find out. The Crown is part of The Manor estate and I've known Bill Thatcher since I was a boy. If anyone knows anything about Benedict Rivers it will be Bill.'

'So we know that *Sadie* is a ship and not a person. If Benedict Rivers is Jago's brother, why is the boy in such a bad way, and who is responsible for the beatings he must have suffered?'

'I intend to find out, Rose. Jago is my patient and the boy is obviously terrified of something or someone.' Tom shrugged on his caped greatcoat. 'I have to call on another patient in the village. Thank goodness the thaw has set in enough to make the roads passable again.'

'What do I need to do for Jago?'

'Keep him warm and make him rest. I don't really need to tell you how to care for a sick boy, Rose. You do it naturally, but I will call in again this evening.'

'Why don't you come for dinner, Tom? We've seen so little of you socially.'

'I would like that. Mama is fully occupied with our guests, most of whom I really cannot stand anyway.'

'We'll look forward to seeing you, and if you have time to call in at the Crown, you can tell us what you've learned.'

Tom laughed. 'I thought there might be an ulterior motive in the dinner invitation, but of course I will keep you informed. Bill loves to chat so it won't be difficult to find out how much or how little he knows of the mysterious Mr Rivers.'

'I would go there myself, but Pa would have a fit if he found out I had entered a public house, even by the back door.'

'Leave it to me, Rose. I'll tell you everything I've learned this evening.'

Rose stood on tiptoe to kiss him on the cheek. 'Thank you, Tom. I can't wait.'

Marianne and Emily were delighted to learn that Tom was going to dine with them that evening, but Cook was not so pleased.

'It's all very well, Miss Rose. I have allowed Winnie to spend this afternoon at home with her family. I will have to do everything on my own.'

'She'll be back in time to help you serve the meal, Cook.'

'That's not the point, miss. I know I shouldn't speak out, but I only have—'

'One pair of hands,' Rose said, smiling. She could see that Cook was offended so she gave her a hug. 'I will help you. I love being in the kitchen where it's warm and smells of cooking. I will be a better help than Winnie, I promise.'

Cook flapped her apron as she always did when she was emotional. 'There's no call for that, Miss Rose. You should not be working in the kitchen.'

'I am simply helping out. I can peel potatoes and carrots, or whatever else needs preparation. I always used to help when you were making jam tarts. I am very good at rolling out pastry, if you recall.'

Cook smiled reluctantly. 'I do remember.'

'Then that's settled. Just tell me what you want me to do. It will make a nice change from sitting at Jago's bedside. Emily can take a turn to keep him company and stop him from trying to get up.'

'Very well, miss. I suppose you will do it whether or not I say so.'

'Of course. You know me too well, Cook.' Rose glanced at a tray neatly set with lace doilies, a pot of tea and a plate of bread and butter. 'Is that for Mama?'

'Yes, I was going to send Winnie up with it before she goes home.'

'I'll take it. I need to sit with Mama for a while.'

'She was quite poorly this morning, Miss Rose.'

'The festive season is almost over and hopefully spring will be early this year. She always loves the first snowdrops.' Rose picked up the tray and took it up to her mother's room.

Grace Northwood was sitting in a rocking chair by the fire. She was still in her nightgown with a woollen wrap around her shoulders and a white, lace-trimmed nightcap covering her hair. Just the odd grey curl escaped to frame her thin ashen face, and grief had erased the last trace of youth and beauty that had captured the heart of a young Matthew Northwood. Rose laid the tray on a table beside her mother's chair.

'I've brought you some food, Mama. Shall I sit with you for a while?'

'Yes, Rose. But I don't feel much like talking. My nerves are getting the better of me this morning.'

'I'm so sorry, Mama.' Rose filled a cup with tea, adding milk and a teaspoonful of sugar. She handed it to her mother. 'Perhaps this will revive you a little.' She pulled up a stool and sat down beside her.

'What day is it, Rose? Is Christmas over yet?'

'Yes, Mama. It's Boxing Day.'

'It's so hard, Rose. My heart breaks all over again every Christmas. No one knows how much I suffer.'

'We all miss him, Mama.'

'But not as much as I do. I am his mother, which is something you might never understand. Heaven knows, I hope you find a husband, Rose, but you are very headstrong, and Marianne is the beauty in the family. She takes after me. I was the belle of the ball when I was young, and then I married your papa. I could have had my pick of the eligible young men in the county, but I followed my heart.' Grace clutched her hands to her heart and her hazel eyes darkened as they filled with tears. 'My poor broken heart.'

Rose knew that nothing she could say would make any difference when her mother was in the slough of despond. She leaned over to brush her mother's cheek with a kiss. 'Can I get you anything else, Mama?'

'No, dear. Leave me with my memories. Felix was such a good boy. He never did anything to upset his loving mama. He used to sit on that stool and tell me everything he had done at school that day. He was such a quiet and gentle boy. Too good for this earth.'

Rose nodded and smiled, but the angelic child her mother described was so far from the truth that in any other circumstances Rose might have laughed. The Felix she remembered had always been in trouble at school. He was mischievous and adventurous, and had broken so many bones that Dr Newton, now retired, had despaired of him. Whatever his faults, Felix had been both funny and lovable. Rose knew she would miss him for as long as she lived. She also knew that when her mother was in this mood there was nothing she could say or do that would make any difference.

'If you need anything just ring your bell and one of us will come, Mama.'

'Ask Marianne to sit with me for a while, Rose. I always find comfort in her presence.'

'Yes, Mama.'

Rose realised she had been dismissed. Marianne

would sigh and assume the air of a martyr about to be burned at the stake, but she would keep their mother company until she thought of a plausible excuse to get away. There were disadvantages in being Mama's favourite, which Marianne always pointed out to Emily when she was feeling put out. Rose was too used to the situation to care, although it had irked her when they were all younger. Now she found it to her advantage and she made her escape before her mother could change her mind.

Rose made her way upstairs to Jago's room. He was lying in bed, staring up at the ceiling, but he raised himself on one elbow as she crossed the floor to his bedside.

'I feel better now, miss. Can I get up?'

'Dr Buckingham said you must rest in order to regain your strength, Jago.'

'I wish I could remember what happened.'

'Do you recall anything about Christmas Eve, or how you came to be asleep in the Nativity scene?'

'I was running. That I do remember. Running away from something, but I don't know what it was. I was cold, so cold. My ankle hurt very badly and it still does.'

'You were only wearing rags and it was snowing.'

'Why do I keep hearing the name Sadie in my head? Am I mad, Rose?'

'No, of course not, Jago. I can tell you that there is a ship in the bay named *Sadie Lee*. Would that be the Sadie you were talking about?'

'A ship?' Jago turned his head away. 'I don't know. I can't remember.'

Rose could see that he was getting agitated and she laid her hand on his shoulder. 'Don't upset yourself, Jago. It will all come back to you, just be patient.'

He gulped and mumbled something into the pillow. Rose had little alternative other than to leave him to rest and recover from his failed attempts to recall the past twenty-four hours. In her own mind she decided that the *Sadie Lee* must have significance for him, otherwise he would not have repeated the name again and again. It was frustrating to have to sit at home and wait for bits of information to filter through. There seemed to be only one person who might know the boy's identity and what had happened to make him run away.

She made her way to the morning parlour where Marianne and Emily were playing cards.

'How is he?' Emily demanded, dropping her hand of cards onto the table. 'Does he remember anything?'

Rose shook her head. 'No, he's just the same, but Mama requests the pleasure of your company, Marianne.'

'Oh, no!' Marianne pulled a face. 'Really? Is she in a bad way?'

'Yes, I'm afraid so. I did my best but she wants you.'

'I'm glad I'm the youngest and not much use to anyone,' Emily said, pouting. 'You are her favourite, Marianne.'

'I'm the eldest.' Marianne laid her cards face up on the table. 'I think I won that hand anyway. You are no match for me, Em.'

'I wasn't trying very hard, Minnie.' Emily shrugged and scooped up the scattered cards. 'Do you want to play, Rose?'

'No, not at the moment, Em. Maybe later. I have something I must do.'

Marianne eyed her suspiciously. 'What are you up to, Rose? I know that look.'

'Nothing bad, I promise. Go upstairs and do your best with Mama. I think Cook needs some assistance in the kitchen as Winnie has gone home for the day.'

Emily jumped to her feet. 'I'll go. Cook likes me and she'll let me have cake if I help.'

Rose tried not to look too pleased. If her sisters were kept busy they would not notice if she put on her outdoor clothes and went on the errand she had in mind. She knew she would not rest until she had discovered the secret behind Jago's sudden appearance in their lives. She sat down and picked up a discarded piece of mending that she was supposed to have completed days ago. Marianne was not easily fooled and she was already suspicious, but she left the room reluctantly, followed by Emily, who was eager to join Cook in the kitchen as it was forbidden territory on most days. Cook did not like her domain crowded with people who were not there to work. Today Emily had a mission and Rose suspected the reward for peeling a few potatoes would be a large slice of seed cake or a couple of jam tarts.

Rose waited until she was sure her sisters would not see her and she went to her room to fetch her fur-lined mantle, gloves and matching bonnet. She crept past her father's study where he was occupied, as usual, with parochial matters and she let herself out of the house.

A pale buttery sun had edged its way between the clouds and continued the thaw that had set in during the night. The ground was slushy, but Rose ignored the discomfort of the icy water that seeped through the buttonholes of her black boots. Clumps of snow toppled off the branches of overhanging trees as she walked past the churchyard, narrowly missing her, but she walked on, determined to reach the Crown Inn before it became too crowded. There were very few people about, partly because it was Boxing Day, but mainly due to the adverse weather conditions. Smoke from cottage chimneys spiralled upwards to merge with heavy cumulus clouds as they threatened to win their battle for precedence with the pale watery sun.

Ned Guppy passed Rose on his cart as he went on his rounds and the delicious aroma of newly baked bread wafted around her, making her stomach rumble. Ned gave her a cheery wave and she acknowledged him with a smile. Constable Dent was patrolling the narrow streets with his hands clasped behind his back, but he stopped when he saw Rose.

'Good morning, Miss Rose. You are up and about early.'

'Good morning to you, Constable. I'm taking a message to the verger,' Rose lied glibly.

'Looks like it might snow again, or maybe it will come down as rain this time. I should be quick, if I was you, miss. You don't want to catch a chill at this time of year.'

'You are right and I will hurry.' Rose walked on, feeling very pleased with herself. She did not often tell out-and-out lies, but this was different. She was on a mission and no one, not even an officer of the law, was going to stop her.

She came to a halt outside the Crown Inn. She knew she could not enter unless accompanied by a male customer. Bill Thatcher was a stickler for the law, although it was rumoured that he had in the past been known to accept the odd barrel of brandy or several pounds of tea from the smugglers who had been operating in this area. However, that was long ago. Now he was considered to be a law-abiding citizen. Rose went round to the back of the building and knocked on the kitchen door. To her relief it was Molly Thatcher who opened it, and her freckled face broke into a grin when she saw Rose.

'Oh, it's you, Rose. I thought it was gypsies selling clothes pegs or lucky heather. They've been doing the rounds in the village.'

'They're brave,' Rose said, smiling. 'There might be a slight thaw but it's still bitterly cold.'

'Come in, do. What was I thinking of, keeping you standing on the doorstep?' Molly stood aside to allow Rose to enter. She closed the door with an exaggerated shiver. 'You're right, it's freezing. Anyway, what brings you here on Boxing Day?'

'Can we talk privately, Molly?' Rose glanced over her shoulder in case any of the kitchen staff were listening, although the women seemed busy enough as they prepared food for the customers.

Molly shut the kitchen door and led the way along a narrow passage to the family's private parlour. She motioned Rose to take a seat.

'What is it, Rose? It's not like you to be so mysterious.'

Rose peeled off her gloves and undid her mantle. 'Is there a man called Benedict Rivers staying here?'

'Yes, why? Do you know him?' Molly perched on the window seat, eyeing Rose curiously. 'Despite the awful weather he turned up on foot late Christmas Eve. He doesn't say much, in fact he's a bit of a mystery.'

'I heard that he'd come off the ship that's moored in the bay.'

'That's what he said, although why he chose to come here in a snowstorm instead of remaining on board is even more of a puzzle. He doesn't like being questioned, although I have tried.'

Rose laughed. 'If you can't get him to talk then no one can.'

'Yes, I'm good at flirting with guests, especially the ones with money because they leave a big tip when they depart. But I don't think I'll get much out of Mr Rivers.'

'Is he here now?'

'I'm not sure. He had breakfast but I don't know if he went out or not.' Molly leaned forward, her green eyes alight with interest. 'Why are you so interested in Mr Rivers?'

'Did I hear you mention my name?'

Rose turned to see Benedict Rivers standing in the doorway. Both she and Molly had been so intent on their conversation that neither of them had heard the door open. Molly blushed scarlet to the roots of her mousy-brown hair, but Rose stood up, facing him with a defiant set to her jaw. She was not going to allow this man to intimidate her for a second time. She was on safe ground in the public house, not on her own in a disused coach house.

'We are naturally curious, sir. You were trespassing on Church property when you found me in our coach house. That wasn't the act of a gentleman.'

A grim smile curved his lips. 'I never claimed to be a gentleman, Miss Northwood.'

Rose was taken aback. 'You remember my name?'

'I have a very good memory.'

Molly stood up. 'Is there anything I can fetch for you, sir?'

'No, thank you, Molly. I just came to say I will be out all day but I will require a meal this evening.' Benedict turned to give Rose a straight look. 'My business here is not yet concluded.'

'You told me that you were looking for your brother, Jago,' Rose said boldly. 'Have you found him yet, sir?'

'No, I have not, and I think you know more about it than you admit. Perhaps I should call at the vicarage tomorrow, Miss Northwood, and your father can give me the information I seek, as you don't seem to trust me?'

Molly's hand flew to cover her mouth and she gazed at Rose, wide-eyed, but Rose faced him down, even though his commanding presence filled the small parlour with menace.

'I don't know what you are talking about, Mr Rivers. I do not know anyone called Jago, and if you have lost your brother, I would say that is sheer carelessness.'

'Your opinion is of no interest to me, Miss Northwood.' Benedict strode out of the room, slamming the door behind him.

'Well! What a rude fellow.' Molly laid her hand on Rose's arm. 'Are you all right, Rose?'

'It would take more than someone like him to upset me,' Rose replied, biting back tears of anger and frustration. 'Although I must admit that he scared me to death when he came into our coach house on Christmas morning, supposedly looking for this brother of his.'

'Do you think it's the boy in the crib, Rose? Everyone in the village knows that your pa took him in.'

'We don't know the boy's true identity yet, and I'm certainly not going to hand him over to a man like Benedict Rivers. I don't trust him an inch. I'm going to follow him, Molly. I want to know if he came off that boat, and if he did, what is his real aim in finding Jago.'

'Is that his name?'

'Unfortunately Jago can't remember anything other than his first name and *Sadie*, which apparently is the name of that ship.' Rose did up her mantle and picked up her gloves, putting them on as she left the room. 'I'll let you know if I find anything out, Molly.'

'Oh, do be careful,' Molly cried anxiously. 'You really should leave this to Constable Dent.'

'Jago is my problem and I'm going to look after him.'

Chapter Five

Rose left the inn and made her way to the harbour. It was difficult going, due to the thick slush, but she was determined to find out more about the ship in the bay. She came to a halt on the quay wall and was staring out at the vessel shrouded in grey sea mist when she heard footsteps. She looked over her shoulders and saw Ned Guppy standing behind her. He was clutching a wicker basket containing a single cob loaf.

'Fine sight, isn't she, miss?'

'Do you know anything about her, Ned?'

He puffed out his chest. 'The mate came ashore Christmas Eve and purchased a couple of sacks of flour, and the last of my mince pies and puddings. He said they'd run out of the necessary to do the normal baking, and he didn't have the time to visit the miller, who had probably shut up shop anyway. Nice chap.'

'Did he say anything else?'

Ned frowned, shaking his head. 'Like what, miss? He just wanted supplies.'

'I mean did he say why they are moored offshore, or where they might be going next?'

'It were none of my business to enquire, Miss Rose.'

'Of course not,' Rose said hastily.

'Can't stand here chatting or the missis will be after me. We've got family coming round for a meal and I'm supposed to be helping out.'

'I mustn't keep you, Ned. I hope it goes well at home.'

'If I upset the mother-in-law I might as well join the crew of that ship out there. Good day to you, Miss Rose.' He hesitated, staring into the basket. 'Have you got a penny on you, Miss Rose? I haven't sold the last loaf.'

Rose felt in her pockets and produced a small coin. 'I'm sorry, Ned. I only have a farthing.'

He picked up the bread and thrust it into her hands, snatching the coin from her fingers as he did so. 'That'll do, thank you.' He sauntered off, whistling.

Rose was left holding a loaf still warm from the oven, but it was more than her life was worth to take it home. Cook was very proud of her baking and shunned any attempts to save her time by purchasing loaves from Ned Guppy. She would consider it a personal insult even if Rose explained Ned's need to sell the last loaf in his basket before he went home to face his family.

Rose shivered as a cold east wind whipped at her skirts and almost tore her bonnet from her head. It was unlikely that she would find out anything else by simply standing and staring at the *Sadie Lee*. She turned and had started walking in the direction of home when she spotted one of the Hawkes children running barefoot towards the village shop, but the boy slipped and fell heavily. Rose hurried to his side and helped him to stand.

'Are you all right, Joe?'

'I dropped me money,' Joe sobbed. 'Can't see it nowhere. I've got to get some food or us won't have nothing to eat today.'

Rose spotted a halfpenny resting on a pile of snow and she picked it up. 'How much did you have, Joe?'

'Tuppence, miss. I was to get a loaf of bread and some cheese.'

Rose thought of the substantial and well-cooked luncheon that was awaiting her at home and she was ashamed. The Hawkes family was large and the children's father was frequently unemployed, or perhaps he was unemployable. He certainly spent a great deal of time in the Crown Inn, and his wife took in washing in order to make ends meet. Rose turned over the slushy snow and picked up another penny, which she gave to Joe, and he found the other two farthings. Forgetting his bruised and scraped knees, he danced about regardless of the fact that his dirty feet were blue with cold.

'Ta, miss. I got to get to the shop before it closes.'

Rose handed him the loaf. 'Take this, Joe. Then you can buy more food than you thought.'

He frowned, screwing up his face. 'Ma says not to take charity.'

'It isn't charity. You'll be doing me a favour by taking the bread. I was given it minutes ago but I will be in trouble with Mrs Philpot if I take the baker's bread into the kitchen, if you know what I mean.'

'Pa says that women are—'

Rose held up her hand. She could guess what Bob Hawkes had to say about women was less than flattering. 'Never mind that, Joe. Just buy the food and take it home to feed your brothers and sisters.'

Joe gave her a mock salute and raced off towards the shop with the loaf tucked under his arm. Rose walked on, but with less of a spring in her step. The Hawkes family were well-known in Abbotsford, and the children ran wild most of the time. They were severely undernourished, and all the efforts of Miss Jones and the other ladies who devoted their spare time to raising money for charity and seeking donations of clothes for the poor and needy, came to nothing where the Hawkes family were concerned. Rose continued on her way home. She might not have found out anything concrete about the *Sadie Lee* or Benedict Rivers, apart from the fact that he was a very unpleasant and possibly dangerous man, but at

76

least the Hawkes children would be fed today. She would have to speak to her father about the parish providing them with some more practical help.

Having discarded her warm outer clothing, Rose went straight to Jago's room and found Emily seated at his bedside while he drank soup from a mug.

'No, you can't give up now, Jago,' Emily said firmly. 'You must finish it off or there's no cake for you.' She turned her head to see who had just entered and she smiled. 'Jago has been a good boy. He's taking his food like a hero.'

'I'm not a little boy,' Jago protested. 'I bet I'm older than you, although I can't remember exactly.'

Rose shot a warning glance at Emily as she opened her mouth to argue. 'We'll soon have you up and about.'

'I'd like to get up, miss,' Jago said eagerly. 'I don't like lying about all day. I'm not used to it.' He frowned. 'I don't know why I said that.'

'Perhaps your memory is returning,' Rose suggested calmly. 'The fever seems to have lessened considerably, but you will have to have Dr Buckingham's permission to leave your bed.'

Emily leaned closer. 'Maybe you were on that boat that's moored in the harbour, Jago. Do you think that's possible?'

'I don't know. Everything is blank, as if I'm in a thick fog.'

Rose could see that he was getting agitated. 'Did

I hear Em promising you some cake, Jago? We can't let her go back on her word now.'

Emily jumped to her feet. 'I'll go down to the kitchen and get some, shall I?'

'That would be a good idea.' Rose sat down on the stool that Emily had just vacated. She waited until her sister had left the room. 'I think you have remembered something, Jago. Would you like to tell me what it was? I won't pass it on to anyone else if you want it kept secret.'

He shook his head. 'Not really, but I keep having the same dream. It's very cold and my clothes are wet. I'm running for my life, but I don't know why.'

'Is that all?'

'Yes. I wake up then but I'm still scared.'

His face was flushed and his eyes suspiciously bright, which made Rose anxious. She laid her hand on his shoulder. 'Don't upset yourself. It's just a dream, probably caused by the fever. We'll find out who you are eventually and you're quite safe here, so please don't worry.'

He managed a wry smile. 'I don't know why you're being so kind to me. I'm a stranger and I could be a bad person.'

'I'm absolutely certain that you are a good boy, Jago. What's more, I'm determined to prove it to you. I won't rest until I find out why you are running away and who hurt you so badly.' Rose stood up as the door opened and Emily hurried in with a plate of cake grasped in one hand and a glass of milk in the other.

'Cook says you may have the cake but you must drink the milk, too. She says it will do you good and help you to get better.'

Rose could see that Jago was struggling and she helped him to a sitting position. 'There you are. Cook has spoken. When Mrs Philpot puts her foot down we all know it's time to take notice.' She turned to Emily. 'Stay with him if you wish, Em. But don't tire him.'

'I won't, I promise. Anyway, it must be nearly time for luncheon so I'll have to come down directly.'

Rose pointed to the small, slightly battered brass timepiece on the chest of drawers. 'Come downstairs at midday. You know how Pa likes us all to be prompt for meals.'

'As if I could forget.' Emily rolled her eyes as she slumped down on the stool. 'Don't fret, Rose. I'll be at table when the hall clock strikes twelve.'

Christmas was officially over, not that it made much difference in the vicarage. There were no decorations to take down and no Christmas tree to either plant out in the garden or to dispose of in a pine-scented bonfire. Grace still kept to her room and the girls took it in turns to sit with her and attempt to make conversation, or to read to her out loud.

The sun won its battle with the clouds and a thaw set in at the beginning of the new week. Rose had not been able to get down to the harbour later on Boxing Day as her father was strict when it came to observing the Lord's Day, and she was expected to attend the church service that evening. Marianne was allowed to play the pianoforte in the evening, but popular ballads and lively dance music were forbidden. Rose had her books, and although she knew that her father frowned on novels, she had borrowed a copy of *Wuthering Heights* by Emily Brontë from the lending library, and could scarcely put it down. Her father would have preferred her to be studying something that would improve her mind, but Rose rebelled silently and surreptitiously.

It was a relief on Monday morning to be able to dress warmly and go out into the winter sunshine, without fear of slipping and breaking a bone or two. The *Sadie Lee* was still at anchor and Rose was desperate to discover more about the mysterious vessel. She called on Molly at the Crown, who was unable to give her any more information. Benedict Rivers was still in residence although he took himself off each morning, Molly said, with pursed lips. He had disappeared for the rest of the previous day, returning late in the evening. As far as the *Sadie Lee* was concerned there had been no sign of any boats bringing crew ashore and its presence was as much a mystery as ever. Rumours were flying around the village as to why it was there for so long, but so far smuggling, although popular, had been ruled out since the Revenue Officers showed no interest in the vessel, and it would be a very daring captain who would advertise the presence of his ship if its business was illegal. Rose had to return home without learning anything more about the mysterious Benedict Rivers or the *Sadie Lee*.

Jago continued to improve physically, but he was still at a loss to remember how and why he had come to Abbotsford in the first place. Four days later, Rose was growing more and more impatient. She had not seen Rivers again, and Molly knew nothing of his movements, although he was still staying at the inn. On a cold Friday morning when the heavy clouds threatened rain or possibly another fall of snow, Rose walked down to the harbour on the excuse of needing fresh air. She leaned on the quay wall, gazing out at the choppy waters on the bay. She was certain the *Sadie Lee* held the key to Jago's mysterious arrival in the village, but she was at a loss as to how to prove her theory.

'So, you are still watching that ship.'

Rose turned with a start. She knew that voice and she was not delighted to come face to face with Benedict Rivers. He always seemed to catch her unawares and at a disadvantage.

'I just like looking at the craft in the bay, sir. I've lived all my life by the sea and I never tire of it.'

'Have you ever been on a boat?' His tone was almost conversational, which made her even more uncomfortable.

'Only small boats, and that was when I was much younger.'

'You are aware that I own the *Sadie Lee*?'

'I did hear something to that effect,' Rose said cautiously.

He moved closer. 'And you still say you have no knowledge of what happened to my brother?'

'You haven't found him then?' Rose tried to sound casual, although his nearness was disturbing. However, she had no intention of allowing him to see that she was uncomfortable in his presence.

'He was seen lying in the Nativity crib on Christmas Eve. What am I to think?'

Rose shrugged. 'You seem to know a lot, so why haven't you found him?'

'I imagine it's because someone is not telling the truth.' A smile curved his lips. 'Although I wouldn't dare suggest that a prim and proper vicar's daughter would tell an out-and-out lie.'

'Are you accusing me, sir?'

He laughed. 'Are you admitting to being prim and proper, Miss Northwood?'

Rose very nearly stamped her foot in frustration. She was unused to having a conversation turned on her in such a way. She suspected that Rivers was laughing at her, but she managed a tight smile.

'You don't know me, sir. And I do not wish to become better acquainted with you. So if you'll excuse me, I will return to the vicarage and read an improving book.'

'Really? I thought you might prefer to visit my

ship. A tender is on its way, but of course if you are a bad sailor or afraid of the sea, I understand.'

'I am neither, Mr Rivers. Perhaps I would like to get a better view of your ship. I must confess I am curious as to the business that has brought you to a quiet fishing port.'

'Are you agreeing to come with me?'

'I'm not afraid of you, if that's what you infer.' Rose followed his gaze and saw the tender making its way towards the shore. She knew it was unwise and she would be in trouble if she missed luncheon, but she could not rest until she discovered the *Sadie Lee*'s secret. 'I will come with you, but I must be home in time for tea.'

'Of course. I understand perfectly. Walk with me to the beach and I promise you will not even get your feet wet.' He proffered his arm, leaving Rose little alternative other than to accept his help as they walked to the foreshore. Without a word, he lifted her in his arms and deposited her in the boat.

Rose experienced a moment of near panic. She knew what she was doing was foolhardy, but she was not about to give up now. She forced herself to sit quietly in the stern while Rivers pushed the boat off and leaped in as if he did this every day of his life. The seaman tipped his cap and began to row towards the moored vessel. He had to battle against a bitterly cold east wind in order to get to the ship, and the small boat pitched and tossed on the choppy sea. However, Rose was a good sailor and if she were to be honest, she found the short voyage exciting and was almost sorry when they reached the shelter of the *Sadie Lee*.

She climbed the companion ladder with comparative ease, considering the length and many folds of her linsey-woolsey skirt, and she refused all offers of help from Rivers and the crewman who extended a tattooed hand to her. She climbed on board and looked around eagerly. It was disappointing to see the holystoned deck spotless and with no sign of the barrels of contraband that she had imagined might be on board. Everything was neat and shipshape, and the first mate who greeted her was clean-shaven, neatly dressed and extremely polite. Moreover, he did not seem surprised by her presence, which led her to wonder if Rivers often brought young women on board.

'Jackson will show you anything you wish to see,' Rivers said firmly. 'I have paperwork to complete and I'll be in my cabin. Let me know when you wish to go ashore, Miss Northwood.'

'Thank you,' Rose had not been expecting this and she was at a temporary loss for words. Rivers strolled off, leaving her with the agreeable boatswain.

'Where would you like to start, miss?'

'I – er – I'd better leave it up to you, Mr Jackson. I'm not familiar with the layout of ships of this size.'

'You look as though you could do with a nice hot cup of tea, miss. It's a bit chilly here on deck. I suggest we start in the saloon.'

Rose nodded. Her teeth were chattering and she was shivering uncontrollably. It was only now she realised how cold she was and she followed Jackson without an argument. The saloon was small but cosy enough. Jackson motioned her to take a seat while he went to the galley to fetch her a warm drink. Rose took off her gloves and bonnet and undid the buttons on her mantle. Despite the strangeness of the situation, she began to relax as she took stock of her surroundings. It was a very masculine cabin with small portholes, the thick glass encrusted with salt on the outside. The walls were oak panelled and the furniture consisted of a square table, a couple of wooden chairs and the padded bench on which she was sitting. An oil lamp swung from the deckhead and the only attempt at decoration were several prints of sailing ships pinned to the bulkheads.

Jackson reappeared carrying a mug filled with tea, which he placed on the table.

'There you are, miss. I took the liberty of adding some sugar.'

Rose sipped the tea, which was very strong but made palatable by the sweetness.

'Thank you, Mr Jackson. It's very welcome.'

Jackson eyed her curiously. 'I'll show you round when you're ready, miss. Although it's the first time I've had to do such a thing, so you'll have to forgive me if I'm lacking in that respect.'

'What cargo do you carry, Mr Jackson?'

'It varies, miss.'

'There's a lot of speculation ashore, Mr Jackson. Some people think you are smugglers, but others are just curious.'

'Nothing as exciting nor as dangerous, miss.'

Rose sipped her tea, eyeing him over the rim of the mug. 'Do you know Mr Rivers' brother?'

Jackson shook his head. 'No, miss. To my knowledge Mr Rivers don't have any family.'

Rose tried again. 'Do you know a boy called Jago?'

'I think not, miss. Might I suggest we do the tour now? I dare say Mr Rivers will want to return to shore before the turn of the tide.'

Rose followed him from the saloon, but a wind had sprung up and she found it difficult to maintain her balance. The rest of the crew were busy going about their daily routine and showed little interest in her. A quick look through the cargo hatch appeared to show the hold was devoid of any sort of cargo. There was nothing suspicious to note, leaving Rose feeling deflated and disappointed. When they returned to the saloon they were met by Rivers.

'Have you seen enough to convince you that we are not smuggling goods into the country, Miss Northwood?'

'The *Sadie Lee* seems to be an excellent ship, Mr Rivers. But I do have one question. Maybe Mr Jackson knows the answer.'

Jackson looked to Rivers, who shrugged and nodded. 'Ask away, Miss Northwood.'

'What have roses to do with the *Sadie Lee*?'

There was a moment of complete silence except for the action of the waves against the hull. Jackson was the first to speak.

'I never heard it said, miss.'

'A curious question.' Rivers eyed her suspiciously. 'Where would you get such an idea?'

'It was just a fancy,' Rose said hastily. She knew she had gone a step too far, but she had to brazen it out or admit to sheltering Jago. 'I must have heard it said in the village.'

'A lot of nonsense is spoken by people who should know better.' Rivers made a move towards the door. 'The tender is alongside, Miss Northwood. We shouldn't waste any more time or you might have to wait six hours before we can get ashore.'

'Thank you for your time, Mr Jackson.' Rose smiled and shook his hand. 'I enjoyed the tour of the *Sadie Lee*. She is a fine vessel.' With her gloves and bonnet firmly secured, Rose followed Rivers onto the deck, but the wind had strengthened and it was difficult to walk against it.

'It's going to be a rough ride,' Rivers said grimly. 'Do you feel able to go down the ladder?'

Rose glanced over the side at the tender bobbing about on the waves and she was suddenly nervous. It hadn't been too difficult of a climb to get onto the *Sadie Lee*, but descending the ladder and making a safe landing into the small boat was daunting.

'I'll try,' she murmured, but before she had a

chance to protest, Rivers had flung her over his shoulder and climbed over the gunwale. There was nothing she could do other than close her eyes and pray.

By the time her feet touched firm ground Rose was feeling queasy and she felt as if the deck was still moving beneath her feet. Rivers had said little during the rough journey from ship to shore.

'You did well,' he said grudgingly. 'Another woman might have had a fit of the vapours after such an experience.'

Rose shrugged. 'I am too prim and proper to behave like that. You said so yourself.'

'You are not going to let me forget that, are you?'

'No. It was condescending and rude.'

'For that I am sorry, but you look frozen to the marrow. You need a tot of brandy to resuscitate you before you go home.'

'I need more than brandy to give me the courage to tell my family why I missed luncheon. I just hope that my father was visiting his parishioners.'

'Perhaps I should go home with you and explain that I practically kidnapped you this morning.'

Rose laughed. 'Do you really think that would make things better? You certainly don't know my father.'

'Then a tot of brandy in the Crown is the only answer.'

'Are you intent on ruining my reputation, Mr Rivers?'

'I thought you were so highly respected that no hint of scandal could ever touch you.' Rivers took her hand and tucked it into the crook of his arm. 'Come, Miss Northwood. I don't want you going down with a chill. A cup of coffee in the Crown's private parlour will do wonders, and if a small tot of brandy should spill into the cup it will be even more efficacious.'

'I would rather have a bowl of Mrs Thatcher's chicken soup. I'm famished.'

Rivers glanced up at the lowering clouds. 'Then we'd best walk quickly. It's either going to rain or maybe there's more snow to come. We could both do with a good meal, and I need to talk to you sensibly and openly about a certain young gentleman.'

'Do you mean the boy you are hunting, who is not your brother?'

'Jackson has been talking.'

'Don't blame him. I asked the question; he was merely being honest.' Rose leaned on his arm. It was easier than fighting against the wind, and the rain that had started to fall in earnest. She did not protest when they entered the pub together, although she could see that the drinkers in the taproom were staring at her in astonishment. It would be all round the village in minutes that the vicar's daughter had entered the public house with the mysterious Mr Rivers.

Chapter Six

A log fire crackled good-naturedly in the hearth and the aroma of chicken soup mingled with the fragrance of freshly brewed coffee. Warmed by the food and the hot coffee, fortified with a tiny nip of brandy despite her protests, Rose sat back in the comfortable armchair and sighed.

'You are a mystery, Mr Rivers. I don't mind admitting that I'm puzzled.'

He put his cup back on its saucer and smiled. 'Perhaps I like it that way.'

'That is no answer. Why would you lie about the boy you were chasing? If he isn't your brother, who is he?'

'I believe you have him in your care. Otherwise why would you be so keen to know my business?'

'What did he do to make you seek him out, keeping your vessel out of commission for such a long time?'

'What do you know about merchant vessels, Rose? I feel I may call you Rose as we've had luncheon alone together for the first time.'

'I've lived in a port all my life and I know a little about the trading that goes on here.' Rose met his gaze with a wry smile. 'Besides which, I don't think sharing a bowl of soup is the beginning of an intimate relationship, least of all yours and mine.'

'You are determined to put me on the wrong foot.'

'I don't have to do anything – you manage very well on your own, Mr Rivers.'

He laughed. 'Perhaps I should take you home now, but should I happen to see your papa, I might be tempted to mention the fact that you drank brandy with me.'

Rose stood up. 'Then I would be forced to tell him that you coerced me into a dangerous crossing to your ship, and an equally perilous climb up a rope ladder. Then you brought me to a public house and plied me with drink. My reputation will be in tatters if word gets round.'

'Miss Northwood, you are a woman after my own heart. Beneath that beautiful and sweet exterior you have the soul of a blackmailer and the spirit of a worthy combatant.' Rivers helped her on with her mantle.

Rose accepted his assistance but she stepped away quickly. 'Thank you, but I can find my own way home.'

'I see the prim and proper Miss Northwood

has re-emerged, but I insist.' He shrugged on his greatcoat. 'However, I promise to leave you at the vicarage gate, and should I see your papa I will merely acknowledge him with a smile and walk away.'

At that moment the door opened and Mrs Thatcher bustled into the room, her round cheeks flushed from the heat of the kitchen range, and her curiosity barely disguised in an eager smile.

'Was it all to your liking, sir?'

'Excellent meal, as always, Mrs Thatcher. You spoil me and make it very hard to return to the offerings of my cook on board.'

'Well, I hope you continue your stay here as long as possible, sir. And it's nice to see you again, Miss Northwood. Molly is very fond of you.'

'And I her, ma'am. But I really should leave now. Please don't let me inconvenience you, Mr Rivers. It is not far to the vicarage.'

'It will be my pleasure to see you safely home, Miss Northwood.'

Rose knew she had lost that particular battle and she left the room without any further argument. Once outside and away from the inquisitive looks of the locals in the taproom, however, she came to a halt.

'This is no good. I need to know why you are chasing this boy who is unrelated to you. What has he done to turn him into the victim of a manhunt?'

'You assumed that he is not related to me. I didn't say that.'

'Then why be so secretive? Who is he and why do you want to find him so badly?'

Rivers glanced over her shoulder. 'Do you know the lady who is bearing down on us with such a purposeful look on her face?'

Startled, Rose turned to see Martha Huggins, the verger's wife, waddling purposefully towards them and there was no escape. Rose managed a smile. 'Good afternoon, Mrs Huggins.'

'Your pa is looking for you, Miss Rose.' Martha cast a critical eye over Rivers. 'We heard you were gallivanting about with a certain gentleman.' Her lips pursed with disapproval.

'My apologies for causing such an upset, ma'am,' Rivers said with such heartfelt humility that Rose gave him a second look. However, he was treating Martha to a charming smile, which seemed to be having an amazing effect.

'I didn't say it, sir,' Martha said hastily. 'It's just what I was told by one of the village gossips.'

'My dear lady, I am sure you are the soul of discretion,' Rivers added humbly. 'I would never place a lady of Miss Northwood's standing in a delicate situation.' He drew Martha aside, lowering his voice. 'She has been assisting me in a very personal matter, but if it has tarnished her spotless reputation I am very sorry indeed.'

Rose had a sudden urge to giggle, which she

suppressed with difficulty. Benedict Rivers was an accomplished liar and Mrs Huggins was clearly taken in by his charm and apparent sincerity.

'You seem to be an honest gentleman,' Mrs Huggins said reluctantly.

'You are very far-seeing, ma'am. I hope those who like to spread rumours learn the whole truth before any harm is done.'

Martha puffed out her chest. 'I abominate lies, sir. I will put the tittle-tattlers right if I happen to hear anyone spreading such stories.' She turned to Rose. 'Your behaviour has always been above reproach, Miss Rose. I wouldn't want your papa to hear otherwise.'

'Thank you, Mrs Huggins.' Rose did not dare look at Rivers for fear of giving herself away by laughing. 'Now I really must get home and put Papa's mind at rest.' She nodded to Martha Huggins and walked on briskly.

Rivers caught up with her just before she reached home. 'Dreadful woman. I hope that silences her for a while at least.'

'You put me in this position,' Rose said icily. 'I hope you're satisfied.'

His confident smile faded. 'It was purely unintentional. I want you to believe that.'

'If that's so then tell me the truth. Who is this boy and why are you chasing him so relentlessly?' She looked round at the sound of Marianne calling her name, and at that moment Rivers swept her into his arms and kissed her on the lips. It was a brief embrace and he released her almost immediately, but it left her shocked, angry and totally confused, especially when he gave Marianne his most charming smile.

'Miss Northwood, you've caught us out. I apologise most sincerely for my forward behaviour and for placing your sister in such an embarrassing situation.'

Marianne was at the garden gate, her face as pale as the lace shawl she had wrapped round her slender shoulders. 'We've been out of our minds with worry. Papa was about to send for Constable Dent. We thought something terrible had happened to you, Rose.'

Rose controlled her breathing with difficulty. 'I don't know what to say, Marianne.'

'You've missed luncheon.' Emily hurried down the path to stand with Marianne. 'Did he just kiss you, Rose? I thought I must be dreaming.'

'Mr Rivers is just leaving,' Rose said with as much dignity as she could muster. 'I can assure you both that I am not having a romantic liaison with him – or anyone, for that matter.'

Rivers caught her by the hand as she was about to open the gate. 'Come now, dearest. You surely don't mean that? I know your loving sisters will make allowances for your reluctance to admit that you have tender feelings for me.' His blue eyes gleamed with amusement but there was also something akin to sympathy in his gaze.

Rose could only play along with the scenario he had set up so unexpectedly, and she knew she would have the support of her romantically minded sisters. Martha Huggins would make up her own story, but perhaps the worst of her escapade could be kept from her father. He had enough to contend with. Rose glanced anxiously at Marianne, who opened the garden gate, rushed out and hugged her, despite being where any passer-by could witness such an outward show of affection.

'Why didn't you tell us, Rose? You know that Em and I would support you, even if we didn't approve.' Marianne shot a sideways glance at Rivers. 'Which as it happens, I do not.'

'My apologies, Miss Northwood,' Rivers said humbly. 'Our feelings for each other came about suddenly, like a maelstrom.'

Emily clasped her hands to her breast, her eyes shining. 'Oh, how romantic. Love at first sight. You are a sly puss, Rose. You never said a word. I thought you hated him.'

'I might have been a little suspicious at first.' Rose guided her sisters back into the garden. 'Why are we standing out in here in the cold?' She stopped and turned to Rivers. 'Thank you for escorting me home. I will say goodbye now.'

He bowed gallantly. '*Au revoir*, Rose.'

She acknowledged this comment with a toss of her head and marched into the house, leaving her sisters to follow.

'Wretched man.' Rose came to a halt in the entrance hall. 'I'd as soon kiss a toad as kiss him.'

Emily stared at her in dismay. 'But Rose, he's in love with you. It's so romantic.'

'I don't believe that for a moment. What is going on, Rose?' Marianne shooed them into the morning parlour and closed the door. 'I think you had better explain.'

Rose tore off her bonnet and fumbled with the buttons on her mantle. Her fingers were numb with cold, despite the hot meal and the coffee laced with brandy. 'I couldn't cause a scene in the street, but I should have slapped his face.'

'You don't love him, then?' Emily sank down on the nearest chair. 'Why did you allow him to kiss you?'

'I didn't. He caught me by surprise.' Rose tugged so hard at a wayward button that it flew off and landed on the floor.

'Let me help.' Marianne brushed Rose's hands away and started to undo the tiny fabric-covered buttons. 'I think you owe us an explanation, Rose. Where have you been all morning? Papa will not be pleased to know you've been consorting with Mr Rivers, especially without a chaperone.'

'I haven't been consorting,' Rose said crossly as she shrugged off her mantle and tossed it onto the sofa. She sank down on the sofa with a sigh. 'Well, not that, but I did go out to his ship and I did have luncheon with him at the Crown.'

Marianne and Emily stared at her aghast, and their shocked expressions might have made Rose laugh at any other time.

'You went out to that ship in the bay?' Marianne's voice was barely audible. 'What were you thinking, Rose?'

'I wanted to find out why Rivers is chasing poor Jago and I needed to discover the *Sadie Lee*'s business.'

'And did you discover his secrets?' Marianne stood with arms akimbo.

'Not exactly,' Rose said reluctantly.

'Anything could have happened to you.' Marianne sighed and shook her head. 'As it is, you've created a scandal that will upset Papa terribly.'

'He might have a seizure and die,' Emily added primly. 'You would be sorry then.'

Rose rolled her eyes. 'Don't be silly, Em. I haven't done anything that would kill Pa. I just wanted to find out what business the *Sadie Lee* has here, but Marianne is right. It was a foolish thing to do and I am no wiser now. Nor did Rivers confide in me during our meal at the Crown.'

'So that rash escapade was for nothing! Heaven knows what Tom will say. His mama will think your behaviour is beyond belief, Rose.'

'I don't care what Lady Buckingham thinks of me, although I am sorry if my actions reflect badly on you, Minnie.'

'Marianne, not Minnie. Don't goad me, Rose.'

'I apologise, but before you lecture me again, I did discover one thing. Jago is not Rivers' brother.'

'Did he tell you that?' Marianne subsided gracefully onto a chair by the fire. 'I think he was leading you on, Rose. He's almost certainly ruined your reputation and is obviously enjoying the power he has over you.'

'You could not be more wrong, Marianne. It was his second in command who told me that Rivers has no siblings, and he has no hold over me at all. I think he enjoyed embarrassing me in front of you and Emily, but that is all.'

'But you didn't tell him that Jago is here,' Marianne said thoughtfully. 'Are you certain he is the boy that Rivers is looking for?'

'He wouldn't tell me anything, but it would be an unbelievable coincidence if he was looking for another errant boy. It has to be Jago.'

'Maybe you should let him see Jago,' Emily said slowly. 'Perhaps it would bring his memory back and we would know for certain who he really is.'

Rose shook her head. 'Rivers is an ill-mannered brute. I wouldn't tell him where Jago is for all the tea in China.'

'You did allow him to kiss you, though,' Marianne said solemnly. 'Are you sure there isn't something going on between you two?'

'No, of course not. How could you think that of me, Marianne?' Rose jumped to her feet. 'I'm going to my room to change out of my damp clothes.

I don't want to hear another word about Benedict Rivers.' She slammed out of the room and almost collided with her father, who had just entered the house on a gust of cold air.

'Rose. You're home at last. Where have you been?'

'Well, Pa, it's like this.' Rose took a deep breath. She had never knowingly lied to her father and she did not intend to start now, no matter the consequences. 'I went out to the *Sadie Lee* with Mr Rivers, and then we had luncheon at the Crown Inn. I'm sorry, Pa. I know it was a stupid thing to do and I'm very sorry for the worry I caused you.'

Matthew shrugged off his black cloak and hung it tidily on its peg. 'Well, now. It was a rash thing to do, but it seems that no harm came of the event.'

Rose stared at him in astonishment. She had expected a good telling-off, at least. 'Really, Pa? I thought you would be angry with me.'

Matthew took off his shovel hat and hung that up next to his cloak. 'In ordinary circumstances I might have frowned on such behaviour, Rose. As it is, I think we should welcome Mr Rivers to our small community. I've just discovered that he has purchased Longfleet Hall. Not only that, but he has donated a large sum to the church funds as well as a considerable amount to the village school.'

Rose stared at her father in disbelief. 'He's done all those things in such a short space of time?'

'I believe he made himself known to Lady Buckingham at her soirée on Boxing Day. He's a very wealthy man, Rose. That opens most doors. Anyway, you will be able to see for yourself at the Buckinghams' New Year's Eve ball this evening.'

Rose stared at him in astonishment. 'You never usually allow us to attend, Pa. Even though we are always invited.'

'Perhaps I have been too strict with my girls. It's understandable since our terrible loss, and I try to keep the outside world away from your poor dear mama, but Tom spoke to me so kindly this morning and with such sympathy that I relented. You may tell your sisters that Dr Buckingham will come to escort all three of you to The Manor at seven o'clock this evening.'

'Thank you, Pa.' Rose was too stunned to do anything other than watch her father walk slowly towards his study. It was hard to believe that he had suddenly changed his mind about the Buckinghams' New Year's Eve ball. All forms of entertainment during the Twelve Days of Christmas had been banned after Felix's tragic death, but now it seemed that had changed.

'Oh, my goodness!' The reality of what had just happened struck Rose forcibly and she turned and ran back to the morning parlour. She burst into the room.

'You'll never believe what Papa just told me.'

Marianne looked up from her embroidery hoop with a sigh. 'I don't suppose we will. What now, Rose?'

'You won't guess in a million years, but Pa has just given us permission to attend the Buckinghams' ball tonight.'

Marianne dropped her sewing. 'You are teasing us.'

'I am deadly serious. Tom is coming round at seven o'clock to escort us to The Manor.'

'Me, too?' Emily asked tremulously. 'Am I to go with you?'

'Pa said all of us,' Rose said excitedly. 'We have less than four hours to get ready.'

'I feel faint.' Marianne closed her eyes and leaned back in her chair. 'My gown will be creased from being so long in the clothes press, and I haven't seen my dancing slippers for ages. There isn't time to do everything.'

Rose gave her a gentle shake. 'Of course there is. We may never get another chance like this. We can use the kettle to steam the creases out of our ball gowns, and we'll do each other's hair. You will have a chance to dance with Tom all evening, Marianne.'

'I haven't got a ball gown,' Emily wailed, her eyes filling with tears. 'My best dresses are too childish.'

Rose gave her a hug. 'You can wear my white taffeta with the pink rosebuds embroidered on it, and Marianne will put up your hair, so you will look like a proper young lady. To be honest, I would happily wear a sack if it meant going to the New Year's Eve ball. Get up Minnie, we can do this together. We are the Northwood sisters, nothing beats us, and while we get ready I have something to tell you about the mysterious Mr Rivers. Pa just gave me the news so it must be true. Come upstairs and I'll tell you while we get ready.'

The carriage sweep leading up to The Manor was illuminated by flambeaux placed at strategic positions, the flickering flames reflecting off the remnants of snow piled up beneath the surrounding shrubs and at the base of the tall oaks that guarded the entrance.

'It looks like fairyland,' Emily said delightedly as they made their way on foot, escorted by Tom.

'It's very pretty,' Marianne agreed, clutching Tom's arm. 'But it's very slippery. Do take care, Emily. If you slip and fall you might hurt yourself.'

'Don't worry, we have our own doctor to make us better.' Emily hurried on ahead and was waiting at the front entrance when Rose finally caught up with her. The footman on duty stood to attention, staring at a point above their heads as he ushered them into the grand hall.

'I hope you're going to behave this evening,' Rose said in a low voice. 'Don't show us up, Em. Marianne will never forgive you if you embarrass her in front of Lady Buckingham.' She took off her gloves and hooded cape and handed them to the maidservant.

Emily's attention had wandered and she was gazing admiringly at the huge displays of hothouse flowers and the crystal chandeliers blazing with light from dozens of wax candles.

'Your cape, Em,' Rose said, nudging her sister gently.

Emily obeyed automatically and the maid led them to a small ante-room where they changed into their dancing slippers.

Marianne was first to return to the grand entrance hall followed moments later by Rose and Emily.

'This is such an elegant house, Rose. It makes the vicarage look like a cottage in comparison.' Emily clasped her hands together, her eyes shining. 'Imagine living here.'

'Never mind all that. Best follow Tom and Marianne or we'll be left behind.' Rose tucked her sister's hand into the crook of her arm. She could see that Emily was bubbling with excitement at the prospect of her first grown-up ball, and she had to keep her own excitement under control. It would never do to appear too much of a country bumpkin in front of all the influential and doubtless very wealthy people who were there before them. It was Rose's first grand ball, but the guests who were already there were the pick of the county and beyond. Lady Buckingham moved in exalted circles far higher than those of the vicar's daughters. Rose glanced at Marianne, but her serene expression was reassuring. At least one of the Northwood sisters would be a credit to the family. Rose was not so sure about Emily, who had spotted a friend and was waving frantically. Rose caught her by the hand and pressed it firmly to Emily's side.

'Decorum, Em.'

'I was only waving to attract Bella's attention.'

Rose knew it was useless to argue, and they moved forward with the line of people waiting to be greeted by their hostess.

When they finally reached Lady Buckingham she acknowledged them with a nod and a brittle smile that did not reach her eyes. 'Do enjoy your evening, Rose.' She patted Emily on the shoulder as if she were a small child and turned her attention to Marianne, whose reception was only slightly warmer.

Tom was about to lead them to a table but his mother demanded that he remain at her side to greet the new arrivals. Despite his obvious reluctance, it would have been impossible for him to refuse without appearing churlish. Rose wondered vaguely if Sir Reginald's long absences from home were a deliberate ploy to keep away from his domineering wife.

Marianne smiled graciously and moved on with swan-like grace to speak to the now retired village doctor and his wife. Emily was claimed almost immediately by Bella Hannaford, whose father was Lady Buckingham's solicitor. They wandered off, arm in arm, giggling over some private joke and leaving Rose on her own at the edge of the highly polished dance floor. The orchestra were playing a pleasant piece that Rose did not recognise and the assembled guests were settling down to wait for the grand parade to begin the proceedings.

'Won't you join me at my table, Miss Northwood?'

Rose looked round to see Rivers standing behind her.

'I didn't expect to see you here, sir.'

'I am the guest of honour. I dare say that surprises you, too.'

'Most certainly. Does Lady Buckingham know who she's dealing with?'

'I am a generous benefactor, come to rescue the village from obscurity.'

'Surely it would have taken a fleet of ships such as the *Sadie Lee* to achieve such wealth by honest means.'

'Are you accusing me of something, Rose?'

'No, I am just surmising.'

'Then I suggest you put all such suspicions to the back of your mind and enjoy the evening ahead.' Rivers proffered his arm. 'Will you join me? Bring your sisters, too. We don't want to start tongues wagging.'

Rose was uncomfortably aware that there were a number of people watching with great interest and no doubt straining their ears in an attempt to hear what passed between them. She laid her hand on his arm. 'All right, but only because people are staring at us and I don't want to create a scene.' She waited until they reached the table he had claimed for them, and she sat down. 'I wanted a few words with you, anyway.'

He took a seat next to her. 'Why do I suspect I am going to be scolded?'

'You are not a five-year-old, sir. Why did you kiss me in front of my sisters and why did you pretend that we have feelings for each other?'

'I do have feelings for you, Rose.'

'No, you don't. You hardly know me.'

'Perhaps it was love at first sight.'

'You are just saying that. I think you want to get close to me because you think I know where your alleged brother is hiding. You have no brother, so who is this poor fellow you are pursuing so relentlessly? Tell me that, Mr Rivers.'

Chapter Seven

Rivers glanced around, as if making sure his response could not be overheard. He leaned closer. 'You're right about one thing. Jago is not my brother, he is my cousin.'

Rose stared at him in astonishment. 'But you said you were looking for your brother.'

'It's complicated.' Rivers smiled ruefully. 'But it was safer for Jago if his presence in the village could be kept secret.'

'I don't understand. Who could wish to harm him more than the hurt that has already been inflicted upon him?'

'So he is in your care? I knew as much.'

'I didn't say that, but I think you owe me an explanation.'

'Yes, I dare say I do.' Rivers eyed her thoughtfully. 'My grandfather Francis Rivers owned a tea plantation in Ceylon. He was a good businessman and he made a fortune, part of which my aunt Lucy inherited. Jago is her son from her first marriage. Sadly, Jago's father died of cholera and Aunt Lucy, who was a wealthy woman in her own right, then married a widower, Hector Dalby, with a son who was much older than Jago.'

Rose nodded sympathetically. 'That must have been hard on the boy.'

'The family returned from Colombo a few years ago and took up residence in the country house Aunt Lucy had inherited on her first husband's death. As ill fortune would have it, Hector Dalby was killed in a shooting accident during a hunting party on the estate.'

'Poor woman,' Rose said sadly. 'She doesn't have much luck, does she?'

'Indeed not. I inherited the family plantation in Ceylon when I was very young, but when I returned to England I was shocked by the change in Aunt Lucy. I hadn't seen her for several years but the lively, beautiful woman I remembered had become frail and timid. She seemed to be afraid of Montague, her adult stepson, and I didn't like the way he treated Jago, who is thirteen or maybe fourteen, still a boy.'

'What did you do?'

'I spoke to my aunt in private, but she was unwilling to stand up to Montague. I don't know what hold he has on her, but there was nothing I could do. Hector had left everything to his son.'

Rose frowned. 'But if Jago's father had owned the house and the land, shouldn't Jago have been the heir?'

'I was pursuing that fact when my aunt sent for me a second time. I went to see her and she was in a terrible state. She told me that Jago had disappeared without trace and she feared the worst.'

'What did you do then?'

'I was certain that any foul play would have been initiated by Montague, and I faced him with it. He denied everything to start with, but I pressed him further. Eventually he admitted that he had paid an unscrupulous sea captain to take the boy on as a deck apprentice, and make a man of him. In other words, to work the child virtually to death.'

'That's terrible. What did you do then?'

'I had my man of business make enquiries and he discovered that the ship on which Jago was virtually imprisoned was plying trade between this port and the continent.'

'I'm confused,' Rose said, frowning. 'I heard that you had purchased Longfleet Hall, as well as having given large sums of money to various good works.'

'That is just a coincidence. I had decided to move back to England months ago, long before I knew of Jago's fate.'

'But the first thing Jago said was "Sadie", and then "Sadie likes roses". What does that mean?'

'I took him for a short voyage on the *Sadie Lee* when he was much younger. He was always a curious child, asking questions all the time, and he wanted to know who Sadie Lee was.'

'And who was this woman?'

Rivers laughed. 'I have no idea, but I made up a story to amuse him. I told him that Sadie Lee was a young flower seller who loved roses. She died of a fever and a beautiful rose grew over the place where she was buried. It was just a story and I thought no more about it.'

'Well, it obviously meant something to Jago. Maybe he was searching for Sadie Lee when he ran away.'

'I think Jago was put ashore in order to get rid of him. The master of the vessel must have known that the *Sadie Lee* was my ship, and he had Jago dropped off a little way down the coast. The poor boy would have died if you had not discovered him in the Nativity scene.'

'What made you think we had him here?'

'I didn't know at first, but you recognised the ship's name and that convinced me you had Jago in your care.'

'But why haven't you involved the police? Surely a crime has been committed?'

'It would be difficult to prove. The captain will swear that he took Jago on in good faith and Montague would deny all knowledge of the transaction. If I returned Jago to his mother's care, he would be a prey to Montague for the rest of his life and Aunt Lucy would suffer, too.'

'It's a terrible story,' Rose said slowly. 'What now?'

'I need to see my cousin and assess his physical state. I assume you have had him treated by Dr Buckingham?'

'I haven't admitted anything yet, Rivers. I need time to think.'

He laid his hand on hers as it rested on the table. 'You've already admitted that he is in your care. You have to trust me, Rose. I promise I am telling you the truth.' Rivers glanced at the dancers enjoying the grand parade. 'Your sisters both have partners and no one will notice if we slip away now. Take me to see Jago for myself.'

Rose hesitated. She did believe his story, far-fetched although it seemed. 'All right. You go first and I'll meet you outside, but I want you to promise you won't upset Jago or try to take him away from us until he is well again.'

'You have my word.' He rose from his seat and walked casually around the edge of the dance floor, smiling and acknowledging people as he went. Rose was suddenly nervous. She should really have discussed this with Marianne before coming to such a decision, but she felt instinctively that this was the right thing to do. She waited for a minute or two and then she followed Rivers.

The servants had left the entrance hall, no doubt under the impression that all the guests were happily enjoying themselves in the ballroom. However, Rose did not dare look for her cloak and she braved the weather in her silk gown with only her dancing slippers to protect her feet.

Rivers stepped out of the shadows as she left the house. He took off his evening jacket and wrapped it around her shoulders.

'I'll ruin my satin slippers,' Rose said reluctantly as they started walking down the carriage sweep.

'Don't worry, I will buy you half a dozen pairs if that makes you happy.'

Rose laughed. 'The only thing that will make me really happy at the moment is to see Jago up and about and with his memory restored. Who knows, maybe the sight of you will bring him back to the present?' She clutched his still-warm jacket around her shoulders, inhaling the individual scent that was his alone, and surprisingly pleasant. She was not entirely sure that she trusted him, but Jago's future was at stake and there were decisions to be made. It was a risk taking him to the vicarage, but Rivers had discovered Jago's whereabouts and Rose had a feeling that nothing would stop him from seeing his young cousin. She trudged on doggedly, trying not to cry out as sharp stones pierced the thin soles of her dancing slippers.

Tiny flakes of snow had begun to fall from the dark velvet sky and the ground below their feet was becoming slippery.

'This is ridiculous,' Rivers said impatiently, and before she knew what was happening Rose found herself lifted off her feet.

'Put me down, Rivers,' she said crossly. 'I am perfectly capable of walking.'

'A snail moves more quickly than you can in those satin slippers. We will both succumb to lung fever if we don't reach shelter soon. We'll get there much faster if you don't wriggle.'

Rose was about to argue, but she realised that it was her pride that was hurt, and Rivers' long strides would get them into the warmth of the vicarage before they were soaked to the skin. They were alone in the dark with snow swirling around, seeming to cut them off from the rest of the world. However, it was a relatively short walk to the vicarage and it was a relief to get indoors and shake the freezing flakes off their clothes and out of their hair.

With her feet firmly on the ground, Rose laid her finger on her lips. 'Don't make a noise. Pa will almost certainly have gone to bed by now, so it's best if we don't disturb him.' She took a lantern from the chest in the hall and lit the way.

Rivers nodded silently and followed her upstairs, but when they reached Jago's room the bed was empty and there was no sign of him.

'Oh, my goodness!' Rose clamped her hand to her mouth to stop herself from crying out in dismay.

'Where would he be?' Rivers asked in a low voice. 'He can't have gone far.'

Rose shook her head. 'I don't know. We'd better go and look for him.' She did not wait for an answer.

The house was eerily silent, but on the first floor

she could see a light shining beneath her mother's bedroom door.

'Best wait here,' Rose said in a low voice. 'I don't want Ma to be upset. She's far from well.'

Rivers nodded. 'I understand.'

Rose entered the room and found Jago seated by the fire opposite her mother.

Grace looked up and smiled. 'Felix has come home, Rose.'

'It isn't Felix, Mama,' Rose said gently. 'His name is Jago.'

'No, dear, it is Felix.'

Rose turned to Jago, who shook his head.

'I never said that, but the lady insists. Maybe she's right. I just don't know.'

Rose moved swiftly to his side. 'My mama is poorly, Jago. You should come with me now.'

'Don't take the dear boy away from me so soon, Rose. He has only just returned.' Grace held out her hand, giving Rose a beseeching look that tugged at her heart, but she knew she must be firm.

'He will come back, I promise.' Rose helped Jago to his feet and guided him out of the room to where Rivers was waiting for them on the landing. Rose held the lantern a little higher so that Jago could see his cousin more clearly. 'Do you know this man, Jago?'

Jago clutched Rose's hand. 'Cousin Benedict?'

'That's right, Jago,' Rivers said calmly. 'I'm here to help you.'

'You mustn't tell Montague where I am. I can't go home,' Jago begged. 'Please don't send me home.'

'I have to let your mother know that you are safe, Jago.'

'Monty will kill me, Cousin Benedict.' Jago sighed and released Rose's hand as he dropped to the floor in a dead faint.

'Oh, poor boy. The shock of seeing you was too much for him.' Rose flexed her numb fingers where Jago's grasp had been so tight. 'We'd best take him back to his room.'

'Certainly not.' The door to Grace's room had opened unnoticed by them and she stood on the threshold. 'Bring the poor child in here and make him comfortable by the fire. Rose, send for that simple servant girl. At least she knows how to make a pot of tea. Tell her to add a nip of brandy.'

'Jago shouldn't be given alcohol, Mama,' Rose protested.

'It's for me,' Grace said firmly. 'I don't know who this gentleman is, but he'll oblige me by doing as I ask.'

Rivers acknowledged her with a bow. 'How do you do, ma'am? My name is Benedict Rivers and I am this young chap's cousin.' Rivers scooped Jago up in his arms and carried him into Grace's room, where he laid the boy on a chaise longue. 'Are you sure about this, Mrs Northwood? I could easily take Jago back to his room.'

'Yes, Mama,' Rose added hastily. 'Don't overtire yourself.'

'I am not in the least weary. When I awoke from my nap he was sitting in the chair and I thought it was Felix, come back to me, but now I am wide awake. This boy is in need of care and attention, which you cannot give if you are to return to the ball.'

'But, Mama, how did you know about that? We didn't want to upset you by speaking of it.'

'The simple girl chatters like a magpie. I might be delicate but I am not in my dotage, Rose. Now ring for Winnie and I'll tell her what I need.' Grace turned to Rivers with a frown. 'And you, sir, should be ashamed of allowing your cousin to get into this state. Go back to the ball and allow me to know what is for the best.'

Rivers nodded respectfully. 'I wouldn't dream of questioning your decision, Mrs Northwood. Come, Rose, we should show our faces at the ball before our absence is noted.'

Rose rang the bell for Winnie as she followed Rivers out of the room. 'Are you sure this is wise? Until a few minutes ago my mother thought that Jago was my brother, Felix, returned from the dead. Her health is very delicate, especially at this time of year. She isn't always in command of her senses.'

'She seems perfectly sane to me, and he might be better off with your mama than on his own, for the time being, anyway.'

Rose could see the sense of this, but she was still reluctant to leave. 'Surely they won't notice our absence. There are so many people at the ball, two less will make no difference.'

'Not to the majority, maybe, but those who saw us together earlier will assume the worst. Your good name could be sullied for ever in a small town like this.'

'That is nonsense. People know me better than that.' Rose gazed down at her ruined dancing slippers. 'Anyway, I can hardly dance in these shoes. They are torn to shreds.'

'Then I had better go back to the ball. I will tell your sisters that you were feeling unwell and I brought you home.'

Rose sighed. 'They won't believe that, but others might. Don't tell anyone that you've seen Jago.'

'No, that would be a mistake. I think the fewer people who know of his whereabouts the better. At least until he regains his memory and can tell us everything. When he does, I will make sure that Montague Dalby's part in this is exposed. It should make convincing evidence to put before the magistrate when I further Jago's case to claim his true inheritance.' Rivers took Rose's hand and held it briefly. 'I am sorry you will miss the rest of the ball. Perhaps we can dance together another time?'

Rose eyed him warily. 'You'd better hurry or it will be over and then we will both be missed.'

Rivers turned to leave just as Winnie came hurrying up the stairs, taking them two at a time.

'You rang, miss?'

'Yes, Winnie. Please bring a tray of tea for three to my mother's bedchamber.'

'I'll see you tomorrow,' Rivers said as he headed for the staircase.

Rose could see that Winnie was listening with interest. 'Now, please, Winnie,' Rose said firmly.

Winnie bobbed a curtsey. 'Yes, miss.'

Rose waited until Winnie had gone downstairs before entering her mother's bedroom. Jago was stirring and Grace was seated on a stool beside him, holding his hand.

'Poor boy,' she said softly. 'I thought he was Felix, but I see now that I was mistaken.'

'His name is Jago and Dr Buckingham has been treating him, Mama.'

'Who is he, Rose? And who is the gentleman who came in with you? I don't know him.'

Rose pulled up a chair. 'If you make yourself comfortable I will tell you everything I know, Mama.'

Winnie arrived with the tray of tea just as Rose finished a brief explanation of how Jago came to be with them. The sound of their voices seemed to have an effect on Jago and he opened his eyes. Rose pressed him back on the chaise longue as he attempted to rise.

'Sit down, please, Jago. A sip or two of tea will make you feel better.'

He brushed his fair hair back from his forehead, staring round the room as if seeing it for the first time. 'What happened?'

119

'You fainted, my dear,' Grace said before Rose had a chance to speak.

Winnie made a show of pouring the tea, all the time gazing curiously at Jago. 'Tea for you, Master Jago?'

Rose took the cup and saucer from her. 'Yes, thank you, Winnie. That will be all for tonight. You should get some rest now.'

'Don't you want me to wait up for the young ladies, miss? And you in your ball gown, drinking tea. It don't seem right.'

'Yes, well, life isn't fair, but you need your sleep. Goodnight, Winnie.'

'Yes, miss. Thank you.' Winnie backed out of the room.

'That girl was behind the door when common sense was given out.' Grace sipped her tea. 'Where's the brandy, Rose? I think we could all do with something stronger than just tea.'

'I'll fetch it in a minute, Mama.' Rose added a couple of spoonfuls of sugar to Jago's tea and handed it to him. 'How are you feeling, Jago?'

'Where's my cousin, Miss Rose? He was here just now.'

'Do you remember him?' Rose asked eagerly.

'It's all a bit hazy, but yes, I recall being on a ship, and being flogged. I think I ran away, but my recollections are muddled. I know I was glad to get off the ship. I think I swam ashore and I was cold, very cold.' Jago sipped his tea. 'I don't know where I am or how I came to be here.'

'This is St Michael's vicarage, and my papa is the vicar. This lady is my mama, and I am Rose Northwood. We've been looking after you for a week now, since Christmas Eve, in fact.'

'Brandy, Rose,' Grace said plaintively. 'I need something or I shall be up all night with a megrim.'

'All right, Mama. I'll go now. I'll be back in a minute or two.'

Rose left the room and went downstairs to the kitchen where she found the brandy that Cook kept hidden behind a flour sack. She was on her way back to the staircase when the front door opened and Emily rushed in on a blast of cold air, followed by Marianne and Tom Buckingham.

'What happened?' Marianne demanded. 'Are you ill, Rose?'

'Why are you holding a brandy bottle?' Emily eyed her suspiciously as she took off her cloak and bonnet. 'Are you a secret drinker now?'

Rose glanced over Tom's shoulder. 'Did Rivers come with you?'

'Of course not,' Marianne said huffily. 'I don't know why you let him bring you home anyway. People are sure to talk.'

'Why don't you let Rose explain?' Tom gave Rose a sympathetic smile. 'I suppose the brandy is for your mama, and there is a perfectly reasonable answer to all this.'

'Jago's memory has returned,' Rose said eagerly.

'Well, perhaps not completely, but he knows who he is and he recognised his cousin, Benedict Rivers.'

'Mr Rivers is Jago's *cousin*?' Marianne leaned on Tom's arm. 'Heavens above!'

'Are you sure about that, Rose?' Tom slipped his arm around Marianne's waist. 'Is it possible he was just saying that to convince you to reveal Jago's whereabouts?'

Rose nodded. 'I agree it sounds far-fetched but he told me the whole story and Jago definitely recognised him.'

'How exciting.' Emily clapped her hands. 'Tell all, Rose.'

'I need to take the brandy upstairs. Mama asked for a tot in her tea. She's been amazing, almost like her old self.'

'Would you like me to go up and see her?' Tom asked gently. 'I could examine the boy while I'm there.'

'Yes, please. That would put my mind at ease.' Rose turned to Marianne. 'I don't think we should all go. It might be too much for both of them.'

'But I want to see Mama,' Emily said sadly. 'She might not be like this tomorrow.'

'It is tomorrow, Em.' Rose gave her sister a hug. 'Perhaps Marianne will be kind enough to help you to bed. You can see Mama first thing in the morning.'

Marianne opened her mouth as if to argue, but Tom laid his hand on her arm.

'That sounds like good advice, Marianne. I'll

make sure your mama is taken care of, as well as Jago, and I'll see you tomorrow.'

'I suppose you're right,' Marianne said reluctantly. 'Come with me, Em. I'll help you to undress.'

'I'd like some hot milk first. Is Winnie still up?' Emily started off in the direction of the kitchen.

'You are a tiresome creature, Em,' Marianne said with a heavy sigh. 'But if a warm drink will help you to sleep I'd better come with you and make sure you don't scald yourself.' She hurried after her sister, leaving Rose to follow Tom upstairs to Grace's bedchamber.

Tom stopped outside the room and Rose went in first, clutching the bottle of brandy.

'What took you so long?' Grace demanded peevishly. 'My tea is almost cold.' She looked round and her expression changed subtly when she saw Tom. 'There was no need to send for you, Doctor. I am quite well now.'

Tom smiled. 'I can see that, ma'am. I've come to check on young Jago, who by the looks of things has had a miraculous recovery.' He walked over to stand beside Jago, giving him an encouraging smile. 'Rose tells me that you recognised your cousin.'

'Yes, sir. It's coming back to me – the beatings and pain. I thought I was going to die.'

'You're safe now, Jago. No one here will harm you.'

'Monty!' Jago said tremulously. 'He'll find me. Don't let him take me.'

'I'll give you something to make you sleep,' Tom said calmly. 'You must return to your room and I'll come and see you again in the morning. You are with friends, Jago.'

'Yes, Doctor.' Jago attempted to rise but sank back onto the chaise longue and Tom had to help him to his feet.

'Easy now. Lean on me, Jago.' Tom guided him to the doorway. 'If you settle down your mama for the night, Rose, I'll take care of the boy. He's going to be fine.'

'You're not going to send me home, are you?' Jago said anxiously. 'I'd rather go back on board than face Montague.'

'Don't worry, Jago.' Rose gave him an encouraging smile. 'Your cousin told me a little of what you've had to suffer. He won't allow you to be ill-treated ever again.'

Jago nodded wearily. 'I'm glad he found me. Monty said that Benedict Rivers is a liar and a thief, but I don't think so.'

'Neither do I,' Rose said firmly. 'He's certainly very concerned about you, and he's gone to great lengths to find you. I'm sure he'll keep you safe from now on.'

'Where's the brandy, Rose?' Grace's plaintive cry made Rose turn back to her mother.

'I have it here, Mama. I'll pour you a fresh cup of tea.'

'Oh, never mind the tea.' Grace picked up her ebony cane and pointed it at a glass on a side table.

'Just a small tot will help me to sleep. Then you may help me into bed. That's the best medicine, isn't it, Doctor?'

'I would think so, ma'am. I will visit you in the morning.' Tom lowered his voice. 'Can you spare me a few minutes downstairs when you've settled your mama, Rose? I have something to tell you and it can't wait until morning.'

Chapter Eight

Rose waited for Tom in the kitchen. Marianne had managed to persuade Emily to take her cup of warm milk up with her to bed, but Rose could hear her younger sister complaining bitterly as Marianne shooed her upstairs. Minutes later Rose was joined by Tom. She knew instantly that something was wrong.

'Why the serious face, Tom? Is it Jago?'

Tom pulled up a chair and sat down at the table. 'No, not directly, although I think the boy will be affected. It concerns Rivers himself.'

'What is it? You can tell me anything.'

'He's been accused of misappropriation of funds from the company he owns jointly with his aunt, Lucy Dalby, Jago's mother.'

'I don't understand. Why would Rivers do such a thing?'

'I only know what was being said, Rose. It seems that Montague Dalby has instigated the case against Rivers, branding him an embezzler.'

Rose eyed him curiously. 'But what has this got to do with Rivers? He's gone to huge lengths to rescue his cousin and he obviously cares for the boy. Not only that, but he spoke very fondly of Jago's mama, and he said he was shocked by the change he had seen in her.'

'Montague Dalby seems intent on ruining Rivers.'

Rose frowned. 'It was Montague who put Jago in the hands of the unscrupulous sea captain, but how did you learn all this, Tom?'

'I heard Sir James Hannaford discussing the case with Mama. It was in the strictest confidence, of course, but they are involved because of the huge donations Rivers intended to make to local funds. I believe a warrant has been issued for his arrest.'

Rose stared at him in disbelief. 'But surely Rivers is a wealthy man and would not need to embezzle his aunt's money?'

Tom shrugged. 'I've told you all I know, Rose. But Jago is a minor and his place is with his mother.'

'That may be so, but he's terrified of his stepbrother and with good cause.'

'I don't see how we can prevent his going home, Rose. Much as I agree with you.'

'I can't do it now, but as soon as it's light I'll go to the Crown and warn Rivers. He needs to know what he's being accused of.'

'Don't do anything silly, Rose. It isn't your business.'

Rose jumped to her feet. 'Of course it is. I can't allow a poor child to be badly treated. How would I feel if it were Felix who had to suffer like that?'

Tom stood up and wrapped his arms around her in a brotherly hug. 'I can only imagine how that makes you feel, but all I can do is to advise you to take care. Don't get involved with people who could ruin you and your family.' He held her at arm's length. 'I must go home now, but I want you to promise me you will think hard before you do anything.'

'I promise, but I will probably do it anyway. Someone has to stand up to that bully Montague Dalby.'

Despite the fact that she was exhausted, sleep evaded Rose for the rest of the night. She left her bed long before it was light, washed in cold water and dressed hastily in a linsey-woolsey morning gown with a white collar and cuffs. It was not her favourite dress but it was warm and serviceable, even though Emily always said it made her look like a governess.

The vicarage was eerily silent as Rose made her way downstairs to the hall where she put on her bonnet, cloak and knitted woollen gloves. She let herself out of the house and a pale silver moon edged between the clouds to light her path. It was only when she reached the Crown Inn that Rose realised she had not given her mission enough thought. She could hardly knock on the door and demand to see Mr Rivers, nor could she assume that Molly would be up and working this early in the morning. There was no sign of activity until she entered the back yard, where she found Jack Hawkes, Joe's older brother, emptying ashes into a hessian sack. He looked up with a start.

'Is that you, Miss Rose?'

'Yes, Jack. Is Molly up yet?'

'I doubt it. She's not an early riser. Some folk can get away with lying in bed until dawn, but not I.'

'Do you know if Mr Rivers is in his room?'

'Constable Dent is looking for him. I reckon that there ship in the bay is used to smuggle goods into the country. I heard it said that's where Mr Rivers gets his money from.'

'That's just gossip, Jack. Will you take a message to him for me?'

'I would, miss, but he went out half an hour since. He must know that the game is up and he'll be away on the next tide.'

Rose did not stop to argue. She picked up her skirts and ran as fast as she could to the quay where she came to a halt, bending over and holding her sides as she gasped for breath. Down below, bobbing up and down, she could see the ship's tender with its lights reflecting off the inky surface of the water. Two men were in deep conversation and one was unmistakably Rivers.

'Ahoy there,' Rose called, muffling her voice with her hand. 'Rivers.'

He looked up, his face pale in the moonlight. 'Rose? What are you doing here? Go home.'

'No. I need to speak to you urgently.'

Rivers said something to the other man in a low voice before taking the stone steps two at a time. He stepped onto the quay wall. 'What is it, Rose? You shouldn't be seen with me.'

'Never mind that. What are you doing?' Rose demanded. 'Are you running away?'

'I'm taking myself out of a difficult situation so that I can address my problems.'

'In other words, you are running away. Well, you can't just disappear and leave Jago behind. What will happen to him when his stepbrother discovers his whereabouts?'

'I hope that Jago will be sent home to be cared for by his mother. You've been wonderful, Rose. But I cannot do anything for the boy if I am locked up in prison.'

'Are you saying you're guilty of the charges against you?'

'No, of course not. But I need a good lawyer to take the case. If I know Montague, he will stop at nothing to have me discredited and financially ruined.'

'You are obviously heading for the *Sadie Lee*. Are you sailing for Ceylon and your plantation?'

'I would be very foolish to impart such information if it were true.'

'Stop playing games, Rivers. You might find all

this very amusing but I've been looking after Jago for long enough to have grown very fond of the boy. I lost my only brother and I can only begin to imagine how Jago's mother must be feeling.'

Rivers hesitated for a moment and then he nodded. It was too dark to read his expression but Rose knew she had won.

'All right. I'll come to the vicarage with you and I'll tell Jago how things stand. He deserves to know the truth.'

'And to be given a choice,' Rose added firmly. 'He might wish to go with you, and that could be the best thing for him.'

'We'll see. But we'd best hurry. It will be light in less than an hour and the *Sadie Lee* needs to catch the tide.'

'All right. Let's go.' Rose started off in the direction of home with Rivers at her side.

Jago was still asleep when they entered his room but he opened his eyes at the sound of his cousin's voice.

Rivers went to kneel at Jago's bedside. 'I need to talk to you urgently.'

'What's wrong? Why are you here in the middle of the night?'

'It's early morning,' Rose said hastily. 'Your cousin has something to tell you.'

Jago raised himself unaided to a sitting position. 'You're going away again, Benedict?'

'I suppose that was deserved. I haven't been a very

steady influence in your life, Jago. I'm sorry for that. Had I stood by you and your mama, none of this would have happened.'

Jago managed a weak smile. 'Mama has a will of her own. She was just unlucky that Dalby was killed and Monty took over. I never liked him.'

'Tell him, Rivers,' Rose urged. 'You have so little time.'

'You're right, Rose.' Rivers turned to Jago, frowning. 'I have to leave quickly or Montague will have me arrested for embezzling your mama's money. It's untrue, of course, but I need to prove it. I'm leaving for France on the tide. I'm offering you the chance to come with me.'

Rose sighed and shook her head. 'That's not very encouraging, Rivers.' She reached out to take Jago's hand in hers. 'Your cousin is trying to tell you that he loves you and he wants to protect you. If you wish to return to your old home and face Montague that is your choice. No one here will force you to do anything against your will.'

'Take me with you, Cousin Benedict,' Jago said eagerly. 'I can't help Mama until I am fully recovered. I know you wouldn't do anything to harm her or me. Let me come with you, please.'

Rivers rose to his feet. 'All right, if you're sure this is what you want, Jago.'

'It is.' Jago swung his legs over the side of the bed. 'Don't think I'm ungrateful, Miss Rose. You and your family have been wonderful.'

'Everyone will understand,' Rose said, smiling. 'You will be safe with your cousin.'

'I wish you would come, too.' Jago clasped her hand as he attempted to stand up, but he sank back on the bed. 'I am a bit shaky, but I will do anything to keep away from Montague.'

'I'll help you, Jago,' Rivers said firmly. 'Get dressed and pack any clothes you have. We need to get to the quay quickly, even if I have to carry you.'

'I'll come with you.' Rose handed Jago his clothes. 'You can lean on me, Jago. I'm stronger than I look.'

'You shouldn't be seen with me, Rose.' Rivers opened the door. 'It's only a matter of time before the village constable comes looking for me. I don't want you to be involved. Please go to your room and stay there until we have gone.'

'I'll do no such thing,' Rose said defiantly. 'I'll wait for you downstairs. This family is already involved and I don't give up easily.'

Jago grinned. 'You should believe her, Benedict. Rose always does what she says. I wouldn't be alive today if it hadn't been for her.'

'All right, but you must leave us at the quay, Rose. With luck you'll get home before daylight.'

'Don't worry about me. Just get yourself and Jago to safety. It doesn't matter to me whether or not you are guilty, I just want to know that Jago is safe from his hateful stepbrother and I trust you to take care of him as we have.' Rose left the room and went downstairs to put on her bonnet, cloak and gloves.

* * *

It took longer than Rose would have expected to get Jago down to the quay. In the end Rivers picked him up and carried him the last quarter of a mile or so. The first grey light of dawn revealed that the tide was already on the turn and there was no time to waste. However, just as they reached the stone steps the sound of footsteps and a warning shout from Constable Dent made Rivers tumble Jago into the waiting tender. Rose stood on the bottom step clutching the bundle of Jago's garments that had once belonged to Felix.

'Is that you, Miss Northwood?' Constable Dent leaned over the wall. 'Come away, miss. You don't want to be seen helping a felon to escape.'

'For heaven's sake, go home, Rose.' Rivers leaped into the boat as Constable Dent negotiated the slippery stone steps. He was just inches away from Rose.

'Do as he says, miss. I'll turn a blind eye to your being here if you go now.' Dent was about to make a grab for the tender when Rose gave it a shove with her foot. She took a mighty leap and landed at Rivers' feet.

'Row, Jackson. Row.'

'What are you doing, Rose?' Rivers demanded angrily.

'I'll come to the *Sadie Lee* with you. Jackson can bring me back later.'

'I can't do that, miss. We have to set sail,' Jackson

said tersely. 'The tide don't wait for no man nor woman, neither.'

Rose scrambled over to where Jago lay huddled where he had fallen. 'I think he's knocked his head. I'll look after him. Let's get Jago to safety. You can put me ashore later.' She knelt down and cradled Jago's head on her lap while Jackson rowed and Rivers took the helm.

Jago had only lost consciousness briefly and it was all that Rose could do to keep him lying down as he recovered. He was dazed and restive at first, but she spoke softly to him and he quickly regained his senses.

'You won't leave me, will you, Rose?' Jago asked as they drew nearer to the ship.

'I have to go home, Jago. It's best if you go with your cousin.'

'But I want you to come with us. It won't be the same without you.'

Rose made reassuring noises but she was worried nevertheless. Jago seemed so young and helpless, and he had suffered so much at the hands of those who should have been supporting and protecting him. Dawn had broken and it was getting light. She could feel the tug of the tide as they reached the *Sadie Lee* and she was worried. Until now her first priority had been for Jago's wellbeing, but she was concerned for her family, too. If she could not get home, her absence would create a scandal that would make life very difficult for her sisters as well as her parents.

But the situation was taken out of her hands. Rivers hauled Jago to his feet and flung him over his shoulder as he climbed the ladder to reach the swaying deck.

'You next, miss,' Jackson said firmly.

'Please take me back to shore.' The realisation of what she was about to do made Rose panic. 'I must get home, Jackson.'

'I can't take you back, miss. The tide is against us and I've got to secure the tender before I climb on board. You first.'

Rose knew then that to argue was useless. A quick glance over her shoulder revealed a small crowd gathering on the quay wall, but even more alarming was Jackson's cry of alarm as the coast guards' cutter came into view. Rose climbed onto the deck with a speed she had not known she possessed. There was no sign of either Rivers or Jago and the crew were busy setting sail. She remembered her way to the saloon and found Jago slumped down on a bench at the table. Rivers turned to her with a wry smile.

'I'm sorry, Rose. It looks as if you are going to join my crew for this particular voyage.'

'Can't you put me ashore somewhere?'

'We're headed for France. I spotted the coast guards' cutter. We're going to have to outrun it until we're in French waters. They can't touch us then.'

'Are you prepared to live forever on the run?'

'It won't come to that.' Rivers held a glass of

water to Jago's lips. 'Will you look after him, Rose? I need to go up on deck.'

'You could hand me over to the coast guards, Rivers. They will see me safely back to port.'

'I think they will be more interested in boarding the *Sadie Lee* and arresting me.'

'How would they know that you intended to flee to France?'

He laughed. 'I don't like the word "flee", Rose. We're leaving the country because it's the best way for me to be free to fight for justice, but I'm certain Montague tipped them off. At least he doesn't know that I have Jago or he would have sent the police in straight away.'

'I liked it at the vicarage,' Jago said miserably. 'I don't think I want to go to France, Benedict. At least not if it means that Rose will leave us.'

'Rose will be with us until I can safely send her home.' Rivers patted Jago on the shoulder. 'Chin up. In a couple of days we'll be at the old farmhouse in Provence and you'll be free to roam around the countryside, if you so choose. With warm sunshine and good food, you'll soon recover your strength.'

'Provence is in the South of France, I believe,' Rose said thoughtfully. 'That's a long way from Abbotsford, Rivers.'

'When we reach Paris I will send a telegram to your papa, telling him that you are safe and well.'

'But I should return home when we land in France. There are boats crossing the Channel all the time.'

'I promise you one thing, Rose. I will not keep you away from your family a moment longer than absolutely necessary. You have my word.'

'Stay with me, Rose,' Jago said faintly. 'I don't feel very well.'

Rivers was about to leave the saloon but he stopped to pass Rose a large china bowl. '*Mal de mer*,' he said brusquely. 'Seasickness. Luckily, I've never suffered from it but, judging by the green tinge of his skin, I think Jago is about to be very ill.'

Rose reached Jago's side just in time. She held his head while he retched and vomited.

'He needs to lie down, Rivers.'

'You and he can share my cabin. It's the largest and most comfortable, and there are two bunks. I'll send one of the crew to show you where it is.'

'I remember,' Rose said shortly. 'You're forgetting that you told Jackson to show me round the ship when I first came aboard. I'll take Jago there when he's recovered a little.'

Rivers nodded and left the saloon. By now the *Sadie Lee* had gathered speed and was pitching and tossing as they reached open sea under full sail. Rose helped Jago to the captain's cabin and made him as comfortable as possible, but he was constantly in need of attention and she did not dare leave him on his own. She lost track of time, but in the end it was hunger that drove her from the cabin. Jago had drifted into a troubled sleep and she left him with a bowl at his side, and was on her way to the galley when she came face to face with Rivers.

'Are we out of danger?' Rose asked, leaning against the bulkhead in order to prevent herself from being thrown into his arms.

'We've lost the cutter and we're set fair for France, but we won't risk going into port at Cherbourg. We'll land a little further along the coast.'

'And you will put me on a ferry to take me back to England?'

Rivers shook his head. 'That wouldn't be right. You aren't used to travelling on your own.'

'You mean I have to go with you whether I want to or not?'

'I'm not compelling you to do anything, Rose. I just need to have time to make suitable arrangements for your return home.' Rivers reached out to steady her as the deck heaved beneath their feet. 'I would be eternally grateful if you would accompany us as far as Avignon. My estate is in a village not too far away and, once there, Jago will have time to rest and recover his health as well as his good spirits. He's just a child, Rose.'

She sighed. 'Of that I am very well aware. I will do as you ask, but only because I care about Jago and I cannot see another way out of this situation. But I want you to promise one thing.'

'Anything in my power.'

'I want you to send a telegram to my papa as soon as possible.'

'I've already given you my word. I'm very grateful to you, and very much in your debt.'

Rose smiled reluctantly. 'I'm sure the time will come when I have to remind you of that.'

'Quite possibly, but in the meantime, I'm starving and you must be, too. Cook has set some food out for us in the saloon.'

'I *am* very hungry, but what about Jago?'

'You go to the saloon and I'll check on the boy. As it is, I doubt if he'll keep any food down until we get him ashore.' Rivers walked off in the direction of his former cabin and Rose made her way to the saloon, where the cook had laid out cold meats, bread and cheese.

She had made a start on the food when Rivers joined her. He sat down at the table and placed a generous helping of roast beef and ham on his plate.

'Are you all right, Rose? I mean, I know this is not an ideal situation, but I will try to make your stay with us as pleasant as possible.'

She buttered a slice of bread. 'I believe you. I just worry about my family at home. They will know I'm on your ship but they have no idea where we're bound. I can only imagine how worried Papa must be, as well as my sisters, and if Mama should find out I hate to think how she will take the news.'

'I'm sorry to have embroiled you in my affairs, Rose. If I could put you ashore safely I would do so without hesitation.'

'I am worried about them, but the damage is done

now.' Rose nibbled the bread and smiled. 'Well, to be honest, I imagine Emily will think it's quite a lark, but Marianne will know better.'

Rivers smiled. 'I am an only child. I envy you your family.'

'You have Jago. He seems more like a younger brother to you than a cousin.'

'That's true, except for the fact that I have been too busy with my various businesses to spend much time with the boy, even when he stayed with me in Provence.'

'Well, you have time to get to know him properly now.' Rose eyed him curiously. 'How do you propose fighting the case against you when you will be so far from London?'

'I have a man of business in Avignon. He handles everything to do with the estate in my absence. I will have to rely on him to find me a good lawyer.'

Rose thought for a moment and she could not let the matter drop. 'Even so, French law must be quite different from the law at home.'

'You have an enquiring mind, Rose. It's a pity to shut young women away at home when they have brains equal to men and a wit often much sharper.'

'I've never heard a man admit such a thing before. Not even Pa, who is very open-minded about many things.'

'I grew up in England, but I've lived abroad for most of my adult life, not just in Ceylon, but in other countries, including France. Perhaps being an outsider looking in gives one a better understanding of the world.'

'It would seem so, but I'm afraid my lot is already cast. If Papa has his way I will marry well and settle down to being a good wife and mother.'

'And you, Rose. What do you want from life?'

'I'm not sure. Until now I haven't had much time to think about myself. I'll let you know if I come to any conclusions.' Rose cut a slice off a large piece of cheese. 'Perhaps I'll find the answer in Provence.'

'It's still winter, of course, but I would like you to see the fields of blue lavender and the olive groves in summer. Not to mention the vineyard.'

'I think by the way you speak you must really love the place.'

'Yes, I confess Le Fleuve is my favourite. I'm genuinely sorry to be taking you there in such circumstances, Rose. But I will try to make it up to you in any way I can.'

'I can't pretend this journey won't alter my life completely. My reputation will be in shreds when I return home, no matter what you say. On the other hand I can't wait to see the area you love so much. It must be really special and I've always longed to travel.' Rose smiled ruefully. 'Although perhaps not like this.'

Rivers laid his hand on hers as it rested on the table. 'I know, and believe me I will do everything in my power to make things right for you. Everything.'

Chapter Nine

Provence, January 1859

The journey to Rivers' estate in a village a few miles west of Avignon had taken much longer than Rose had anticipated. Jago had suffered terribly from sea-sickness, which thankfully disappeared the moment he put a foot on dry land. Even so, he was still not fully recovered and tired easily. They travelled by hired carriage and then several different trains, breaking their journey at night in order for them all to get some sleep before moving on again next day. Rose had made sure that Rivers sent a telegram to her father, after which there was nothing she could do other than cope with the rigours of a long journey south, cutting through the centre of France. However, no matter how fatigued Rose felt, she was fascinated by everything she saw and heard. She had a smattering of French that she had learned in the schoolroom and it was surprising how much of it came back to her as the days went by. It was, of course, midwinter and sometimes the journey south was delayed by bad weather.

However, when they finally arrived at the estate, despite the chill in the air, the sun shone from an azure sky, tinting the sleeping vines with gold as they waited for spring to bring them back to life. The silvery leaves on the gnarled branches of the trees in the olive grove cast a tracery of shadows on the grass below, and in the distance a line of blue-green mountains, capped with snow, provided a spectacular backdrop.

As the carriage drew up in a paved courtyard, Rose caught her breath at the sight of the old farmhouse. The rambling two-storey building had stuccoed walls, painted a rusty pink, and the windows were framed with green shutters. There were wrought-iron balconies outside each of the rooms on the first floor, giving the old building a romantic look. Rose could imagine a scene from *Romeo and Juliet* enacted on the gravelled courtyard where a lion's-head fountain trickled melodiously into a pool surrounded by a stone wall. Rose was enchanted by everything she saw, and when they entered the house she was not disappointed. The beamed ceilings and well-trodden flagstone floors dotted with colourful rugs made the old house feel homely. A log fire blazing in one of the stone fireplaces added to the feeling of warmth and welcome, as did the tempting aroma of something savoury emanating from the kitchen. The scent of herbs and garlic mingled with the fruitiness of red wine and Rose's stomach rumbled with hunger. She was so preoccupied taking in the ambience she had not noticed the small woman wearing a white apron, her hair confined to a starched white cap, who came hurrying to greet them.

'Rose.' Rivers tapped her on the shoulder. 'I want you to meet my excellent housekeeper, Madame Laurent.'

Rose turned with a start. 'I don't know what to say. My French is very poor, as you already know.'

Madame Laurent inclined her head graciously. 'No matter, Mademoiselle. I speak English.'

'Oh, thank goodness.' Rose sighed with relief. 'It's a pleasure to be here at last. We seem to have been travelling for such a long time.'

'I will show you to your room.' Madame Laurent glanced anxiously at Jago, who was leaning heavily on Rivers' arm. 'Monsieur Jago is ill?'

'He has been unwell,' Rivers said smoothly. 'But he is recovering nicely. A few weeks' rest and your delicious meals, and he'll be back to his old self. I'll take him to his room.'

Madame eyed the small valise that Rose had placed on a nearby settle. 'Is that all your luggage, Mademoiselle?'

Rose felt herself blushing. She was not about to admit that Rivers had given her money to purchase a very basic wardrobe from a street market in a small town where they had spent a whole day in order for Jago to rest.

'I travel light, Madame,' Rose said hastily.

'No matter. I know a very good seamstress. I am sure she will be happy to oblige. Come this way, if you please.' Madame Laurent bustled off, leading the way into a long corridor and up a flight of stairs to the first floor, where she opened a door to a bedroom overlooking the front courtyard and the huge evergreen oak tree that stood like a sentinel protecting the old building from intruders. The furniture was carved oak, simple but elegant, with a four-poster bed in the centre of the room, complete with heavy damask curtains and a patchwork coverlet.

'It's beautiful,' Rose said, warming her cold hands in front of the coal fire that burned merrily in the hearth. 'So lovely. Are you sure this is my room, Madame?'

Madame Laurent smiled benignly. 'It is the room that the lady of the house always uses, Mademoiselle. Monsieur Rivers thought you would be more comfortable here. He sent a messenger with specific instructions before you arrived.'

Rose moved to the dressing table and fingered the silver-backed hairbrush and hand mirror. 'It is so much more than I expected. Thank you.'

'I will leave you to make yourself comfortable. Just ring the bell if you need anything, Mademoiselle.

Luncheon will be served in the dining room in half an hour.' Madame Laurent left the room, closing the door behind her.

Rose unpacked her few belongings and placed them in a chest of drawers beneath the window. It was so quiet here and such a contrast to the hectic days spent travelling that it felt as if she had stepped into another world. As always, if she found herself alone, her thoughts went to those she loved most. She hoped that everyone at home would understand why she had allowed Rivers to bring her to France, although it was a question she had asked herself on numerous occasions. She could have left him and Jago at the quay, or she could have remained at home and waved them both goodbye from the safety of the vicarage. The answer was staring her in the face but she chose to ignore it. No sane person would risk everything for a man she barely knew and a young boy who was no relation. She went to the washstand and splashed lukewarm water onto her face, drying it on the towel provided. This, she decided, was not the time for self-recriminations. What was done was done, and she must take the consequences. She could only hope her family would forgive her.

Feeling refreshed and extremely hungry, she left her room and went downstairs to find the dining room.

She almost walked past it but the door was open and she spotted Rivers standing by the fireplace with a glass of red wine in his hand. There was no sign of Jago.

Rivers met her curious gaze with a smile and he raised his glass. 'Can I tempt you to join me?'

'It's only midday.'

'You're in France now, Rose. We drink wine when we feel like it.' Rivers went to the richly carved sideboard and filled a glass, which he handed to her. 'Welcome to my home.'

She sipped the rich red wine and smiled. 'Thank you. I can understand why you love it here. It is very beautiful, even in the depths of winter.'

He gave her a searching look. 'You are missing your family. I suppose I should send you home. After all, we are here now and Jago is safe. He should make a full recovery.'

'We've only just got here,' Rose said, alarmed. 'Are you going to send me away?'

'Do you want to stay? I don't wish to keep you here against your will.'

Rose swallowed a mouthful of wine. 'I do miss everyone at home, but I came to help you with Jago. He is still far from well and I don't want to leave him.'

'He will be well cared for here.'

'Nevertheless, I would never forgive myself if I left to go home and Jago took a turn for the worse. I believe he is quite fond of me.'

'That's true. Then you'll stay? For the time being, at least.'

Rose nodded. 'I may never get another chance to live abroad. I didn't realise how dull my life was in Abbotsford, or what I was capable of. I want to stay on, Rivers. I also want to see you clear your name.'

Rivers raised his glass. 'Thank you, Rose. That's all I needed to know. Here's to Jago, and to me proving my innocence. And,' he added, smiling, 'here's to you, for courage and determination. Rose Northwood, I salute you.'

'Thank you, but I think you are giving me more credit than I deserve.' Rose followed him to the table and he pulled out a chair for her. She sat down. 'Where is Jago? Isn't he eating with us?'

'The poor boy is exhausted. Madame Laurent will have his food taken to his room. I dare say he will join us for dinner this evening. After luncheon I'd like to show you round the estate, if you are not too tired.'

'I would like that very much. It looks so beautiful.'

Rivers took a seat opposite her and rang a silver bell. 'It is, even at this time of year. But in the spring and summer it's quite breath-taking.'

'I will have to return home long before then.' Rose sighed. 'I am enjoying this adventure but I will have to face the consequences sooner or later.'

'I feel very guilty for putting you in such a position, Rose, but I will make it up to you one way or another. I just need to clear my name before I can do anything.'

Conversation ceased as Madame Laurent entered

the room carrying a large tureen, which she placed on the table. A young maidservant followed her with a basket of freshly made bread and a large slab of butter on a green china plate in the shape of a cabbage leaf. She glanced curiously at Rose but scuttled away quickly when Madame shot her a stern glance.

Madame ladled beef casserole onto two plates and placed one in front of Rose and another for Rivers. 'Will that be all, Monsieur?'

'Thank you, yes, Madame. Have you sent food up to my cousin?'

'Yes, Monsieur. Angeline took it to his room just now. She needs to be kept in her place, that one. She has too much to say for herself.'

Rose stifled a giggle. Angeline did not look angelic, as her name suggested she should be, but perhaps a little companionship from someone his own age might be the tonic that Jago needed to bring him back to full health. She waited until Madame had left them to enjoy their meal.

'I think Jago will enjoy having a young friend. Angeline looks as if she might be fun.'

Rivers laughed and raised his glass. 'I had not thought of that, but I hope you're right.' He was suddenly serious. 'By the way, I have my man of business coming to dinner with us tonight. I meant to tell you earlier, but it's important that I get my legal situation sorted out as quickly as possible.'

'I agree.' Rose spooned some of the casserole into her mouth. 'This is so delicious. I must get the recipe for Cook at home. Although I doubt if she would have all the herbs needed to make this dish.'

'I'm sure Madame would be only too happy to share her secret with you, Rose. She would take it as a great compliment. By the way, I think you will like Guy Colbert. He's a charmer but he is also very efficient and I trust him to handle my affairs while I am absent. I can't give any higher praise.'

Rose was suddenly curious. She could not wait to meet this amazing man of business. She settled down to enjoy her meal.

That evening, Jago had chosen to have supper brought to him in his bedchamber, leaving Rose and Rivers to enjoy a glass of wine in the main reception room. Rivers was answering Rose's questions about the history of the farmhouse when Madame announced the arrival of Monsieur Colbert. Rose turned her head to see a tall, well-dressed man in his thirties enter the room. His black frock coat and pin-stripe trousers were impeccably tailored and he wore a spotless white shirt with a blue silk cravat. His fair hair waved back from a high forehead and his pale blue eyes were fringed with thick lashes that would have been the envy of any woman.

Rivers rose to his feet. 'Ah, Guy, many thanks for joining us.' They shook hands.

'Good evening, Benedict.' Colbert turned his attention to Rose. 'And this must be Mademoiselle Northwood, whom you praised so highly in your letter.' He took Rose's hand and raised it to his lips. 'It's a pleasure to meet you.'

'You might allow me to introduce you properly, Guy.' Rivers laughed and motioned him to take a seat. 'Rose, this is Guy Colbert. He handles all my business matters here in France.'

'How do you do, sir?' Rose said politely.

Colbert sat down opposite Rivers. 'We have much to discuss.'

'Yes, indeed, but that can wait until after dinner.' Rivers went to a side table and filled a glass with wine, which he handed to Colbert. 'Jago is here, too. That in itself is a long story, but we'll go into that later. He's suffered greatly at the hands of Montague Dalby, but he's on the mend, although it will take time.'

Colbert nodded. 'You told me some of it in your letter. It's a shocking business.' He sipped his wine. 'But if you'll forgive me for raising the subject, Benedict, surely it is not in Miss Northwood's best interests for her to be here without a suitable chaperone. It would certainly be frowned upon by any respectable family in France.'

Rivers frowned. 'I hadn't considered it in depth, Guy. I suppose I assumed that having Jago here and Madame Laurent would suffice.'

'I think you know that isn't the case.'

Rose put her glass down with a thud. 'Excuse me, gentlemen, but you are talking about me as if I were not here.'

'I'm sorry, Rose.' Rivers smiled apologetically. 'Guy is right. I should have thought of it myself. I need to find someone suitable to keep you company while you are here.'

'If my reputation is ruined then the damage has already been done,' Rose said calmly. 'I do not need a chaperone.'

'Perhaps we could persuade one of your sisters to join us,' Rivers said thoughtfully. 'Do you think Marianne would be willing to travel to France in order to save your reputation, Rose?'

'Even if she could be persuaded to leave home, Marianne would need a chaperone herself to accompany her on such a long journey. As I said, the harm is already done. I knew that when I agreed to accompany you to Provence, Rivers.'

'I am sorry, Rose,' Rivers said earnestly. 'I've been extremely selfish.'

Colbert cleared his throat. 'I seem to have started something by my comments. I'm sorry if I have made you feel uncomfortable, Miss Northwood.'

'It's Rose. Please call me Rose. You have only brought the truth to the surface, Monsieur. I don't regret my actions, although I do miss my home. However, I considered that Jago's wellbeing was more important than social mores, so may we forget all about it, for now at least?'

Rivers was about to reply when Madame Laurent entered the room. 'Dinner is served, Monsieur.'

* * *

The food was excellent and the wine flowed, although Rose took care to take small sips and declined a second glass. However, Rivers and Colbert were quick to relax in the comfortable ambience of the farmhouse dining room. A log fire warmed the oak-panelled room and added more light to that from sturdy white candles in ornate iron holders. Rose could imagine generations of French farmers and their families seated around the same table, enjoying wonderful food and drinking their own vintage wines as they chatted about the day's events. She did not contribute much to the conversation but preferred to sit quietly and listen to Rivers and his advisor as they discussed the current situation. Fruit and a selection of cheeses followed a rich dessert. A combination of a hearty meal together with even a modest amount of wine was having an effect, and Rose was finding it hard to stay awake. The days of travelling had taken their toll, too, and she longed for the quietness and comfort of her room.

'You must be exhausted, Rose,' Rivers said suddenly. 'Here we are, discussing things that have little interest to you. I am sorry.'

Rose managed a smile. 'No, really. I do understand, but I am rather tired. Would you mind very much if I went to my room?'

Rivers pushed back his chair and stood up. 'Of course not. Once again I apologise for neglecting you.'

'I hope we meet again soon,' Colbert added with

a disarming smile. 'I would be more than happy to show you some of the local sights.'

Rose managed to stand without swaying, although she felt for a moment as if she were back on board the *Sadie Lee*. 'Thank you, Monsieur. I'm sure I would enjoy that very much.'

She nodded to Rivers as she made her way out of the room and into the comparative cool of the dark corridor. She had not thought to ask for a candle, but there was just enough moonlight filtering through the windows to show her the way. However, when she reached the first floor she was suddenly confused. Everything looked different in the dim light. She opened one door and realised her mistake as the furniture was shrouded in dust covers. A feeling close to panic almost overwhelmed her but she took a deep breath and tried the next door. This time the room was empty of furniture, although she could just make out the shape of a baby's cradle beneath the window. She closed the door and made her way to the window at the end of the landing. She realised then that she had become disorientated when she looked down and saw the stables at the side of the house. She laughed softly, imagining how her sisters would giggle when she told them of her mistake. Marianne would tell her that it was because she had been drinking wine and Emily would tease her mercilessly. Convinced that she was now facing the front of the house, Rose opened the door and stepped into a room that was almost identical to hers. On a wall table by the door there was a conveniently placed candlestick. She lit a candle, but almost dropped it when she saw a tall white shape reflected in a cheval mirror. Rose was tempted to turn and run, but common sense reasserted itself and she held the candle higher. She realised then that she was not in her room and the spectral figure was a dressmaker's dummy displaying a beautiful white lace wedding gown with a veil that seemed to float its way to the floor. A set of silver-backed hairbrushes and a mirror were laid out on the dressing table as if the occupant of the room was about to sit down and get herself ready for bed. A silk nightgown and voluminous wrap were set neatly on the counterpane and a pair of dainty, fur-trimmed slippers peeped out from beneath the bed frame. A shiver ran down Rose's spine. Who was the owner of the garments and where was she now?

Feeling like an intruder, Rose backed out of the room and closed the door. She was still clutching the silver candlestick and her hands were shaking, sending drops of hot wax onto the polished floorboards. She was tempted to go downstairs and tell Rivers what she had seen, but that might look as if she was being a busybody. Perhaps the woman in question had been his intended? That thought was more than disturbing. Rose took a deep breath and tried each door until she came to her room.

Warmth from the fire and light from candles on the mantelshelf greeted her and she was so relieved she wanted to cry. A knock on the door made her turn with a start.

'C-come in.' Rose placed the candlestick on a side table and waited as the door opened so slowly she half expected to see a wraith-like figure wearing the white lace gown, but it was just Madame Laurent and she clutched a dainty china cup and saucer in one hand and a pitcher of warm water in the other.

'Monsieur Rivers told me you had gone to bed, Mademoiselle. I took the liberty of bringing you some hot chocolate and some water for the washstand. You must be very tired after travelling so far from home.'

Rose took the cup and saucer from her. 'Thank you, Madame.'

'Jago told Angeline about your long journey from England. Angeline is very young and doesn't know when to keep silent, Mademoiselle. I, on the other hand, am a soul of discretion.' Madame Laurent walked over to the washstand and filled the prettily patterned jug. 'I will say goodnight. I trust you will sleep well.'

'Madame . . .' Rose simply had to ask the question, 'I lost my bearings just now and went into the wrong room. I saw what looked like a wedding gown displayed on a dressmaker's dummy.'

'It must have been a trick of the light, Mademoiselle. There is nothing of that description in any room. I would advise you not to bring it up in conversation. Goodnight.' Madame Laurent hurried from the room and closed the door firmly behind her.

Rose was left with a host of unanswered questions, but there was little she could do other than to sit down and sip her hot chocolate before getting ready for bed.

Next morning Rose was up at dawn. She had slept badly, haunted by dreams of a young woman wearing the lace dress and, even with her face concealed by the veil, Rose knew she was crying. Having dressed quickly and tied her hair back with a ribbon, Rose retraced her steps of the previous evening, going from room to room, but there was no sign of the gown, the veil or the nightclothes, let alone the silver-backed hairbrushes and mirror. Perhaps she had imagined it all, but that was hard to believe. Rose could only think that Madame Laurent knew more than she admitted and had removed all trace of the bridal garments. Even the crib had disappeared and the furniture in all the other rooms on this side of the central staircase was shrouded in dust covers. Rose went slowly downstairs, hoping to have a word with Rivers before Jago came to join them for breakfast. But the dining room was empty and the table laid for one only. She was about to ring the bell when Angeline erupted into the room, stopping abruptly and dropping to a clumsy curtsey.

'I'm sorry, Mademoiselle. I didn't know you were in here.'

'Is Monsieur Rivers up yet, Angeline?'

'He left for Paris an hour since, Mademoiselle. Shall I fetch your breakfast now?'

'Jago might join me.'

Angeline shook her head. 'I took him some hot chocolate but he said he wants to eat in his room.'

Rose frowned. 'We'll see about that. Lay another place at table, please, Angeline. I will go upstairs and speak to him. It's not good for a boy of his age to take to his bed.' Rose did not wait for an answer. She made her way purposefully to Jago's room at the far end of the house. She knocked and opened the door. 'Are you awake, Jago?'

'Yes. Is that you, Rose?' Jago sat up in bed, peering at her in the half-light.

Rose marched over to the window and threw back the curtains. Pale wintry sunlight filtered into the room. 'It's breakfast time, Jago. I think you should come downstairs and sit at table with me. Your cousin has gone to Paris on business, so Angeline told me.'

Jago pulled the covers up to his chin. 'I think I'd rather have my food brought up here.'

Rose eyed him suspiciously. There were no outward signs of illness, apart from the healing scars on his back, and it was unnatural for a boy of his age to want to lie around in bed all day. 'I would like it if you came down and had breakfast with me, Jago. Otherwise I will be on my own.'

'I am unwell,' Jago said plaintively.

Rose pulled the coverlet back with one quick flick of her wrist. 'I don't believe you. Or if you do feel poorly it's because you have decided to play the part of an invalid. My mama has done that ever since my brother died and it's not a good thing.' She tossed a dressing robe onto the bed. 'Put that on and I'll help you downstairs. You may return to your bed if you get too tired, but in the meantime I think I have discovered a mystery and I need your help to solve it.'

Jago sat up and swung his legs over the side of the bed. 'No, really? What could there be of interest in this old farmhouse at this time of year? It's all right in summer, but what is there to do now but sit by the fire all day?'

'You and I will work that out. I expect your cousin will be gone for a day or two, so it's just you and me, Jago. Come downstairs and I'll tell you all about it over breakfast. I think I smelled croissants baking as I came up here.'

'I am rather hungry.' Jago allowed her to help him into the robe and a pair of slippers. 'My ankle hurts and I'm a bit shaky on my legs.'

'You'll get stronger every day. The more you stay in bed the worse it gets. Maybe we can go for a walk this afternoon. You can show me round the vineyard and olive groves.'

'Maybe,' Jago said doubtfully. 'But what is the mystery? That sounds exciting.'

Rose helped him on the stairs, but otherwise he

seemed to be walking well enough on his own. She decided that what he needed now was exercise and something to occupy his mind. Obviously the trauma he suffered during his brief time at sea would not go away easily, but she would do her best to make him forget the worst of his treatment. She had not been able to protect Felix, but if she could help Jago it would go some way to justify the upset she knew she had caused her family.

Once settled at the dining-room table she made sure that Jago had finished his food before she told him of her experience the previous evening. He leaned his elbows on the table, watching her intently.

'So you see,' Rose concluded eagerly, 'I've searched the whole of the first floor this morning and there is no sign of the gown or anything I saw last night.'

'You might have been dreaming.'

'No, that's the point, Jago. I saw all that before I went to bed. I didn't take a candle with me and I got confused in the darkness.' Rose thought for a moment. 'But I took a candlestick from the room where I saw the wedding dress. It must still be on the mantelshelf in my bedchamber. I'll go up and fetch it. That will prove to you that I did not imagine the whole thing.'

Rose was about to leave the table but Jago laid his hand on her arm. 'Better wait until the cleaning women have done their bit, Rose. I remember them from the last time I was here. They come in from the village every day, or so it seemed.'

Rose nodded. 'You're right. I can wait, but maybe you could speak to Angeline. She might know something. The wedding gown must have belonged to someone who lived in this house. Madame Laurent wouldn't tell me anything.'

'I will talk to Angeline. She loves to chatter about goings-on in the village. Not that I remember many of the people she mentions.'

'Then she's an ideal person to ask, but be careful. I don't want her to tell Madame Laurent. There's obviously some mystery attached to all the things I saw. If all else fails I'll speak to your cousin when he returns.'

'Or Monsieur Colbert might know something,' Jago said thoughtfully. 'He was always here when I used to stay with Cousin Benedict, although that was in the summer months. I've never stayed here in the winter.'

'If he comes here while your uncle is away I will definitely speak to him. Someone must know who the dress was made for.'

Jago clutched her hand. 'You won't leave me here on my own, will you, Rose? I know you want to go home.'

'Of course I'm worried about my family, but they will get along well enough without me for a while. I have no intention of abandoning you, Jago.'

'Thank you.' Jago lowered his voice. 'Please don't tell my cousin that I asked you to stay. He'll think I'm totally useless.'

'I won't say a word, but I'm sure your cousin thinks nothing of the sort. He understands what you've been through and he's doing his best to make things better for you.'

Jago put his head on one side, eyeing her curiously. 'You like him, don't you, Rose?'

'He's not the easiest man to get on with, but I respect his determination to keep you safe, Jago. I think he's a good person despite what everyone says.'

'You're right. He's always tried to look after Mama and me, but when she married my stepfather, everything started to go wrong. He was not a nice man and Montague takes after him. I hate Montague Dalby. He's the cause of all our problems.'

Rose patted him on the shoulder. 'Let's hope your cousin finds a good lawyer and Montague Dalby will get his just deserts.' Rose glanced over her shoulder as the door opened and Angeline hesitated on the threshold.

'Madame told me to clear the table.'

Rose jumped to her feet. 'Yes, do that, Angeline.' She sent a meaningful look in Jago's direction. 'I'll be back in a few minutes, Jago. Then I'll help you to your room and you can get dressed. We might even go for a short walk as the sun has come out.' Rose hurried from the room. There was a slim chance that Angeline might know something about a young woman who must have lived or at least stayed in the farmhouse before her wedding. Had she gone through the ceremony? If so, who did she marry and what happened then? The more she thought about it the more curious Rose felt.

She went straight to her room, intent on finding the silver candlestick, but on opening the door she found two of the village women still at work. One was making the bed and the other was dusting, but there was no sign of the candlestick. Rose muttered an apology and left them to finish their tasks. She did not go downstairs straight away, but headed for the room where she had found the wedding gown. As before everything was shrouded in Holland covers and it was almost no surprise to see the candlestick back in place on the mantelshelf. Someone had replaced it since she had gone downstairs to breakfast. Rose suspected it was Madame Laurent, but she could hardly march downstairs to the servants' quarters and accuse her of lying. She closed the door and retraced her steps to the dining room to find Jago on his own.

'Well?' Rose said eagerly. 'Did she know anything?'

Jago shook his head. 'No, not really, but she has a brother my age and three sisters. She said I would be welcome to visit them if I so wished.'

'And do you? I mean, it might be good for you to have some young company, Jago.'

'I don't know. Not yet, anyway. I couldn't walk that far.'

'Then we must see about getting your health and strength back, my boy.' Rose held out her hand. 'Come along with me. We'll find your clothes and we'll take that walk. We won't go far and we'll do a little more each day. You'll soon be back to normal.'

'Thank you, Rose. I wish you were my sister.'

Rose laughed. 'You should speak to Emily, my younger sister. She might disagree with you.'

Jago stood up with difficulty. 'I am so weak, Rose. Will I ever be strong again?'

'Yes, of course you will. Good food, rest and gradual exercise will have you back to your former self again.'

Jago grinned. 'It's my birthday next week. I'll be fourteen, almost a man.'

'Really? Then we must celebrate.'

Chapter Ten

Madame Laurent confirmed that the master had gone to Paris to see a lawyer, as arranged by Monsieur Colbert, who would be calling daily to make sure that Rose and Jago wanted for nothing. Madame said the last words with a curled lip, making it clear that she was perfectly capable of running the household without the help of a mere land agent. Rose made sympathetic sounds, but she was rather looking forward to getting to know Monsieur Colbert. She had grown fond of Jago during their time together but it would be nice to have adult male company, and the fact that Guy Colbert was good-looking, smart and had a twinkle in his eye made him even more attractive. Maybe he knew something about the mysterious wedding gown and the disappearing crib. She could not wait to find out.

However, when Colbert was questioned later

that morning he seemed to be as mystified as both Rose and Jago. He stayed for luncheon, but then he had business in Avignon and drove off in his chaise, having promised to return next day and stay longer so that he could drive Rose and Jago around the property. Rose was left none the wiser as to the mysterious wedding gown.

She devoted all her attention to Jago. Having persuaded him to go for a walk in the winter sunshine, she made sure that he did not overexert himself. When they returned, she settled him down by the fire and answered his questions about her life in Abbotsford. He was particularly interested in Felix. At first Rose was reluctant to talk about her younger brother, but she discovered that memories could also be comforting, and to tell Jago about the things that Felix had done in his short life seemed to bring him back in a good way.

Next day, as promised, Colbert arrived soon after breakfast, but to Rose's surprise Jago did not want to go for a carriage ride.

'I've seen everything there is to see round here, Rose,' he said sulkily. 'Besides which, there isn't really enough room in Colbert's chaise. I would feel uncomfortable sitting between you.'

Rose shot him a worried glance. 'But the fresh air will do you good.'

'I'd rather stay here and talk to Angeline. She makes me laugh.'

'But you can chat to her at any time,' Rose protested. 'Besides which, she will get into trouble with Madame Laurent if she doesn't do her work.'

'I will have a word with Madame,' Colbert said, smiling. 'Let the boy do as he wishes, Rose. We won't be out for long and perhaps Jago will feel better tomorrow.'

'If you're sure you don't wish to come with us, Jago?' Rose was reluctant to leave him. However, she had grown accustomed to the stubborn mulish expression that wiped the smile from his face when he was pressed into doing something against his will.

'I'll go for a walk with you later, if that makes you happy, Rose.'

She laughed. 'You are a cheeky boy, Jago. But I will go with Monsieur Colbert. We'll be back before luncheon.'

Colbert picked up her cloak and gloves and handed them to her. 'It's cold outside even if the sun is shining. *Au revoir*, Jago. I'll have a word with Madame, as I said. Perhaps she will allow Angeline to sit with you for half an hour.' He held the cloak up and wrapped it gently around Rose's shoulders. 'Come, Rose. Jago is a sensible boy. He'll be fine.'

Madame Laurent was reluctant to allow Angeline any time off with Jago, but after a little cajoling from Colbert she agreed to half an hour, although she made it plain that she disapproved of Rose going out with a gentleman unchaperoned.

'I am not a gentleman, Madame,' Colbert said with a mischievous gleam in his pale blue eyes. 'I am Monsieur Rivers' business manager, therefore above suspicion.'

Rose managed to keep a straight face as Colbert proffered his arm and led her out into the wintry sunshine. He helped her into the chaise and sprang up to sit at her side, taking the reins with the assurance of someone used to handling a spirited horse. The groom, who had been keeping the horse under control, stood aside and with a flick of a carriage whip they were off at a walk and then a fast trot. Rose had to hold on to her bonnet as they left the shelter of the ancient oak tree and headed into the open with the wind whipping at her bonnet strings and tugging at her hair. Rose had gathered the layout of the land on her arrival, but Colbert drove past the serried ranks of vines and the neatly organised olive groves. On either side of the road were small cottages with smoke rising from the chimneys and lines of washing hung out to dry.

It was market day and the tree-lined village square was filled with stalls selling home-grown produce, eggs, butter and cheese. A young girl had two goats tethered to a pole and was milking them to order, filling jugs and basins with the rich, creamy milk. Chickens wandered in and out of the busy crowds, and there were knots of people standing about, chatting and gesticulating as if conducting an imaginary orchestra. The air was filled with the scent of French tobacco, garlic and something very savoury. Rose craned her neck to see a baker carrying a tray of hot pies, which were being snapped up by hungry shoppers.

'Would you like one?' Colbert said, reining the horse in so that they came to a standstill.

'It would spoil my appetite. I don't want to offend Madame Laurent. She does make delicious meals.'

'Nonsense, she gets paid for her efforts. That woman thinks she rules the roost when Benedict is absent.' Colbert leaned over to speak to the baker and exchanged several coins for two pies, wrapped in cabbage leaves. He passed them to Rose.

'Hold on to them, Rose. I'll drive on to a pleasant spot I know and we'll eat them there. It will be our secret. I won't tell Madame if you don't,' he said with a conspiratorial wink.

Rose smiled and began to relax as he drove off. Her feelings towards Colbert were mixed and that, together with knowing she was breaking all the rules set down by society in going out unchaperoned, made her feel uneasy. However, it was an adventure and something more to tell her sisters when she returned home. She decided to sit back and enjoy herself. The horse negotiated its way slowly through the busy marketplace, breaking into a trot as they reached the edge of the village. Colbert drove on until they came to a ruin of what must once have been an impressive mansion, nestling amongst the willows on the river bank. He alighted and tethered the horse to a gnarled branch of a skeletal tree.

'Allow me,' Colbert said, holding up his arms to help Rose from the chaise. With her hands full of hot pies and wilting cabbage leaves, she was in no position to argue and she allowed him to lift her bodily to the ground.

'Thank you.'

'I came prepared,' Colbert said as he lifted a blanket from beneath the seat and a bottle of wine, two glasses and a corkscrew.

'You planned this?' Rose eyed him warily. 'Did you know that Jago would prefer to remain at home?'

Colbert laughed. 'I had an inkling, but he would have been more than welcome, had he chosen to accompany us. However, I am glad it is just you and me. We have had little time to become acquainted.' He spread the blanket on a dry patch of ground in front of the tumbled grey stones capped with moss and lichen. 'Make yourself comfortable, Rose, and I'll pour the wine.'

Rose perched on what was left of the wall that had once surrounded the great house. 'Who used to live here, Monsieur Colbert?'

'Guy, please. The old house has been derelict for a hundred years or more. The local people say it's haunted, but I don't believe in ghosts.' Colbert extracted the cork with the ease of long practice and filled a glass, which he handed to Rose.

'I'm not sure if I do, but something strange has surely happened at the farmhouse.'

Colbert poured wine into the remaining glass and

set the bottle down before raising the glass to his lips and taking a sip. He nodded seriously. 'You are referring to the lace dress you think you saw.'

'I didn't imagine it,' Rose said firmly. 'It was on a dressmaker's dummy together with the veil, and I definitely saw the crib.'

'Could it have been a trick of the light? After all, you must have been very tired. You are a long way from home, Rose. This business can't be easy for you and you must be concerned for your family.'

'No, it isn't easy, but I hope my family will understand.'

'I am sure they will.' Colbert picked up a pie and unwrapped it. He took a bite and smiled. 'Delicious. What more could a man wish for than a glass of wine, a savoury pie and a beautiful companion?'

Rose was not used to flirting, especially with a foreign gentleman, even if he was very good looking and quite charming. She felt a cold shiver run down her spine just as the sun vanished behind heavy grey clouds and it started to rain. Colbert abandoned the food and leaped to his feet. He held his hand out to Rose.

'We'd best take shelter. I think it is just a shower.'

She grasped his hand and allowed him to help her up. Colbert snatched up the rug and wrapped it around Rose's shoulders. They found some sort of shelter amongst the rubble and partly demolished walls of the tumbledown house. It was a small space and Rose found herself pressed up against Colbert in proximity that was both intimate and quite inappropriate. She could only be thankful that there was no one to witness their enforced closeness. If Pa could see her now he would have a fit. Rose tried hard to put all thoughts of home out of her mind. Colbert's breath was warm on her cheek as he used his body to shield her from the rainstorm. A flash of lightning made Rose jump but Colbert stroked her back as if comforting a small child, and a loud crack of thunder rumbled around the crumbling stone walls.

'It's all right, Rose. The storm will soon pass.' Colbert peered out into the rain as the horse whinnied anxiously. 'I need to see to the animal. I don't want him to panic and attempt to bolt or he'll wreck the carriage.'

'Yes, of course. You must.' Rose sighed with relief as he released her and left the comparative protection of the thick stone wall, bending his head against the wild wind and relentless rain. Rose could do nothing other than huddle against the cold stones, clutching the damp rug around her.

Time seemed to have stood still as the thunderstorm raged overhead and then, as suddenly as it had started, the storm faded away and the wind died down to a stiff breeze. As the downpour ceased, Rose emerged to see Colbert walking the frightened horse up and down. He was speaking to it in soft soothing tones, although Rose could not understand a word of what he said. However, it seemed to have an effect on the horse and Colbert brought it to a halt close enough for her to reach easily, even though she had to step over deep puddles.

Colbert held out his hand. 'Allow me,' he said cheerfully as he helped her to climb into the chaise. The seat was wet even though partially covered by the folding hood.

Rose glanced at his sodden clothing and giggled. 'You are soaked to the skin, Guy.'

He smiled. 'It was worth it to keep you reasonably dry and to hear you speak my name.'

'Are all Frenchmen as romantic as you, sir? I mean, we barely know each other.'

'I think after today we are much better acquainted.' Colbert climbed up to sit beside her. 'I had better get you home quickly before you catch a chill, or worse.'

'I hate to think what Madame Laurent will say when she sees the state we are in.' Rose smoothed her damp skirts. 'We've left the pies on the ground, and the wine.'

Colbert flicked the reins. 'Walk on.' He turned to Rose with a grin. 'Perhaps the ghosts will enjoy them and raise a glass to us.'

Rose laughed and settled down to enjoy the drive back to the farmhouse as the sun struggled out from behind the clouds.

Madame Laurent was nowhere in sight when they arrived back at the farmhouse.

Colbert assisted Rose from the chaise. 'I would see you inside,' he said apologetically. 'But I need to go home and change into some dry clothes, and my horse could do with a rub down.'

'That is quite all right. I will creep in and hope Madame doesn't see me.' Rose managed a smile. Something between them had changed after the enforced intimacy during the storm, and she regretted her boldness in accepting his invitation to see more of the countryside. Whether or not he felt the same was questionable, but he seemed oblivious to any change in their relationship.

'I have business to conclude in Avignon but I will call tomorrow afternoon. Perhaps Jago will feel like going out then.'

Rose nodded. 'I'll speak to him about it. *Au revoir.*'

He laughed and saluted. '*Au revoir.* You are learning my language.'

In her hurry to get away, Rose almost walked into one of the large terracotta pots that contained spiky plants and were spaced out on the terrace. A trailing frond of ivy tickled her forehead as she hurried into the house. She crossed the entrance hall and peeped nervously into the drawing room where she had left Jago. To her relief he was on his own, sitting by the fire with an open book on his lap, although he did not seem to be paying much attention to the contents. He looked up and grinned.

'Where have you been? It's ages since you and Colbert went for a drive.'

Rose took off her bedraggled bonnet and her damp

cloak. 'We got caught in a thunderstorm. Didn't you have one here?'

'No. The sun has been shining all morning. I was beginning to think you and Colbert had run away together.'

'That's not funny, Jago.'

'I think it is. Colbert likes the ladies. I heard Madame telling Angeline not to get friendly with him. Did he try to kiss you, Rose? Your cheeks are very pink.'

'No, of course he didn't.' Rose tossed her head. 'As if he would behave so badly. Your cousin would be very put out to hear you saying things like that.'

'Well, you've been warned, Rose. Perhaps I had better go with you next time.'

'That is an excellent idea. I'm going to change into dry clothes and then I'll come down for luncheon. I am starving.' Rose hesitated in the doorway. 'By the way, did you ask Angeline if she knew anything about the wedding gown and the baby's crib?'

'I did, but she said she hasn't been working here for long. She did say that there was always gossip about this place. All sorts of stories have done the rounds, but she doesn't bother to listen. I can't say I blame her.'

'Oh, well, it was worth a try,' Rose said casually. It was disappointing, but someone must know the truth.

She left Jago and went upstairs to her room where she took off her damp outer garments and changed into a woollen skirt and a cotton blouse. She glanced at her reflection in the mirror, and shook her head. She was in desperate need of more clothes, but how long would she remain in France was the burning question. She wanted to go home and yet she needed to stay and make sure that Jago was fit and well before she could even consider returning to Abbotsford. By now her family would be used to her absence, although she knew that Marianne and Emily would be longing to hear all about her escapade. How Papa would react was another matter. Rose was not looking forward to the inevitable interview with her father. As to Mama, Rose doubted if anyone had thought to mention her absence to her. Sometimes she envied her mother, living in a world she had created for herself, untouched by anything that happened on the outside.

Rose picked up a brush and tidied her hair. Then, of course, there was Rivers. She wondered if he had been successful in finding a good lawyer and, more importantly, if he would be home for Jago's birthday the following week. She had no money with which to purchase a present for him, and she doubted if Madame would go so far as to bake a birthday cake. Jago was recovering well, but he did not seem to remember much about the beatings and ill treatment he had suffered on board ship. Perhaps that was for the best. He was just a child, after all. The loss of memory might be merciful in the short term, but one day it would all come flooding back to him and then he would suffer all over again.

She put the brush back on the dressing table and left her room to go downstairs and join Jago for luncheon.

*   *   *

After the episode during the thunderstorm, and bearing in mind Madame's warning to Angeline about Colbert, Rose was careful not to be alone in his company. Jago was getting stronger with every passing day and looking forward to his birthday, although Rose was growing more and more anxious. She wanted to make it a special time for him but it was going to be difficult. However, although Madame said she was too busy to bother with making a birthday cake, she gave Rose permission to use the kitchen one evening when all the dinner things had been cleared away. Rose had never made a cake in her life, but she had spent a lot of time in the kitchen watching Cook and enjoying the results of her efforts.

It was the day before Jago's birthday and, although he still had to use a stick, he had walked a long way that afternoon, much further than usual. He was obviously exhausted and he went to his room after dinner, leaving Rose free to try her hand at baking. She had to wait until Angeline had gone home and Madame Laurent had retired to her sitting room.

Rose stood in the middle of the flagstone floor, gazing at the unfamiliar territory with apprehension. Then she remembered how Cook set about making a cake and she took a deep breath, picturing herself in the vicarage kitchen with Cook standing at her side giving instructions. She stoked the fire in the range before going to the larder and taking out what she thought were the necessary ingredients. She set about the onerous task, finding it harder than she had anticipated. However, she managed to fill a cake tin with a reasonable-looking mixture of eggs, sugar, flour and a little milk, and placed it in the oven with a feeling of triumph.

It was only when she stood back that she saw the chaos she had caused in the normally tidy kitchen. A fine snow of flour shimmered on the floor and the large pine table had disappeared beneath packets, bottles, jars and eggshells. She wiped her hair back from her forehead with a floury hand and began clearing things away, but she had not got very far when the smell of burning assailed her nostrils. She wrenched open the oven door and a cloud of smoke hit her in the face, filling the kitchen with its acrid smell. She found a cloth and removed the cake tin from the oven, dropping it with a cry of pain as she burned her fingers. The charred mixture spread across the floor and Rose collapsed onto a chair with tears of anger and frustration running down her cheeks.

'What on earth is going on? I thought the house was on fire.' Rivers stood in the doorway, still dressed in his caped overcoat as he gazed at the scene of the disaster. 'Rose, are you all right?'

Rose jumped to her feet. 'I tried, Rivers. I wanted to make a cake for Jago's birthday tomorrow. I've ruined it.' She bit back a sob. 'I thought I could do it but it's a disaster.' She glared at Rivers, realising that he was laughing. 'It's not funny.'

'I'm sorry, Rose, but it is hilarious. Your face is covered in flour and the kitchen looks as if a hurricane has swept through it.' Rivers crossed the floor in long strides and wrapped his arms around her. 'You tried, and that's the main thing.'

Rose dashed tears from her face with her sleeve as she pulled away from him. 'It was stupid to think I could do it.'

He held her at arm's length. 'I'd say it was heroic. I've left you here on your own to cope with a sick boy and a devoted but difficult old woman. Anyway, I'm back now, and I've brought someone with me who will help us all to put things right.'

'We need a miracle, Rivers. Poor Jago will have nothing on his birthday and I've ruined Madame's kitchen.'

'There's someone I want you to meet, Rose.' Rivers glanced over his shoulder. 'Come in, Lucy, but mind how you go. The floor is quite slippery.'

'Lucy?' Rose wiped her eyes, gazing at the fair-haired woman who stood in the doorway. She looked pale and tired, but she must have been a beauty when she was young. 'You are Jago's mama?'

'I am, and you must be Rose. I've heard so much about you.'

'But I thought you were in England, ma'am.' Rose looked from one to the other. 'You went to Paris, didn't you, Rivers?'

'I did, and then I went on to London where I met my aunt and we visited a solicitor. We both have a vested interest in proving that Montague lied and has cheated his stepmother out of almost everything that her first husband, Leonard Hanbury, left to her.'

'Jago will be overjoyed to see you,' Rose said earnestly. 'He is much better now but still has a long way to go. I was trying to make tomorrow a proper birthday for him, but his mama is the best present he could have.'

'Thank you, Rose.' Lucy peeled off her gloves and untied her bonnet. 'I haven't been the best of parents to my poor boy. I allowed Montague to bully me into letting Jago go to sea, but he promised me it was a genuine apprenticeship and would benefit Jago. It was a dreadful mistake on my part.'

'The blame is all Montague's,' Rivers said firmly. 'But now I think we had better clear up this mess. I wouldn't want to face Madame in the morning if she found a speck of flour where it shouldn't be.'

'I agree. We'll soon get this kitchen tidy.' Lucy took off her cloak and laid it over the back of a chair. 'I think I remember where the sweeping brushes and mops are kept. Roll up your sleeves, Benedict.'

He grinned. 'Yes, Aunt Lucy. Right away.'

Rose stared at him in amazement. 'You are going to help me clean this up?'

'I've had to take care of myself in the past, Rose. I wasn't always in a position to hire servants or to live in hotels. We'll soon get everything put away and Madame won't notice anything different.'

'But the cake,' Rose said, sighing. 'It's ruined and I have nothing to give Jago tomorrow.'

Lucy handed a broom to Rivers. 'You start on the floor, Benedict. I'll take care of the table.' She turned to Rose with a wide smile. 'Don't worry about Jago, my dear. I went to Fortnum's and purchased a delightful cake and some treats for my son's birthday. Although I'm sure he would have appreciated your efforts much more. Benedict told me how good you've been to him.'

'It was me who found him,' Rose said shyly.

Lucy reached out to clasp Rose's floury hands. 'You saved my boy's life. I can never thank you enough.'

Rose withdrew her hands gently. 'I would have done the same for anyone in such distress, but I suppose Jago reminded me of my brother, Felix.'

'Benedict also told me of your loss. I am so sorry, Rose. It must have been terrible for you and your family.'

'Yes, it was. Mama has never fully recovered from the shock, although we do our best to help her.'

'Are you leaving all the hard work to me, ladies?' Rivers demanded, leaning on the broom handle. 'You will have plenty of time to talk later.'

'Are you planning to stay here?' Rose asked eagerly.

Lucy nodded. 'I have no home now. Montague has made it plain that I am no longer welcome in what he has claimed as his late father's house. He has inherited everything, including the money that my first husband left me, which became Hector Dalby's property when we married.' Lucy busied herself piling up the empty packets on the kitchen table. 'Benedict has spoken to his solicitor to see if there is anything that can be done. If not, then I have to depend upon my poor nephew. Life is hard for widows, Rose.'

'You know you can stay here for as long as you like, Lucy. We are family so what is mine is also yours.' Rivers stowed the broom back in the cupboard. 'And now I am going to have a tot of brandy. Would anyone care to join me?'

Lucy shook her head. 'I'm exhausted. If you'll excuse me, I'll go to my room. I assume it will be the one I always occupied on my visits here.'

'I asked Madame Laurent to have it ready for you before I left,' Rivers said casually. 'I thought you might be glad of some respite from your stepson's bullying.'

'Indeed I am.' Lucy smiled wearily. 'Goodnight, Benedict. Goodnight, Rose. I look forward to getting to know you better.' She left the kitchen and Rose was about to follow her but Rivers barred her way.

'Could you spare me a few minutes, please, Rose? I have something I need to tell you.'

Chapter Eleven

Rose followed Rivers into the drawing room where he paused to help himself to a generous tot of brandy. He glanced at her, holding up the cut-glass decanter. 'Are you sure I cannot persuade you to join me?'

'No, thank you.' Rose regarded him watchfully, wondering what was coming next. Was he going to send her home? Although she longed to see her family again, she was reluctant to leave just yet. 'What did you want to say to me?'

Rivers motioned her to sit down. He took a seat opposite her, stretching his long legs out before the glowing embers of the fire. 'I fully understand that you want to return to your family, Rose. However, I am going to impose a little longer on your good nature.'

'In what way?' Rose was intrigued. 'What can I do for you? Jago will have his mother to take care of him now.'

'Yes, that's true, and part of the reason that I brought my aunt here, and now you have a perfectly respectable chaperone.'

'I can see that, but it doesn't explain why you want me to remain here.'

'I have to return to London to prepare for the court case that Montague Dalby has brought against me, and I'm also acting on behalf of my aunt in an attempt to restore at least a portion of her rightful inheritance, including Landon Hall, which was left to her by her first husband, but is now inhabited by Montague.'

'I understand all that, Rivers. But that still doesn't answer my question.'

Rivers sipped his brandy, eyeing her speculatively. 'I am afraid that Montague will come here in my absence and try to bully my aunt into giving up her claim on the money he has taken from her, as well as the estate, which is considerable. He is young but he is greedy and he is devious. I fear that Lucy will give in to him, but if she has you at her side she will stand fast.'

Rose smiled ruefully. 'You think I will frighten this person off?'

'I think you have courage and moral strength. I've seen the way you've protected Jago and I know you would do the same for his mother, should the need arise.'

'Is this person, Montague Dalby, so formidable?'

'Not to me, but Lucy is another matter. Not

only that, but Montague tried to rid himself of his stepbrother, and I believe he is quite capable of making another attempt on Jago's life.'

Rose stared at him horrified. 'Why would he do something so dreadful?'

'Landon Hall was left to Jago, although Hector Dalby claimed it as his own when he married my aunt. It is a magnificent country house with a large estate and, as I said before, Montague wants it for himself.'

'But Jago is in the way,' Rose added, frowning. 'Do you really think Montague is capable of murder?'

'I think he is capable of doing anything if it means that gets him what he wants. He placed Jago in the hands of a sadistic sea captain, most likely hoping that the boy would not survive.'

'Jago was in a terrible way when I found him.'

Rivers put his glass down and leaned forward, his expression intense. 'I need your help for a little longer, Rose. I know it's asking a great deal but I also know I can trust you implicitly.'

'When do you plan to return to London?'

'Tomorrow, if at all possible. I need to see Guy before I leave to make sure that everything is running smoothly here, and then I will travel to London.' Rivers smiled. 'Did he look after you in my absence?'

'He did his best,' Rose said vaguely. She thought fast. 'I will do what I can for your aunt and for Jago, but I must go home first. I have to make things right with Pa before I can go any further.'

Rivers frowned. 'I understand, but do you think your father will allow you to return to France? Will you tell him everything?'

'My father is a good man, Rivers. He will understand, and he is always telling us that we must do our duty.'

'All right, but I must come with you and speak to him personally. It's something I should have done at the outset and I would have, had things been different. But are you sure that you are happy to return to France, Rose? Might you not wish to stay at home?'

'I've grown very fond of Jago. It's almost as if he is another brother, although of course no one could take Felix's place. But I think I will find it very difficult to get back to the quiet life I led before,' Rose added with a wry smile. 'When do we leave?'

'Tomorrow evening at the latest. I will see Guy and he will arrange for the workers to be on the lookout for any stranger who might try to gain admittance. I might even ask him to stay here until you return. The *Sadie Lee* is in port and she will take us directly to Abbotsford. After I have seen your papa I will travel on to London.' Rivers picked up his glass and drank the last drop. He rose to his feet. 'I will have another before I retire. Are you sure you wouldn't like a small tot to help you to sleep?'

Rose sighed. 'Maybe I will, just this once, but don't tell Papa.'

'It will be our secret,' Rivers said as he poured a

small amount of brandy into a glass and handed it to her.

'There seem to be many secrets in this house.' Rose took a small sip. 'Do you know of any, Rivers?' she added, emboldened by the fiery spirit.

He shook his head. 'None that comes to mind. The best person to ask is Madame Laurent. Her family has been associated with the farmhouse for a very long time.' He raised his glass in a toast. 'Here's to turning the tables on Montague Dalby and clearing my name.'

'Yes, indeed.' Rose raised her glass to her lips but she did not drink. Already her head was beginning to feel light and exhaustion threatened to overcome her. She rose to her feet. 'If you'll excuse me. I really need to get some sleep, especially if we are to travel tomorrow.'

'Goodnight, Rose. And thank you again.'

Despite the fact that his mother had come to stay to look after him, Jago was obviously upset when Rose told him that she would be going away for a few days. She had to promise faithfully that she would return as soon as possible and that seemed to calm him. Even so, his birthday was a subdued affair and the gifts he received from his mother did not cheer him significantly.

Colbert arrived soon after breakfast and Rivers took him to his study, closing the door behind them. They emerged half an hour later and shook hands.

'Don't worry about a thing,' Colbert said confidently. 'There is nothing I cannot handle and I will prime the workers. You need not worry about Jago or his mama. They will be perfectly safe with me.'

'Madame has had a room made up for you. Just ask her if there is anything you require, Guy. Once again I am very grateful to you.' Rivers turned to Rose, who had been on her way to the drawing room as they emerged from the study. 'Are you ready to leave? It happens that everything is arranged earlier than I had anticipated.'

'I am,' Rose said firmly. 'All I have to do is get my bonnet and cloak.'

Rivers nodded. 'Good. We'll wait for you outside. Monsieur Colbert is going to drive us to the railway station, and then we'll be on our way.'

Rose shot Colbert a sideways glance as she hurried past him. Memories of their last carriage ride were still fresh in her mind. She was glad that it was Lucy who would be staying at the farmhouse and not her. Colbert was being particularly charming, but she was still wary of him, although she could not put her finger on what she found disturbing. He had not tried to take advantage of her during the thunderstorm, but he had treated her in a familiar way that had made her feel uncomfortable. Perhaps it was all in her imagination, but she was still unsure. She took the stairs two at a time in her eagerness to be on her way. Now that she knew she would see her family very soon she could not wait.

'You will return, won't you, Rose?'

She looked up to see Jago leaning over the banister rail.

'Of course I will, Jago. I am going home to persuade my pa to let me come back here and stay with you until everything is sorted. You know that.'

'Yes, but I wanted you to tell me again. You wouldn't lie to me, would you, Rose?'

'No, never!' Rose reached his side and slipped her arm around his thin shoulders. 'Why would you even think that?'

'Other people have told me lies. I never know who to believe.'

'Well, this is me, your friend Rose Northwood, and I would never tell you things that were not true. I hope to be back with you in a few days' time, but the sooner the better.' Jago wrapped his arms around her, hugging her as if he would never let her go.

'I trust you, Rose. I wish you were my sister.'

She held him at arm's length, smiling. 'I will be your best friend, and I promise I will return as soon as possible. Make sure you do your exercises and eat up all the good food that Madame prepares for you, and, above all, look after your mama. She loves you very much, Jago.' Rose could see tears in his eyes and she gave him another quick hug before hurrying to her room to put on her bonnet and cloak and collect her valise. Soon she would be with her own family, although it was hard to leave Jago. The boy had claimed a large part of her heart in such a short time and she could not shake off the feeling of responsibility for him. She would return to Le Fleuve, no matter what Papa said, but she owed it to all her family to tell them that face to face. She went downstairs and stepped outside in the cold, sweet air of Provence.

It was early morning a couple of days later when the *Sadie Lee* anchored in the bay. Abbotsford village was bathed in a cool clear light and frost glittered off the rooftops and the narrow, cobbled streets that sloped down to the harbour. Rivers joined Rose on the top deck.

'Home at last, Rose. How does it feel?'

She shot him a sideways glance. 'Exciting, but I confess to being a little nervous.'

'I will see your papa first. All the blame lies on my shoulders. I won't allow you to take any part of it. I hope to be able to persuade your father to allow you to return to France, but if he refuses there is nothing I can do. You understand that, don't you?'

'Yes, I do. But if he forbids it then I must make my own decision. I am almost twenty-one, Rivers. In a few weeks I will reach my majority.'

'Let's hope it doesn't come to that. I don't want you to suffer a rift with your family. I know how much you love them.'

'You do?' Rose looked up at him, finding it hard to believe.

'I've come to understand you during the past few

weeks. It feels as if we have known each other for a much longer time. I won't do anything to hurt you, Rose. That I promise.'

'Tender's waiting, boss.' Jackson pointed to the boat bobbing up and down on the waves. 'Luggage is loaded.'

'Thank you, Jackson.' Rivers turned to Rose with a smile. 'I'll see your father and then I'll travel on to London. Whatever happens in the next few days, let's hope we meet again back on board the *Sadie Lee.*'

'I hope so, too,' Rose said with feeling.

'If I succeed in my court case I will send you an armful of hot-house roses to mark the occasion, as in the legend of *Sadie Lee.* You will know then that I am coming for you. If not, I might well be in prison.'

Rose felt tears sting her eyes but she blinked them away. 'If that happens, I will visit you.'

'Let's hope it won't come to that.' He held her hand briefly. 'I would like to say that you are my Rose, but that must wait for fate and a good lawyer to decide.'

'I don't understand,' Rose said breathlessly, but her words were carried away on a gust of wind.

'Boss,' Jackson said urgently, 'we'd best get into the boat.' He made a move towards the rope ladder. 'The wind is getting up and the sea will be too choppy if we leave it any longer.'

'We're coming now. I'll go first, you follow me, Rose. I can catch you if you fall.'

'I wish you hadn't said that, Rivers. I'm not fond of that wretched ladder.'

'You'll be all right, miss,' Jackson said heartily. 'I'll help you. You're a good 'un. We can't afford to lose you.'

Rose had to close her eyes during the perilous descent from the ship to the waiting tender. The ship was at the mercy of the wind and waves, and needle-sharp spray slapped her face and soaked her garments. Rivers lifted her into the boat and Jackson leaped in after them. Rose huddled against in the bows as Jackson rowed them to the landing place, where Rivers leaped out first and lifted her in his arms before she had a chance to attempt to climb into the swirling shallows. He carried her to a spot beyond the reach of the ebbing tide and put her down before going to retrieve their luggage.

'Anchor offshore, as we discussed, Jackson. I'll send word when I'm ready to return to France.'

'Aye, aye, sir.' Jackson took the oars again as Rivers pushed the boat back into deeper water.

Rose waited for him to join her. 'It's still very early.'

'All the better. We can walk to your home without the whole village knowing our business.'

'That won't last long. I see a light in Guppy's bakery. We'll be lucky to get past there without being seen.' Rose smiled as she walked on, taking care not to slip on the icy cobblestones, and sure enough, the first person she saw was Ned Guppy. He opened the bakery door to pass a large basket of delicious-smelling hot loaves to Joe Hawkes, who had emerged from the shadows. They both turned to stare at Rose and Rivers.

Ned touched his forelock. 'Good morning, sir. Good morning, Miss Rose.'

Joe just stared.

'Good morning,' Rose said cheerfully.

'Is all well with you, Guppy?' Rivers acknowledged him with a nod.

'Aye, sir. All well here. We thought as how you'd been abducted, Miss Rose.'

'No, as you see, I am home again now.' Rose walked on quickly, knowing that young Joe would broadcast her arrival in the company of Benedict Rivers. She needed to get home before news reached the vicarage.

Unfortunately, the next person they saw was the verger's wife, renowned gossip Martha Huggins. She was surreptitiously emptying the night soil onto the flower bed furthest from her cottage, but she stopped, staring at them open-mouthed.

'Miss Rose. We heard as how you'd run off with that villain. I'm surprised you can show your face here again.'

'You should mind your own business, ma'am,' Rivers said icily.

Rose clutched his arm, shaking her head. 'There's no need for that, Rivers.' She turned to Mrs Huggins with an attempt at a smile. 'Mr Rivers has done no wrong by me or anyone else.'

'Has he made an honest woman of you then?' Martha placed the chamber pot on the grass at her feet. 'Your poor dear mama will be driven to her grave by such behaviour.'

Rivers was about to speak but Rose tugged at his arm. 'I'm sure that Mrs Huggins means well, Mr Rivers. She is too sensible to pass on gossip, but for your information, ma'am, I am not married, nor do I intend to marry in the near future. Now if you'll excuse us, we need to get home before tongues start to wag. Good day, Mrs Huggins.' Rose stalked on towards her home with Rivers following.

He caught her up at the vicarage gate. 'Rose, I am so sorry. I would rather cut off my right hand than place you in such an invidious position.'

'I chose to accompany you, Rivers. Perhaps not, as it turned out, to France, but that just happened because of unforeseen circumstances. I won't allow anyone to say that you forced me to do anything against my will.'

'I'm not sure I deserve such generosity, Rose. But I will speak to your father and I will assure him that I have done everything in my power to protect your good name.'

Rose laughed. 'I think it's a little late to be worrying about my standing in society, but I appreciate the thought. Just tell him the truth, Rivers.' She opened the gate and walked swiftly up the path to the front door. She rang the bell and moments later it was opened by Emily, who was in her cotton nightgown, her hair still in rags. She held up a lamp, staring at Rose as if she had just seen a ghost.

'I saw you both standing at the garden gate. I thought I was dreaming.'

'I don't know why you are up so early, Em, but please let us in. It's bitterly cold out here and my clothes are damp.'

Emily stood back to allow them in. 'My goodness. Where have you been all this time? Marianne and I had given you up for dead.' She shrugged dramatically. 'Well, not dead, perhaps, but certainly lost to us for ever.'

Rivers placed the two valises on the floor at the foot of the stairs. 'Is your papa up yet, Emily?'

Emily stared at him as if he had spoken in a foreign language. 'You wish to see Papa? I would have thought he was the last person you might want to meet, considering what you've done to my sister.'

'Emily, that's enough,' Rose said crossly. 'Please curb your tongue. You know nothing, so wait until you hear what I have to say before you start making accusations.'

'Papa was called out urgently to baptise a sickly newborn babe.' Emily pouted and her eyes filled with tears. 'You have no right to be angry with me, Rose. It's me and Marianne who have suffered because of your goings-on.'

Rose looked up as Marianne appeared at the top of the stairs. She was struggling into a wrap and, like Emily, her hair was still tied up in rags.

'Rose, is that you?'

'Yes, it is and she's come with that dreadful man who is wanted by the police,' Emily said triumphantly.

'Doesn't anyone in this village believe that a person is innocent until proven guilty?' Rose demanded, taking off her damp cloak and laying it on the carved wooden chest.

Marianne hesitated with one bare foot on the top tread. 'I think charity flew out of the window when we lost all hope of you returning to set matters straight.'

'Now you are being over-dramatic, like Em.' Rose sighed. 'May we continue this conversation somewhere warm and more comfortable? I don't know about Rivers but I have not had any breakfast and I am cold and hungry.'

'I expect Winnie has lit a fire in the breakfast room,' Marianne said grudgingly. 'I suggest that Mr Rivers might prefer to wait in there, but you must come upstairs and tell me everything while I get dressed.'

'Me, too. I'm not missing this.' Emily pushed past them and ran upstairs, leaving Rose to follow more slowly as she was hampered by her wet skirts.

'I'm sorry about all this, Rivers,' Rose said over her shoulder. 'Please wait in the breakfast room. I'll ask Winnie to bring you some tea.'

'Now I know I'm back in England. Tea makes every situation seem easier and solves any problem thrown at a man.' Rivers smiled and saluted her as he took off his wide-brimmed hat and heavy greatcoat.

At the top of the stairs Rose stopped. 'I'm going to my room to change. Then I'll join you both and tell you everything you want to know.'

'Well, do hurry,' Emily said sulkily. 'I'm dying to hear what's been going on and where you've been.'

Marianne eyed Rose suspiciously. 'You haven't married him, have you, Rose? I mean, it might look better to everyone if you have.'

'No, we are not married, and have no such intention, as I told Martha Huggins just now.'

'Martha saw you and you spoke to her?' Marianne said faintly. 'Where are my smelling salts? I feel faint, Em. Run and get them for me.'

'Get them yourself. I'm not your slave, Marianne.' Emily followed Rose to her room. 'Please be quick. Tell us before Papa gets home or he'll make us swear on the Bible that we won't tell anyone what's been going on.'

Rose took the lantern from her sister. 'Thank you, Em. I need that. I'm not saying anything until I'm washed, dressed and ready to face the world. Now go away, please.'

Rose took her time, but washing in ice-cold water in a room without a fire was not the most comfortable experience. She had grown used to the comparative luxury of the farmhouse in Provence where Angeline was available at the tug of a bell pull, and Madame might sometimes appear to be grumpy, but she made sure that meals were promptly on the table at set times, and if hunger beset Rose she had only to ask and food would be provided. Rose dressed quickly and brushed her hair, tucking it into a neat chignon at the nape of her neck. She picked up the lamp and was about to go downstairs to join Rivers when Emily pounced on her.

'No you don't. Come to Marianne's room. We want to know everything.'

Somewhat reluctantly Rose agreed. She followed Emily to their sister's room and entered to find Marianne seated at the dressing table, arranging her springy golden curls in the most flattering style. She met Rose's smile with a frown.

'You have a lot of explaining to do. Lady Buckingham is furious because she was taken in by Rivers and I'm afraid to go round there in case she blames me for allowing you to travel abroad with him.'

'That's ridiculous.' Rose perched on the edge of Marianne's bed. 'What happened has nothing to do with either you or Emily. As to Lady Buckingham, she was happy enough to accept the large donation to the village funds from Rivers. I doubt if she asked where it came from, but now, apparently, she is prepared to believe the worst of him.'

Marianne turned to face Rose. 'You went away with Mr Rivers. You didn't give a thought to how it would look or how it might affect us. Where have you been all this time?'

'I've been taking care of Jago, as you well know. I didn't plan to accompany Rivers to France. It was more or less an accident that I was on board when the ship sailed.'

'Papa said the coast guard was on hand,' Emily said suspiciously. 'Surely you could have allowed them to rescue you.'

'I wasn't in any danger.' Rose looked from one to other. 'But I can see that nothing I say will make any difference. I just hope that Papa shows more understanding.'

'At least you are home now,' Marianne said, sighing. 'I suppose the scandal will die down eventually, but I will never forgive you for putting me in such a difficult position, Rose. I really thought that Tom was going to propose but now his mother will never allow him to tie himself to such a family as ours.'

'What nonsense.' Rose jumped to her feet. 'Anyway, you won't have to put up with me for long. I will return to France with Rivers when he has set things in motion regarding the court case to clear his name. I promised Jago that I would stand by him, and that is what I intend to do. You will no doubt think you are well rid of me.' Rose marched out of the room and slammed the door. She headed for the staircase but stopped when she saw Winnie coming towards her.

'Oh, miss. I was looking for you. I have to tell you

that your papa wants to see you. He's in his study with that Mr Rivers.' Winnie lowered her voice. 'I was told that the police are after that person, miss.'

'Thank you, Winnie. That will be all for now, but I would be grateful if you could light a fire in my room. I will be staying for a while.'

Winnie's brown eyes widened and her lips formed a circle of surprise. 'Oh! Don't say you are going to that heathen country again. Cook says . . .'

Rose did not wait to find out. She chose to ignore Winnie's last remark and hurried downstairs to her father's study. She took a deep breath and knocked on the door.

'Enter.'

Rose opened the door and stepped into the small room lined with bookshelves. A fire had been lit in the grate and a candle still burned on the mantelshelf, even though it was now light outside. 'You wanted to see me, Papa?' Rose shot a sideways glance at Rivers, who was standing with his back to the fireplace.

Matthew Northwood took his seat behind the kneehole desk, littered with papers, hymnals and a leather-bound Bible. 'This is a sorry business, Rose. I can't pretend otherwise.'

Rose shifted uncomfortably from one foot to the other. Suddenly she felt ten years old again when she had been brought before her father having been accused of slapping the face of a girl at school. She had actually given Alice Warren a hefty push for tormenting one of the younger children in the class, but Alice had turned the tables on Rose and had accused her of assault. Unfortunately, their teacher, Miss Purvis, believed Alice, who was her favourite. Rose had been sent home in disgrace.

'I'm sorry, Pa,' Rose said hastily. 'I did what I thought was right. I had to look after Jago.'

Matthew leaned his elbows on the tooled leather top of the desk, gazing at his daughter with a sigh. 'You always were headstrong, Rose. But Mr Rivers has told me the circumstances and has praised your steadfast loyalty to his cousin. He also tells me that he is innocent of all the charges against him, and I am inclined to believe him.'

Rose turned to Rivers with a smile of sheer relief. 'I told you my papa is a fair-minded man.'

'I never doubted it,' Rivers said earnestly. 'But I must agree with your father, Rose. I know you wanted to return to France to be with Jago, but on thinking it over, I believe that you ought to remain here with your family.'

Rose stared at him aghast. 'But we agreed that I should go back to the farmhouse and stay there with Jago and Mrs Dalby. They need me, Rivers. I am not needed here.'

'How can you say such a thing, Rose?' Matthew stared at her in disbelief. 'We kept your absence from your mama until very recently, which was difficult for everyone. You simply cannot do as you please. Think of your sisters.'

'They are better off without me in this instance,'

Rose said angrily. 'I promised Jago that I would return quickly. Would you have me break my word, Pa?'

'You were not thinking straight, Rose. I want you to stop this nonsense and behave reasonably. I am sure that Mr Rivers and his aunt are perfectly capable of looking after the boy. You will remain at home and maybe, in the fullness of time, when the court case is settled and the boy returns to England, you will be able to visit him. I am sure that he will understand.'

Rose turned to Rivers. 'You agreed to this without speaking to me first?'

'We both care about you, Rose. I was being selfish by encouraging you to flout convention. In the end we all have to live by the rules or face the consequences.'

'You are a hypocrite, Rivers. You pretend to be above the mores of society, but really you are as afraid of censure as anyone else.' Rose ignored her father's pleas for calm and strode out of the room with Rivers close on her heels.

'Rose, stop. Please listen to me.'

She turned on him, fighting back tears of disappointment and anger. 'Go to London, Rivers. Sort out your court case and then return to France. Oh, and keep your armful of roses. I never want to see that flower again. It would remind me of you and your duplicity.'

'I am only thinking of you, Rose.'

'You used me and now you have no need of me. Goodbye, Rivers. I don't imagine we'll meet again.'

Rivers took a step towards her with his hand held out, but meeting her furious gaze he stopped and lowered his hand. 'I'm sorry you feel like this, Rose. But perhaps it would be safer for you to remain with your family. You don't know Montague Dalby and it's best kept that way. He has set out to destroy everyone whom he considers a threat.'

'I don't want to hear any more. You are just making things worse.' Rose turned her back on him and headed blindly for the breakfast room. Marianne took one look at her face and came towards her with her arms outstretched.

'I am so sorry, Rose. Don't upset yourself. That man has made fools of many people in the village.' She enveloped Rose in a hug.

'Yes, he has,' Emily added, wrapping her arms around both her sisters. 'We were happy before he came to Abbotsford. We don't need him.'

Chapter Twelve

Rose spent the next few days struggling with feelings of self-recrimination. She had allowed herself to become involved with Rivers and his family, and all because she had taken pity on a helpless boy. She was angry with him as well as with herself, and what made matters worse was the tender loving care she received from her whole family. Someone must have told Mama a little of what had occurred and she made a point of taking tea with Rose so that she could relate all her own past trials and tribulations in endless detail. Rose sat and listened politely but she had heard all the stories before, and none of these confidences had any bearing on her own situation. Marianne and Emily were constantly at her side, thinking up activities that they thought might help and Rose was grateful, but sometimes she wished they would simply leave her alone to get over things in her own way.

Cook made all Rose's favourite dishes and even Winnie did her best to make things better. She brought Rose hot chocolate every morning and lit her fire so that she did not get up to a cold bedroom. Sometimes in past cold seasons their father had urged economy and had banned a fire in any room other than the drawing room, but there was no mention of that this winter, which made Rose feel guilty for bringing her own troubles to her family. What bothered her most was the thought of Jago recuperating in the old farmhouse with only his mother for company. She was worried that Lucy would not understand Jago's need for fresh air and exercise, and, more than that, he needed companionship. Rose had a suspicion that Lucy Dalby would frown upon her son spending too much time with Angeline, labelling her as a common girl from the village. Jago would be upset, but Madame Laurent would be only too happy to have Angeline back full time on household duties.

The only person who seemed to understand Rose's need to get out of the house and do something useful was her father. He found all sorts of errands that would take Rose into the village and involve her with old friends, most of whom were too fond of her to ask difficult questions.

Lady Buckingham, however, was not so considerate. She sent for Rose and spent the first five minutes of their meeting berating her for being a silly young woman, easily taken in by a charlatan. Rose was too polite to point out that her ladyship had welcomed Rivers into Abbotsford society like a long-lost son, especially when he opened his purse strings and offered to share his wealth with the community. Rose suffered the lecture but only realised the purpose of her summons to The Manor when Lady Buckingham demanded answers to questions regarding Rivers' business in France, and the possible source of his fortune. Rose could honestly deny all knowledge apart from the tea plantation in Ceylon, and she said as much, after which she was promptly dismissed from Lady Buckingham's drawing room with a warning not to be taken in so easily next time, should a handsome man show interest in her. Rose left the property fuming silently.

She did not go home but walked on into the village, taking deep breaths of the frosty, salt-laden morning air. She nodded automatically, acknowledging the greetings from Ron Huggins and George Finch, who was on his way to bell practice. He was followed by Miss Jones, who stopped Rose to show her the latest wound on her hand caused by Spike, her spiteful cat.

'I don't know what to do with him, Rose,' Fanny Jones said tearfully. 'He has the best food I can afford and a nice warm bed. My mother thinks he is so sweet, but he doesn't attack her. It's just me.'

Rose wanted to laugh but she could see that Miss Jones was genuinely upset. 'He is very ungrateful.'

'I was just trying to keep him from going out into the cold last night,' Fanny continued, sniffing. 'I had quite a struggle because he's a big cat. Then he caught me with his claws and tried to bite my hand. I cried like a baby.'

'Perhaps you should let him go out at night,' Rose suggested tentatively. 'Maybe he has a lady cat he might like to visit.'

Fanny's grey eyes opened wide. 'Oh, no. He isn't like that. He isn't one of those cats who howl all night and keep people awake.'

'Perhaps he likes to go outside and protect you and Mrs Jones from the wicked creatures who do disturb your sleep?' Rose suggested tactfully.

'Do you really think so?' Fanny gazed at her as if she had said something amazing. 'Maybe I should allow him to be our guardian.'

'I think you should.' Rose smiled. 'Good morning, Miss Jones.'

'Thank you, Rose. You are so sensible, most of the time, anyway. I'm sorry you were taken in by that man who robbed his aunt of her fortune. We were all so shocked to hear about it, my dear. I must go now or I'll be late for bell practice.' Fanny hurried away in the direction of the church.

Rose shook her head and walked on. She smiled, thinking of Miss Jones's innocence when it came to a very ill-tempered tom cat who had been prevented from going about his nocturnal escapades. Perhaps Spike would be better behaved in future if allowed to have his freedom at night.

'Rose. Stop.'

Rose turned her head to see Molly waving to her

from the side entrance to the Crown Inn, and she retraced her steps. 'Good morning, Molly.'

'I heard you were back. What happened to you, Rose? The whole village is talking about you.'

'May we go inside, Molly? People keep staring at me.'

Molly opened the side door and stepped into the yard. 'I'm not surprised. Come into the kitchen. It's nice and warm in there.' She flapped her apron at Jack Hawkes, who had stopped what he was doing to give Rose a curious glance. 'Get on with your work, Jack, or you'll be in trouble with my pa.'

He hefted a crate filled with bottles and staggered off with it, muttering beneath his breath.

'That family are a bunch of idlers,' Molly said crossly as she led the way into the large pub kitchen. 'The only one who's worth anything is young Joe, but he works for Mr Guppy now, or I'd offer him the job of potboy.'

The tempting aroma of roasting meat mingled with the yeasty smell of ale and the ever-present hint of stale tobacco from the taproom.

'Yes, Joe is a good boy.' Rose followed Molly through the busy kitchen, acknowledging Mrs Thatcher with a nod and a smile as she walked past her.

Molly opened the door leading into the hallway and stopped at the foot of the stairs. 'Come to my room, Rose. It's the only place we can be private.' She put a foot on the first tread but stood back to allow one of the guests to pass.

'Who is that?' Rose whispered as the handsome stranger gave her a casual glance as he walked past. He entered the parlour, closing the door behind him.

Molly grinned. 'You'll never guess, Rose. I was really surprised when he introduced himself to Pa last night.' Molly picked up her skirts and bounded up the stairs as if they were in a race to reach the top landing.

Rose followed her eagerly. 'So many strange things have happened since Christmas Eve, that I doubt if anything will come as a shock. But don't keep me in suspense.'

Molly sat on the edge of her bed, patting the space at her side. 'Sit down and I'll tell you.'

'You always did make a drama out of everything, Molly.' Rose sat, folding her hands in her lap. 'Now tell me.'

'That incredibly good-looking gentleman is Rivers' brother, Edmond.'

'Rivers hasn't got a brother. He told me so himself.'

Molly shrugged. 'Well, I'm only telling you what Mr Rivers told my pa. He said he is Rivers' younger brother and he has just returned to England from having spent years abroad, working on the family tea plantation.'

'Why would Rivers say he was an only child if he has a brother?'

'You seem to know Mr Rivers better than anyone,' Molly said slyly. 'What do you think, Rose?'

'I think I need to meet Mr Edmond Rivers. I am

more than curious.' Rose stood up. 'I want you to introduce me, Molly.'

'All right. I was hoping you might say that.' Molly leapt to her feet. 'I am dying to know the truth. Life has become so much more exciting since all this happened, and you are at the heart of the mystery, Rose. I still want to know what happened in France.'

'Introduce me to Mr Edmond Rivers and I'll tell you everything.'

Downstairs in the smoky hallway, Molly ushered Rose into the parlour. 'Excuse me, Mr Rivers, but might I have a minute of your time?'

Edmond Rivers put down the copy of *The Times* he had been reading and turned to face them. 'I hoped you might be bringing me my luncheon, Molly.'

'I will go and see if it's ready, sir. But first I would like to introduce my good friend, Rose Northwood. She has just come back from France.'

Rose stepped forward, eyeing the man curiously, despite her mother's often repeated dictum that staring at a person was ill-mannered. She was looking for some resemblance to Rivers, but she saw none. However, she had to agree with Molly – Edmond Rivers was a handsome young man. He was probably in his mid-twenties and his classic features reminded her of an illustration she had once seen of a statue representing a Greek god. His fair hair was in complete contrast to his dark brown eyes fringed with long eyelashes. His skin was lightly tanned as if he spent much of his time out of doors, and his disarming smile revealed perfect teeth. Despite her reservations Rose found herself attracted to him.

'I didn't know that Rivers had a brother,' she said lamely.

Edmond laughed. 'I am the black sheep of the family, Miss Northwood. Or may I call you Rose? I hear that you have been in my brother's company quite a lot recently.'

Molly backed towards the doorway. 'I'll fetch your food, sir.'

'Thank you, Molly. You know how to make a guest feel very welcome, my dear.' Edmond turned to Rose, motioning her to take a seat. 'Will you join me in a cup of coffee or something to eat, perhaps?'

Rose shook her head. 'No, thank you, sir.' She sat down, hoping that Molly would return soon. Edmond Rivers was undeniably attractive, but she was not entirely comfortable in his presence. 'Might I ask why you are here in Abbotsford? You seem to know a lot about your brother even though you say you have just returned from abroad.'

'You are a very intelligent young lady, Rose.'

'You haven't answered my question.'

'When I first arrived in London I made enquiries from people known to my family. I learned that my brother embezzled our aunt's fortune and left her more or less destitute. At least that was what my aunt's stepson told me.'

'You had all this from Montague Dalby?'

'Do you know him, Rose?'

'Only by repute, sir.'

'You mustn't believe everything you are told. I grew up with Monty and I know he is an honest fellow. However, Benedict is my brother and I reserve judgement until I have spoken to him and heard his side of the story. I have it on good authority that you know where I might find him.'

Rose met his questioning gaze with a straight look. Despite her recent falling-out with Rivers, she remained loyal. If Edmond really was his brother there must be a good reason for their estrangement, and his description of Montague Dalby did not ring true. However, she was saved from answering by Molly erupting into the room with a tray of food clasped in her hands. She came to a halt, staring from one to the other.

'Are you ready to eat, sir?'

'More than ready.' Edmond sat back in his seat to make it easier for her to set the food down in front of him.

Rose stood up and backed towards the door. 'Perhaps we could talk later, Mr Rivers?'

'No, sit down, please. I will eat and you will tell me all about France. I heard that you had recently returned from a trip with my brother, therefore you must know his address.'

Molly gave Rose a nudge and a meaningful nod. 'Go on, Rose. Tell him what he wants to know.'

'Why don't you ask your brother yourself?' Rose

said suspiciously. 'I believe he is still in London, although I don't know where he is staying.'

'I went to his town house and was told that he had returned to France.' Edmond cut into the thick slice of ham. 'I was also told that Mrs Dalby is already there. It is important that I see both of them as I have news that concerns the court case in which my brother is involved. However, I need to know their exact location.'

'Then shouldn't you pass the information on to Mr Rivers' solicitor?' Rose asked warily. It seemed strange that Edmond Rivers did not know where his brother lived in France. From the way that Rivers spoke about the place and what Madame Laurent had led her to believe, Rose had assumed that Le Fleuve had been in the family for many years.

'I would prefer to speak directly to Benedict as well as to Aunt Lucy. You must understand that.' He shot a glance at Molly, who was loitering in the doorway. 'That will be all for now, thank you, Molly.'

'Thank you, sir.' Molly's cheeks flushed and she shot a meaningful glance in Rose's direction as she backed out of the room.

'I can see that you distrust me, Rose,' Edmond said, smiling. 'I can't say I blame you, especially as my brother chose not to mention me, but I can assure you that I have everyone's best interests at heart.'

'I have no reason to doubt it, sir. Perhaps I should go and leave you to enjoy your meal.'

He held up his hand. 'Please stay awhile longer, Rose. I have evidence that will prove my brother's innocence, but I need to see him urgently to discuss the matter.'

'I don't know the exact address,' Rose said hesitantly, which was true. She knew how to find the farmhouse and vineyard but she had paid scant attention to learning its whereabouts on a map.

Edmond's smile faded and he leaned forward, fixing her with a penetrating stare. 'But you could take me there?'

'I suppose so.'

'And you are not averse to a little excitement. I can see that in your eyes, Rose. I imagine you have not found it easy to return to life in the village after travelling to the Continent with my brother. Benedict loves to do things in style.'

Rose recalled the first-class travel arrangements that Rivers had made so effortlessly, and the excellent meals they had enjoyed on their journey through France, staying overnight in high-class hotels. Not for Rivers a country inn or a ride on a farm cart when a luxurious carriage could be hired. She realised that Edmond was watching her closely and she put all thoughts of Rivers and the pink-painted farmhouse out of her mind.

'What exactly are you saying, sir?'

'I want you to accompany me to Provence, Rose. You will be my companion and my guide. What do you say?'

Rose reached for the door handle. 'I would have to think about it, sir.'

'There is no time for that. I have hired a vessel to take us to France. We leave tonight.'

'I cannot go away again, sir. It would upset my whole family.'

'But you would save Benedict from public humiliation and possible bankruptcy. I believe you are quite fond of him and you wouldn't like to see him go to prison for a crime he has not committed.'

'That's true,' Rose said slowly.

'And your reputation is already in shreds, so I believe.'

'How would you know that?'

'I'm a man of the world, Rose. It's quite obvious that when you travelled with my brother, you did not have a chaperone. I can imagine how that must look in a small place like this. You, a vicar's daughter, together with a rascal like Benedict Rivers spells scandal in my book, at least.'

'My papa knows everything. He realises that I had little option.'

'Then let's hope he is so understanding this time.'

'I haven't agreed to help you.'

'But you will, Rose. I can see that you believe in my brother's innocence and that you are a true and loyal friend. I will wait for you at the jetty at midnight.'

'You know I cannot go with you. It's unthinkable.'

'Maybe, but I can assure you that Benedict's

future lies in your hands. You are the only one who can save him from disaster. If you won't help, it will take me a long time to discover his whereabouts, and that will be on your conscience. I've said all I can to try to persuade you to do the right thing.' Edmond turned away to concentrate on his rapidly cooling meal.

Rose knew another refusal would be ignored and she left the room.

Molly was waiting for her in the entrance hall. 'What goings-on!' she said, grinning. 'Are you going to run away with him, Rose? He's very handsome.'

'Of course not.' Rose tossed her head. 'I wouldn't be so stupid.'

'I don't know. If he spoke to me like that I might be sorely tempted.'

'Molly, where are you?' Bill Thatcher's strident voice echoed off the ceiling, making Molly turn with a start.

'Oh Lord! I'm in trouble. Coming, Pa.' Molly lowered her voice. 'I was supposed to be helping in the taproom. Let me know what's happening, Rose. I can't wait for the next act in the drama.'

'There is no second act,' Rose said firmly. 'I must be going, too.' Rose let herself out of the main entrance and turned in the direction of home. Edmond Rivers must be mad to think that she would risk her reputation further by accompanying him to France, despite her concern for Jago's welfare. It was odd that he had made no mention of the boy, but it was the Rivers family's business, nothing to do with her. She walked on briskly.

For the rest of the day Rose tried hard to put Edmond Rivers' request to the back of her mind, but despite all her efforts she kept remembering her last meeting with Rivers and the ill will that existed between them. Her thoughts continually strayed to Jago, with worries that refused to go away. She attempted to maintain an outward display of normality but when she was alone in her bedroom that night she was having second thoughts. Perhaps she had dismissed Edmond's desire to save his brother from disgrace too lightly. The thought of Rivers languishing in prison was too much to bear. For some reason she had kept the valise she brought home with her in a cupboard and she retrieved it now, flinging in garments that she might need for a long journey and a protracted stay. What she was about to do was probably foolhardy and might prove the ruin of her, but she knew she would never forgive herself if she did not do everything to help a friend.

As she made her way to Marianne's room she heard the clock in the hall strike the half-hour. There was not much time in which to get from the house to the jetty, but she could still do it if she ran. However, she was not going to go without telling Marianne and she tapped gently on her door. She went in without waiting to be invited.

Marianne was seated at her dressing table, tying

the last rag into her golden hair. Her mouth opened in a silent gasp of surprise as she saw Rose's reflection in the mirror.

'You are not going with that man, are you, Rose?'

'Yes, I had to come and tell you, Minnie. It's something I feel I must do.'

Marianne swivelled around to face her. 'You can't go, Rose. Your reputation won't stand for another disastrous trip abroad. It's already in tatters.'

'I know that, but this is important. I believe Edmond Rivers when he says he can save his brother from prison, and I can't go on without knowing that Jago is progressing well.'

'You are putting that family above ours, Rose. Have you thought what this will do to me? If Tom *is* getting round to proposing marriage, another scandal will put an end to our happiness.'

Rose shook her head. 'I don't believe that for a moment. I know that Tom loves you as you love him. He will defy his mother if she tries to prevent your marriage. I'm certain of that.'

'I wish I was so sure.' Marianne sighed. 'But I can see that you are set on this, Rose. I know I should try to stop you, but I also know that you will do it anyway.'

Rose dropped the valise and rushed over to give her sister a hug. 'I knew you would understand. I have to leave now or Edmond will have left without me.'

'Are you absolutely sure you are doing the right thing?'

'No,' Rose said, smiling ruefully as she retrieved her suitcase. 'But if I don't do this I will regret it for the rest of my life, especially if Rivers is punished for a crime he didn't commit. That isn't justice.' Rose left the room before Marianne had a chance to say another word. At least she had told someone of her plans, and Marianne would be able to tell the rest of the family why her sister had absconded in the middle of the night. Rose did not envy her that task.

Edmond was waiting on the jetty, as promised. He said little as he helped Rose into the boat that was to take them out to the vessel at anchor. It felt to Rose that she was re-enacting the last time she had gone to France, only with a different brother. However, Edmond's behaviour changed subtly now that she had complied with his request. He was polite but distant and did not try to engage her in conversation. If Rose had not believed his story she might have demanded to return to shore, but the accommodation on the ship was comfortable and a steward was on hand to attend to her needs. She resigned herself to a long and arduous journey, buoyed on by the prospect of reaching the farmhouse and being reunited with Jago. She had many questions she wanted to put to Rivers, but that would have to wait. There was nothing for it but to make herself as comfortable as possible and endure the long journey to Provence.

Despite the circumstances, Rose slept well and was awakened in the morning by the steward bringing her a cup of strong coffee, which she drank although she would have preferred tea. Having washed and dressed, she went to the saloon, where she ate breakfast on her own. She was wondering where Edmond was when the door opened.

'We dock in five minutes, Rose. Please be up on deck and ready to leave the ship.'

'Yes, of course.' Rose was about to ask about their travel plans for that day, but he left without another word. She was puzzled by the change in his attitude towards her, but she thought he might be anxious about the journey. There could be any number of reasons and she decided to put it out of her mind. She returned to her cabin and collected her things.

They disembarked and Edmond hired a cab to take them to the railway station where they boarded a train for Paris. However, when they reached the city Rose thought they would take another train heading south, but Edmond guided her out of the station into one of the waiting fiacres, giving the address of a hotel.

Rose sat down in the corner of the carriage. 'Wouldn't it make more sense to travel on, Edmond?'

'No, Rose. I have business to conduct in Paris. We will be staying for a couple of days.'

'I suppose we could see some of the sights?' Rose said hopefully.

'Maybe.' Edmond stared out of the window.

Rose had already had second thoughts about the journey and now she was really worried. Edmond had convinced her that seeing his brother was a matter of urgency, but now he seemed to have changed his mind. The charming man who had persuaded her to travel with him had vanished, leaving in his place a cold, off-handed individual who treated her like an inconvenience. She realised now how rash she had been in placing herself totally in his care. Without a penny to her name, she was dependent upon Edmond Rivers for everything. She could demand money to pay for her return journey to Abbotsford, but she knew without asking that this would be denied. Edmond had a plan of his own and she was merely a pawn in the game he was playing. Perhaps she could appeal to his better nature, or, if all else failed, she might try to make her way to Provence on her own. That also presented problems, but Rose was not about to concede defeat.

The carriage ride was relatively short and they were dropped off outside a hotel in a side street. Rose had enough experience of travelling with Rivers to know that this was not a high-class establishment and her suspicions were confirmed when Edmond ushered her into the foyer. He ignored her protests and they were shown up two flights of stairs to a room overlooking the rear of the building.

'This will be yours,' Edmond said tersely. 'Make yourself at home.'

'Wait a minute.' Rose clutched his sleeve. 'Why are we stopping here, Edmond? You told me you needed to see your brother urgently.'

'And I told you that I have business to deal with first.'

'Then allow me to accompany you. I don't wish to be shut up in this dingy room.'

'You placed yourself in my care, Rose Northwood. You will do as I say.' Edmond walked out of the room and closed the door, turning the key in the lock.

Rose grasped the handle and shook it, but the door remained firmly closed. She beat on it with her fists but no one answered her cries for help. Edmond must have given the staff instructions to ignore her and she was now a prisoner. She ran to the window and flung up the sash but the drop was too great even to consider climbing down to the ground. She was trapped and she did not know why. What good would it do Edmond Rivers to keep her imprisoned? Rose slumped down on the bed and waited.

She must have fallen asleep as she was rudely awakened by someone shaking her. She sat up with a cry of alarm. It was dark in the room but the outer hall was gaslit, creating shadows, with Edmond seeming to loom over her in a way that sent a shiver down her spine. She swung her legs over the side of the bed.

'This is an outrage, Edmond. I demand that you set me free.'

Chapter Thirteen

'Stop behaving like a child, Rose. You came with me willingly so don't pretend otherwise.' Edmond moved to the doorway.

'You locked me in this room,' Rose said angrily. 'Why are we here in Paris? You said that reaching your brother quickly was a matter of urgency.'

'Stop complaining and come downstairs to the dining room, or do you want me to have food sent up here? I can keep you confined to your room if you wish.'

Rose jumped to her feet. 'Of course not. But you have got me here under false pretences and I want to know why.'

'Come now or I might change my mind and you will go hungry.'

She could see that Edmond was in no mood to talk and there was nothing she could do other than follow him to the dining room. Perhaps a good dinner would put him in a better mood and make him more reasonable. Besides which, she was very hungry and she did not fancy having to wait until breakfast next morning for her next meal. She would dine first and then make her demand to be sent home, even if she had to travel on her own.

Rose followed him downstairs to the dining room where a waiter led them to a table partially obscured by two potted palm trees.

A man in a black frock coat stood up to greet them.

Rose gazed at him in amazement. 'Monsieur Colbert?'

Guy stepped forward, taking her hand and raising it to his lips. 'Miss Northwood, I thought we were on first-name terms, especially after that episode in the thunderstorm.'

'Take a seat, Guy. There is no need to flatter her. Everything is going to plan.' Edmond pulled up a chair and pressed Rose down on the seat.

'I don't understand. If you are acquainted with Guy Colbert, why did you need me to take you to the house in Provence?' Rose turned to Colbert. 'And you, sir – you are supposed to be working for Mr Rivers. How do you explain this?'

Guy resumed his seat and unfolded his table napkin. 'It seems you have not been open with Miss Northwood, Monty.'

'Monty!' Rose stared at Edmond in horror. 'Montague Dalby?'

He bowed and pulled up a chair. 'In person. I'm surprised you believed all that nonsense about me being Benedict's younger brother.'

Rose made as if to rise, but was prevented from doing so by Montague's tight grip on her wrist.

'Sit down and be quiet, Rose. You will be compliant or else you will have to be restrained physically.'

'Why are you doing this?' Rose demanded in a low voice. She turned to Guy, frowning. 'And why are you colluding with this man? You know that he is trying to ruin your employer.'

'It is none of your business, Rose,' Guy said calmly. 'Monty and I are old friends.'

'But Benedict Rivers pays you to work for him,' Rose protested angrily. 'You are a traitor.'

'Harsh words.' Montague laughed, shaking his head. 'Poor little Rose. You have succumbed to the Rivers charm. But Benedict isn't interested in a penniless girl like you. He is going to marry a wealthy widow. I don't suppose he told you that, did he?'

Rose was too shocked to speak for a moment. She could see that they were both laughing at her and she struggled to regain her composure.

'Obviously not,' Guy added. 'I told you she was an innocent, Monty. I knew that the moment I met her. Rivers has been using her, as he does everyone who comes in contact with him.'

'That isn't true. You don't know what you're talking about.' Rose could not stop herself. She knew that by protesting it made her seem weak and

226

vulnerable, but she could not believe that Rivers had been anything but honest in his dealings with her. It was Montague who was the cheat and the liar.

Conversation ceased for a few minutes while Montague ordered food and wine. He did not ask Rose what she wanted to eat, but that was the least of her worries. She was desperate to get away from both Montague and Colbert, but first she needed to find out exactly what they were planning. With that information she might be able to do something to help Rivers in his fight to clear his name. Despite the allegations that Montague made against him, she could not believe that Benedict Rivers was a criminal or that he had intended to make use of her. If he chose to marry a rich woman, that was his right, and maybe that would explain the mysterious wedding gown that was there one moment and gone the next.

One of the waiters brought wine and filled their glasses, and another served the food. Rose was too hungry to refuse the tempting dishes set before her. She ate eagerly and sipped the wine, saying nothing during the meal. Not that Montague and Colbert seemed to notice. It appeared that they had forgotten her existence as they talked in low voices, discussing business matters about which Rose knew nothing. Rose was angry and frustrated but she realised that there was little she could do at the moment other than go along with the situation. However, at the first opportunity she would make her escape and find a way to warn Rivers that his trusted agent was plotting against him. All thoughts of making her way home were temporarily abandoned, and she allowed Montague to escort her to her room. He opened the door and thrust her inside.

'You will remain here until I let you out in the morning, Rose. I am not a harsh man and I promise you will be treated well enough, providing you do exactly as I bid.'

Rose bit back a sharp retort. 'It seems I have no choice,' she said mildly.

'Precisely. Tomorrow we travel on to Avignon. Be ready when I come to collect you.'

'Why are you taking me with you? Surely I can be of no further use to you?' The question slipped out before Rose could stop herself, and she knew by the triumphant expression on Montague's face that he relished her discomfort.

'Because, my dear, you are going to be very useful when it comes to striking a bargain with my stepmother's nephew.'

'You are holding me hostage?'

'That's a strong word, but accurate in the circumstances. Now stop asking questions and go to bed. We have a long journey tomorrow.' Montague closed the door and Rose heard the key turn in the lock.

She undressed slowly and put on her nightgown. With neither money nor friends in Paris, the only course she could take was to appear to be compliant. Perhaps when they reached Avignon she could find a way to escape and get to Le Fleuve to warn Rivers. She climbed into bed, expecting to be awake all night, but was soon drifting off to sleep in a welcome, if temporary, escape from the predicament in which she now found herself.

The journey to Avignon took almost all day, involving train journeys followed by several hours in a hired carriage. Neither Montague nor Colbert spoke to her, but they kept her close, and escape was out of the question. Rose managed to appear docile but inwardly she was furious, and even more so when they arrived at a small house on the outskirts of the town, which apparently belonged to Colbert. She was shown to a tiny bedroom and left with a plate of bread and cheese and a jug of water.

'We are going out to dine, Rose,' Montague said brusquely. 'You cannot escape so don't waste your time trying.' He closed the door and Rose heard the now familiar sound of the key grating in the lock. She went straight to the window and looked out into the bleak darkness of a wet and windy night. She drew the curtains and turned her attention to the plate of food. The bread was fresh and the cheese was soft and creamy. There was little point in starving herself so she sat down to eat, washing the food down with gulps of cool water. Ash and cinders filled the grate but there was no means of lighting a fire and Rose huddled on the bed, wrapped in a blanket. She was being treated like a prisoner and that was unlikely to change as Montague intended to use her as a pawn in whatever nefarious game he was playing. Perhaps he would demand a ransom for her or, even worse, maybe he wanted to get his hands on his stepbrother. Rose could only imagine what Jago's life would be like if Montague exerted his influence over the poor boy. He had tried once, unsuccessfully, to rid himself of a rival for the family fortune, and now he had proved himself to be totally ruthless. Overcome by exhaustion and still fully clothed, Rose pulled the rest of the bedcovers over herself and lay down to sleep.

She was awakened suddenly by the sound of raised voices and heavy footsteps coming up the stairs. Someone was rattling her door handle.

'Give me the key, Monty.' Colbert's voice was slurred and it was obvious that he had been drinking heavily.

'Go to bed, Guy.' Montague sounded almost as intoxicated, and there were sounds of a scuffle.

'Give me the key. I want to finish what I started during the thunderstorm. She's not going to get away so easily this time. I'm done with playing the part of a gentleman.'

'Keep your hands off her, Guy. Rivers won't want second-hand goods.'

Rose covered her mouth with her hands to prevent herself from crying out. She remembered the close embrace she had suffered in the ruins of the old house, and she shivered with revulsion. Colbert had only thinly disguised his intentions towards her and now she had heard his drunken admission.

'He won't know. Open the door, Monty.'

Rose stifled a scream as the key turned in the lock, but the fight outside intensified. There were grunts and thuds, and the scraping of booted feet along the bare boards. Then, as quickly as it had started, there came a pause, followed by what was unmistakably a heavy object being dragged along the landing. Rose held her breath, clutching her hands beneath the blankets as she prayed silently that Colbert had lost the fight. A door banged and there was silence.

Rose threw back the covers and slid off the bed. She tiptoed across the room and tried the door. To her astonishment it opened and the key lay on the floor outside. She hesitated, listening intently for sounds of activity, but all was quiet. She knew this might be her one and only chance, and escaping was the only thing on her mind. She went back into the bedroom and piled the pillows on the bed, covering them with the blankets so that it resembled a body beneath. She had not taken off her boots before getting into bed and now all she had to do was to grab her belongings. She closed the door and locked it, hoping her captors would not think to check on her until late morning, which would give her time to put a fair distance between herself and them.

Rose crept downstairs and let herself out of the front door. She was met by a gust of icy wind and pellets of rain, but nothing was going to deter her from making her escape. She would get to the farmhouse no matter how long and tortuous the journey. All she had to do was to head west and hope that she would find the right road. However, in the dark, and with the wind tugging at her clothes and sharp spikes of rain almost blinding her, it was difficult to tell east from west. She could not afford to wait until dawn and so she trudged in what she hoped was the right direction, relying purely on instinct.

The road outside Colbert's house narrowed into a muddy lane, scarred with potholes created by horses' hoofs and rutted by wagon wheels. Rose stumbled on in the dark, unable to see where she was heading. The going was hard and the rain soaked her clothes, making her skirts wrap around her legs as she tried to quicken her pace. She had no idea of time or how far she had walked, and the night seemed endless. It was only when the first pale light of dawn split the sky in the east that she saw a stone wall ahead of her. She stopped and leaned against it in an attempt to catch her breath. Where there was such a boundary there must be a house, and perhaps she could find a servant up and about at this early hour. She needed to ask directions and to make sure she was on the right road.

Sure enough, after a while she came to stone columns on either side of a gateway, and what appeared to be a carriage sweep leading up to a building hidden by a stand of trees. She started walking towards the house but a sudden shout made her come to a halt.

A man emerged from the deep shadows. She could not understand a word of what he was saying and she tried to explain but he took her by the shoulders and twisted her round so that she faced the road. He gave her a sharp push and she stumbled, clutching at thin air as the ground hurtled towards her.

The first thing Rose felt when she opened her eyes was warmth. The smell of freshly ground coffee and baking bread registered in her brain. At first she thought she was in the kitchen at home, but as she gazed dazedly around she realised she was in a house much larger and grander than the vicarage in Abbotsford.

A young girl was fanning her with her apron and an older woman, wearing a voluminous white apron and a starched mob cap, was leaning over her. They were chattering in French but Rose could only catch a word here and there.

'*Madame*,' Rose murmured, '*je suis Anglaise.*'

The older woman threw up her hands, repeating '*Anglaise!*' She shooed the young girl away with a string of instructions. Then she took a glass from the table and held it to Rose's lips, nodding as if to encourage her to drink.

Rose took a sip of water and managed a smile. '*Merci, Madame.*'

The woman, whom Rose took to be the cook, rattled off more questions, but Rose could only smile and shake her head. Eventually Cook shrugged and moved away to open the oven door and take out the tray of hot bread. Rose tried to stand but she was overcome by dizziness and she sat down hastily. Just at that moment, the kitchen maid burst into the room, followed by a beautiful woman. She was wearing a silk wrap over her voluminous lace nightgown. She moved quickly to Rose's side.

'You seem to be in a state of distress.' The young woman's smile was warm and her dark eyes glowed with sympathy. 'Are you unwell?'

Rose shook her head. 'I only want directions, Madame.'

'I am Blanche de Fontenay. Might I know your name?'

'Rose Northwood. You speak very good English, Madame.'

'I lived in London for several years when I was younger.' Madame de Fontenay eyed Rose's damp clothing, shaking her head. 'You will catch cold or lung fever if you do not get out of those wet garments. What were you doing, walking on your own in the dark? Were you running away from something or someone?'

Rose nodded wearily. 'It's a long story, Madame. But all I want is directions to Le Fleuve vineyard.'

Madame de Fontenay paled visibly. 'To Le Fleuve? Do you know its owner?'

'Of course,' Rose said dazedly. The heat from the range coupled with exhaustion was making her feel dizzy. 'I need to get a message to Mr Rivers.'

'You are in no fit state to go anywhere, Mademoiselle Northwood. You must come with me. My maid will find you something dry to wear.'

'I could not impose upon you, Madame. If I could just have directions I will be on my way.'

Madame de Fontenay clutched her wrap closer around her slender body. 'What is so important that it's worth risking a severe chill?'

'I have urgent news for Benedict, if he has returned home, that is. If not, it is even more important for me to get there. Poor Jago, he must not go with his stepbrother.' Rose realised that she was rambling, and she brushed her hand across her forehead in an attempt to clear her mind. 'I'm sorry. I am not making much sense. But I must leave now.'

Madame shook her head. 'It is still very early and you are soaked to the skin. I'm sure whatever it is you have to say will wait for an hour or two.' She turned to the cook and issued a string of instructions. 'Follow me, Miss Northwood. There must be no more arguments. I need to get dressed and you must change your clothes.' She left the kitchen, walking quickly so that Rose had to make an effort to match her steps, despite aching limbs and the beginnings of a sick headache.

The old château began to reveal itself to Rose as she did her best to keep up with her hostess.

A narrow passageway led to an elegant entrance hall with a wide staircase leading up to a galleried first floor. The ornate scrollwork iron banisters were complemented by plaster cornicing in a delicate tracery of leaves and fruit. The marble stair treads struck cold beneath the thin soles of Rose's boots and her feet squelched with each painful step.

Madame's bedchamber was large enough to be a ballroom, with a four-poster bed and dainty Louis Quinze furniture, which Rose assumed must be genuine antiques and probably priceless. Her feet sank into thick Aubusson carpet and the scent of hot-house lilies filled the air. A lady's maid hovered by the dressing table, eyeing Rose with suspicion, but after a few words from her mistress she bobbed a curtsey and disappeared into what Rose thought must be a dressing room. From a distance she could see a whole wall lined with cupboards and shelves filled with shoes, hats and other accessories necessary to a lady of standing. She reappeared moments later with garments for Madame, which she laid out neatly on the bed. A few words from her mistress sent her back into the dressing room and she returned with a more modest outfit, which she placed on a chair close to Rose.

Madame de Fontenay turned to her maid with what seemed to be an instruction to assist Rose, who was too tired to argue. She stepped out of the pile of sodden clothing and held up her arms as obediently as a small child while the maid slipped a silk chemise over her head, followed quickly by a fine woollen gown. Then, leaving Rose to finish her outfit with a pair of pantalettes and silk stockings, the maid gathered up Rose's wet clothes and placed them in a linen laundry bag.

Rose caught sight of her reflection in a tall cheval mirror and thought for a moment she was looking at a stranger. The soft blue-grey gown made her eyes look bluer, or perhaps it was the rosy flush on her cheeks. Guy Colbert's words rang in her ears and she felt suddenly hot and dizzy.

Madame gave Rose a critical look. 'You need shoes, Rose. I'll tell Francine to find a suitable pair for you.'

'No, really. I can put on my boots. They will dry out quickly,' Rose said wearily. She was overcome by the feeling that this was all too much and everything seemed unreal.

'Nonsense.' Madame issued another set of instructions to her maid, who disappeared once again into the dressing room and returned with two pairs of dainty leather shoes. 'Try them both on, please, Rose.'

'I – no, thank you.' Rose raised her hand to her forehead and felt the heat radiating from her body. 'I'm afraid I am rather unwell, Madame. I don't want to bother you further. I should leave now.'

'You should be in bed.' Madame came towards her, frowning. She turned to Francine issuing more instructions and the maid hurried from the room.

'I think you know Rivers,' Rose said breathlessly. 'I have to warn him. Will you get a message to Le Fleuve for me?'

'I am very well acquainted with Benedict. What is so urgent that it cannot wait until you are fit to travel?'

'Tell him that Montague is in Avignon. He and Colbert are plotting to kidnap Jago.' Rose sank down on the nearest chair and held her head in her hands. She was shivering one moment and then she was so hot that she wanted to strip off her clothes, but this was not the time to be ill. She had to get to the vineyard to warn Rivers before Montague arrived. However, before she realised what was happening, she found herself being helped from the room by Francine and another servant who had miraculously appeared at her side. After that everything became a muddle of voices speaking French so rapidly that she could barely catch more than a word or two, and then she was being undressed like a baby and put to bed, despite her protests. Exhaustion overcame her and she slid into a feverish sleep, disturbed by wild dreams that featured Montague and Colbert in increasingly desperate situations.

Rose lost all sense of time and place. She was dimly aware of being examined by an elderly doctor and dosed with bitter-tasting medicine, after which she slept fitfully. Sometimes when she opened her eyes and swallowed spoonfuls of the vile-tasting medication it was by candlelight.

The next time there was pale winter sunshine reflecting off a mirror somewhere in the room. Gentle hands washed and dried her and someone dressed her in clean nightwear, but she was only vaguely aware of what was going on around her. Daylight faded into darkness and then it was light again. She was burning with fever and then shivering with cold. She knew she was chattering but the words that left her lips had little meaning.

Then, just as suddenly as the fever had claimed her, it went away. The next time Rose opened her eyes she found the fog had lifted. She raised herself on her elbow and gazed round the room with its pretty floral curtains and matching bed hangings. There were vases of flowers on a white-painted chest of drawers with carvings picked out in gold. The rest of the furniture fitted in beautifully and the walls were covered in wallpaper depicting trailing leaves, butterflies and exotic birds. Tall windows let in sunlight, forming square patterns on the delicately coloured carpet. It was a room fit for a princess, but how she came here was only just beginning to dawn on her.

Rose sat up in bed as the door opened and Madame de Fontenay walked into the room.

'Oh, Rose. You are feeling better. I am so pleased.'

'Madame, I am so sorry to have been a burden on you and your household.'

'Nonsense. You were very unwell but now you have recovered. However, the doctor says you must not overexert yourself.'

'But I have to get to Le Fleuve, Madame. I have to warn Rivers, although I'm afraid I might be too late. How long have I been here?'

'Five days, Rose.' Madame smiled gently. 'But don't worry. You told me of the danger that Jago might be in before the fever overcame you. I sent a servant with a message that morning.'

Rose sighed with relief. 'Thank you so much. Jago's life might have depended upon it, and Benedict needs to know that Guy Colbert is a dangerous man.'

Madame de Fontenay looked down at her tightly clenched hands. 'He is and always was a villain.'

'All the more reason for warning them at Le Fleuve. Montague is even worse.'

'Don't upset yourself, Rose. I will have some breakfast brought to you, but you will need to take things very slowly until the doctor says you are well enough to leave. Madame Laurent knows the situation and she is looking forward to seeing you again when you are well enough to travel.'

'I feel much better, Madame.' Rose swung her legs over the side of the bed and attempted to stand, but sat down again, exhausted by the effort. 'Perhaps I will wait until tomorrow.'

'I should think so, too. I will leave you now and have some food sent up for you.' Madame helped Rose back into bed. 'Perhaps you can get up and sit by the window this afternoon, if you so wish.'

Rose gazed at her, puzzled. Madame de Fontenay was a beautiful woman, probably in her late twenties, with dark hair and eyes, and skin the colour of peaches and cream. Rose caught a waft of expensive perfume that reminded her of the lilies of the valley in the vicarage garden. 'May I ask how you come to know Benedict Rivers, Madame?'

'Please call me Blanche.' She tucked Rose in and stood back. 'His papa bought Le Fleuve about thirty years ago. My papa was the head vintner and it was natural for us to become acquainted. I was just thirteen when I met Benedict and we were about the same age. We became friends.'

'But I thought he lived in Ceylon, at the family's tea plantation.'

'He did, but his father loved Le Fleuve and they came every summer until Monsieur Rivers passed away.'

'And you must have married Monsieur de Fontenay.' Rose eyed her curiously.

'My husband was many years my senior. I'm sorry to say he died just a few months ago. Despite the difference in our ages, it was a good marriage. Now you must rest, Rose. I will come and see you again later.'

Blanche left the room before Rose had a chance to ask any further questions. The way that Blanche looked when she spoke about Benedict made Rose suspect that there might have been something more than just friendship between the beautiful vintner's daughter and the son and heir to the Rivers family fortune. The memory of the wedding gown and veil came to Rose's mind and she lay back in bed, imagining a romance that for some reason had ended when Blanche married a wealthy but much older man. What could have happened that made such an improbable match happen?

Chapter Fourteen

The following day, Rose was feeling stronger and became even more restive and anxious to get to Le Fleuve to see Jago and to find out what was happening regarding Rivers' court case. She had almost forgotten about Montague and Colbert, but they had obviously not forgotten her. She ventured downstairs to the drawing room at Blanche's invitation and was seated by the fire drinking tea, which Cook had brewed especially for her, when Lisette, one of the parlour maids, rushed into the room without knocking.

She spoke rapidly and was obviously distressed. Blanche rose to her feet and hustled the upset maid out of the room, leaving Rose wondering what on earth was going on. However, as the minutes went by she had a nasty feeling that Montague or Colbert might have discovered her whereabouts. Perhaps one of the servants had been gossiping in the village. The sudden presence of an unknown English woman in their midst would have caused quite a stir. Rose waited anxiously for Blanche's return.

'Rose, I'm afraid that news of your whereabouts has reached Colbert.'

'Is he here?' Rose jumped to her feet. 'I don't want to see him.'

'He knows better than to come to my home. He is well aware that there would be no welcome for him. My groundsmen have instructions to send him on his way, should he dare to show his face. It was a messenger from a man called Montague Dalby, the other person you mentioned. He said he had good news for you and wanted to pass it on in person.'

'You didn't believe him?'

'No, of course not, but I think he was sent here to find out if this is where you are living at present.'

'All the more reason for me to return to Le Fleuve. I can't thank you enough for everything you have done for me, but it isn't fair to put you in danger.'

Blanche stared at her in dismay. 'Do you really think that man is dangerous?'

'I wouldn't put anything past Montague. He already has money his stepmother inherited from her first husband, but I believe there is property left to Jago, which Dalby also has his eye on. He wants to get rid of Jago, which is why I have been so anxious. He almost succeeded when he apprenticed the boy to an unscrupulous sea captain. I am still very concerned for Jago's safety.'

'You are much better now, Rose. If it's your wish to return to Le Fleuve I will take you in my carriage, but I suggest we travel very early tomorrow morning, just in case Colbert has set his spies to watch the château.'

'Do you think he would go that far?'

'I know him of old. There is nothing that man will not do if he thinks it will profit him.'

Rose frowned. 'I don't understand why Benedict hired him in the first place. He must be aware of Colbert's reputation.'

'Not necessarily. Don't forget that Benedict spent most of his time in Ceylon or even in England, where I believe he owns a house in Dorset.'

'He owns a large estate on the outskirts of Abbotsford, which is where I live.'

'I will accompany you tomorrow, Rose. If Benedict is back from Paris I need to see him.'

'You always speak fondly of him.' Rose eyed her curiously.

'We are old friends,' Blanche said casually. 'Now, would you like some more tea . . .?'

They left the château next morning, just as dawn was breaking. Rose was still feeling a little weak but her determination to return to Le Fleuve overcame any physical discomfort she was suffering. At first she was nervous, staring out of the window in an attempt

245

to spot anyone behaving suspiciously, but the only sign of life was a stream of farm workers trudging doggedly towards their place of employment. In the end she sat back and relaxed. Soon she would be back at Le Fleuve, which had always felt homely and safe from the outside world.

'Perhaps Colbert and his friend Dalby have had a change of heart,' Blanche said cheerfully. 'They must realise that kidnapping you would not further their purpose, whatever that is.'

'I hardly know Colbert, but I know that Montague is totally ruthless, which is why he has accused Rivers of fraud.'

'You are very fond of Benedict, aren't you?'

The question startled Rose and she shook her head. 'That's not true. I mean, of course, I like and respect him for taking care of Jago, but I don't like to see anyone accused falsely.'

'Benedict is a very attractive man.'

'Is it much further to Le Fleuve?' Rose asked, changing the subject.

'No, we're nearly there. I hope Madame Laurent has baked some of her special croissants. I am starving.'

Rose smiled. 'So am I. She is an excellent cook when she is in the right mood.' Rose remembered her own disastrous attempt at making a birthday cake for Jago after Madame had refused to oblige. Rivers had arrived just in time to save the occasion; perhaps he would be there already and then everything would be all right. Rose sat back in her seat and gazed out of the window, only this time she was genuinely admiring the view of olive groves and serried ranks of vines waiting for spring to wake them into life again after a long winter. Then, to her relief, she saw the gates leading into the estate and she knew she would be safe and secure.

Madame Laurent greeted them with her usual stoical reserve, although Rose detected a hint of disapproval in her attitude when she spoke to Blanche. But it was Jago who gave Rose an enthusiastic welcome. He was beginning to lose the haunted look of a runaway, and there was colour in his cheeks. His eyes were clear and he was grinning widely. He bowed politely when Rose introduced him to Blanche and she clutched his hand, holding on to it a little longer than was necessary.

'I am very happy to meet you, Jago.' Blanche released him reluctantly. 'It is good to see you looking so well. I mean, Rose told me about your terrible ordeal.'

Jago grinned. 'I am fine now, thank you, Madame. It is kind of you to care.'

'Anyone with any sensibilities would feel for you,' Blanche said earnestly.

'Will you be staying for some breakfast, Madame de Fontenay?' Madame Laurent did not sound encouraging but, seemingly oblivious, Blanche turned to her with a grateful smile.

'That would be delightful, Madame. We left the château very early this morning.' She lowered her voice. 'Perhaps I could have a few words with you in private, Madame?'

'Yes, of course. Come to the kitchen while I make breakfast.' Madame Laurent turned to Rose. 'Your old room has been kept ready for you, Mademoiselle.'

'Yes, I insisted upon it,' Jago said proudly. 'Madame thought you would stay in England with your family, but I knew you would return here to see me. Come and sit by the fire in the drawing room. I want to hear everything that has happened, and how you came to be with Madame de Fontenay. I remember her from a long time ago when she used to visit Le Fleuve. She was always very kind to me.' He caught Rose by the hand and led her into the drawing room, where he sat down on the sofa and patted the empty space beside him.

She sat down, smiling. 'It's so good to see you fully recovered, Jago. I've been quite unwell myself.'

'I want to know everything. Where is my uncle? Did he stay in London?'

'Hasn't he been in touch with your mama, Jago? I would have thought she might have received a letter by now.'

'Not that I know of. She hasn't said anything to me but I know she's been very anxious. She doesn't sleep at night. I hear her walking up and down in her room, and then she doesn't wake up until almost midday. I hope you have some good news for us.'

Rose thought for a moment, wondering whether she ought to tell him what had happened to her or to wait until his mother joined them. However, the sudden appearance of Lucy in the doorway solved that dilemma. Jago jumped to his feet.

'Mama, you're up early.'

'I heard the carriage arrive. I thought perhaps it was Benedict, but I just saw the de Fontenay crest. I thought you were still in England, Rose.'

'It's a long story, but I've been staying with Madame de Fontenay,' Rose said hastily. She could see that Lucy Dalby was upset. 'You look pale, ma'am. Would you like me to fetch some coffee for you, or a cup of tea, perhaps?'

'No, nothing, thank you. I don't understand how you came to know Madame de Fontenay. Is she here?'

'Yes, she accompanied me this morning. She's in the kitchen with Madame Laurent.'

'I'm confused, Rose. I thought the plan was for you to get permission from your papa to stay here a little longer.' Lucy sank down on a chair by the fire. 'Tell me what has happened. Why is Blanche here?'

'I was abducted by your stepson, ma'am. Montague tricked me into thinking he was someone else before virtually taking me prisoner. He brought me to Avignon with Colbert, who is not the trusted friend that Rivers thought him to be.'

'Montague and Guy Colbert?' The colour drained

from Lucy's face. 'I think I need brandy more than a cup of tea. Jago, pour me a tot, if you please.'

Jago stood up and crossed the floor to a small table. He picked up a decanter and poured a little of the spirit into a glass, which he handed to his mother.

'Are you all right, Mama?'

She sipped the brandy and almost immediately the colour returned to her cheeks. 'I don't know what to think. We all trusted Colbert. Are you sure of all this, Rose?'

'They locked me in a room in what appeared to be Colbert's property on the edge of Avignon. Montague Dalby intended to hold me hostage. I don't know his exact demands but it had something to do with you and Jago.'

'He wants my son's inheritance,' Lucy said faintly. 'He has already taken my property and placed the blame on Benedict. Now he wants to take my son from me.'

'I'm not a child, Mama.' Jago puffed out his chest. 'I'm fourteen. I've been to sea and I was flogged every time I displeased the captain. I'm a man now and I'll take care of you, so don't worry.'

Lucy's eyes filled with tears and she reached out to clutch her son's hand. 'You are all I have, Jago. Always remember that I love you.'

'You mustn't worry about me, Mama,' Jago said stoutly. 'I'll always be your boy.'

'Thank you, my love, but you don't know what we are up against. Montague is ruthless, although I find it hard to believe that Guy Colbert would turn against Benedict, who has always treated him like an equal.'

'On the night that I escaped, Montague and Colbert had been out drinking.' Rose looked from one to the other. 'Colbert tried to get into my room but Montague stopped him and they fought. Then all went quiet and when I tried the door I found it unlocked. I grabbed my things and fled.'

'How appalling,' Lucy said, shivering. 'What a terrible experience.'

'I will make them sorry for treating you like that,' Jago added, fisting his hands.

'I ran, but then I had to slow down because it was dark and the road was rutted and muddy. Fortunately for me it was one of Blanche's employees who found me wandering in the grounds of the château. I collapsed and he took me into the servants' quarters. I was in a fever for several days and I've only just recovered.' Rose looked round as Blanche entered the drawing room. 'I was just telling them how you looked after me when I was unwell.'

'It was nothing,' Blanche said hastily. 'How are you, Lucy? It's been too long since we last met.'

Lucy nodded. 'It seems that we are in debt to you, Blanche.'

'Rose has obviously told you her story. I only did what any decent person would do in the circumstances, but I should be leaving now. It's good to know that she is in safe hands.'

'Aren't you staying for breakfast?' Rose asked anxiously. 'Please don't go just yet.'

'Madame Laurent gave me one of her delicious croissants while we had a chat in the kitchen. It's probably safest if I go now. I am in no danger personally, but if my presence is noted, Colbert will know that I brought you here, Rose.'

'I am sure he will work that out for himself,' Lucy said hastily. 'Please don't go on my account. You are welcome to stay for a while.'

'Yes, please do,' Jago added. 'I would like to thank you for looking after my best friend, Rose. She saved my life, you know.'

Blanche gave Rose a curious glance. 'She did not tell me that.'

'Anyone would have done the same.' Rose smiled. 'Jago was our Christmas miracle. I found him asleep in the crib outside the church. He was in a bad way.'

'I would have died if you hadn't come along when you did and taken me home.' Jago went to sit beside Rose and he gave her a hug. 'You and I seem to get ourselves into trouble. I don't know how we do it.'

'You need to be very careful from now on,' Blanche said seriously. 'You should not venture far from the house, Jago.' She turned to Lucy with a worried frown. 'Please tell your ground workers to be on the lookout for strangers, and in particular you must warn them against Guy Colbert. You and I both know him of old, Lucy. You understand what I'm saying.'

Lucy nodded. 'Yes, I do. Indeed I do.'

Rose looked from one to the other. There seemed to be some secret they were sharing and it concerned Colbert. She could only imagine what he must have done in the past and it did nothing to calm her worries.

'Benedict is going to be very upset to discover that someone he trusted has turned against him,' Rose said, frowning. 'Have you heard from him recently, Mrs Dalby?'

Lucy placed her empty glass on a side table. 'I wish I had never married that man. I have a good mind to revert to my maiden name and become Lucy Rivers once again.'

'But I am a Hanbury, Mama,' Jago said plaintively. 'I am your son.'

'Yes, of course you are.' Lucy managed a weary smile.

'Any woman would be proud to have a son like you, Jago.' Blanche gazed intently at Jago. 'But now I really must leave. Remember what I said about warning your outside staff, Lucy.' She turned to Rose with a genuine smile. 'Look after yourself, Rose. I know you will keep an eye on Jago. You are his guardian angel.'

Rose jumped to her feet and followed Blanche from the drawing room. Madame Laurent came bustling from the kitchen.

'Are you leaving so soon, Madame?'

'Yes, Berthe. I have to go now.'

'It is just as well, Madame.'

Quick to note the disapproving tone in Madame Laurent's voice, Rose retrieved Blanche's cloak from the rattan chair where it had been carelessly abandoned, and helped Blanche to put it on.

Madame Laurent did not attempt to help. She remained standing, arms folded tightly across her chest, with a sour expression marring her features. Rose found it difficult to think of her as Berthe, but of course, even someone as strait-laced and judgemental as Madame Laurent must have been a pretty little baby many years ago. No doubt she had been someone's pride and joy, at least Rose hoped so. It would be sad to think that a child came into the world unwanted and unloved.

Rose followed Blanche to the front entrance where her carriage was waiting.

'Once again, thank you for looking after me,' she said earnestly. 'I might have died but for your kindness, Madame.'

'Blanche, please. I hope to see you again before too long, Rose. But promise me that you will be very careful. You don't know Colbert as well as I do. That man will stop at nothing to get what he wants.' Blanche nodded to her footman as he held the carriage door open for her. She climbed inside and sat down.

Rose watched until the carriage was out of sight before returning to the drawing room. She was curious. There was something going on between

Blanche de Fontenay and Lucy Dalby, or Lucy Rivers, as she wished to revert to her maiden name. What it could be was a mystery, but then Le Fleuve was a puzzle waiting to be solved and it seemed that Blanche de Fontenay was a part of it.

Lucy's face was flushed, which might be accounted for by the second glass of brandy clutched in her hand. She looked up and managed a tight smile.

'Blanche has gone back to the château?'

'Yes, ma'am. She repeated her warning about Colbert.' Rose sat down opposite Lucy. 'Have you known Madame de Fontenay for long?'

'Too long, one might say.' Lucy rose somewhat unsteadily to her feet. 'All this talk about Colbert's treachery and Montague having followed us here has unsettled me. I need to go to my room and lie down.'

Jago stood up. 'Shall I help you, Mama?'

'No, thank you. I am quite capable of finding my way on my own.' Lucy held herself very upright as she walked slowly from the room.

'Should I go with her?' Rose asked anxiously.

Jago sat down with a sigh. 'No, she can manage. I've seen her like this before when she has had a tot or two of brandy, but it was only after she married Dalby. I never liked him, Rose.'

'I'm sorry. It must have been hard for you to have a stepfather you did not get on with.'

'He didn't like me either. It wasn't a happy household. Mama used to cry a lot, although she thought I didn't know. Monty was a bully from the start. He used to make up stories about me and get me into trouble.'

'I can believe that,' Rose said with feeling. 'He is a despicable character and so is Colbert. I don't know why your cousin put so much faith in him.'

'We need Cousin Benedict to come home. He would stand up to Monty, which of course is why Monty wants to discredit him and send him to prison. If I was a man I'd challenge Monty to a duel.'

Rose laughed. 'I think duelling is illegal nowadays, even here in France.'

'Well, all right, but I'd challenge him to a boxing match. I was very quick on my feet until my illness.'

'You are getting better every day. When all this blows over, and the weather improves, we will go on long walks. You will soon build up your strength.'

'Everything will be all right now you're here, Rose.' Jago reached out to touch her hand. 'I wish I had a sister, just like you. You won't go away again, will you?'

'I promise to stay at least until your cousin returns. Now how about a game of chess? As I recall, you beat me last time we played. I think it's my turn to win.'

Jago grinned. 'I love a challenge.'

They played chess until it was time for luncheon, with Rose getting thoroughly beaten, much to Jago's amusement. After they had eaten Jago fell asleep in his chair by the fire and Rose went in search of

Madame Laurent. There were so many questions that only she might be able to answer. Angeline was in the scullery washing the dishes and she directed Rose to Madame's private parlour at the back of the house. Rose knocked on the door and received a faint answer, which she took to be permission to enter.

Madame did not look too pleased, but she invited Rose in and motioned her to take a seat.

'What can I do for you, Mademoiselle?'

'You've worked here for a long time, Madame.' Rose remained standing. She had a feeling that this interview would not last long. 'Why do you think Monsieur Colbert has turned against the family?'

'Who knows?' Madame shrugged and looked away.

Rose was not about to be put off so easily. 'But Mr Rivers trusted him, Madame. It seems that Monsieur Colbert has been a friend of the family for a long time.'

'He is no friend of mine.' Madame rose to her feet. 'I cannot help you, Mademoiselle. Who knows what has changed? Now if you don't mind, I value my rest time in the afternoon.'

'Of course. I am sorry to have bothered you.' Rose left the room, closing the door firmly behind her. Of one thing she was certain – Madame Laurent knew much more than she was prepared to divulge. There was nothing Rose could do other than to return to the drawing room and sit quietly, waiting for Jago to wake up. It was warm in front of the roaring log fire and outside rain beat rhythmically against the window panes. Rose lay back in one of the well-worn but comfortable armchairs and closed her eyes.

She was awakened by the sound of horses' hoofs on the gravelled forecourt and a carriage being drawn to a halt. Jago opened his eyes and sat up straight.

'Who can that be? If it's Colbert or Monty I will send them on their way.' He stood up and went to the window, peering out into the twilight.

Rose was on her feet and making for the doorway. 'I'll find out, Jago. You wait there.'

'I'm not a child and I'm quite well now. I'm coming with you.'

'No, Jago. Please wait there. If it's your stepbrother, I don't want him to know you're here.' Rose hurried into the entrance hall just as the front door opened and a man stepped inside, wrapped in a caped greatcoat with a wide-brimmed hat pulled down low over his face.

Rose stifled a scream.

Chapter Fifteen

He was laughing as he took off his hat. 'I didn't know I was such a horrifying figure, Rose.'

She stared at him in amazement. 'Rivers! You frightened the life out of me.'

His smile faded. 'What's the matter?' He took off his coat and flung it over the back of the rattan chair. 'You look as if you've seen a ghost.'

She shook her head. 'No, it's not you. I mean, I'm just relieved it's you.'

'Who did you think I was?' Rivers moved towards her, a worried look darkening his blue eyes to indigo.

'You obviously don't know what's been going on in your absence.'

'I want to hear all about it, but first there's someone you should meet.' Rivers turned to a shadowy figure standing behind him. 'Come in, Will.'

Rose found herself facing a young man, perhaps

a couple of years her senior. He took off his top hat to reveal a head of neatly trimmed hair the colour of horse chestnuts, gleaming in the candlelight. His warm, toffee-brown eyes twinkled as he gave her a shy smile.

'Will Jameson. How do you do, Miss Northwood?'

'Will is my barrister,' Rivers said hastily. 'He came with me to discuss the case. We've been through the magistrates' court and the court case is in a few weeks.'

Rose shook Will's hand. 'How do you do, sir?'

'Please call me Will.' Again that charming, slightly shy smile.

'Yes, Rose,' Rivers said firmly. 'We're going to be living in close proximity for a few days while Will and I go over the case that Dalby has fabricated against me.'

'That's just the trouble.' Rose lowered her voice. 'Montague Dalby is in Avignon with your man, Colbert, whom you trusted to take care of your affairs. He's a rat, Rivers.'

'Colbert and Dalby?' Rivers stared at her, his brows drawn together in a frown. 'What makes you think that, Rose?' He reached out to open the drawing-room door, but Rose laid her hands on his sleeve.

'Please don't. Not yet, anyway. Jago is in there. I really don't want to talk about this in front of him. He's doing so well now and I don't want to give him a setback.'

'What has happened since I left you in Abbotsford?'

'I met a man who was staying at the Crown. He told me that he was your younger brother, Edmond.'

'But you knew that I had no siblings, Rose.'

'Yes, but he was very convincing. He told me he had news of your court case, needed to speak to you and that he wanted me to take him to Provence.'

'And you put yourself in his hands?'

'Don't look at me like that, Rivers. I really thought he was genuine. I only discovered the truth when Colbert joined us in Paris. The man who said he was Edmond Rivers is actually Montague Dalby, and, worst of all, he and Colbert are working against you, both of them.'

'Colbert came from nothing and I gave him a chance to make something of himself.' Rivers turned to Will. 'Make a note of all this, Will. I can believe anything of Dalby, but I trusted Colbert.'

'I couldn't get away from them,' Rose said with a break in her voice. 'I was a virtual prisoner until we reached Avignon.'

Rivers took her hand in his, holding it close to his heart. 'I am so sorry, Rose. I should never have involved you in my family's troubles.'

'It isn't your fault. I chose to come with you because I care for Jago. I am even more determined to stay until he is fully recovered and you have cleared your name.'

Rivers shook his head, frowning. 'I don't deserve

261

that degree of loyalty. But what I don't understand is what Dalby hoped to gain by abducting you.'

'I think I was to be held hostage. They took me to Colbert's home in Avignon, but the pair of them went out one evening and got very drunk. I managed to escape in the middle of the night after they had a drunken brawl and left my door unlocked.'

'Hell and damnation, Rose. I am so sorry.'

She managed a wry smile. 'I admit that I was terrified. Alone and penniless in a foreign country. I didn't know if I was on the right road for Le Fleuve and it was pitch dark, but somehow I wandered into the grounds of the Château de Fontenay. Madame took me in and looked after me when I was struck down by a fever.'

'Blanche knew that you were running away from Colbert and Montague Dalby?'

'Yes, she did.' Rose eyed him curiously. 'I believe she knows Colbert. She seems to dislike him but she didn't tell me why.'

'What's in the past should stay there. It all happened a long time ago.'

'Whatever the reason, Colbert and Montague mean to harm Jago and I won't allow that to happen.'

'I will handle this, Rose. You need not worry any more. I am home for now, anyway. Although if Dalby is still intent on harming Jago we might have to leave Le Fleuve sooner than I planned. What do you think, Will?'

'Rose's testimony will help your case, Benedict.'

Will shook his head. 'An incredible story. Perhaps I may be permitted to take a full statement from Rose tomorrow. In the meantime, the boy is safe here with us, isn't he?'

Rivers nodded. 'Yes, of course. But we won't mention any of this to him. I think it's time you returned to your family, Rose. I can't allow you to take any more chances on our behalf.'

'You have no further use for me.' Rose stared at him with mixed emotions. She had put so much of herself into caring for Jago and bringing him to safety and now Rivers was dismissing her as if she meant nothing to him or his family.

'I thought you would be happy to be free from all this.'

'I won't be happy until I know that Jago is no longer in danger. I really do care about him, Rivers. I don't want everything I've been through to be for nothing.'

'We'll talk later, but now I must see my aunt and make her aware of the situation. How much does she know already?'

'I told her everything. She has not taken it well.'

'Lucy is not a strong woman. She needs someone to protect her, especially where Dalby is concerned. Make no mistake, Rose. That fellow may be young but he's ruthless.'

'You must see Jago first,' Rose said firmly. 'He needs you.'

Rivers nodded and opened the drawing-room door.

'Jago, I've brought my barrister from London. Will is going to help us get the better of your stepbrother.'

Rose smiled at Jago's obvious pleasure and the rekindling of hope in his blue eyes. She closed the door, leaving them to speak in private, and she hurried to the kitchen to give Madame the news that there would be two extra for dinner that evening.

Next day Rose went down to breakfast and was told by an excited Angeline that the master had called a meeting of the senior outside staff and had already sent them on their way. She did not know what he had said, but the men had departed looking serious, and she was overtly curious. Rose, however, had nothing to say other than to request a fresh pot of coffee and some croissants.

Rivers passed Angeline as he entered the dining room. 'I've told Lucy and Jago to pack what they need. That goes for you, too, Rose.'

'We're all leaving?'

'No, Rose. You, Jago and my aunt are going to Abbotsford. I intend to remain here with Will as a witness. We will wait for Colbert and Montague Dalby to show their faces. I won't allow them to harm the people I care about.'

Rose met his gaze with a determined lift of her chin. 'You may send Lucy and Jago to safety, but I intend to stay with you. I want to see Dalby get his just deserts, and Colbert, too. They are both despicable.'

'I admire your courage, Rose. But you should return to your family. I don't want to put you in any more danger. Besides which, you have your reputation to consider.'

There was a hint of a smile in his eyes as he spoke, and Rose found herself responding, even though she knew he was right. 'My reputation is in shreds already, and I have a score to settle with Colbert in particular. I'm sure I can persuade Blanche to give Will a statement. She alone knows how ill I was when she took me in.'

'I don't know, Rose. I would feel better if you were safe at home.'

'I am safe here with you. I can be of more use here.'

Rivers turned to Will, who had just joined them and taken a seat at the table. 'What do you think?'

'I think that Miss Northwood has made up her mind, Benedict.' Will met Rose's questioning look with a wry smile. 'Is that not so?'

Rose nodded. 'Most certainly. I want to see those villains brought to justice. So long as Jago is in the care of his mama and safely back in Abbotsford, there is little that either Colbert or Dalby can do.'

'All right, Rose. I can see that you've made up your mind.' Rivers sighed. 'I'm sure you can help more by being here, but your family must be anxious.'

'They know nothing of my abduction by Dalby. As far as they are concerned, my leaving home was all arranged for Jago's benefit. I will tell them everything when I do return home.'

'I can see it's no use arguing with you,' Rivers said with a wry smile. 'However, I think the first thing I will do is to call on Blanche. She, of all people, knows Colbert the best.'

'How is that?' Rose was curious. She had always suspected that there was something behind Blanche's story that she had withheld.

'It's not my place to say anything. Blanche will tell you if she thinks fit. I'll leave you to make your statement to Will, Rose.'

She shook her head. 'Oh, no. I'm coming with you. I want to hear what Blanche has to say.'

For a moment she thought that Rivers was going to refuse, but he merely nodded.

'All right. I'm not going to argue. Be ready to leave in ten minutes.'

Blanche greeted them with such obvious pleasure that it made Rose wonder again if there had ever been anything more than mere friendship between her and Rivers. However, he treated Blanche with the deference due to someone of her standing, and as far as Rose could see there was nothing else behind his customary charming manner.

Blanche sank down gracefully on one of the Louis Quinze sofas in her drawing room, motioning her visitors to take a seat.

'This is an unexpected pleasure, Benedict. What can I do for you?'

Rivers pulled up a chair and sat down, his tall,

well-muscled body making the delicate chair look even more fragile. A serious expression replaced his smile.

'I'll get straight to the point. Rose says she told you everything that passed between her and the two criminals who held her against her will.'

Blanche nodded. 'She was in a terrible state when she arrived here, but the story came out gradually as her health improved. What else can I tell you?'

'Anything you know about Colbert. I thought he was trustworthy, but now I know he was lying to me while taking my money. Dalby is another matter. I know that he is a nasty character and completely ruthless. He will do anything to get the money that Jago is to inherit from his father's estate.'

'But surely he has no claim on it?' Blanche's brow puckered in a frown.

'The money has been put in trust for Jago until he reaches his majority,' Rivers said firmly. 'His mama and I are the trustees.'

'So what can Dalby do about it?' Blanche looked from one to the other. 'I don't understand. Rose said that Dalby had sent his stepbrother to sea, it seems in the hope that the boy wouldn't survive. I can't see that would take Dalby any closer to getting his hands on the estate.'

'He has made Lucy totally dependent upon him,' Rivers said angrily. 'My poor aunt is not a strong woman. She cannot stand up to Dalby on her own. By getting rid of Jago, Dalby would be one step closer to the fortune that would be at Lucy's disposal.'

'That is terrible, but I don't see how I can help.'

'You can't do anything about Dalby, but I need to learn everything I can about Colbert from the time before I took him on. I know there was some sort of scandal attached to his name, but it was never spoken about in the family. I assumed it must have been some youthful indiscretion, but perhaps there is something you can tell me.'

'I could leave the room if you don't want me to hear what you have to say,' Rose said reluctantly. She was more than eager to learn the truth about Blanche's past, but she did not want to embarrass someone who had been so kind to her. She stood up. 'I can wait in the ante-room.'

'No, please stay, Rose. My past is always there to haunt me, but I was very young when I met Guy. I was only fourteen when he came to work in the vineyard. Guy was twenty-one and very handsome. We fell in love – at least I did, and I thought that Guy felt the same.' Blanche shot a sideways glance at Rivers. 'You weren't at Le Fleuve when all this happened. It was your aunt Lucy and her first husband who were living there at the time.'

'I think I was at boarding school in England then. You and I were good friends when we were very young, Blanche. I used to look forward to our sojourns at Le Fleuve when we returned from the tea plantation.'

'I was glad that you didn't know about my disgrace, Benedict.'

'I would have stood by you, no matter what. If you don't want to talk about it, I quite understand.'

Blanche sighed. 'When I told Guy that I was in the family way he was angry and wanted nothing to do with me, but my father found out and forced Guy to propose. I was happy at first and my wedding dress was made.'

'Was it white lace with a long veil?' Rose asked eagerly.

'How do you know that?' Blanche eyed her curiously. 'As a matter of fact, it was.'

'I saw a dress and veil in one of the bedrooms at Le Fleuve. I asked Madame Laurent about it but she denied all knowledge.'

Blanche pulled a face. 'That sounds like Berthe. She blamed me for leading Guy astray, but it wasn't like that.'

'Of course not.' Rivers rose from his seat and walked over to the window. 'You were a child and he was a grown man.'

'We were to have a quiet wedding.' Blanche took a lace hanky from her reticule and wiped her eyes. 'But then Guy disappeared, having stolen money from Mr Hanbury. We found out later that Guy had left his home town after being accused of theft.'

'I am so sorry.' Rose jumped to her feet and went to sit beside Blanche, wrapping her arms around her in a comforting hug.

'I knew nothing of all this,' Rivers said angrily. 'I would never have taken Colbert on, had I known.

I'm surprised that no one told me about his shady past.'

'The people here are good at keeping secrets,' Blanche said sadly. 'I've managed to get by, despite my previous entanglement with Guy Colbert.'

'What happened to the child?' Rose clutched Blanche's cold hand, chafing it gently. 'Did you have the baby?'

'My father arranged for me to marry Henri de Fontenay, who was a widower in his seventies, but I had to give birth first and the baby boy was to be adopted. I had no choice other than to accept, otherwise I would have been turned out with a fatherless child to raise. I would have been scorned by the whole village.'

'So you had the baby and gave him away?' Rose wiped tears from her eyes. 'How sad for you.'

'He went to someone who could love him and give him a good home. I married Henri. He was a good man and treated me well, but he died a few months ago, leaving me a wealthy widow.'

'Do you ever see your son?' Rose had to ask.

'Yes, he's a fine boy. But he doesn't know me and never will. That was part of the agreement, and I've kept my word.'

'I'm not sure I could be so high-minded,' Rose said, sighing. 'I think I would have to make myself known to him.'

Rivers turned to give Blanche an apologetic smile. 'I'm sorry to have brought all this back to you,

Blanche. I didn't know your full story, although I thought it very odd that a beautiful girl like you should agree to marry such an old man. Now I understand.'

'I am sorry, too,' Rose said earnestly. 'You've been so good to me.'

'It's all right, Rose. I have to live with my past. I think about my beautiful boy every day, but I know he is loved and cared for. Having said that, if anyone tries to harm him they will have to deal with me, and I would be like a tigress if my boy was in real danger.'

'You've given me the information I needed, Blanche,' Rivers said gently. 'I was a fool not to have looked into Colbert's past more carefully, but he will be brought to justice, I can assure you of that.'

'I try hard not to think about him, Benedict. I have to take my share of the blame for what happened.'

'You were an innocent child,' Rivers said angrily.

Blanche shook her head. 'It's something I have to live with every day of my life.'

Rivers strode over to the door and opened it. 'Let me know if Colbert should try to contact you, Blanche. I'm going to make him pay for what he did to you, and for his treatment of Rose. He will wish he had never shown his face around here.'

Rose kissed Blanche on the cheek. 'I wish I was as brave as you, Blanche.'

'You should return to your family in England, Rose. Forget Colbert and go back to your old life.'

'I don't think I can,' Rose said, frowning. 'I have changed. I was never meek and mild, although I tried to be a good daughter. Now I am ready to fight those hateful men and make sure they are brought to trial. Jago is like the brother I lost and I will defend him with all my might.'

'We'll leave you in peace, Blanche.' Rivers held the door open for Rose. 'We'd best get back to Le Fleuve. Who knows what those two villains are planning? But we won't allow them to get the better of us.'

'I agree.' Rose blew a kiss to Blanche as she left the room. She waited for him to close the drawing-room door, before adding in a low voice, 'I am more determined than ever to see this through, Rivers. I'll do anything you ask of me.'

'I doubt that,' he said drily. 'But I appreciate the sentiment.'

'I mean it, Rivers. I was shocked by Blanche's story. She was about the same age as my sister Emily is when Colbert took advantage of her and then refused to marry her. I can only imagine what she went through.'

'That would explain the wedding gown you saw at Le Fleuve.' Rivers walked slowly towards the entrance hall. 'Why would Madame Laurent deny all knowledge of it?'

'I don't know. It was there one day and gone the next. Madame Laurent must know it was there, neatly arranged on a dressmaker's dummy.'

'That was very strange. Why would she have kept a bride's gown and veil, especially if she disapproved of the match?'

'That's not all, either.' Rose fell into step at his side. 'There was a wooden crib in one of the other rooms.'

'I suppose that vanished, too?'

'I'm not making this up, Rivers. I am telling you what I saw.'

'I don't doubt you, Rose. I am going to have a very serious talk with Madame Laurent when we get home.' Rivers nodded to the footman who opened the heavy oak door at the main entrance. A groom had been walking the horses and he brought the chaise to the bottom of the flight of stone steps. Rivers assisted Rose into the carriage and climbed in beside her.

'I wonder what happened to Blanche's child,' Rose said thoughtfully. 'I don't know how she can bear to see him growing up in another family.'

'She has suffered and is still suffering.' Rivers leaned back against the leather squabs. 'I've always admired Blanche, even as a boy. She is a strong woman and that makes Colbert's treatment of her even worse in my eyes.'

Rose shot him a sideways glance. She could not shake off the feeling that Rivers had stronger feelings for Blanche than he cared to admit. It was not a comfortable thought.

* * *

273

Will was waiting for them when they arrived back at Le Fleuve. He greeted them warmly but Rose could see that something was bothering him.

'Might I have a word with you, Benedict?'

Rivers shrugged off his greatcoat and handed it to Angeline, together with his gloves and hat. She moved away slowly as if hoping to overhear something of interest.

'Yes, of course,' Rivers said equably. 'We'll go to my study.'

'I think Rose should come, too.'

'If you think so, then yes, of course.' Rivers strode off in the direction of the study with Will following him.

'I'm coming.' Rose needed no second invitation. She abandoned her outer garments and hurried after them.

'What's all this about, Will?' Rivers asked as he took a seat behind his desk. 'Has something happened in our absence?'

'Not exactly.' Will pulled up a chair for Rose and one for himself. 'But Mrs Dalby, or Miss Rivers, as she now wishes to be called, is very nervous about travelling on her own with Jago.'

'I was going to send one of my most trusted men to accompany them as far as Cherbourg, where Jackson will be waiting for them.'

'She is frightened of Dalby, even though he is her stepson. She thinks he will go out of his way to find them before they can get to safety. I have tried to reassure her, but she has shut herself in her room.'

'Do you want me to talk to her?' Rose asked anxiously. 'I will try to convince her that she needs to get Jago back to England.'

Rivers sighed and shook his head. 'I know my aunt only too well. Once she has got an idea into her head it is almost impossible to reason with her.'

Rose thought for a moment. 'Then perhaps we should all remain here until you have to leave for London.'

Rivers stared at her in surprise. 'Why would you say that?'

'This house is as safe as anywhere. You have an army of outside workers ready to obey your slightest command, and we are better kept together. Every day that Jago rests makes him stronger and more able to travel.'

'I think Rose is right,' Will said slowly. 'While we are here, I can prepare your case for the courts. What do you think, Benedict?'

Chapter Sixteen

Madame Laurent had the look of a cornered animal as Rivers pressed home his demand for an explanation as to the vanishing wedding gown, veil and the crib. Rose felt almost sorry for her, but Madame clearly knew much more than she was prepared to admit. However, once Rivers had started questioning her there seemed to be no excuse she could offer that would satisfy him. Will stayed in the background, saying nothing, although it was obvious that he was listening intently.

'Madame Laurent, I have been very patient,' Rivers said with an exasperated sigh. 'But you have run this household for many years. There is nothing at Le Fleuve that does not escape your attention. I am asking you for the last time – where is the lace gown and the veil? Was it the wedding dress made for Blanche Bonnard, the vintner's daughter?'

Madame Laurent shot a malevolent glance in Rose's direction. 'You should not believe the fantasies of a young woman who has been through a shocking experience.'

Rose opened her mouth to protest but Rivers held up his hand. 'I believe Rose saw the gown. Where is it now, Madame?'

Madame took a deep breath. 'All right, have it your way, Monsieur Benedict. The truth is that I burned it and the veil, and I chopped the crib up for firewood. Are you satisfied now?'

'Why would you do such a thing?' Rose stared at her in astonishment. 'Why did you keep them in the first place?'

'That is my business, Mademoiselle.'

'No,' Rivers said firmly. 'Everything that happens here is very much my business. Why did you keep them, if only to destroy them now?'

Will moved closer. 'Might I enquire as to your relationship with Guy Colbert, Madame? It seems to me that he might be at the bottom of this.'

'Do you think so, Will?' Rivers turned to him with a questioning look.

'Why else would a respectable, reliable housekeeper do something that was against the best interests of her employer?'

Rivers turned back to Madame Laurent. 'That is a fair question. What have you to say to that, Madame?'

'Guy Colbert is my sister's son, my nephew,' Madame said reluctantly. 'I witnessed him being humiliated and sent away because of Blanche Bonnard, the little slut.'

'That is enough of that language.' Rivers made a visible effort to control his temper. 'Blanche was a child when your nephew took advantage of her, and then he abandoned her. I would never have employed him had I known about his past. You kept that very quiet and I can see why.'

'He is family,' Madame said sulkily. 'We protect our own.'

'Not if they have done something very wrong.' Rose turned away, too disgusted even to look at Madame Laurent.

'I suppose my employment here is terminated.' Madame folded her arms with a defiant toss of her head. 'I will pack my bags.'

'You have been a good servant, Madame,' Rivers said slowly. 'Apart from this, you have worked hard and served my family well. But you have a chance to make amends now.'

Madame Laurent sniffed, eyeing him suspiciously. 'What do I have to do?'

'You will promise not to contact your nephew from now on. Should he get in touch with you I want you to inform me immediately. There is more at stake here than a lace wedding gown and a wooden crib.'

'I don't know what you mean, Monsieur.'

'Your nephew has allied himself with a man who put Jago in harm's way, hoping that the boy would not survive.'

Madame's eyes opened wide. 'Why would anyone do that to a young boy?'

Rose could see that Madame Laurent's shock on hearing this was genuine. She knew that Madame had grown fond of Jago, and her reaction made this obvious.

'Montague Dalby is the person who abducted me, Madame. He pretended to be Monsieur Benedict's brother, and I foolishly believed him.'

'That's right,' Rivers said before Madame had a chance to speak. 'Dalby and your nephew have banded together. Dalby is trying to ruin me and blacken my name, and Colbert seems to think he was treated unfairly by my family.'

'Well now, as to that, I couldn't say.' Madame looked nervously at Will, who was watching her intently. 'Am I going to be prosecuted?'

'I am a lawyer, not a policeman, Madame,' Will said with a wry smile. 'I suggest you cooperate fully with your employer. Your nephew has gone beyond your help now.'

'What must I do, Monsieur Benedict?'

Benedict eyed her coldly. 'As I said before – if your nephew attempts to contact you I need to know immediately.'

'I understand, and I will do as you ask.'

'Thank you, Madame Laurent.' Rivers leaned forward, allowing his stern expression to soften. 'I know it cannot be easy when your family is concerned, but I trust you to do the right thing by me, and in particular by Jago. I can assure you that his life depends upon it.'

Madame Laurent drew herself up to her full height, holding her head proudly. 'I have things to do in the kitchen. May I go now?'

Rivers nodded his assent and she marched out of the study, closing the door behind her.

'Can you trust her, Benedict?' Will asked earnestly. 'She seems very devoted to that nephew of hers.'

'She is also very fond of Jago,' Rose said hastily.

Rivers gave her an encouraging smile. 'I agree with you, Rose. Madame has been a loyal servant for many years. Despite her obvious affection for Colbert – and it was largely on her say-so that I engaged him as my agent – I think she will do as I asked.'

'So we will stay here while you and Will go over the details of your court case?' Rose looked from one to the other.

'Yes, I think you are right. Lucy isn't in a fit state to travel and Jago will probably be safer here with us. I just wish I knew what Dalby and Colbert were planning.' Rivers turned to Will. 'Perhaps you would like to take Rose's statement now? I'm going to check on the outside workers to see if they've seen anything suspicious.'

'Yes, of course. We can do that now.' Will took a pad of paper from his document case. 'Is that all right with you, Rose?'

'Definitely. I'll tell you exactly what happened to

me. I want to see those wretches put behind bars for all the hateful things they've done.'

Rivers left them to get on with the task in hand and Will took his place behind the desk.

'Are you comfortable with this, Rose? Just tell me if it all gets too much for you and we'll stop until you feel you can carry on.'

Rose leaned her elbows on the tooled leather top of the desk. 'I'm not such a faint-heart, Will. I've been through this a couple of times already. Once more isn't going to send me into a fit of the vapours.'

He laughed and reached for the inkstand, taking a pen from the tray and dipping in the ink well. 'Start at the beginning then, Rose. How and where did you meet Dalby?'

It was a slow process with Will writing everything down in neat copperplate. He had to stop Rose every so often in order to clarify points in her story for the sake of accuracy. They worked until luncheon was served and again afterwards until Will was satisfied that he had everything in enough detail.

When they had finished, he glanced out of the window. 'I could do with some fresh air. Do you fancy a short walk, Rose? I don't think we would be doing anything too rash if we stick to the grounds?'

'I would love to go for a walk,' Rose said with feeling. 'The sun is shining and I long to go outside. It's been such a long, hard winter.'

'We'll wrap up and brave the weather.' Will rose

to his feet. 'We'll pretend it's springtime and the worst weather is over.'

Rose stood up and stretched. 'That sounds lovely.'

It was cold outside but the sun shone from a clear sky and although it was only the end of February there was definitely a feeling that spring could not be far away. Rose and Will walked side by side through the olive groves. They chatted as if they had known each other for years instead of days, and Rose found herself liking him more by the minute. He was quiet and reserved when compared with Rivers' outgoing, almost larger-than-life presence, but his sense of humour appealed to Rose and it was good to laugh, forgetting all the difficulties that they were bound to face before the court case was settled.

They were on their way back to the house when, at the sound of an approaching vehicle, Will drew Rose to the side of the carriage sweep. Rose had expected the chaise to continue to the house but, on seeing them, the driver reined in and drew the horses to a halt.

'Mademoiselle Rose.' He took a note from his pocket and leaned down, holding it out to her.

Rose opened it and frowned as she read the contents. 'Blanche asks me to return to the château with the driver.'

Will gave the man a searching glance. 'Are you sure he is employed by Madame de Fontenay?'

Rose nodded. 'Yes, I remember him. He's one of

her coachmen. I think he was the one who drove us here when I returned from the château.'

'Are you thinking of going with this fellow?'

'Blanche wouldn't send for me unless it was something urgent.'

'I think you ought to check with Benedict before you accept the invitation.'

'She must have something important to tell me.'

'Even so, I think you ought to talk it over with Benedict. It could be a ruse to get you away from here.'

'This is Blanche's headed writing paper. I'm sure it's a genuine request.' Rose could see that the coachman was growing impatient. 'I must go, Will.'

'Then I should accompany you.'

'No, you need to find Rivers and tell him what's happened. If I get to the château and it doesn't seem right I will come back straight away. I know I can trust Blanche's servants. They all seem to be devoted to her.'

'I don't like it, Rose.' Will handed her into the chaise. 'Don't stay there a minute longer than necessary. If you are away longer than an hour I will come and fetch you myself.'

Rose laughed. 'Like a knight in shining armour. I like that, Will.' Her last words were lost as the coachman flicked his whip over the horses' heads and the chaise drove off at a smart pace. She was a little concerned by the terse note, but she would not have admitted that to Will. He would have stopped her going. But Blanche needed her, and that was all that mattered. Rose wished that she had enough command of French to question the driver, but she had to content herself with sitting patiently until they arrived at their destination. However, her suspicions were confirmed when the door was opened by someone who was definitely not Blanche's butler. He looked more like a person who would be at home in the prize-fighting ring. She was tempted to demand that the coachman took her back to Le Fleuve, but she was even more anxious about Blanche now, and she walked boldly into the entrance hall.

'Madame de Fontenay.' Rose controlled her nerves with difficulty as the unsmiling man closed the door and strode off across the marble tiles without uttering a word. She followed him with a sinking heart. There was no sign of any of the servants who would normally have been in attendance, and her fears were confirmed when she entered the drawing room and came face to face with Guy Colbert. Behind him, seated on the sofa, was Blanche. She looked pale and drawn, and her lips trembled when she saw Rose. She attempted to stand but Colbert laid his hand on her shoulder, pressing her back onto her seat.

'You can see that Madame de Fontenay is delighted that you accepted her invitation, Rose,' Colbert said, baring his teeth in a grin. 'Dalby and I missed you when you left us in the middle of the night. That wasn't a nice way to treat us, was it, Rose?'

'I am so sorry,' Blanche said tearfully. 'I didn't want to bring you into this, Rose.'

'I know that.' Rose made a move towards the sofa but Colbert barred her way. 'Don't look so worried. This is a happy occasion. You are to be Blanche's bridesmaid when we marry this evening. It is all arranged, and not before time.'

'Why are you doing this?' Rose demanded. 'You know she doesn't want you.'

'I have no choice, Rose.' Blanche looked away. 'I must do as he wishes.'

'I don't understand,' Rose said slowly. 'Why would you try to force Blanche into a sham marriage?'

'She was willing enough to have me all those years ago, but I was in no position to marry even had I wanted to. However, I am now making up for lost time.'

'He wants my fortune,' Blanche said on a sob. 'That's the only reason he intends to marry me, but I would rather die.'

'You loved me once, my dear.' Colbert leaned over to kiss Blanche on the forehead. 'You shrink away from me now, but this evening, when the priest arrives, I will take you to be my wife.'

'This is terrible,' Rose said angrily. 'You can't do this to her, Colbert. No man of the cloth would perform such a ceremony.'

'You would be surprised how easy things are when there are large sums involved.' Colbert moved a step closer to Rose. 'And you are worth a considerable amount in ransom money, which is what we intended in the first place. A note has been sent to Le Fleuve to that effect.'

Rose shuddered as she glanced round the room. 'Where is Montague Dalby? He obviously has a hand in this.'

'He is on his way to fetch Father Daugherty,' Colbert said, grinning. 'An Irishman who has fallen foul of his parishioners in his own country, but is as yet still legally able to perform nuptials.'

'Why would Dalby want to help you, Colbert?' Rose demanded suspiciously. 'I thought he was only interested in taking Jago from his loving family.'

'Jago is part of the bargain,' Colbert said, grinning.

Rose shook her head in disbelief. 'Jago has done nothing to deserve such treatment.'

'No, he hasn't.' Blanche clasped her hands tightly, closing her eyes. 'The disgrace is mine, and not his.'

Rose stared at her, frowning. 'I don't understand any of this, Blanche.'

'Of course you don't.' Colbert laughed, but there was no humour in the sound. 'You have led a privileged, sheltered existence. You have no idea what it is like to be born poor.'

'We are not a wealthy family,' Rose said crossly. 'A vicar does not receive a large stipend.'

'But you have never gone hungry, Rose. You were never barefoot as a child, or dressed in rags. Some of us have clawed our way up the social scale.'

'You told me that you loved me.' Blanche opened

her eyes wide, glaring at him. 'I was fourteen, little more than a child myself.'

'Old enough to give birth to my son,' Colbert said through gritted teeth. 'You sold the boy to the highest bidder, Blanche. I was threatened with prison and sent away without a penny to my name.'

Rose stared at him aghast. 'Are you inferring that Jago is your son?'

'That is exactly what I am saying. Blanche Bonnard took a dowry from the Rivers family in exchange for my son.'

Rose turned to Blanche, who was openly weeping. 'Is this true? Did you give Jago to Mrs Dalby?'

'She was Mrs Hanbury at the time, and she was childless,' Blanche took a deep breath, wiping tears from her pale cheeks. 'Her husband was desperate for a son and heir, and she was terrified that he would abandon her.'

'It seems odd that her husband was prepared to accept someone else's child as his own,' Rose said slowly.

'Mrs Hanbury was staying at Le Fleuve when Papa discovered my secret.' Blanche mopped her eyes on a lace-trimmed handkerchief. 'Mrs Hanbury was very kind to me. It was she and Berthe Laurent who persuaded me to give up my baby as soon as he was born.'

'But surely Mr Hanbury would have discovered the truth?'

'He owned a tea plantation in Ceylon, close to

the Rivers' property. He was away for months at a time. I don't think Mrs Hanbury had any difficulty in convincing him that she had borne him a son. He was overjoyed and he held a huge party for all the neighbours and the workers, too. I was forced to attend and watch them cooing over my baby boy.'

'I am so sorry, Blanche,' Rose said earnestly. 'It must have been awful for you.'

'I was heart-broken but I was just fifteen when Jago was born. I was lucky not to have been cast out by my family. Marrying de Fontenay seemed like a way to escape from everything.'

Colbert held his hands to his heart. 'What a sad story, Blanche.' His simpering smile changed to a sneer. 'But you did well out of it and now you will pay for giving up my son. You will marry me and we will live here as a family.'

'Jago had a good life until Mr Dalby died and left Montague as his heir.' Blanche regained her self-control with an obvious effort. 'I won't allow you to bring him down to your level, Guy.'

'Would you rather I left matters in Montague's hands?' Colbert moved closer to Blanche, causing her to shrink away. 'If Monty had his way he would arrange for the boy to have a tragic accident. He would then have control of Mrs Dalby and the fortune she inherited from her first husband.'

'Benedict would never allow that to happen,' Rose cried angrily.

Colbert turned to her with a savage grin. 'Benedict

Rivers will be in prison, my dear. He won't be able to do anything for anyone, least of all you.'

'I can't believe I'm hearing this. You are both evil.' Rose made for the door but Colbert was too quick for her. He threw her down onto the sofa next to Blanche.

'I know that Rivers has a soft spot for you, Rose Northwood. He will pay handsomely for your release and you will be sent home to face your father and the town gossips. I imagine your reputation will be in shreds and no decent man will look at you with marriage in mind. You will suffer accordingly.'

Blanche placed her arm around Rose's shoulders. 'You are a despicable creature, Guy Colbert. I would rather kill myself than marry you, and if your hateful partner brings Jago here I will deny everything. He has only known me as Madame de Fontenay, and it will be your word against mine.'

'You always were a little idiot,' Colbert said coldly. 'But as my wife you will learn how to behave. You might have run rings around de Fontenay, the old fool, but you will have to obey me in everything or suffer the consequences. Your father is no longer around to protect you.' He strode out of the room, slamming the door behind him.

'What will we do, Blanche?' Rose twisted round to face her. 'Surely he hasn't really found a priest who will officiate at the ceremony?'

'Guy is capable of anything, Rose. You know what sort of man he is.'

'Yes,' Rose said thoughtfully. 'But there must be something we can do. Rivers won't allow Colbert to keep us here, and Jago is safe while he's at Le Fleuve. Does Rivers know the truth about Jago's birth?'

'I doubt if Mrs Hanbury or Berthe Laurent would have let him into the secret. He was away at boarding school when Jago was born, and there would be no reason for him to suspect his aunt. It's not the sort of thing that families discuss openly, and I was married to de Fontenay when I met Benedict again.'

'I'm sure he would be horrified if he knew the truth.' Rose patted Blanche's hand. 'There must be a way out of this. Where are your servants, Blanche? Surely they won't stand by while you are treated like a prisoner in your own home?'

'I don't know exactly, but I think Guy locked them in the servants' quarters with one of his men on guard. He seems to have brought a small army with him.'

'Dalby won't receive a warm welcome at Le Fleuve. No matter what he says, I am certain that Rivers will give him short shrift.'

'They spoke openly in front of me, Rose. That man Dalby is going to use your capture to force Benedict to give up Jago by threatening to harm you. I know Jago, he's my own flesh and blood, and he adores you. He will do anything to prevent anyone hurting you.'

'I've risked everything I hold dear to protect Jago, and Rivers knows that. He will come for me,

Blanche. I know he will. But if he doesn't come soon I'll find a way to escape, even if I have to walk all night to get to Le Fleuve.'

'Well, I hope your sense of direction is better than it was last time you tried to make it there in the dark,' Blanche said with a wry smile.

'That's right, Blanche. Keep your spirits up. We have Rivers and Will on our side. They won't let anything happen to us. I'm certain of that.' Rose spoke with more conviction than she was feeling. She got to her feet and walked over to one of the tall windows that overlooked the carriage sweep, but her heart sank when she saw a man on guard at the foot of the stone steps and another patrolling the grounds with a fierce-looking dog on a lead. If she were to try to escape it would have to be under the cover of darkness, and even then there was no guarantee that she could evade the guards. The light was fading fast but, try as she might, she could not think of a plan that had any chance of success.

Rose glanced over her shoulder and it was obvious from her dejected appearance that Blanche was losing hope. Everything she had suffered in the past by giving up her child had been to no avail, and now Colbert wanted the son he had refused to acknowledge when she had told him of her plight. Rose pressed her forehead on the cold glass windowpane. She could only hope that Rivers had received the ransom note and that he would arrive before Dalby brought the priest to the château.

The sound of the door opening made Rose turn with a start. Her hand flew to cover her mouth when she saw the familiar lace gown and veil draped over Guy Colbert's arm. He threw them at Blanche.

'Put these on. Father Daugherty will be here very soon and will require sustenance. We need to get the ceremony over while he is still sober enough to officiate.'

Blanche fingered the lace. 'This was to be my wedding gown.'

'Madame Laurent said that she had burned it,' Rose said dazedly. 'I found it laid over a dressmaker's dummy in one of the bedrooms at Le Fleuve.'

'What does it matter?' Colbert took a step towards Blanche. 'I'll give you five minutes to put it on. If you haven't done so, I will have to dress you myself.' He shot Rose a malevolent look as he left the room.

Blanche turned to Rose with a dazed look. 'What shall I do?'

'He was deadly serious. I think you ought to humour him.' Rose moved swiftly to stand in front of Blanche. She took the wedding gown and held it up. 'It is lovely. I don't wonder that Madame Laurent could not bear to destroy it.'

'It might not fit,' Blanche protested. 'I was a child when that was made for me.'

'Try it on, anyway. Maybe we can convince the priest to leave without going through the motions. At least we can play for time. If you can make a scene, I might be able to slip away.'

'But what good would that do?'

'Your faithful servants have been locked up. If I can get to them through one of the passages that only they use, I'm sure they will want to help you. It's our only chance unless Rivers gets here first. What do you say, Blanche?'

Chapter Seventeen

Reluctantly, Blanche took off her outer garments and allowed Rose to help her into the delicate lace bridal gown. Despite her former concerns, the dress fitted her as perfectly now as it must have done when it was made for her, but she looked anything other than a happy bride. Blanche refused to put on the veil and Rose had to prevent her from seizing a pair of scissors from her sewing box and cutting the delicate fabric into small pieces. Blanche sank back onto the sofa, covering her face with her hands as she wept. Rose tried her best to comfort her but there was little she could say, and nothing left to do but sit and wait for Colbert to reappear with Father Daugherty and Dalby.

An hour passed and then another. It was now completely dark outside. Rose took a seat by the window, waiting anxiously. She hoped it would be

Rivers and Will who rode up to the house first, but when she was giving up hope of rescue she saw the gleam of approaching carriage lamps and a carriage drew up outside. She jumped to her feet, hoping against hope that it was Rivers, but her heart sank when she saw Dalby alight first, followed by a man in clerical dress. She turned to Blanche.

'Dalby is here with the priest.'

Blanche stood up, only to sink back onto the sofa with a groan. 'I don't know if I am brave enough to stand up to them, Rose. I'm afraid I will give in, if only to make Colbert leave me alone.'

Rose hurried to her side. 'You've been strong in the past. Just remember that. Make a fuss, cry or have hysterics and leave the rest to me. Create a diversion and I'll get to your servants even if I have to break a window and climb in so that I can reach them. I'll return with a small army.'

'I don't doubt it,' Blanche said with a reluctant smile. 'I will try to find the courage to face Guy alone, but he has a way of making me do as he wishes. Please come back quickly.'

'I will, I promise.' Rose moved away, standing as close to the doorway as she could without being too obvious.

They did not have long to wait before the sound of approaching footsteps was followed by Colbert bursting into the room, the priest not far behind him. Rose nodded to Blanche, who jumped to her feet and picked up a china ornament, which she hurled at Colbert, narrowly missing his head. The priest crossed himself, closing his eyes and muttering something in Latin, which Rose did not understand.

Screaming abuse at Colbert, Blanche threw a book at him.

'What's this?' Colbert demanded. 'Why are you behaving like this? We are about to become man and wife, and not before time, my darling.'

Rose did not wait for the outcome, although she could see that the priest was not entirely comfortable with the situation, which was a good sign. She slipped out of the room and only just managed to evade Dalby, who was walking purposefully towards the drawing room. During her stay at the château Rose had occasionally used the passageways that led eventually to the kitchens and the servants' quarters. She doubted if whoever was on guard would be aware of these narrow corridors, which were designed to make it easy for the maids to carry out their duties swiftly and unobtrusively.

The door leading into the kitchen area was situated at the far end of a broom cupboard and had been left ajar by one of the scullery maids, enabling Rose to look into the large room without attracting the attention of the man on guard. However, it seemed that he was occupied gnawing on a meaty bone that the cook had given him. He tore chunks of roasted lamb off with his yellowed teeth, and chewed hungrily as if he had not eaten for many hours. Rose could not see anyone else who might be a threat and she managed to sidle into the room, unseen by all but one of the kitchen maids. She was glad now that she had made friends with many of the staff at the château, and she put her finger to her lips, warning the girl not to acknowledge her as she made her way to the servants' hall.

There, as she had suspected, the rest of the indoor staff were huddled together at the large dining table, sitting in silence as a tough-looking man leaned against the wall. His bony fingers played on the cudgel tucked into his belt, and Rose was quick to notice a sheathed knife there also. She was trying to think of a suitable distraction when a maid hurried into the hall and beckoned to the man, telling him that there was hot food in the kitchen. He turned to the servants, who were eyeing him nervously, and fingered the hilt of his knife in a manner that suggested he might use it on anyone who dared to move.

'Stay there and keep quiet.' Apparently satisfied that the mere threat of violence was enough to subdue them, he followed the maid into the kitchen.

Rose emerged from the shadows, once again raising her finger to her lips for hush. In a low voice, and in her halting French, she told them of her plan to rescue their mistress. She exhorted them to pick up anything that might serve as a weapon, and urged them to follow her. They were hardly her idea of a threatening mob, but she hoped that sheer numbers and the element of surprise would be enough to halt the nuptials and convince the priest that Blanche was being coerced.

The butler, sporting a black eye patch he had adopted when he lost an eye in an accident many years previously, snatched up a broom and brandished it like a sword. His waxed moustache quivered with emotion as he swore to protect his mistress, giving him the appearance of a pirate about to go on the rampage. The elder of the two footmen seemed to forget the aching joints about which he had complained to Rose on many an occasion, and he leaped to his feet. He moved swiftly to the window and climbed onto a chair to release a curtain pole from its hangings. His younger colleague followed his example, grasping an even longer metal rod with both hands. The three housemaids armed themselves with knives and forks, leaving Cook to pick up a china pitcher. Judging by the fierce look on the woman's florid and crumpled features, Rose had no doubts that she would smash the jug over the head of anyone who tried to molest her or her mistress.

'We will save Madame,' Rose said in a hoarse whisper. 'Follow me.'

She led her small, oddly assorted band of warriors back the way she had come, squeezing through the narrow corridors until they came to the hallway outside the drawing room. With a three-legged wooden stool in her hands, which she had collected on the way out of the servants' hall, Rose kicked the door so that it flew open. She rushed into the room with the angry servants close behind her.

'Stop this at once.' Rose raised her voice to a

shout. 'Leave Madame de Fontenay alone, Colbert. She doesn't want you.'

Colbert, Dalby and the priest all turned to stare open-mouthed, giving Blanche a chance to break free from Colbert's grasp. She moved swiftly to stand beside Rose.

'Get out of my house, Colbert. And you too, Dalby.'

Colbert's furious expression dissolved into a wide grin. 'You are no Jeanne d'Arc, Rose, and your rag-tag army is pathetic. How do you expect old men, a boy and some female servants to stand up to the ruffians I have at my disposal?'

'We will put up a good fight,' Rose said boldly and the butler levelled his broom at Colbert. The other servants closed ranks behind him.

'And they are not alone.'

There was a sudden silence and Rose's small band of would-be saviours made way for Rivers and Will as they strode into the room.

Rose gasped with relief. 'I knew you would come, Rivers. But we were winning.'

'You can't stop me, Rivers,' Colbert said through gritted teeth. 'I am going to marry this woman.'

'She doesn't want you, Colbert.' Rose slipped her arm around Blanche's shoulders. 'She told you that, but you didn't take any notice.'

'She will agree or I'll make her secret public. You won't like that, Rivers. Your family will have to deal with a scandal that will shock the whole community.'

Rivers shook his head. 'Lucy told me everything.' He turned to Blanche, lowering his voice. 'Don't worry, I understand. I just wish I had known sooner and I might have been able to save Jago from the ordeal that he has been put through.'

Dalby took a step towards Rivers. 'What are you saying?'

'You should ask your stepmother. It was a secret shared by herself, Blanche and Madame Laurent for fourteen years.'

'I have no idea what you are talking about.' Dalby spun round to face Colbert. 'Where are the men we hired? I paid good money for them, so where are they?'

Despite Dalby's angry questions, Rose could see that Colbert was not listening. He was attempting to persuade the priest to continue with the ceremony, even though it was abundantly clear that Blanche had refused to participate.

Will stepped forward. 'Your men are explaining themselves to the local gendarme, Mr Dalby. I think they might have some questions for you and Monsieur Colbert, also.'

'You are a fool, Colbert,' Dalby punched him on the shoulder as if to emphasise his words. 'I gave you a simple task and you've failed in that as you've failed in everything else.'

Colbert faced up to him. 'You are an upstart and too much of a coward to carry out your own evil deeds. I am done with you, Monsieur.' He gave Dalby a vicious shove that sent him staggering towards the door. 'You'll go back to that cold and foggy little country you came from if you have any sense.'

Rivers took Colbert by the collar. 'You have questions to answer, Colbert. You'll find several officers of the law waiting for you, and Dalby, too.' He marched Colbert out of the room in the wake of Dalby, who had managed to crawl into the entrance hall.

Rose could hear the commotion that ensued and she smiled. Perhaps Colbert at least would get the punishment he deserved, although Dalby, being a foreigner, might live to cheat someone else another day. She patted the butler on the shoulder. 'You did well, Monsieur. I think it is quite safe for you and your staff to return to your duties.'

'Yes, of course,' Blanche added hastily. 'I can't thank you enough, Gaston. You were all splendid. I am touched that you were prepared to risk your lives to save mine.'

Gaston passed the broom to the younger footman. 'Of course, Madame.' He bowed from the waist and, waving his arms expressively, he mustered his staff and ushered them from the room.

Blanche was about to speak to the priest, but he had packed away everything he had brought with him and was already heading for the door. He brushed aside her offer to recompense him for his loss of earnings.

'I wouldn't bother about him, Blanche,' Rivers

said, laughing. 'I doubt if that particular person has ever been ordained. I'm sure he demanded his fee before he came here today. I don't imagine you will see that particular gentleman ever again.'

Blanche sank down on the sofa. 'I doubt if I will ever trust anyone enough to marry again, but thank you both for bringing this terrible episode to an end.'

'It may be over for you, Blanche,' Rose said thoughtfully, 'but it is still very much a problem for Rivers.' She gave him a steady look. 'That's so, isn't it? I doubt if Dalby will drop the case against you.'

'He will try to extort money from me, or anyone who gets in his way.' Rivers glanced out of the window. 'The gendarmes are taking him and Colbert away. He will have to convince them that he has not committed any offence in France.'

Will pulled up a chair and sat down. 'He will need a good lawyer. Luckily I am occupied elsewhere, and I think he has just lost his case against you, Benedict, although it will still go to court.'

'That, I suppose, will depend upon whether Jago's true parentage becomes known.' Rivers gave Blanche a sympathetic smile. 'I know how much all this must have hurt you, Blanche. I wish you had told me the truth a long time ago. I might even have been able to prevent all this.'

'I will be ruined if it becomes public knowledge,' Blanche said sadly. 'Although it would be worth it to be able to acknowledge the child I was forced to give up so soon after his birth.' She blinked back tears. 'But the decision must come from Jago and the woman who has been his mama for all these years.'

Rose sat down beside her. 'I am so sorry, Blanche. I wish there was something I could do to help.'

Blanche grasped Rose's hand. 'You've done more than enough. I might have been forced to go through that ceremony, but for you.'

Rivers smiled. 'Yes, I apologise for our late arrival. It's true that Rose is the heroine of the day. She came here like a warrior queen to save you. I'm afraid that Will and I were mere onlookers in the end.'

'We did our best,' Will said modestly. 'But you were amazing, Rose. I am filled with admiration for you and your cohorts, especially the gentleman with the patch over one eye and the moustache that seemed to have a life of its own. I thought he might run Colbert through with that vicious broom handle.'

Rose smiled reluctantly. 'I suppose it does seem funny now, but the servants were willing to risk life and limb in order to protect Blanche.'

'They had an inspiring leader.' Will patted Rose on the arm. 'I think it was a wonderful thing to do. We might not have been able to stop the ceremony but for you, although I doubt very much if the marriage would have been legal.'

'It's over now.' Blanche held her hand out to Rivers. 'Thank you, Benedict. You were always a good friend.'

He shook his head. 'If I had paid more attention

to what was happening here, I might have been able to help you sooner.'

'It's all out in the open now, and that's possibly a good thing. I need to talk to Lucy before I speak to Jago. I'm afraid he will hate me for giving him up.'

'I'm sure that won't be the case,' Rose said hastily. 'Jago is a kind-hearted and intelligent boy. I think he will do his best to understand, and it's obvious that he is very fond of you.'

Blanche sighed. 'Lucy has been his mother for all these years. I cannot hope to take her place, nor would I want to. I would just like to be part of Jago's life from now on, if that were at all possible.'

'He might find the truth hard to take at first,' Rivers said, frowning. 'But he'll get used to the idea, given time.'

Rose could feel Blanche's pain and her indecision. 'Might I suggest something?'

'Of course.' Blanche turned to her with a glimmer of hope in her dark eyes. 'What is it, Rose?'

'You will be returning to England very soon, isn't that so, Rivers?' Rose met his gaze with a straight look.

He nodded. 'Yes, I have to be in London for the court case.'

'And Dalby will be there, too?'

'Yes, naturally.'

'Even so, he can't be trusted. I think that Jago might be in danger if he were to remain at Le Fleuve without the benefit of your protection, especially if

Dalby still sees him as some kind of threat. After all, Dalby has his sights set upon Jago's inheritance from Mr Hanbury. He doesn't know the truth about Jago's birth, and he might try to use him as a bargaining chip. We know that Lucy is very much afraid of him.'

'Having met the fellow, I wouldn't be at all surprised,' Will said thoughtfully. 'What are you suggesting, Rose?'

'I think they should keep together, perhaps at your estate on the outskirts of Abbotsford, Rivers. Blanche should come too so that she can spend time with Jago and get to know him properly.'

'Dalby will also be in England,' Rivers said slowly. 'Have you taken that into consideration, Rose?'

'Yes, but he will be in London during the court case, and he might even go to prison. In any event, you will be there to make sure he doesn't abscond. I don't know how much money is involved, but he was prepared to go a long way in order to get his hands on it.'

'I believe that Hanbury died a very wealthy man. However, the fortune belongs to my Aunt Lucy. Dalby has no claim on it.'

'It is hard for a woman on her own, Benedict,' Blanche said softly. 'I know from experience. I don't think Lucy would be strong enough to stand up to her stepson. After all, she is virtually homeless now that Dalby has inherited the house she shared with her late husband.'

305

'Therefore it makes sense for her to come and live with you, at least for a while, Rivers. As I recall, it was your suggestion in the first place.' Rose faced him eagerly. 'When Dalby is committed to prison, she will be able to buy a property suitable for herself and Jago.'

'You're right, Rose. It was my idea originally.' Rivers looked from one to the other. 'Anyway, do I have a choice in the matter? You and Blanche seem to have thought this out together.'

'I think you should accept their suggestion, Benedict,' Will said slowly. 'It does make sense.'

'I agree.' Rivers met Rose's amused glance with a smile. 'I will leave it to Rose to persuade Lucy that this is the best course to take at the moment. Is that what you want, Rose?'

She nodded. 'You would have come to the same conclusion yourself.'

'Now you are trying to flatter me.'

'I wouldn't stoop to such a low trick.' Rose assumed an air of innocence, having had plenty of practice in the past when caught out in some misdemeanour at home. Marianne and Emily always swore she got away with things for which they would have been punished, but Rose argued that it was self-preservation, and they would do well to copy her. She smiled to herself.

'You've made your point well,' Rivers said with a wry smile. 'Perhaps you ought to represent me in the dock, Rose. Maybe Will could learn something from you.'

Will laughed. 'I already have, Benedict. I admire Rose wholeheartedly, and I hope I might be a welcome visitor to the vicarage in Abbotsford when this is all over.'

Rivers frowned. 'I pay you for your legal expertise, William Jameson. Remember that, if you please.'

'I think we should set off for Le Fleuve as soon as possible,' Rose said hastily. 'Will you be all right here with just the servants to look after you, Blanche?'

'Yes, of course. I'm exhausted, in any event. You are all welcome to stay for the night if you so wish.'

'I think we should leave now.' Rivers kissed Blanche on the cheek. 'You were very brave tonight. I hope you will seriously consider Rose's suggestion. You would be safe with us at Longfleet Hall, and it might be good for you and for your son.'

Blanche paled visibly. 'You are not going to tell Jago the truth, are you, Benedict?'

'He will need to know eventually, but it is not my decision to make.' Rivers gave her a sympathetic smile. 'I think you need to talk things over with Lucy. You both love him and I know you'll do what is right.'

'You could come with us now,' Rose said gently. 'You don't have to stay here on your own.'

'I have my small army to look after me.' Blanche sighed. 'Would I ever be able to return home?'

'Of course you would,' Benedict said impatiently. 'I don't think there's any doubt that Colbert will end up serving a long sentence, and if justice prevails we will see Dalby punished for what he has done. You will be back here before you know it.'

'I'm so tired.' Blanche held her hand to her forehead, closing her eyes briefly. 'I need to sleep and I'll let you know my decision in the morning.'

It was late evening by the time they arrived back at Le Fleuve. Rose was surprised to find Madame Laurent waiting up for them, and she appeared to be in a state of distress.

Benedict took her aside. 'If you are worried about Colbert, I think you and your family should be prepared for the worst, Madame.'

'What do you mean by that?' Madame Laurent eyed him warily.

'Your nephew has been arrested and no doubt all his crimes will come to light when he appears in court. I am genuinely sorry to be the bearer of bad news, but I am certain he will get a custodial sentence.'

'What has he done now?' Madame asked faintly. She turned to give Rose a desperate look. 'Tell me, Mademoiselle.'

'He lured me to the château where I discovered that he was holding Madame de Fontenay a prisoner in her own home,' Rose said bluntly. 'He had hired a priest to perform an illegal marriage ceremony.'

Madame Laurent rolled her eyes. 'The stupid boy. I warned him against such an action.'

'But you gave him the wedding dress and veil,

which you said you had burned.' Rose glared at her. 'You lied to us, Madame.'

'Yes, I admit it, but I did not know he was going to force himself on Madame de Fontenay. I thought he might use his charm to persuade her to wed him. Guy was always impetuous. He is not a bad man.'

'You will find that opinions differ, Madame.' Benedict walked away.

'You are fond of him,' Rose said gently. 'I understand, but he will have to face up to his crimes in court and there is nothing you can do about that.'

Madame Laurent wrung her hands. 'Monsieur Benedict could speak up for him. Guy worked well for him for many years.'

'I expect that will be taken into consideration,' Rose said, with more hope than conviction.

'You could persuade Monsieur Benedict.' Madame Laurent's eyes narrowed and her lips pursed. 'He listens to you, Mademoiselle. It is obvious that he cares what you think. It would be such a shame if Jago were to discover the truth about his birth.'

Rose stared at her aghast. Was Madame trying to blackmail her? Or was she simply casting around for any verbal weapon she could think of in order to protect her nephew?

'What are you saying, Madame?' Rose tried to keep the note of panic from her voice.

'I know the truth. I know who really gave birth to the boy. Guy is his real father, and his mother is—' Madame broke off, staring over Rose's shoulder.

'What is she saying?' Lucy's querulous voice made Rose spin round.

Lucy's face was as white as her long nightgown. She was halfway down the wide oak staircase, her hand trailing on the banister rail, and her bare feet making no sound on the bare wooden treads.

'Were you talking about me and my child, Madame Laurent? What lies have you been spreading?'

'No lies, Madame. Just the plain unvarnished truth. Unless Monsieur Benedict speaks up for my nephew, your secret will be revealed to the world.'

Lucy swayed, clutching the rail with both hands. 'You evil witch. I never trusted you.'

Rose hurried to the foot of the stairs, holding her hand out to Lucy. 'Come down before you fall down. Let me help you.'

'No. This is between me and that woman.' Lucy descended the last few steps in a flurry of white cotton and lace. 'Say it to my face.'

'Please stop.' Rose placed herself between them. 'For the boy's sake, please keep your voices down.'

'I'll tell everyone.' Madame Laurent was on the edge of hysteria. 'I've looked after that boy as if he was my own flesh and blood, but he needs to know the truth, and I'm going to wake him up and tell him everything.'

Chapter Eighteen

Lucy thrust Rose aside with surprising strength. She clawed her fingers and flew at Madame Laurent.

'You are evil. You shan't destroy my child.'

Rose attempted to separate them but she was thrown to the ground. Rivers emerged from his study, followed by Will, and they dragged the two screaming women apart.

'Keep her away from my son,' Lucy cried hysterically. 'She is as bad as Colbert. They bring nothing but misery to the world.'

Madame Laurent struggled, shouting what were obviously insults in French. She would have gone for Lucy again, but Will managed to hold her back.

'Let me go. She is the cause of all this trouble.' Madame Laurent kicked out with her foot but Will had her in a firm grip.

'Stop that, or I will have to lock you up for the night.'

Will did his best to restrain her, but she managed to slip free from his grasp.

Rivers thrust Lucy into Rose's arms. 'Stay back, Madame Laurent. Don't make this any worse for yourself, or you will end up in prison with Colbert.'

She came to a sudden halt, her lips curled back in a snarl. 'You will pay for this, I swear it.'

'It's too late now,' Rivers said grimly. 'First thing in the morning you will pack your bags and leave my house. Be thankful that I don't turn you over to the authorities. Now go to your room and stay there or I will have to lock you in.'

'I'm leaving Le Fleuve now.' Madame Laurent drew herself up to her full height. 'I wouldn't stay in this old ruin any longer if you begged me on bended knees.' She marched off, slamming the door to her room so that the windows rattled.

Lucy burst into tears. 'That dreadful woman. Don't let her get anywhere near Jago.'

'Rose, will you take my aunt to her room, please?' Rivers said with a weary smile. 'We will leave for England tomorrow, so I suggest we pack what we need for the journey.'

'That sounds eminently sensible.' Will turned to Rose. 'Can I help you with her?'

Rose shook her head. 'No, but thank you. I'll see her settled and then I'll check on Jago. I hope he hasn't heard all this.'

'My poor boy,' Lucy sobbed. 'We have all done wrong by him.'

'I won't allow that,' Rivers said firmly. 'You have been an excellent mother and you can't be held responsible for Dalby's actions. You and Jago are welcome to come and live with me at Longfleet, if that is what you so wish, but there's plenty of time to make a decision. We leave first thing in the morning. Try to get some sleep.'

Rose helped Lucy to her room. Having seen her safely to bed, she went to check on Jago. Fortunately, his bedchamber was at the back of the building and he was sleeping soundly. She closed the door and made her way to her own room. It was only when she sat down on the bed that the events of that day came rushing back to her in a series of shocking memories. She lay back on the bed, too exhausted to think of undressing. The fire had not been lit and the room was cold. Rose shivered as she pulled the bedcovers up to her chin and closed her eyes. She had not expected to sleep but within minutes she had drifted off and slept without dreaming until she was rudely awakened by someone shaking her and calling her name.

'Rose, get up immediately. The house is on fire.'

She snapped into a sitting position, peering into the darkness. All she could see was Rivers' silhouette against flickering light from the hall.

'On fire?' she said dazedly.

He pulled back the covers. 'Get up. Leave everything. I have to get Jago. Will is waking my aunt.'

'But the servants . . .?' Rose slipped her feet into her boots.

'Angeline went home for the night. Madame Laurent set the fire. I'll swear to that. It didn't happen by mistake. Come on, Rose. Don't linger. The fire will take hold quickly in this old building.'

Rose grabbed her cloak and reticule from the chair where she had left it just hours earlier. She could smell the acrid smoke and hear the crackle of burning timbers. She followed Rivers onto the landing. It was difficult to see as the smoke billowed up the staircase, obscuring her vision and making it hard to breathe. She stumbled, but Rivers picked her up and carried her bodily down the stairs. Will was already in the entrance hall with Lucy, who seemed to have fainted.

'I had to carry her, Benedict. I didn't have time to get to the boy.'

Rivers set Rose on her feet. 'Go outside, get away from the building before it comes crashing down. Will, go to the stables and rouse the grooms. Get the horses to safety in case the fire spreads. I'm going to get Jago.'

Rose caught him by the sleeve. 'You can't go back into that inferno.'

'Let go, Rose. I'll take the back stairs. I know what I'm doing.' Rivers disappeared into the smoke-filled building.

'Come on, Rose.' Will hoisted Lucy over his shoulder. 'Do what he says. I'll need you to take care of Mrs Dalby while I go to the stables.' He shooed her out into the darkness away from the burning building.

Coughing and gasping for breath, Rose had little choice other than to do as he said. Will set Lucy down on the ground beneath the old oak tree and Rose sat beside her, cushioning Lucy's head in her lap, as she watched the fire take an even greater hold. Flames licked out of the broken windows, blackening the pink walls as the fire engulfed the building. Roof tiles splintered and tumbled to the ground while the blaze roared like an angry animal as it consumed centuries of history.

Time seemed to have stood still as Rose waited for Rivers to appear with Jago. Tears ran unstopped down her cheeks. She wondered vaguely if this was simply a dreadful nightmare. Perhaps she would awaken suddenly when Angeline brought a cup of hot chocolate to her bedside. Then, just as she was giving up hope, she saw a figure emerge from the side of the house. Rivers had Jago in his arms and he was crossing the forecourt. He was coming towards her and he was real. She laid Lucy on the ground and jumped to her feet.

'Rivers! Thank God.' She ran towards him. 'Is Jago all right?'

'He tried to get downstairs on his own but he must have fallen. I think he just knocked himself out. He'll come round in a minute. Where's Will?'

Almost before the words left his lips there was the sound of horses' hoofs and Will appeared, driving one of the several carriages from the coach house. Behind him came the grooms, still in their nightshirts as they led the rest of the horses to safety.

Rivers set Jago down on the ground beside his mother.

'Are you all right, Rose?' he asked anxiously. 'You're crying.'

'You look like a chimney sweep, Rivers.' Rose smiled through her tears.

Rivers brushed her cheeks with his fingertips. 'You should take a look in a mirror yourself, Rose.' He drew her closer and bent his head so that their lips met in a kiss sweetened by desperation and their close escape.

His lips tasted of smoke, and charred pieces of his greatcoat crumbled beneath her fingers, but Rose was oblivious to anything other than the breathless hush that wrapped her in a world of her own. Then Rivers released her and stepped away, and she was engulfed by a wave of noise. The shouts from the grooms and the terrified whinnying of the horses added to the roar of the raging inferno and the ear-splitting sound of masonry crashing to the ground.

Rose felt as if her limbs were suddenly turned to stone and she could not move, but suddenly she was lifted off her feet and flung into the carriage. She found herself seated beside Lucy, who was moaning softly, Jago trying to comfort her. The door slammed and Rose's first thought was for Rivers.

'Stop,' she cried, banging her fists on the wall behind the driver's seat. 'Please stop. You've left Monsieur behind.'

Jago laid his hand on her arm. 'He's bringing the horses, Rose. And Will is driving the dog cart. We're all safe, but I don't understand what happened. How did the fire start?'

Lucy slipped her arm around his shoulders. 'That wicked woman wanted to kill us all, Jago. She pretended to be a good person who cared for the family, but she is evil. I never want to come back here.'

Rose huddled in the corner. 'There will be nothing to come back to after a fire like that. I think perhaps that is what Madame Laurent wanted.'

'What happened this evening, Rose?' Lucy leaned forward. 'I can hardly see your face, but I know something terrible must have occurred.'

'Not now, Lucy.' Rose sat back against the padded squabs and closed her eyes. 'I'll tell you everything when we're in a safe place. I don't want to think about it now.'

'But that's not fair,' Lucy said childishly. 'We were almost burned to death and you don't want to tell us why.'

'Leave her alone, Mama. Can't you see that she's had enough for one day? I don't know what's going on any more than you do, but this is the second time

Rose has come to my rescue. She'll tell us everything when she's ready.'

Lucy sighed, but she subsided in silence and eventually, as the journey went on into the night, Rose knew by their rhythmic breathing that both Lucy and Jago had fallen asleep. There was no such respite for her. The events of the last few hours were replaying themselves over and over again in her memory and she could not shut them out. She had a sudden longing for Rivers' presence and the comforting nearness of him. The taste of his kiss lingered on her lips and she wanted an explanation. Had he kissed her in the heat of the moment? Or had it meant something to him, as it had to her? She was shocked by her own reaction and the feelings that such an intimate moment had aroused. She closed her eyes, listening to the rumble of the carriage wheels on the rough tracks and the drumming of the horses' hoofs. Outside the window there was only darkness and it felt as if they were hurtling into a terrifying void. Everything was uncertain now. Rivers had to face Dalby in the courtroom and even with Will to help him it might be difficult for him to disprove the claims against him. She would have to go home, but parting from Rivers, Jago and even from Will and Lucy, would feel like leaving her family all over again. Her life seemed to involve nothing but farewells.

It was still dark when they arrived at the railway station. Rivers directed the coachman and grooms to take the horses and vehicles to Château Fontenay with a hastily written note for Blanche. Then they boarded the train, still half-drugged with sleep and the shock of recent events. Rose slept fitfully, waking every now and then to look round the carriage to make sure that everyone was there. She had a horrible feeling that they might disappear one by one until she was travelling alone in a foreign country, but common sense won in the end and she relaxed, leaning against Lucy, who had Jago's head cradled in her lap. Sad as it might be for Blanche, it was obvious that there was a deep connection between adoptive mother and son. Lucy might not be his birth mother but in every other sense of the word she had raised him and loved him just as if he was her own.

Rose glanced at Rivers, but he was staring out of the window, deep in thought. Will was snoring gently in the far corner of the carriage. Rose closed her eyes and fell into a fitful sleep. At some point in the night they changed trains, but Rose, Lucy and Jago were barely awake when Rivers and Will shepherded them along the platform to another train. It was late afternoon when they arrived at Cherbourg. A cab took them to an inn where they waited for Jackson to bring the *Sadie Lee* into harbour. Rose could not help but be impressed by the way Rivers managed to organise everything with seeming ease. She felt as though he could snap his fingers and everything would fall into place.

She was seated by the window, sipping coffee, when Rivers walked over and sat down next to her.

'You'll be home with your family tomorrow, Rose.'

She shot him a sideways glance. 'I dare say you will be pleased to see the back of me.'

'You know that's not true.'

'Do I? I don't think I know anything for certain, Rivers. What are your immediate plans? Are you going to Longfleet when we land?'

'That's the next step, after I've taken you home, of course. I need to speak to your papa.'

'No, you don't. He understood why I had to return to France with you. He won't question your motives.'

Rivers smiled. 'Your papa will expect me to do the right thing by you, Rose. It's as simple as that. I will ask him for your hand in marriage, of course.'

'Marriage?' Rose almost dropped her coffee bowl. She stared at him in amazement. 'Why would you do that?'

'I know it doesn't seem a very good bargain on your part. I have a court case hanging over me, which could bring about my ruin.'

'No, that's not possible, Rivers. You've done nothing wrong, and even if you had, it wouldn't make any difference to me if I were—' Rose broke off, biting her lip.

'If what, Rose? Could it be that you have feelings for me?'

'Yes, no. I mean I don't know. Stop putting words in my mouth. I don't want you to speak to Papa. I will tell him everything. I've nothing to be ashamed of.'

'I know that, but I remember what village life is like, Rose. All those people who have known you since childhood will have been putting two and two together while you've been away. Your reputation is already lost and it's my fault for taking you on board the *Sadie Lee* in the first place.'

'I could have refused to get into the tender,' Rose said slowly. 'You didn't kidnap me, Rivers.'

'Why did you come with me that day?' Rivers leaned towards her, his blue eyes darkening to the colour of storm clouds. 'Be honest, Rose.'

She glanced over his shoulder. 'Jackson has arrived, and in answer to your question, I don't know why I went with you. Perhaps I wanted an adventure, and I certainly had that.'

Rivers stood up with a wry smile curving his generous lips. 'We'll continue this conversation later.' He held out his hand. 'Come, this might be the last time we board the *Sadie Lee* together.'

Rose laid her hand in his and felt a tremor run down her spine as his strong fingers closed over hers. She allowed him to help her to her feet and then she snatched her hand free.

'I can manage perfectly well without you, Rivers. You need to look after Lucy and Jago first.'

He laughed. 'Stubborn to the last, Rose Northwood.

But Will is taking care of the others. Do I have to carry you aboard or will you walk with me?'

'I'll be by your side from my own choice, Rivers. I don't care what the gossips say.'

Jackson looked from one to the other, his expression carefully controlled.

'The *Sadie Lee* is ready to sail, Captain.'

'Thank you, Jackson. I knew I could rely on you. Lead on. We'll follow.'

Rose hesitated, glancing over her shoulder to make sure that Lucy and Jago had heard the command. She was relieved to see Will helping Jago to his feet, Lucy fussing round him as if she feared that someone might suddenly appear and steal her child from her. Rose quickened her pace, following Jackson and Rivers out into the biting east wind. In a few short hours she would be at home with her family. It would be a bittersweet parting from the people who had become dear to her.

The sun was setting as they boarded the *Sadie Lee*, and the sea looked calm, almost as if it were a summer's evening. Rose felt the gentle movement of the deck beneath her feet and she experienced a sense of freedom even though they were still in port. It was true that her short voyages on the vessel had not been from choice, but somehow they were linked with pleasant memories, as if *Sadie Lee* was an old friend. She glanced at Jago and to her surprise he seemed to have suddenly shrugged off the look of an invalid. There was a hint of colour in his previously ashen cheeks, and his blue eyes were sparkling as he watched the seamen going about their preparations to sail back to England.

Lucy had already gone below, hinting that she felt poorly the moment she set foot on a ship and Will had accompanied her. Rivers was talking earnestly to Jackson, leaving Rose alone with Jago.

'Your first words to me were about the *Sadie Lee*,' Rose said softly. 'Even when you were so badly injured and poorly you spoke her name.'

Jago grinned. 'I loved being at sea, Rose. If the captain had not been such a bully, and the crew little better, I would have enjoyed a career as a seafarer.'

'Try not to think of the bad times,' Rose said hastily. 'Why don't you ask Jackson if there's something you can do to help during the trip home? He can only say no. He won't bite.'

Jago laughed. 'I'm not scared of him. You should have seen old Captain Blakeley. He only needed a long beard and a gold earring in one ear and he could have been Blackbeard the pirate.'

Rose could see that Rivers had finished his conversation with Jackson and he was heading for the saloon. 'Now's your chance, Jago. Go and speak to Jackson before he gets too busy.'

Jago walked away, limping only slightly. The broken ankle he had suffered in his headlong flight from brutality had healed, but gave him pain at times.

Rose was still of the opinion that exercise would help him complete his recovery. She smiled to herself as she saw him engage Jackson in conversation. It was obvious that Jago was genuinely interested in anything to do with the ship, and Jackson seemed to understand this. He patted Jago on the shoulders and leaned down, speaking to him in an encouraging tone, although Rose could not hear the words as the ship's engine purred into action, and suddenly they were moving away from the shore. She was on her way home.

It was early morning when they reached Abbotsford quay and, typically for March, the heavy clouds seemed to hang overhead, threatening rain. There were two carriages awaiting them on the quay wall. Rivers left Will to deal with Lucy and Jago, but Rose shook her head when he offered to take her to her front door.

'No, thank you, Rivers. I prefer to walk.'

'You'll be the talk of the village, Rose. Let me do this for you.'

'It's less than a mile. I want to see people and acknowledge them. I've nothing to be ashamed of.'

'That's true, but the gossipmongers will be delighted to spread the news of the errant Miss Northwood's return.'

'Let them,' Rose said firmly. 'Goodbye, Rivers. I hope all goes well with the court case. When is it?'

'The week after next, as you well know. You aren't

getting away so easily, Rose. I will call upon you tomorrow morning and I hope you will receive me.'

'Of course. Now, if you'll excuse me I don't like the look of those clouds so I will make my way home.' Rose turned away, hoping he had not noticed the tears in her eyes. Really, he was being very obtuse. Could he not see that parting from him was like an arrow in her heart? And yet all Rivers cared about was etiquette, which seemed hypocritical in a man who flouted convention in every other way. She picked up her skirts and started walking at a brisk pace without looking back. She had the feeling that he was watching her but she had made her decision. It had been a shock when he had told her of his intention to ask for her hand in marriage, and the more she thought about it, the more she hated the idea of receiving a proposal as a matter of duty. She might not be the romantic young girl that she once was, but to marry merely to protect her good name was almost an insult.

'Rose?'

She came to a halt at the sound of a familiar voice and when she turned her head she saw a familiar figure hurrying towards her. 'Tom. I didn't expect to see you so far from home.'

He hurried to her side, glancing over her shoulder. 'Is that Benedict Rivers?'

'Yes, it is. We've only just landed. It's a long story, Tom. I'll tell you when I've discussed everything with my family.'

'Good morning, Doctor.' Bob Hawkes was about to walk past but he stopped to stare at Rose. 'Miss Rose. You've been gone awhile, so I heard.'

'I'm home now, Mr Hawkes. Please pass my respects to your good wife.' Rose tucked her hand in the crook of Tom's arm. 'Will you walk me home, Tom? I thought I could do this on my own, but it's more difficult than I thought.'

'Of course. I had a visit to make at Miss Jones's cottage. Her mother is quite poorly again.'

'Poor Miss Jones. What with that spiteful cat she owns and her ailing mother, she has a very difficult task on her hands.'

'I agree, and the old lady will probably live to be a hundred, all the while wearing her daughter out with her demands.' Tom patted Rose's hand as it rested on his sleeve. 'But what about you? Marianne told me just yesterday that you were still in France.'

'I was, but there was a fire at the farmhouse and we had to leave. I didn't have a chance to send a telegram to tell them I was on my way home.'

'That would have been a first for Abbotsford, I think. We're always a bit slow to accept innovations.' He tipped his hat to Martha Huggins, who had emerged from Guppy's bakery. Her eyes widened when she saw Rose, who acknowledged her with a nod and a smile.

'Good morning, Mrs Huggins.'

'Miss Rose. You're back from foreign parts and on your own, I see.'

'Dr Buckingham is escorting me to the vicarage, Mrs Huggins. I dare say I will see you in church on Sunday.'

Tom quickened his pace. 'That will ensure a large congregation,' he said in a low voice. 'You have certainly given the gossips something to talk about.' He slowed down again as they reached the village school. 'Why didn't Rivers bring you home, Rose? If you don't mind me asking. I mean, I am engaged to your sister . . .'

Rose came to a sudden halt and released her hold on his arm. 'You proposed to Marianne and I wasn't there?'

'Well, I'm sorry about that. If I had known you were going to arrive so suddenly I might have waited for your approval.'

'Don't be silly, Tom. I didn't mean that. I'm delighted, of course, but what does your mama think of your choice?' Rose took his arm again and started walking. 'I hope she didn't make a fuss.'

'You know my mother almost as well as I do, Rose. She wanted me to marry an heiress but I think she is accustomed to the idea that I make my own choices now and, to be fair, she is very fond of Marianne. Who would not be delighted to have such a beautiful, charming and kind daughter-in-law?'

'I'm glad for your sake.' Rose giggled. 'I expect Lady Buckingham is relieved that you picked Marianne and not me.'

'Don't be so hard on yourself, Rose. Any man

327

would think himself very fortunate to earn the love of someone like you.'

They walked on arm in arm and in comfortable silence until they reached the vicarage. Tom opened the gate.

'Aren't you coming in?' Rose asked when he remained outside on the pavement. 'Surely you want to see Marianne?'

'I do, and I'll be back in time for dinner tonight, but you should have some time on your own with your family. I'll see you later.'

Rose took a deep breath and walked up the path to the front door. She was suddenly nervous as she raised the knocker and let it fall again. She waited, listening for the sound of footsteps.

Chapter Nineteen

Winnie stood in the doorway. Her mouth opened but no sound came out and she seemed to be at a loss for words, which was unusual for her.

'Good morning, Winnie. It really is me.' Rose stepped inside and stripped off her cloak, leaving Winnie still standing in the same spot, staring at her as if she had seen a ghost. Rose laid her cloak on a carved wooden chest together with her reticule. It occurred to her suddenly that these were the only worldly possessions that she had managed to save from the inferno. 'Is my papa in his study, Winnie?'

'Yes, Miss Rose,' Winnie said faintly as she closed the front door. 'We wasn't expecting you, miss.'

'That is true, but I am here now. Be kind enough to tell Cook that I have come home so there will be another place needed at table from now on. Where are my sisters, Winnie?'

'They are in the drawing room, miss. Shall I tell them you are here?'

'No, just tell Cook. I'll go and see my papa first and then I'll give my sisters a surprise. Don't spoil it, Winnie.' Rose walked slowly to her father's study, knocked and entered. 'Papa, I've come home.'

Matthew Northwood took off his spectacles and stood up, staring at Rose in disbelief. 'Rose! My dear child, why didn't you let us know you were coming home?' He walked round his desk and, unusually for him, he wrapped his arms around her in a brief hug before releasing her with an embarrassed sigh. 'Why are you here now, my dear? Has something happened? Is the boy all right?'

Rose kissed him on the cheek. 'It's good to be home, Pa. I didn't have a chance to send a telegram, even if I knew how to do so. The fact is that the farmhouse was set on fire, quite deliberately, and we all had to leave. Rivers has his court case the week after next, so he would have come home anyway.'

'You're saying it was arson? How dreadful, Rose. Are you all right, my dear?' Matthew gazed at her short-sightedly. 'You weren't harmed?'

'No, Pa. Fortunately the alarm was raised quickly and it was just a matter of getting everyone out of the house. Although it was a terrible experience.'

'We must just be thankful that you escaped unharmed, and you are home for good, I hope.'

'Yes, Papa. I will try to settle down and be a good daughter from now on.'

'I don't doubt that, Rose my dear. Your intentions are always the best, although sometimes things don't go quite as you planned. Where is Mr Rivers? I thought he would have had the decency to bring you home in person.'

'He wanted to, Pa, but I told him not to bother.'

'A gentleman would have offered marriage, Rose. I'm sad to say that your gallivanting abroad will not have done much for your good name.' Matthew threw up his hands. 'I know that sounds cruel, my dear, but such is life in a small rural community. We are not like those in London society who get away with all sorts of bad behaviour without ruining their reputations.'

Rose sighed. 'In Rivers' defence, he did intend to speak to you on the subject but I refused to consider his offer. I don't want a man to marry me out of chivalry. It would be a disaster for both of us.'

'You are so independent, Rose. I hope you don't regret your decision in the future.'

Rose leaned forward to kiss him on the cheek. 'I only care what my family thinks of me, Pa. You know that I have not done anything wrong. That's good enough for me.'

'You had better go and explain everything to your sisters, and then you must see your mama.'

'Does she know that I've been away, Pa?'

'Of course she does. I tell her everything, or almost everything, anyway. To be honest, I think you will be surprised to find that she understands more than you give her credit for.'

'I'll go to her room when I've seen the girls, and congratulated Marianne on her engagement. I met Tom in the village and he walked home with me. You must be proud of Marianne.'

'I am proud of all my girls.' Matthew went to sit behind his desk. 'But the Sunday sermon won't write itself. I must get on.'

Rose left the study and went straight to the drawing room. She had the satisfaction of seeing her sisters' surprise and delight when she entered.

Emily jumped to her feet and rushed over to give Rose a hug. 'You're home.'

'Yes, I am and very happy to see you both.' Rose disentangled herself from Emily's enthusiastic embrace, and crossed the floor to throw her arms around Marianne.

'I've missed you both,' Rose said, wiping tears from her cheeks. 'But congratulations, Marianne. I always knew that you and Tom would make a fine couple.'

Marianne blushed and lowered her eyes, gazing at the ruby ring on her left hand. 'I never took him for granted, Rose. But I've loved Tom since we were little more than children.'

'You will be very happy together and have lots of beautiful babies,' Rose said, laughing. 'I will be their favourite aunt.'

'That's not fair,' Emily protested. 'I am going to be their best aunt because I am not as old as you are.'

'I'm not married yet, but we thought a June

wedding would be lovely.' Marianne sat down and picked up her embroidery hoop. 'I hope you will both be my bridesmaids.'

'Of course,' Rose said eagerly. 'Although as Emmie is so young perhaps she ought to be your flower girl.'

Emily picked up a cushion and tossed it at Rose, who caught it deftly with one hand.

'Now you're being mean to me, Rose. And you've only just got home.'

'I was just teasing you.' Rose glanced at the brass clock on the mantelshelf. 'It will be time for luncheon soon. I promised Pa that I'd go upstairs and see Mama after I'd let you know I am home for good.'

'Yes, please do.' Marianne's smile faded. 'She was very upset to learn that you had gone to France. She'll be relieved to know that you're home safe and sound.'

'I very nearly wasn't.' Rose walked to the door. 'The old farmhouse was burned down by a madwoman. She tried to kill us all.'

'No!' Marianne and Emily spoke as one.

'You can't leave it like that,' Emily cried. 'Come and sit down and tell us everything.'

Rose laughed. 'You'll just have to wait. It's much more exciting than any of the stories I used to make up for you.'

'That's just not fair,' Emily said, pouting.

'She's just tormenting us.' Marianne smiled serenely. 'Rose is back, Emmie.'

Rose left the room. Nothing had changed – at least, there was very little different at home – it was she who had changed. She was not the Rose Northwood who had been taken forcibly to France. She was a woman who had experienced a whole range of events and emotions, not least falling in love with a man who wanted to propose as a matter of protocol rather than because he wanted her as his wife. That person was someone she would have to learn to live without for the rest of her life. Maybe she would regret refusing him so bluntly, but better that than to live a lie.

Rose hurried upstairs to her mother's room and knocked on the door.

Grace greeted her with a smile that was so reminiscent of Marianne that Rose was taken aback. It was the first time she had noticed the likeness and it was a relief to see her mother alert and happy.

'Rose, my dear. It's good to have you home. Come and sit down and tell me all about your travels. Your papa told me that you had returned to Provence to take care of that dear boy. How is he?'

'Jago is on the mend, Mama. His broken bones are healed and he has regained much of his strength. In fact, he has returned to Abbotsford and will be living not too far from here – at Longfleet Hall.'

'I know it, of course. I used to go there quite often when they held their garden parties and balls. That is where your papa and I met all those years ago. Although the house fell into a state of disrepair after

Sir Charles passed away. Lady Faulkner apparently lost all interest in day-to-day living, poor soul.'

'I didn't know that, Mama.'

'I heard that she had gone to join her husband in heaven some time ago. I suppose that was when Mr Rivers purchased the estate.'

'That must be so, Mama.'

'Your papa keeps me up to date with the goings-on in the village. Anyway, Rose, do tell me about your time in France. Why did you leave so suddenly?'

Rose could see that her mother was genuinely interested. It was good to speak to her openly without having to watch every word for fear of upsetting her. In fact, Grace seemed to be very much her old self. Rose sat down on a stool next to her mother and gave her an account of the events that had led to her return home.

Grace sighed. 'I would dearly love to become reacquainted with Mr Rivers, Rose. Why haven't you brought him to see us again? After all, you have known him for quite some time.'

'I suppose so, Mama. It was Christmas Day when he came upon me in the old coach house. I thought he was the villain who had harmed Jago and I wanted nothing to do with him then, but it was the beginning of everything.'

'You must bring him here now I am feeling better so that I can judge for myself, and I want to see Jago again. He did so remind me of Felix.'

'I can certainly bring Jago to see you, Mama.

I don't know about Rivers. He has a court case to fight. Someone wishes to ruin him.'

'Well, we can't allow that to happen, Rose. Your papa must know someone who can help. Perhaps Lady Buckingham will speak up for him.'

'I don't know about that, Mama. Lady Buckingham changes her mind so often.'

'She has a lot of responsibilities, Rose.' Grace's expression lightened. 'You do know about Marianne and Tom, I suppose.'

'Indeed I do, Mama. I think it's wonderful, and I told them so. I love Tom like a brother.'

'You've come home just in time for their engagement party. Lady Buckingham has kindly offered to have it at The Manor, which is good of her as we cannot afford to entertain in such a way. Nevertheless, you will enjoy yourselves, of that I am certain.'

'I dare say I'll hear all about it over dinner tonight, Mama. Do you think you might join us?'

Grace shook her head. 'Not today, Rose. Maybe tomorrow. I'll see how I feel. My nerves are getting the better of me, I'm afraid. I am quite happy here in my room.'

Rose leaned over to kiss her mother's soft cheek. 'All right, Mama. But it's high time you rejoined the family, and it is getting quite spring-like. I saw primroses in the churchyard on my way home, and the daffodils are out in the garden.'

'I'm not promising anything, but I will see.'

Rose left the room. She was not convinced that her mother would keep her word, but she could only hope. Perhaps a visit from Jago would do some good. She made up her mind to visit Longfleet and invite him to visit them at the vicarage, but first she would have to satisfy her sisters' curiosity.

Then, of course, there was the forthcoming engagement party, which would be interesting. Lady Buckingham had made it plain in the past that the Northwoods were beneath the Buckinghams in the social strata. Rose wondered how Lady Buckingham really felt at welcoming Marianne into the family. She could only hope for her sister's sake that Lady Buckingham had realised that her prejudices were old-fashioned and slightly ridiculous. Marianne was as good as, if not better than, the young women from the county families, and more importantly, she and Tom were genuinely in love. Rose went downstairs to join her sisters, ready to answer the torrent of questions she knew they would hurl at her.

Rose did her best to fit in with life at the vicarage, but it was not easy. She had hoped that Rivers might visit, and found herself making excuses for him the next day and the day after that. She missed Jago and the easy-going way of life at Le Fleuve, and she wondered how Blanche was coping now that Colbert was safely in the hands of the authorities. Rose was beginning to feel that she had lived two separate lives, and being at home with the family, although delightful in many ways, was no substitute for springtime in Provence. Rivers might manage well without her, but that did not prevent her from worrying about the criminal charge brought against him. If Dalby had evaded arrest in France he would have to make his way back to London in order to appear in court. Rose felt as if she had been reading a particularly enthralling novel and, on getting close to the end, had discovered the last chapter missing.

On the third day since her return home she decided that if Rivers was not going to come to see her, she would visit Longfleet. She was eager to see everyone again and, if she were to be honest, she wanted to get away from the fever-pitch excitement leading up to the engagement party at The Manor, which was due to take place the following evening.

As usual, Rose was up before her sisters and she ate a hasty breakfast in the dining room. She was joined by her father, who after giving her a brief kiss on the forehead, retired to his seat at the head of the table and opened the newspaper. It was yesterday's news as the paper boy rarely managed to deliver the current day's copy until almost midday, but that did not seem to bother Matthew. He ate a slice of toast and sipped his coffee. Rose finished her meal and stood up.

'I'm going to walk to Longfleet, Papa.' She waited for his response, but he did not raise his head. 'I think I should call on Mr Rivers and his aunt,' Rose continued, raising her voice. 'I want to see how Jago is faring after our flight from Le Fleuve.'

'Yes, my dear, of course,' Matthew said absently. 'Have a nice walk, Rose.'

She knew that he had not heard a word of what she had said, but that was good enough. She had told him where she was going and she was prepared for a long walk, but at least the sun was shining and when she stepped outside there was a hint of spring in the air. Rose set off purposefully, but she was less than halfway to Longfleet when she had to step aside to avoid an approaching chaise being driven at a brisk pace.

On seeing her, the driver reined in the horse. 'Rose. Where are you going? Allow me to drive you.'

'Good morning, Rivers,' Rose said breathlessly. 'I'm obviously going in the opposite direction to you.'

He laughed. 'Could it be that you were on your way to Longfleet? I was definitely heading for the vicarage. Where would you like to go? Just say and I will take you there.'

Rose hesitated. 'I suppose it is rather amusing. We are obviously at cross purposes.'

Rivers stepped down from the driver's seat. 'I'm not laughing, Rose. If you were on your way to see me, then I am very touched.'

'I wanted to see Jago and make sure that he hasn't suffered any adverse effects from our sudden flight from Le Fleuve.'

'He is very well, all things considered, and I'm sure he would love to see you.'

'I was going to invite him and his mother – I mean Mrs Dalby – to visit us at the vicarage. My mama took a liking to Jago and she has asked to see him.'

'Then I suggest we go to Longfleet and you can invite them yourself.'

'Yes, thank you. Anyway, I am curious to see your home. I can't imagine you living in a great house.'

Rivers handed her into the chaise and climbed up to sit next to her. 'You don't see me as lord of the manor?' His blue eyes twinkled as he took the reins.

'I don't know about that,' Rose said, smiling. 'You might be a wealthy landowner or spending time in prison, should the court case go against you, that is.'

He flicked the reins and guided the horse gently so that they were facing the opposite direction. 'Well, who knows? Anyway, for the moment it's a lovely day and we are going to Longfleet so that you can assess my worth.'

'You make it sound as if you were about to offer marriage again.' Rose shot him a sideways glance. 'Or do you think it amusing to play such games?'

'I never play games. I did suggest marriage, although I wouldn't call it a proper proposal.'

'I know that. You raised the subject to save my face. I appreciate that, but when a gentleman asks me to marry him I don't think it's asking too much for a little romance. It isn't a business transaction, at least not in my humble circumstances.'

'You are anything but humble, Rose.'

She laughed. 'You know what I mean, Rivers. When there is a fortune involved on either side it does become a business arrangement in some classes, although I'm happy to say that didn't affect my sister. Tom Buckingham and Marianne are engaged, and the formidable Lady Buckingham is holding a party for them tomorrow evening. Perhaps she will invite you to attend.'

'Will you be there?'

'Of course.'

'Then I might invite myself. With the court case pending and Dalby out to ruin me I doubt if Lady Buckingham would consider me a suitable guest.'

'You would do that?' Rose turned her head to meet his amused glance. 'You would walk into The Manor uninvited?'

'If you wished me to attend there is nothing that would stop me.'

Rose eyed him warily. She was never sure whether or not Rivers was simply teasing her. She decided to change the subject.

'How far is it to Longfleet now?'

'A couple of miles or so. Too far for you to have walked.'

'I am used to walking. We haven't had a horse since poor Clover was put out to grass several years ago.'

'How does your papa get about when he visits outlying farms and houses in the parish?'

'Pa walks or, occasionally, if the weather is too bad or he has far to go, he borrows a horse from Lady Buckingham. Occasionally he uses the old doctor's pony and trap.'

'That's very generous of the good doctor.'

'It's a mutually useful arrangement. I'm not supposed to know about such things, but in return for the favour Papa turns a blind eye to the fact that Dr Newton has what you might call a special relationship with his housekeeper, Mrs Burnett.'

'That sounds intriguing.'

'Well, Mrs Monroe has been confined to her bed with long bouts of illness for the last twenty years, and you might say that Mrs Burnett has filled the void in the doctor's life.'

Rivers' lips twitched but he merely nodded. 'Yes, I understand. However, it's a pity your papa doesn't have his own transport. It must be awkward at times . . .'

'Good heavens!' Forgetting everything else, Rose leaned forward, gazing at the red-brick wall that followed the road as far ahead as she could see. 'That isn't part of Longfleet estate, is it, Rivers?'

'It most certainly is. I believe it's one of the longest continuous walls in the whole of the West Country. It was erected by the first owner of Longfleet, who was rumoured to have made his fortune by heading a very profitable smuggling ring, but that is just hearsay.'

'Was he one of your ancestors?'

'No. I'm sorry to disappoint you. There's nothing as exciting as privateering or pitting one's wits against the revenue men in my family.'

'What about the olive grove and the vineyard? Do they belong to you, too?'

'Yes, my grandfather bought Le Fleuve and the land when he decided to hand the tea plantation over to my father. I think he was of the opinion that tea might go out of fashion, but people always drink wine and need olive oil for culinary purposes.'

'He sounds like a very forward-thinking gentleman.'

'I believe he was.' Rivers reined the horse in to a walk. 'Here we are at the gates. I hope you are still as impressed, Rose.'

Rose said nothing as she gazed in awe at the avenue of copper beech trees that lined the straight driveway. Their branches were bare although there were bronze-tipped buds just visible on the swaying branches. At the very end, the early Georgian façade of Longfleet Hall came into view, its elegant contours visible against a pale blue sky. As they drew closer, she could see the front entrance beneath a classical pediment surmounting Corinthian columns, and guarded by two stone lions. However, on closer inspection the gravel carriage sweep was dotted with weeds and the lions wore coats of green moss.

'Mama said that Lady Faulkner had allowed the house to deteriorate,' Rose said slowly. 'But it is still beautiful. No wonder you wanted it for yourself, Rivers.'

'There are some things that money can buy, but others that are priceless.' He drew the horse to a halt and almost immediately a groom appeared from the side of the building and ran to take the reins, and a footman emerged from the house to open the door of the chaise. Unused to such regal treatment, Rose alighted from the carriage. Rivers was at her side before she had a chance to catch her breath and he proffered his arm.

'Welcome to Longfleet, Rose.'

She allowed him to lead her into the grand entrance hall. She was impressed by its perfect proportions. However, it was painfully obvious that her mother had not exaggerated the condition of the building. It had been allowed to fall into a state of disrepair and the ornate plasterwork appeared to be crumbling, the paintwork was chipped and the marble-tiled floor in need of renovation. A curved staircase led to a galleried first floor. The house was undoubtedly beautiful but it felt neglected and sad.

'What a shame,' Rose said softly. 'This must have been such a wonderful home years ago. It needs a great deal of loving care to restore it to its former glory.'

'I agree wholeheartedly, but it will have to wait until after the court case. Everything hangs on that at the moment.'

Rose looked up at him, frowning. 'You don't think you'll lose, do you?'

'Will is confident that we will win, but from what

I've learned of Dalby he is quite ruthless when money is concerned. That's why Lucy and Jago are staying here indefinitely.'

'Do you know if Dalby has returned to England?'

'Will has gone back to London. He hopes to find out whether or not the French police detained Dalby, although I hope he was allowed to return home. I want to get the case over and done with. Then we can all get on with our lives.'

'But Dalby isn't the one defending himself, is he? That means when you are exonerated he will also walk free from the court. He will still pose a threat to Jago.'

'Not necessarily, Rose. Now we know the truth about Jago's parentage, it is clear he is no longer an heir to the Hanbury estate. However, Lucy is a very rich woman and Dalby is her stepson. I imagine he will try everything to divest her of as much money as he can, by fair means or foul. He has no scruples.' Rivers broke off at the sight of Lucy, who was crossing the entrance hall with a welcoming smile.

'Rose, this is an unexpected pleasure.'

Rose smiled. 'It's good to see you again, Lucy.'

'Jago is in the library. Do come and see him.'

'A library? How wonderful. I've always thought that to be the height of luxury.' Rose glanced at Rivers. 'Maybe you will show me the rest of the house later?'

'Of course. Go with Lucy. Perhaps you would like to stay for luncheon? I do have an excellent cook.'

'Thank you. I would like that very much.' Rose followed Lucy into the depths of the house. Beyond the entrance hall it was easy to see how much needed doing in order to restore the old building, but the house seemed to wrap its arms around her in a genuine spirit of welcome. She could see it in her mind's eye as it must have been years ago, and if she closed her eyes she could hear the voices of the family and the laughter of young children. At one time this must have been a wonderful home.

Lucy opened a door and the smell of old books wafted out into the corridor. Rose followed her into the room and was thrilled by what she saw. The walls were lined with bookshelves and crammed with tomes of every shape and size. Jago rose from his seat in the window and hurried across the room to give Rose a hug.

'I knew you'd come and see me, Rose. I've really missed you.'

Rose returned the embrace. 'You're looking so well, Jago. You must be delighted to have all these books around you.'

'I am, but I'm looking forward to riding again. Cousin Benedict says he will find me a suitable horse. There is so much to do here. It's even better than Le Fleuve.'

Lucy shuddered. 'Don't mention that place again, Jago. I still dream about the fire and our narrow escape. We lost everything we had there, but fortunately I have been able to send for my belongings from my old home, and Jago's of course. My maid went yesterday morning so I expect her to return later today.'

'Let's hope Monty isn't there, Mama,' Jago said, grinning. 'He'll probably cut up all our clothes and send them back in pieces.'

'Don't say things like that, Jago. I believe he's capable of anything.'

The words had hardly left her lips when there was a knock on the door and the footman announced that Miss Brown had returned, but his announcement was rudely interrupted.

Montague Dalby pushed past him. 'So this is where you've been hiding, Stepmother, and you too, Jago.'

'Get out,' Lucy cried tearfully. 'Leave us alone, Montague.'

Jago advanced on him with his hands fisted. 'You heard my mama. Leave now, Monty. We don't want anything to do with you.'

At that moment Rivers strode into the room. Rose knew by the look on his face that he was in no mood for polite conversation.

'Get out of my house, Dalby. I'm not telling you again.'

'I will only go if my stepmother and stepbrother accompany me. You are going to prison, Rivers. I refuse to leave them here.'

Rivers took a step towards him but Rose threw herself in between them. 'Stop this now. Can't you see that this is what he wants, Rivers? He's doing this deliberately to put you in the wrong. How would it look in court if you had laid your hands on him? Please don't do anything rash.'

'But that doesn't include me.' Jago put his head down and charged at Dalby, sending him crashing to the ground.

Chapter Twenty

Rivers dragged Dalby to his feet. 'I don't know what you think you might gain by coming here, but this is my home and you are less than welcome.' He marched Dalby out of the room, leaving Rose to help Jago to his feet.

'Are you hurt?' she asked anxiously.

Jago leaned against her for a moment, but he was laughing as he shook his head. 'I'm fine, Rose. I hope Monty has a few bruises.'

'I am sure he has.' Lucy fussed round them. 'Go and sit down, Jago. You are still unwell.'

'No, Mama. I am completely recovered and it's time I did something other than sit around reading books.' Jago straightened up, brushing his fair hair back from his forehead. 'First of all I will keep Cousin Benedict up to his promise of a horse, and the first thing I will do then is to ride over to the vicarage and call on you, Rose.'

'That will be lovely, Jago. My mama was asking about you. She said she wants to see you again, and my sisters will be glad that you are fit and well. You were in a very poor state of health when you left Abbotsford for France.'

Jago straightened his jacket. 'I'm going to see if Cousin Benedict needs any help with Dalby. I would love to throw him out and see him grovel. It would be a payment for all the times he bullied me when I was younger.' He hurried from the room followed by Rose.

'Don't do anything rash, Jago. You know the court case is coming up.' She caught hold of his sleeve. However, the sight that met their eyes brought them both to a halt.

At the far end of the entrance hall Rivers was about to eject Dalby bodily, but he hesitated and turned to them with a wry smile.

'Mr Dalby is just leaving.' He released Dalby and gave him a none-too-gentle shove, which sent him stumbling onto the gravel carriage sweep. Rivers took Dalby's coat and hat from the straight-faced footman and tossed them after their owner. 'I'll see you in court, Dalby. But I'm warning you to keep away from Jago and his mother. From now on you will have nothing to do with either of them.'

Dalby regained his balance, clutching his coat and hat in his arms as he backed away. 'Your actions prove my point. I'll tell the court that you are

350

holding Mrs Dalby and her son here against their will in order to extort money.'

Rivers slammed the door, cutting off Dalby's string of expletives.

'He is no gentleman. I would never use language like that in front of a child and a lady.' Rivers patted Jago on the shoulder. 'I hope you didn't hurt yourself when you tackled Dalby.'

'Not me. I'm tougher than you think, Cousin. What's more, I am coming to London with you. I want Will to call me to the stand as a witness.'

Rose stared at him in surprise. 'Are you sure you're fit enough for that, Jago?'

'I am almost back to normal, but I won't allow Dalby to blacken Cousin Benedict's name. I want to tell the court what sort of man my stepbrother is.'

'There's just one thing against that, Jago,' Rivers said slowly. 'If Dalby knows that you are going to testify against him it's quite possible that he will instruct his lawyer to reveal the truth of your parentage. Are you prepared for that to happen?'

Lucy crossed the floor quickly and Rose could tell by her face that she had overheard enough to alarm her.

Jago turned to her with a sweet smile. 'I won't do anything to upset you, Mama. I know that Madame de Fontenay gave birth to me and that the villain Colbert is my real father, but that doesn't matter to me. You have brought me up and loved me, and I love you.'

Lucy's eyes filled with tears and she flung her arms around him. 'Oh, my dear boy, I know you love me as I love you, but we can't allow Montague to blacken Benedict's name and possibly send him to prison. You must do whatever your conscience decides. I won't blame you for telling the truth.'

Rivers shook his head, clearly moved. 'I am touched by your loyalty, both of you. However, I will fight my own battles. I won't allow Dalby to win.'

'No matter what you say, you need me,' Jago said firmly. 'I am going to London with you, and I will let the world know what sort of man Monty is.'

'I don't think you ought to go to London, Jago.' Lucy caught hold of his arm. 'You are only just recovered from all those terrible beatings and the illness you suffered.'

'I am well enough, Mama.'

'I will go with you,' Rose said firmly. 'Will you allow that, Lucy? I promise I will look after him.'

Rivers looked from one to the other. 'Are you sure about this, both of you?'

Rose nodded emphatically. 'I will support Jago in whatever he decides. I've been to London before – well, once anyway – and I'm not afraid to say my piece in court if needed.'

'I will tell the truth to the judge. I am not afraid of the consequences.' Jago gave his mother a hug. 'I love you, Mama. I will always be your boy.'

'Then it's settled.' Rose smiled triumphantly. 'We will make sure you remain a free man, Rivers.'

'I don't want to involve either of you, but we'll see what Will says. I believe the head of his chambers has given him the opportunity to act as my defence in court.'

Rivers glanced at the grandfather clock that stood to attention at the foot of the stairs. 'I didn't realise the time, but I can see Herbert hovering in the background, waiting to tell us that luncheon is served.' He proffered his arm to Rose. 'May I escort you to the dining room, Miss Northwood?'

Rose laid her hand on his sleeve. 'Thank you, sir. That would be delightful.'

Lucy took Jago's arm and they processed to the dining room, where Rose began to relax and allow herself to enjoy the delicious meal.

Later that day, at home in the vicarage drawing room, Rose related the events at Longfleet in detail to Marianne and Emily.

'Why does nothing exciting like that ever happen to us?' Emily said, pouting. 'You have all the fun, Rose.'

'I wouldn't call the scene with Dalby "fun" exactly.' Rose pulled a face. 'He is a horrible individual. I cannot stand the sight of him, and I thought that Rivers was going to strangle him at one point.'

'The man is a menace,' Marianne said, nodding. 'But I don't think you should go to London, Rose. Look what happened when you took off for France:

you were kidnapped and then you were almost killed in a fire at the farmhouse. What could happen to you in London?'

Rose laughed. 'Not much else, if you put it like that, Marianne.'

'Exactly my meaning. I don't think Papa will allow you to go to London with Rivers and Jago. It's all very well doing something like that, but what about your reputation? What will Lady Buckingham say when she finds out?'

'Is that all you're worried about?' Rose sighed in exasperation. 'I hope you are not going to turn into a frightful bore when you marry Tom. You will finish up being just like his mother.'

Marianne rolled her eyes. 'Heaven forbid.'

'You will, Minnie.' Emily giggled. 'I can see it now. We'll have to be terribly polite and formal when we visit you at The Manor.'

'Maybe I'll change the way they live,' Marianne said, tossing her head. 'I am nothing like Lady Buckingham.'

Rose could see an argument looming and she hastily changed the subject. 'What are you going to wear for your engagement party, Marianne? I haven't anything new, but then it will be your night, not mine.'

'Mama persuaded Pa to let me have a new gown,' Marianne said, smiling. 'It is rather lovely, isn't it, Emmie?'

'Yes, but I will have to borrow Rose's white taffeta

again – that is, if you'll lend it to me, Rose. It's not fair.'

'You look lovely in it, Emmie.' Rose could see another squabble on the horizon. 'What do you think I should wear when I attend the court?'

'You won't be put on the witness stand, will you?' Emily's eyes widened, her choice of gown apparently forgotten.

'I don't know, although I think it more likely I will be seated in the public gallery.'

'Where will you stay?' Marianne asked eagerly. 'Not in a hotel, I hope. Imagine how that would look.'

'Rivers said Will has a relative who owns a house not too far from the law courts. We will all stay there and it will be perfectly respectable.'

'I wish I could come with you,' Emily said wistfully. 'Life here is so dull. Nothing exciting ever happens.'

'I thought that once.' Rose smiled. 'And look what happened to me. Your turn will come, Emmie.'

'There's my engagement party tomorrow night for a start.' Marianne stood up and tugged at the bell pull. 'I suggest we have some tea and cake. Everything looks better after a slice of Cook's delicious fruit cake.'

'She is a much better cook than Madame Laurent at Le Fleuve,' Rose added seriously. 'And after tea you may go through my trinket box, Emmie. You can choose whatever you like to wear to the party tomorrow.'

Tom arrived early next evening to escort Marianne and her sisters to The Manor. Emily was dressed in the white taffeta, with a string of seed pearls, also borrowed from Rose, around her neck, as well as a pair of silver earrings. Rose wore the only ball gown she possessed, which was a modest creation in sprigged muslin with a lace shawl. Matthew had tried to persuade his wife to accompany them, but Grace had suffered one of her attacks of nerves and had to be put to bed with a cold compress on her forehead. Winnie promised to look in on her every half-hour while the family were out.

While Rose sympathised with her mother, she could not help feeling that Mama might have made an effort to attend a function that was so important to Marianne. However, she put all such thoughts to the back of her mind and set off with the others, intent on enjoying herself.

As Rose had expected, Lady Buckingham was effusive in her greeting to Marianne and she was kindly disposed towards Emily, but, although polite, it was obvious that she did not approve of Rose. However, her attitude changed subtly when Benedict Rivers arrived, accompanied by Jago, and they waited next in line to be welcomed by their hostess.

'We called for you at the vicarage, Rose,' Rivers said loud enough for Lady Buckingham to hear. 'But your maid told us you had left, so we followed on.'

Rose smiled. 'Thank you, that was kind, but we came with Tom and Papa.'

'I see you've brought your brother with you, Mr Rivers.' Lady Buckingham beamed at him. 'You are looking so well now, young man.'

'Jago is my cousin, ma'am,' Rivers said firmly. 'He and his mother are living with me at Longfleet Hall until they find accommodation suitable for them.'

Lady Buckingham leaned forward, lowering her voice. 'Yes, I heard of your problems, Mr Rivers. I hope all the misunderstandings will be cleared up by the court case, which I believe is within the fortnight.'

'You are well informed, ma'am. I hope to be fully exonerated of the charges against me,' Rivers said, smiling. 'But we mustn't take up more of your valuable time, Lady Buckingham.' He proffered his arm to Rose. 'Shall we join your family, Rose? I'm sure that Jago would like to dance with your younger sister.'

Jago frowned. 'Must I, Cousin Benedict?'

'I think you must, my boy. Good manners require it.'

Rose turned her head to give Jago an encouraging smile. 'Emily is quite entertaining when you get to know her and, to be honest, she is as bored as you are, Jago. Take pity on her.'

'I suppose I should.' Jago followed them to the table where Tom had settled Marianne. Matthew, in the meantime, had gone off to mingle with his parishioners.

Jago approached Emily as warily as a hunter

357

stalking a dangerous animal. 'Good evening, Miss Emily,' he said cautiously.

Emily looked up and, to Rose's relief, a smile replaced her sulky expression. 'You look so much better than when I last saw you, Jago. Shall we get some fruit punch?'

'Lemonade for you, I think,' Marianne said severely. 'I'm sure your mama would agree with me, Jago.'

He nodded. 'Yes, Miss Northwood.'

Rose hid a smile. She knew by the looks on their faces that both Emily and Jago were determined to sample the fruit punch, which was probably laced with brandy or some other spirit, but she was not going to spoil their fun. After all, they would relax and join in the dancing, and any effects that the punch might have would soon wear off. Rose glanced at Rivers and he gave her a conspiratorial wink.

'May I have this dance, Rose?'

Rose laid her hand in his and he led her through the crowd of guests to the dance floor, where he took her in his arms and whirled her into the waltz. There was little chance to speak but gradually the tension leached out of Rose's body and she relaxed, allowing him to lead her into the romantic world of the Viennese waltz. When the dance came to an end and they left the floor, Rivers held her back.

'Rose, are you really intent on coming to London with us? We leave on Monday morning.'

She nodded emphatically. 'Yes, most certainly.

I wouldn't dream of allowing Jago to go unaccompanied.'

'He'll be with me.'

'You know what I mean, Rivers. You will be occupied with your legal advisors and then you will be in court. Jago is just a boy and he'll be on his own in London unless I go with him.'

'Very well then. We'll be staying in Doughty Street. Will's aunt owns a house there and she has kindly offered to put us up for as long as we need to be in town.'

'That's kind of her.'

'I am going to speak to your papa and ask his permission to take you to London, but at least I can assure him that you will be residing in a respectable household.'

'I'm of age, Rivers. I can do as I please, within reason.'

He smiled. 'I know that, but there is such things as manners, Rose. I would be very disrespectful if I did not speak to your papa first, especially after our escapades in France. He must be a very forbearing gentleman.'

'You're right, of course. And he is a good man and a kind one. But there is one person I would like you to speak to before we go away.'

'Your mama?'

'How did you guess?'

'It follows, Rose. I know how fond you are of both parents, as well as your sisters. You've told me how your mama suffers every Christmas since your brother died. The least I can do would be to tell her how much I think of you and how I would never do anything to hurt you.'

Rose turned away, her breathing suddenly erratic. 'You mean that, don't you?'

'You know I do. Anyway, this isn't the time or the place to talk about my feelings for you, Rose. They've just struck up a mazurka. Would you care to dance?'

Rose nodded. 'I would.'

They merged into the crowd of dancers. Rose was amused to see Jago and Emily attempting the steps with set expressions on their faces as they tried to remember their dancing lessons.

'Do you know, Rivers, I'm glad I'm not fourteen now.'

He laughed. 'And so am I, very glad, Rose.'

Rivers took her back to their table at the end of the mazurka, but Jago and Emily stayed until the next dance, which was a lively polka. After that, Rose lost sight of them and she suspected they had gone to the refreshment room. Marianne and Tom were constantly besieged by well-wishers. Rose watched as Rivers managed to get her father away from George Finch, who had been monopolising him for the last half an hour or so. Rose hoped that Rivers' undoubted powers of persuasion would work on her father. If Papa objected to her accompanying Rivers to London, it would make things difficult, but she was going anyway. She hoped that Rivers realised that.

There were several gentlemen of her acquaintance who asked her to dance but none came up to Rivers' standard, which surprised her. She had never thought of him as a man who was gifted with social graces, but then she had only known him for a few short months, although it felt as if he had been part of her life for much longer. He seemed to be getting along splendidly with her father, and that also was unexpected. Papa was reserved when it came to expressing his personal feelings, but he did not appear to have any difficulty in communicating with Rivers. They were laughing and chatting as if they were old friends. Rose realised with something of a shock how little she really knew Benedict Rivers, and that left her eager to learn more.

As he made his way back through the crowd he was still smiling. 'Your papa is a remarkable man, Rose. He was prepared to listen to what I had to say without prejudice, which was remarkable considering I might be convicted of the charges against me.'

'Papa is a very good judge of men. I know all about his admirable qualities, but did he give permission for me to accompany you and Jago to London?'

Rivers eyed her with an amused smile. 'Would it make any difference if I told you he refused?'

'No, not really. I would have had to use my considerable powers of persuasion, but if that failed

I would still go with you. I was the one who found Jago half dead in the snow and I feel responsible for him. I want to see Montague Dalby punished for the way he has treated Jago, and Lucy, too.'

'Then it's just as well that your papa said you could accompany us to London. I assured him that you would be staying with Will's aunt Esther, who is a very respectable lady, and that seemed to satisfy him. Now, I think they are about to play another waltz. May I have this dance, Rose?'

Supper was served in the ante-room. Lady Buckingham made a speech welcoming her son's new fiancée into the family, which was met by enthusiastic applause. Rose was both relieved and delighted to know that Marianne's future was secured, although she did not envy her sister having a mother-in-law like the formidable Lady Buckingham. However, Rose knew that Marianne's generous nature and her kindness would win over her harshest critic. She might not be bringing money and a long lineage to the union, but Tom would have a gentle and loving wife, who would stand by him no matter what happened.

Rivers handed her a glass of champagne. 'Tom Buckingham is a lucky man, Rose.'

She smiled. 'I think he knows that. They were childhood sweethearts and soon they will be man and wife. I am so happy for them both.' Rose raised the glass. 'A toast to the engaged couple. And I hope above all things that the court case goes in your favour, Rivers.'

'I'll say aye to both, Rose. But I don't intend to lose. I have right on my side, and Dalby will regret the day he decided to take me on, especially with you beside me.'

'I'm so glad that Papa agreed to my going with you and Jago,' Rose said, sipping the champagne.

'Although we are leaving for London on Monday morning, the case doesn't come up for a few days, but I need more time with Will. Blanche's confession has changed everything, Rose.'

'You aren't going to shame her and Lucy in public, are you, Rivers?'

'I need to talk it over with Will. The last thing I want to do is to make things difficult for my aunt and my old friend Blanche.'

Rose laid her hand on his as it rested on the table top. 'I know you'll make the right decision. I trust you implicitly.'

He raised her hand to his lips. 'I need to earn that trust, Rose. Believe me, it's foremost in my mind. I would never do anything to hurt you or your family, let alone my cousin Jago.'

Rose met his intense gaze with an attempt at a smile. 'I'm with you, no matter what, Rivers.'

Chapter Twenty-One

Doughty Street was a gated community with porters' lodges at both ends, keeping the street free from passing traffic and the terraced Georgian houses unbothered by door-to-door salesmen, gypsies and others who might be unwelcome in the select homes. Rose could not help but be impressed by the porter in his mulberry coat with brass buttons and gold lacing in his hat. She wished that her sisters were here to see how far up she had come in the world. Even so, London was busier than she remembered it and the area around the railway station was dirty, with beggars on every corner. However, the cab had whisked them to their destination and a neatly dressed housemaid opened the door and ushered them into the narrow hallway.

Mrs Esther Pilbeam received them in the drawing room that occupied the width of the first floor. Two tall windows swagged with blue velvet curtains looked down onto the tree-lined street, and a coal fire burned in the grate. The room was furnished tastefully but without ostentation. Mrs Pilbeam rose from her armchair by the fireplace and greeted them with a warm smile.

'My nephew is at the office, but he will be home shortly. In the meantime, Nancy will show you to your rooms. I'm afraid you and the young man will have to share, Mr Rivers.'

'That is perfectly fine,' Rivers said before Jago had a chance to speak.

'I don't mind at all.' Jago shrugged and turned his attention to the view of the street below. 'I just want to go out and explore.'

'All in good time,' Rivers said calmly. 'But this isn't Abbotsford, Jago. You need to know where you may and may not go safely.'

'This is a good neighbourhood, but Mr Rivers is right, Master Jago. You do need to know which areas are unsafe, especially at night.' Mrs Pilbeam turned to Rose. 'You will have the smaller room on the second floor, Miss Northwood. I trust that will suit you.'

'It's very kind of you to put us all up, Mrs Pilbeam,' Rose said earnestly. 'I am sure the room will be delightful. I'm very excited to be here in London.'

Mrs Pilbeam smiled. 'Is this your first trip to the city, my dear?'

'I was here once with my parents and sisters.

We went to the Great Exhibition and stayed in a small hotel near Paddington station, but it was nothing like this.'

'Perhaps we will have time to see some of the sights,' Rivers said, smiling. 'I will be happy to take you anywhere you wish to go, Rose.'

'There you are, Miss Northwood. That is a most generous offer.' Mrs Pilbeam motioned to her maid, who had come into the room. 'Show Mr Rivers, Mr Hanbury and Miss Northwood to their rooms, please, Nancy.'

Nancy bobbed a curtsey. 'Shall I show you first, miss?'

'Yes, thank you.' Rose followed her from the room, leaving Rivers to make conversation with Mrs Pilbeam while Jago continued to gaze out of the window.

The bedroom allocated to Rose overlooked the backs of the houses in the next street, with their small gardens, outbuildings and sheds. It was a small room but cosy, with a fire in the grate, crackling and spitting cheerfully. A square of pink and green floral-patterned carpet covered most of the floorboards, and those visible were polished to a conker-bright shine. A pink and green coverlet with a matching pillow sham made the single bed look inviting. A chair, upholstered in pink velvet, and a white painted chest of drawers completed the furnishings. It was a pretty room, warm and welcoming.

Nancy placed Rose's valise on a side table.

'Would you like me to come back and unpack for you, miss?'

Rose smiled. 'No, thank you, Nancy. I didn't bring very much with me as we're only here for a few days. I'll do it myself.'

'Very well, miss. If there is anything you want you just have to ring the bell.' She bobbed a curtsey and left Rose to unpack and put her things away. She had just finished when there was a knock on the door and Jago entered without waiting for an answer.

'I might have been in a state of undress, Jago,' Rose said, laughing. 'You should always wait for someone to invite you into their room.'

'Sorry, but I couldn't wait. I really would like to go for a walk, Rose. Will you come with me?'

Rose glanced out of the window. It was still early afternoon and the sun was shining.

'Did you ask Benedict if it was all right to go out?'

'He said he has some paperwork to do, so as long as we don't stray too far, he doesn't mind.'

'As a matter of fact I would like to get some fresh air and exercise.' Rose picked up her bonnet and put it on, followed by her mantle and gloves. 'I'm ready. Let's go and explore the neighbourhood, Jago.'

There was no sign of Rivers as Rose followed Jago downstairs and out into the street, but there seemed to be no valid reason to sit indoors on such a pleasant afternoon. The London plane trees were in full bud and sparrows hopped cheekily in the gutter and around the base of tree trunks, taking no notice of passers-by. They stopped at the porter's lodge at the north end of the street and Rose asked if there was somewhere of note within walking distance. Thanking him for his advice, they set off, heading west in the general direction of the British Museum. Jago was doubtful at first, complaining that he had not come to London to spend time looking at dusty old artefacts, but Rose insisted that it was a good start, and they had a few days before the court case. Rivers was bound to be fully occupied during that time and they would have to amuse themselves. In the end they reached a compromise and Jago agreed on the British Museum, if the next day they might get a cab to the Zoological Gardens. Rose thought that an excellent plan, and they walked arm in arm, chatting about the exciting things they might do in London.

The museum was further than the porter had suggested, but they spent an hour walking from gallery to gallery and Jago was mildly interested in some of the exhibits. Eventually Rose could tell he was getting bored and she suggested that they return to Doughty Street. He agreed instantly. They had entered the museum in bright sunshine, but the clouds had rolled over and it was raining when they left.

Rose huddled beneath the portico. 'We didn't think to borrow an umbrella from Mrs Pilbeam and I haven't enough money for a cab, Jago.'

'I should have asked Benedict for some coins,'

Jago said ruefully. 'I'm not used to being on my own in a big city.'

'It looks as though the rain has settled in for the afternoon.' Rose sighed. 'We'll get very wet if we walk back to Doughty Street in this downpour.'

'I suppose we could go back inside and hope it stops soon.' Jago looked up at the darkening clouds. 'But maybe we ought to risk a soaking.'

'You've only just recovered from bouts of lung fever,' Rose said doubtfully. 'Your mama would never forgive me if you went down with it again because we didn't prepare for something like this.'

'Excuse me, miss.'

Rose turned to see a tall gentleman, standing a few feet away, presumably sheltering from the rain. She eyed him warily, but he seemed to be quite respectable and his clothes were of good quality.

He smiled and inclined his head. 'I couldn't help overhearing. I sent a boy to fetch a cab and I happen to be going in the direction of Doughty Street. Might I offer you both a lift?'

Jago smiled delightedly. 'That would be excellent. Wouldn't it, Rose?'

'That's very kind of you, sir,' Rose said doubtfully. 'But are you sure it wouldn't take you out of your way?'

'Absolutely not. I am always happy to help anyone in difficulty.'

'Perhaps we ought to wait a while.' Rose was not entirely convinced. It seemed too good to be true that a stranger would offer to go out of his way for them. After all, Doughty Street was not a thoroughfare in the common sense of the word. However, before she could think of a good excuse a hackney carriage drew to a halt at the foot of the steps. The gentleman tipped the boy who had braved the weather to bring it to them.

'Come along, my dear. There's no sense in delaying. I will drop you off at the door of your residence.' He held out his hand. 'My name is Crouch, if that makes it more acceptable. We are no longer strangers.'

'And I am Jago Hanbury, and this lady is Miss Rose Northwood,' Jago said, grinning. 'Now we are all friends. Do come along, Rose. I'm beginning to shiver.'

Jago was already halfway down the steps and Mr Crouch was smiling genially as he proffered his hand. Rose was also feeling chilled to the bone and, if anything, the rain was coming down faster than before. She allowed him to lead her to the cab and she climbed in to sit beside Jago. Crouch followed her and sat down on the opposite seat. He tapped the roof of the cab with his furled umbrella.

'Very sensible, Miss Northwood. Make yourselves comfortable.'

The cab pulled away and rejoined the traffic on the main road. Rose could see that Jago was shivering and she could only hope he had not contracted a chill while waiting in the cold. She tried to relax, but she had a nagging feeling that something was wrong.

Crouch was staring out of the window, his profile set and stony. She had a sneaking suspicion that she had experienced something like this before, and it had ended in her abduction by Dalby. She was tempted to call out to the driver and order him to stop, but a sideways glance at Jago made her hesitate. He was very pale and it was obvious that he needed to be indoors by a warm fire. Perhaps she was being oversensitive but her suspicions were confirmed when she realised that they were going in completely the wrong direction. She leaned forward.

'I think we should get out here, Mr Crouch. The driver seems to have taken a wrong turn.'

Crouch turned to her with a cold stare. 'I don't think so, Miss Northwood.'

'Who are you? I don't believe you are taking us to Doughty Street.'

'I'd advise you to sit very still, Miss Northwood. And you, too, Master Hanbury. I am not a violent man but I have to deliver you both, whole and unharmed, to my employer. He will tell you what you wish to know.'

'Stop!' Rose shouted at the top of her voice. 'Driver, stop the vehicle. We are being kidnapped.'

'He can't hear you, Rose. Even if he could, he is in my employ, so you are wasting your time.' Crouch's hand shot out and he grasped Jago's wrist so tightly that it made him cry out. 'I could break the boy's arm with one quick twist, and don't think I won't do it, my dear. I suggest you cooperate.'

'My cousin won't allow this,' Jago said defiantly. 'He will send the police to look for us and then you will be the one in trouble.'

'That has been taken into account, my boy.' Crouch released Jago, but with a quick movement he produced a leather sheath from beneath his tweed overcoat. He drew a vicious-looking knife and held it close to Jago's throat. 'Now we don't want to get blood all over this nice clean cab, do we? Keep quiet and no harm will come to either of you.'

Rose had no doubt that Crouch would carry out his threat and she moved closer to Jago.

'We will do as you say, but you won't get away with this.'

Crouch laughed as he sheathed the weapon. 'How wrong you are.'

The carriage ride seemed to last for ever and night had enveloped the city by the time it came to a halt.

Crouch opened the door and alighted swiftly. A man dressed all in black leaned in and lifted Jago from the seat as if he weighed less than nothing. Jago's attempts to resist were futile and he was flung over the man's shoulder. Crouch beckoned to Rose.

'Come quietly and the boy will not be hurt.'

There was nothing she could do other than to obey him and she climbed stiffly to the ground. It was too dark to see very much, but the sound and smell of the river were enough to petrify her. Were they going to be drowned in order to prevent Jago from testifying? This criminal act must be to do with the court case, although it seemed unlikely that Dalby knew they were in London. She stumbled as Crouch gave her a shove so that she followed the man, who had a furious Jago slung over his shoulder like a side of meat or a sack of coal.

They seemed to be in a narrow alleyway with a mixture of buildings leaning top heavily towards each other. The cobblestones were wet and very slippery and Rose almost fell several times before they reached what looked like a very old, half-timbered house. The man carrying Jago kicked viciously at the door. It opened and a waft of foul-smelling air caught the back of Rose's throat, making her cough.

'Get inside.' Crouch pushed her so that she stumbled into the narrow hallway. She had only smelled that noxious odour once before and that was in a cottage on the edge of Abbotsford where one of her father's poorest families lived in total squalor. The stench was a mixture of cockroach and rodent droppings, an overflowing privy and unwashed bodies. It did not bode well, especially when the person who let them in lit a candle and the flickering light revealed the true state of the building. The staircase was in a shocking state of disrepair. Rose had to tread carefully to avoid the rotten pieces of wood, and the banister rail was broken. Despite this, they reached the first floor and were taken to a room at the rear of the building, where they were left without any explanation. Rose heard the key turn in the lock as Crouch and his accomplice left. The flickering light of a single candle sent grotesque shadows moving stealthily in the corners of the room, which was empty apart from a table, two chairs, and a palliasse laid out on the bare boards.

Jago sniffed loudly. 'This is Monty's doing, Rose. He wants to prevent me from testifying against him.'

'He must think that I am a danger, too,' Rose said thoughtfully. 'If I told the court that he had kidnapped me and held me prisoner, that would go against him.'

'And so it should. Monty was jealous of me and Mama from the start. He used to bully me so badly that I was glad of the chance to get away from home. I think Monty paid the captain to make my life hell because the way I was treated on board ship was even worse.' Jago sank down on one of the wooden chairs. 'I'm so cold, Rose.'

She sighed. 'I know you are, and I am, too.' She went to the fireplace, where ashes and cinders tumbled onto the hearth. It was obvious that it had been like this for some time. There was nothing to make a fire with, and several of the small windowpanes were cracked and others missing altogether. Jago warmed his hands by cupping them around the candle flame.

'What will we do, Rose?'

'I don't know, Jago, and that's the truth.' She went to peer out of the window. There were gaslights on the wharfs and she could see several barges being unloaded, but the men working there were too far

374

away to hear any cries of help. Looking down, she saw there was a sheer drop into deep, seemingly endless shadow, and the whole area was surrounded by a high brick wall. 'They can't keep us here for ever.'

'I'm hungry.' Jago rested his head in his arms. 'Do you think Benedict will come looking for us?'

'I'm sure he will have all the police in London scouring the area, but whether they will find us is another matter. Hopefully someone will bring us some food and something to drink.'

Jago raised his head. 'Do you really think so?'

'We're more valuable alive than dead, so they won't starve us,' Rose said with more conviction than she was feeling. She pulled up a chair and sat next to Jago, slipping her arm around his thin shoulders. 'We'll be all right. If the worst comes to the worst, we'll wait until morning and when it's daylight we can see what lies below and if there's a chance of escape through the window.'

'Do you think they'll send Benedict a ransom note?'

'I suppose they might. Who knows what Dalby has in mind? He deserves to be sent to prison for a very long time.'

How long they sat together in the cold and semi-darkness Rose did not know. She lost count of time and the feeling in her hands and feet. In the end it seemed unlikely that anyone would come and bring them anything to eat or drink. In desperation and out of complete exhaustion, Jago lay down on the palliasse and Rose curled up beside him in an attempt to keep him warm. He fell asleep almost immediately but Rose was wide awake, listening to every sound in the old building from the creaks of the contracting wood to the scrabble of rats and mice behind the skirting boards. Eventually, however, she dozed off and slept fitfully until dawn, when she awakened with a start at the sound of footsteps on the stairs and a heavy tread outside the door. She snapped into a sitting position and scrambled to her feet as the door opened slowly, creaking on rusty hinges.

A girl edged her way into the room. In one hand she carried a jug of what smelled like tea and tucked under her arm was a small loaf of bread. She scuttled across the room and set them down on the table. She turned to leave but Rose barred her way.

'Who sent you here?' Rose demanded. 'Give me the key.'

The girl was probably fourteen or fifteen but small and ill-nourished. Her clothes were patched, worn and in need of a wash, and she looked as though she could do with a bath. Her long light brown hair was matted and she might have been pretty if she smiled instead of scowling. She clutched the key to her flat chest and backed away.

'Tolley is downstairs. If I cries out he'll come to my aid. You don't want to get on the wrong side of Tolley.'

'Who are you?' Rose asked in desperation. Anything to keep the girl talking so that she might find out where they were being kept prisoner. 'My name is Rose.'

'What's it to you who I am?'

'What do people call you?'

'Persistent, ain't you? I suppose it won't hurt. I'm Jess and I was told to bring you bread and tea, that's all. Now I got to go.'

'At least tell me where we are, Jess. We've been kidnapped by an evil man called Crouch. I believe he works for Montague Dalby.'

Jess backed towards the door. 'I don't know nothing about them. I does what Tolley tells me.' She glanced at Jago, who was waking up slowly. 'What's up with him?'

'He's not well. He needs warmth and good food and a change of clothes.'

Jess laughed, although there was no humour in the sound. 'Tell him this ain't a posh hotel. As for where you are, look out of the window and tell me what you see.'

Rose did as she asked. 'I see wharfs and barges. I see the river and down below there's a yard filled with what looks like rubbish.'

'That's all you know. I don't know who you are except for the fact that you've never done a day's work in your life. You've had a bed of roses, so far, Rose.' Jess laughed at her own joke. 'That rubbish is worth a fortune when it's sold on the black market, and don't ask me what that is, because I don't know. I got to go, Rose. But I dare say they'll send me with your dinner at some time today or even tomorrow. I just does what I'm told.' Jess left the room, locking the door behind her.

Jago scrambled to his feet. 'Is that food on the table?'

Rose picked up the bread and examined it for mould, but to her surprise it was still warm from the oven. She broke it in half, and then in half again, which she divided into two portions. 'We'd better keep some for later as we don't know when Jess will bring more food.'

'I could have tackled her, Rose. Why didn't you wake me sooner? She looked as if a puff of wind would blow her over.'

'Maybe, but she has a brute called Tolley waiting for her downstairs. I think he might do us both a mischief if we tried to get away. We have to bide our time, Jago.' Rose bit off a chunk of bread and chewed it slowly. Even as she swallowed the food she felt her energy and optimism start to return. She sipped the hot, sweet tea from the jug.

'Don't they have cups or plates?' Jago said through a mouthful of bread.

'It seems not, but the tea is still quite hot, so they haven't come far. Have a drink – it will make it easier to eat the dry bread.'

Jago obliged, pulling a face. 'I prefer coffee. Madame Laurent used to make really good coffee.'

Rose took the jug from him and sipped. 'You've spent so much time locked up for one reason or another, but I'll get us out of here, Jago. Just be patient.'

'Maybe we could bribe that girl to take a message to Benedict.' Jago took another bite of the bread and chewed thoughtfully.

'The only problem with that is that neither of us has any money. I can't believe that I set out for a walk in London with nothing in my purse. I haven't even got any jewellery or anything she might want.'

'She looked very poor to me. And she needed a bath.'

'I expect we smell a bit after spending the night here. Maybe Jess is the victim of her upbringing, but she was right in one thing. I have never had to work to earn my living, and I have taken for granted that I get all my clothes and meals paid for by Papa. I've visited the poor people in the village and taken baskets of food to the neediest, but I never gave it a second thought. When we get home I will try to do better, Jago. I really will.'

'If we get home,' Jago stuffed the last of his piece of bread into his mouth. 'They might dump us in the river after the court case, Rose. There's no knowing what Monty might do, given half a chance, even though he knows now that I am not a Hanbury. We've either got to escape or persuade Jess to take a message to Benedict. It's as simple as that.'

Rose sat down at the table and drank some more

tea. She stared out of the window, wondering exactly what was packed away in the crates and tea chests down below in the yard. There might be a significant reward if the haul was reported to the police or the customs officers. 'I wonder if Dalby knows what's down there in the yard,' she said softly.

Jago was suddenly alert. 'He seems to be well in with the criminals who deal in the black market, as that girl said. He had dealings with Colbert, but has obviously escaped arrest in France. He must be cleverer than I thought.'

'Whatever is in the yard must be worth a fortune. Maybe that's why Dalby has been so eager to discredit Rivers and dispose of us. Your mama thought he was after the money you would inherit from your father's estate in Ceylon.'

'Except that Leonard Hanbury was not my father,' Jago said gloomily. 'I am the son of a French villain and the young girl he wronged.'

'You mustn't think like that, Jago,' Rose said urgently. 'Blanche didn't want to give you up, and Lucy has loved you just as much as if you were her natural-born son. It's unfortunate that she married Hector Dalby and you had to suffer at the hands of Montague, who is more of a criminal than we imagined.'

Jago's gloomy expression lightened. 'If we could find evidence to link him with whatever is down there it might be enough to send him to prison, never mind proving his false accusations against Benedict.

We've got to get out of here, Rose. We need to move quickly.'

'I agree, but first I want to find out exactly what is in those crates and tea chests.'

'How are you going to do that? We're locked in.'

Rose stood up and went over to the window. She lifted the sash. 'Not completely.'

'You can't climb down there, Rose. You'll break your neck. I'll go.'

'No, Jago. You haven't recovered your full strength and if you fall there will be no one to help you.'

'You can't climb in those long skirts.'

Rose tucked her skirt into her belt. 'There's always a way. I think I look quite oriental, like the Indian dancers we saw at the Great Exhibition.'

'I don't know what you're talking about,' Jago said moodily. 'Let me go, please.'

But Rose already had one leg over the sill. 'Keep watch. If you hear anyone coming, call out.' She took a deep breath and closed her eyes as she clung on, desperately feeling for a foothold. Despite her brave words she was terrified of heights, but there was no going back now. She opened her eyes and reached for the iron drainpipe. The cold metal numbed her fingers and she glanced down, checking that the pipe ran all the way to the ground. There was nothing for it now but to take a chance. She swung her body so that her feet curled around the pipe and she released her grip on the sill. For a moment she hung suspended, her free hand clutching at thin air not once but twice, missing each time.

'Hold on, Rose.' Jago leaned out of the window. 'You're almost there. Try again.'

She had lost all feeling in her right hand as it clutched the drainpipe and she was cold, so cold. Jago's words echoed in her head and she made one last almighty effort.

Chapter Twenty-Two

Rose was never to remember the last part of that perilous descent to the back yard, but somehow she found herself standing on a pile of wooden boxes, from where she managed to slither to the ground. Quite what she had expected to find in the barrels and tea chests she did not know, but it was a surprise to discover that there were bolts of cloth, some of it silk and chintz, in the tea chests, which were stamped on the outside 'Produce of Ceylon', and the oak barrels filled with alcohol. The fact that no effort had been put into disguising the contents made it seem unlikely that all this was contraband, and she remembered hearing her father say that the lowering of taxes had largely put a stop to smuggling. Bearing all this in mind, she suspected that the goods were part of a ship's cargo that had been purloined and, as Jess had suggested, would be sold illegally. With his connections to the importation of tea from his stepmother's family's plantation, Rose suspected that this was a profitable sideline for Montague Dalby, and one he would not want the authorities to know about.

Curiosity satisfied, her next move was to find a way into the building through the back door so that she could release Jago before Jess and Tolley descended upon them again. She found the door eventually, but it was locked. She searched for a suitable implement and found a broken brick, which she used to smash one of the glass panes. Fortunately, the key was still in the lock and she managed to open the door and slip inside. There was no way of knowing whether anyone else lived in the building, but Rose was past feeling nervous. Her success in conquering her fear of heights had made her bold and she made her way quietly to the staircase. It seemed much longer than a few hours since she had been forced to ascend the rickety staircase in semi-darkness but now daylight filtered through a filthy fanlight over the front door, revealing the rotten boards and broken banister rail.

Once again their captors had been remiss, leaving the key in the lock, and Rose was able to open the door. Jago rushed across the room and hugged her so that she could hardly breathe.

'I thought you must have fallen, Rose. I leaned out of the window but I couldn't see you. I was imagining all sorts of things.'

'Well, I didn't fall, as you can see. We'd better get

out of here before Jess and that man return to check on us.' Rose wriggled free from Jago's frantic grasp and she crossed the floor to close the window. 'It will take them a few moments to realise that one of us managed to get down to the yard. It will be obvious that we know what's being stored down there.'

'What is it? Tell me.'

'I'm quite certain it was goods that never reached their proper destination.'

'Do you think that Monty was profiting from the illegal sale of them?'

'It seems likely, but we'd better go quickly. I don't fancy meeting Tolley on the stairs. I can imagine that he looks like a great bear with a shaggy beard and unkempt hair.'

'I'm starving, Rose. The first thing I want is to get breakfast.'

'I'm sure Mrs Pilbeam's cook will be only too happy to oblige, but we have to find our way back to Doughty Street. I've no idea where we are, except that we're by the river.' Rose led the way downstairs. She opened the front door and looked up and down the narrow alley before stepping outside, followed by Jago. She hesitated. 'If we walk that way, along the main streets, we might bump into Jess and Tolley, but if we follow the river as far as possible we might miss them.'

'I think we should find a policeman,' Jago said anxiously. 'We don't even know where we are.'

Rose set off towards the wharf area. 'No, but we

can ask someone. Let's get as far away from here as possible.'

She quickened her pace with Jago close on her heels. The rainfall yesterday had left everything sparkling in the early morning sunshine, creating sun-pennies on the river as it flowed down to the sea on the ebb tide. The wharfs were busy with dockers unloading barges and lightermen going about their daily business of ferrying people to and from ships moored mid-channel. No one took much notice of them and when Rose judged that they had gone far enough upstream she took the first turn on the right and headed north into Upper Thames Street, not that either of them had any idea where this was in relation to Doughty Street. Rose was wary of asking strangers the way, but eventually Jago spotted a police constable and he hurried across the street, weaving his way recklessly through the traffic and narrowly avoiding a collision with a brewer's dray. Rose followed more slowly and arrived in time to see the constable take a notebook from his pocket.

'Are you Miss Rose Northwood?' he said, eyeing her up and down.

'Yes, Constable, and this is Jago Hanbury. We were kidnapped and held prisoner.'

'You'd better come to the police station with me, miss. There's been a search going on for you two.'

'We need to get back to Doughty Street, but we haven't any money,' Jago said nervously. 'And I'm hungry.'

The young constable grinned. 'I'm sure they can find you a cup of tea and a bun or something, sir. Come with me and we'll do this by the book. Someone will take you home after the formalities.'

Rose sighed with relief. 'Thank you, Officer. It's been a trying few hours and I have something to report.'

In the police station they were asked to give a statement to the desk sergeant, but when Rose mentioned Montague Dalby they were hustled into a more private office and interviewed by another officer, who identified himself as Detective Sergeant Somerton. Rose was only too happy to tell him everything that had happened from the moment they were abducted by Crouch outside the British Museum, to their imprisonment in the near-derelict property. She went on to describe the yard piled high with goods that were almost certainly stolen.

'Do you know the address of the house where you were kept prisoner, Miss Northwood?' Detective Sergeant Somerton eyed her sternly and she had a feeling he did not entirely believe her.

'No, sir. It was dark when we were taken there and I was so relieved to have escaped that all I wanted to do was to get as far away as possible.'

'So you can't give me the exact location of the stolen property?'

Rose bowed her head. She was beginning to feel

weak and exhausted. A combination of very little to eat and even less sleep was sapping her energy. 'No, sir.'

'Stew Lane,' Jago said triumphantly. 'I noticed the name because I am so hungry, Officer. Could I have something to eat and drink?'

'Stew Lane.' Somerton wrote it down in his notebook. He picked up a bell and rang it. 'We've sent word to Doughty Street to inform your people that you are safe.' He looked up as the door opened and the desk sergeant looked into the room. 'Hoskins, will you be kind enough to bring two cups of tea and some buns or biscuits? Anything that will prevent Mr Hanbury from dying of starvation.'

'Yes, sir. Right away.' Hoskins closed the door behind him.

Somerton rose to his feet. 'I will have to leave you here for a while, but you will be sent home as soon as we can arrange transport for you.'

'Are you sending officers to Stew Lane?' Rose asked eagerly. 'If so, and they happen to find Jess there, please be lenient with her. She did her best to look after us.'

Somerton hesitated in the doorway. 'She will get a fair hearing, Miss Northwood. As do all our suspects.' He left the door ajar as he headed for the front desk, shouting instructions to muster a raiding party on the property in Stew Lane.

'I'm worried,' Rose said in a low voice. 'When Dalby finds out that we've reported his activities to the police he will be even more determined to win his case against Rivers.'

'He wanted to keep me from testifying in court, but he's failed. I'll tell them what a brute he is and how he apprenticed me to a sea captain with a bad reputation, where I was cruelly treated, beaten and starved. I was lucky to survive, Rose. It's a miracle I'm here, largely thanks to you, as I've said so many times before.'

Rose reached out to take his hand in hers. 'I know, Jago. You've had a terrible time. I wish I could make it up to you, but I can't.'

'You can and you already have, Rose. You are my dear friend and I'll never forget how you climbed down that drainpipe this morning.' Jago laughed. 'I can't wait to see Cousin Benedict's face when I tell him what you did.'

Rose was prevented from replying by the desk sergeant entering the office carrying a tray of tea and a plate of sticky buns. Jago fell upon them eagerly.

'Careful, lad. Don't choke yourself,' Sergeant Hoskins said, smiling. 'We can't have a death on our hands in the police station.'

Rose laughed. 'You don't know what a relief it is to be here, Sergeant.' She sipped her tea and sat back on the hard wooden chair. It was hardly luxury but it seemed so in comparison to the discomfort of the night she and Jago had just endured. Soon they would be back safe in Doughty Street. She knew that Rivers would be angry, but at least she could return Jago to him unharmed.

Jago seemed oblivious to anything other than satisfying his hunger. He munched his bun and washed it down with a mouthful of tea. 'Try one, Rose. They are very good.'

She smiled and took a sugar-coated bun from the plate. She shot a sideways glance at Jago. He could bounce back from almost any situation. His courage and resilience never ceased to amaze her. She had a sudden vision of Felix and her eyes filled with tears. She was sure that, had he lived, he and Jago would have been the best of friends.

'What's the matter, Rose?' Jago demanded anxiously. 'Why are you sad? We're safe now.'

She managed a watery smile. 'When we go home I want you to be very kind to my mama, Jago. She hasn't seen much of you, but she was very impressed. It would be lovely if you could spend a little time with her.'

Jago nodded wisely. 'I know, Rose. I think I remind her of your brother, who died. That must have made her very sad.'

'It did and it still does, particularly at Christmas.'

'I think Madame de Fontenay is sad, too. I can't think of her as my mama, even though I know that's true, but I do like her. Maybe by the time next Christmas comes round we could share it with her as well. I don't like people I love to be unhappy.' He took another bun. 'These are really delicious. I wonder what Mrs Pilbeam's cook has made for luncheon.'

Rose glanced over her shoulder as the door opened and she jumped to her feet. 'Rivers! You came quickly.'

He smiled. 'Are you pleased to see me, by any chance, Rose?' He laid his hands on her shoulders, looking into her eyes, his smile replaced with a concerned frown. 'Are you all right? Did they hurt you?'

Rose was overcome with relief. She sensed that he cared as much for her as for Jago, but she managed to resist the impulse to hug him and she turned away. 'I'm perfectly all right and so is Jago, except that he's hungry.'

Rivers gave Jago a playful slap on the back. 'You can't keep out of trouble, can you? If I take my eyes off you for a second you are in some kind of fix, and this time you've taken Rose with you.'

Rose tried not to feel envious of the deep affection that Rivers demonstrated for his young cousin. She sighed. 'Who would have thought that the British Museum would be a dangerous place?'

'How did you come to get into a cab with a strange man?' Rivers demanded, frowning. 'After all you've been through in the past, weren't you even a tiny bit suspicious, Rose?'

She tossed her head. 'It was pouring with rain. Neither of us had any money for a cab and Crouch seemed to be a respectable gentleman.'

'It's not her fault, Cousin Benedict,' Jago said hotly. 'Rose has been a real heroine. She climbed down a drainpipe to get into the back yard. She found stolen property.'

'I'm sorry, Rose. I didn't mean to sound harsh,' Rivers said with an apologetic smile. 'I've been out of my mind with worry about the pair of you. I know what Dalby is capable of. At least I thought I did, but now I think he's really dangerous. I want you both to return to Abbotsford and leave me to get on with my business here.'

Rose opened her mouth to argue, but Rivers shook his head. 'We'll discuss it later. Come along both of you. I'll take you back to Doughty Street.'

Rose was too stunned to argue. Being sent home was the last thing she had expected, and she turned to Jago, who appeared to be just as surprised.

'That's not fair, Benedict,' he protested. 'We've given the police information that could well lead to Monty's arrest on criminal activities. If he was proved to be totally dishonest there would be no need for you to go to court.'

Rivers held the door open. 'You can tell me all about it in the cab. Come along. We're in the way here. We don't want to get arrested for obstructing the law.'

'You're not being fair, Rivers.' Rose marched past him, narrowly avoiding the desk sergeant who was in the hallway. She turned her head to glare at Rivers. 'Jago and I have been through too much to go running off home like scared rabbits. We are here to stay until you are exonerated and a free man.'

The desk sergeant winked at Rivers. 'I should take heed if I were you, guv. The young lady has a mind of her own.'

'Of that I'm very well aware,' Rivers said ruefully. 'Come, Rose. I promise to listen to whatever you have to say.'

'I should think so, too.' Rose sailed past the sergeant with a nod and a smile. 'Thank you for the tea and buns, Sergeant. You saved our lives.'

Sergeant Hoskins saluted. 'If only things were that easy, miss. Good luck to you, I say.'

Mrs Pilbeam and Will welcomed them home with genuine smiles of relief.

'You poor things.' Mrs Pilbeam glanced at Rose's soiled gown and scuffed shoes. 'You look as though you've had a hard time.'

'I am so sorry,' Will added earnestly. 'I should have taken better care of you both.'

'It really isn't anyone's fault,' Rose said firmly. 'My mistake was to go out in London without any money in my purse. None of this would have happened had I been able to hail a cab.'

'I'm the man. I should have looked after you better, Rose.' Jago puffed out his chest. 'I'll know better next time.'

Rivers followed them into the parlour. 'We will all be more careful from now on. Rose has told me about what she discovered on the property in Stew Lane where they were kept overnight. It seems that Dalby has been involved in illegal trading, although that's no surprise to me. If the police are able to prove that he organised the theft of certain shipments before they were even landed it will make his case against me easier to dispute.'

'I have some news for you, Benedict.' Will went to stand with his back to the fireplace. 'I found out this morning that the ship that Dalby chose for Jago has been lost at sea with all hands. It is now an insurance claim at Lloyd's.' He turned to Jago, who had slumped down on the sofa. 'It looks as if the ill treatment and injuries you suffered saved your life, or you might have been on board when it went down.'

Mrs Pilbeam threw up her hands. 'How terrible. But thank the Lord you are here safe with us now, Jago. Cook has prepared a special meal, which we will have as soon as you are ready.'

Jago grinned. 'I'm ready now, ma'am.'

Rose turned to Will, frowning. 'Are you suggesting that the loss of the ship was suspicious?'

'That is the general consensus of opinion. It's totally illegal, of course, but some ship owners who are in difficulties have been known to use this method of collecting insurance money.'

Rivers shook his head. 'I thought that practice had gone out in the last century.'

'One would hope so, Benedict.' Will looked from one to the other. 'But I don't think you'll be surprised to learn the name of the person who owned the ship.'

'Do you mean Montague Dalby?' Rose said aghast.

Will nodded. 'He attempted to conceal the fact, but I have proof. After today's happenings and your evidence, Rose and Jago, I think we have enough proof to send him to prison for a very long time, and you'll be exonerated, Benedict.'

Mrs Pilbeam reached for the bell pull. 'I think we should have luncheon. All this excitement is too much for me, and Jago looks quite pale.'

'Thank you, ma'am,' Jago said with a heavy sigh. 'My cousin doesn't realise how we suffered last night and first thing this morning in that dreadful house. Rose was so brave when she climbed out of the window and slid down the drainpipe. She is a real heroine.'

'Don't tell me more. I feel quite faint.' Mrs Pilbeam leaned back in her chair, closing her eyes. 'Pass me my smelling salts, please, Will. The bottle on the mantelshelf.'

Will seemed at a loss, but Rose spotted the small glass bottle and she reached for it, taking out the cork and handing it to Mrs Pilbeam, who sniffed the contents and sneezed.

'Where is Nancy?' she said, sitting upright. 'Luncheon should be on the table by now. Ring the bell for me, Rose. That girl is probably flirting with the butcher's boy. I know what goes on behind my back.'

Nancy answered the summons almost immediately

and received a sharp rebuke from her mistress, which did not seem to surprise her.

'Luncheon is ready, ma'am.' Nancy backed out of the room.

'Help me up, Will.' Mrs Pilbeam struggled to her feet, resting her hand in Will's. 'All this excitement isn't good for my poor heart. Pour me a glass of sherry, Benedict. I will sip it at table. You may imbibe if you wish, all of you, except Jago, of course. And I don't want to hear any more of your experiences last night, my boy. Please keep them to yourself.'

'Yes, ma'am. I'm sorry to have upset you, ma'am.' Jago followed Will as he helped his aunt from the parlour.

Rivers caught hold of Rose's hand. 'Rose, my dear, much as I would like to have you here to support me, I think Jago would be better off at home in Abbotsford. I don't want to cause Mrs Pilbeam any more distress than the poor lady has already suffered.'

'I understand, but I really would rather stay here with you, Rivers.'

He raised her hand to his lips. 'I can't risk you or Jago being used as a pawn by a man who will stop at nothing in order to further his own ends. I think a written statement from Jago might be all that is needed, if at all. I will feel much happier if I can be certain you are both safe.'

Rose met his intense gaze with a sigh. 'All right, Rivers. I'll do it. I'll take Jago back to his mama.

If Mrs Hanbury agrees I will stay there with him until you return. Does that make you happy?'

He stroked her cheek with the tip of his forefinger. 'Not happy, but at least I can stop worrying about you.' He laughed. 'Don't make me say more now, Rose. When I can speak to you as a man exonerated from any wrongdoing I have so much I want to say to you, but it will have to wait until then. Do you understand what I'm saying, Rose?'

Rose felt the blood rush to her cheeks. 'I think I do, Rivers.' She allowed him to lead her to the dining room where the others had already taken their seats.

Mrs Pilbeam gave her a searching look. 'I hope you aren't coming down with a fever, Rose, my dear. Your cheeks are very flushed.'

Rose would much rather have stayed in London until after the trial, but with the new evidence against Dalby it seemed likely that the hearing might be postponed indefinitely. Will took a statement from Jago, who was extremely unhappy about being sent home. However, all his protests fell on deaf ears. Next day, after Detective Sergeant Somerton confirmed that there was no need for either Rose or Jago to remain in London, Rivers took them to the station and saw them ensconced in a first-class carriage. He promised to telegraph Lucy to advise her of their return and to arrange a carriage to meet them on arrival in Abbotsford. Fortunately, there was no need to change trains and in three hours or so they would be safe at Longfleet Hall. Rose declined his offer to send a telegram to her papa informing him of her return to Dorset, but she promised to visit the vicarage as soon as possible so that she could tell them in person without causing her parents any worry.

As promised, there was a carriage waiting for them at Abbotsford station and Harry, the more junior footman, gathered up their luggage and loaded it on the back of the barouche. Rose acknowledged Joe Jenkins, the stationmaster, who welcomed her home, and she spotted his wife, Clara, hanging out the washing in the garden of their house. Rose's heart sank because Clara was known to be a great friend of Martha Huggins. No doubt she would be off hotfoot to spread the news that Miss Rose had come home. Rose came to the conclusion that she had better send a note to her father as soon as she arrived at Longfleet.

She took a deep breath of the salty sea air, which was delightfully fresh after the soot-laden mixture of odours in London. Jago seemed to have forgotten his reluctance to return, and he bounded on ahead to open the carriage door before the footman had a chance to do so. Rose shook her head at him as she climbed in and made herself comfortable in the luxurious interior.

'You should allow the servants to do their job, Jago.'

He slumped down opposite her. 'You're just

crotchety because you had to leave Benedict in London. I might be young but I am not blind, Rose. Anyone can see that there is something going on between you.'

Rose laid her finger on her lips as Harry hurried to put up the step and close the carriage door. 'Don't tell everyone, Jago,' Rose said, smiling. 'Let it be our secret. It's just mutual attraction between your cousin and me, that's all.'

Jago laughed. 'You can't kid me, Rose. I've had people telling me untruths all my life and I know when I'm being had.'

'Don't let your mama hear you talking such common language. She'll think I am to blame.'

'You're a vicar's daughter. You could only teach me hymns and biblical tracts.'

'Sadly, that is not true. I am a poor example of my upbringing, but I trust you to keep what you know to yourself.'

'Of course,' Jago said smugly. 'How are we going to amuse ourselves at Longfleet, Rose? It's going to be so very dull.'

Rose shrugged. 'I doubt that, Jago. Trouble seems to follow you around. We'll just have to do our best to survive until your erstwhile stepbrother is arrested and Rivers is cleared of the charges that Dalby raised against him.'

'I'm not very good at being patient,' Jago said ruefully. 'But I will try, Rose. I promise.'

Chapter Twenty-Three

Lucy was delighted to have Jago home, but she was appalled to learn of their abduction and imprisonment in the near-derelict house. Rose withheld the worst parts of the account and Jago refrained from comment, although he admitted afterwards that it had been difficult to keep quiet. Rose decided that it was important to keep him occupied, although now he was virtually back to a normal state of fitness it was going to be hard.

Next day she decided to go home and she invited Jago to accompany her. He agreed without hesitation and sent to the stables for two horses to be saddled and brought round to the front entrance.

'You should ride side-saddle, you know, Rose.' Jago watched with obvious disapproval as Rose mounted the animal with apparent ease. 'It's not ladylike to sit astride like a man.'

Rose laughed. 'Jago, you surprise me. I didn't think you were so conventional.'

'Maybe . . .' Jago shrugged. 'But I think Benedict would agree with me.'

Rose flicked the reins and dug her heels gently into the horse's flanks. 'Walk on.' She turned her head to smile at Jago. 'I do what I want, Jago. I think Rivers has realised that by now. Come on, I'll race you to the vicarage.'

Jago's reply was lost as the wind whipped Rose's hair from beneath her bonnet and tugged at her skirts, but the feeling of freedom that came with riding a spirited animal was exhilarating and she was a capable horsewoman. Lady Buckingham had her faults, but she had been generous when it came to letting Rose and Marianne make use of the horses in The Manor stables. Marianne was a careful rider and preferred a sedate trot across the fields, whereas Rose enjoyed a long gallop and even took a few fences, given the chance.

Rose glanced over her shoulder and saw that Jago was about to catch up with her. She urged her horse to go faster and she reached the vicarage just ahead of him. They dismounted and took the horses to the stables at the back of the house, where they rubbed the animals down and left water within their reach before heading into the house, using the back entrance in preference to the front door.

When Rose breezed into the kitchen, Cook almost dropped the saucepan that she was about to place on the hob.

'Lawks, Miss Rose. You gave me a proper fright. What are you doing coming in the servants' way?'

Rose laughed. 'I'm sorry, Mrs Philpot. We rode here and it was quicker to come in the back door than walk all the way round to the front of the house.'

Cook glanced at Jago. 'Goodness me, is that the same boy who arrived here half dead on Christmas Eve?'

Jago stepped forward and proffered his hand. 'How d'you do, Cook? I hope you've made some of your delicious jam tarts. I dream about them, you know.'

Cook's cheeks reddened with pleasure. 'Flattery will get you everywhere, young man. It's good to see you fully recovered. I rarely get above stairs so I don't know what goes on until young Winnie tells me.'

'We are home for a while, Mrs Philpot,' Rose said quickly. 'But I'm staying at Longfleet Hall until Jago's cousin returns from London.'

'Now, that Mr Rivers is a charming gentleman,' Cook said, smiling. 'He took the trouble to come below stairs and introduce himself to us. Not many people would be so thoughtful.'

Rose was surprised, but she did not want to get into an involved conversation, which could go on for a very long time if Cook was given her head.

'Jago and I will be here for luncheon, if that's not too much trouble, Mrs Philpot. I know it's short notice.'

'It's no trouble, Miss Rose. I'm glad to see you back safe and sound.' Cook turned her attention to the pan on the stove and Rose took the opportunity to slip away, followed by Jago.

Upstairs, the first person Rose saw was Emily, who uttered a cry of delight and ran towards her with her arms outstretched.

'Rose, you've come home, and you've brought the boy with you.'

Rose gave her a hug. 'Yes, but we're staying at Longfleet until Rivers comes home.'

'That's odd. Why would you do that? Don't you want to live with us any more, Rose?'

'She's just doing me a favour,' Jago said hastily. 'Rose and I were kidnapped in London. We were almost murdered.'

Emily gave him a condescending look. 'You can't *almost* be murdered. You either are killed or you're not. As you are both standing here, I take it that you survived.'

Rose laughed. 'You take things so literally, Emmie. Where is Marianne? And Papa – is he at home?'

'Marianne has gone to Dorchester to be fitted for her wedding gown and Papa went out an hour or so ago. I suppose he'll be back in time for luncheon. But Mama is in the morning parlour. She's taken to coming downstairs when she feels so inclined. I'm sure she would love to see you both.'

'Of course. That sounds promising. She usually recovers a little in the spring, and the daffodils in the churchyard are better than ever. I noticed them as I rode past.'

'Come along then, Rose. You, too, boy.' Emily started off in the direction of the morning parlour.

'I have a name. I'm Jago.' He fell into step beside Rose. 'Why is she being horrid to me? Just because she's pretty doesn't mean she can speak to me like that.'

'I think she likes you, Jago,' Rose said, smiling. 'Take no notice and she'll come round. Mama will be very pleased to see you.'

Grace's smile when she saw Jago proved Rose's point and left Emily pouting.

'Pull up a stool for Jago, Emily,' Grace said eagerly. 'Come and sit by me and tell me all about your time in London.'

Rose shook her head, frowning. 'Only the good bits, Jago. Remember what I said before we left Longfleet.'

'Why are you whispering, Rose?' Grace demanded. 'Of course I am more than delighted to see you, my dear. But I remember that Jago has been very unwell and now he looks the picture of health.' She patted the stool that Emily dumped unceremoniously at the side of her mother's chair.

Somewhat reluctantly Jago went to sit beside her.

'Why is he the favourite?' Emily demanded in a low voice. 'He's done nothing other than cause trouble, and I've been a good daughter.'

Rose slipped her arm around Emily's shoulders. 'Of course you have, and Mama knows that. I think Jago reminds her of Felix and that gives her some comfort, but it doesn't mean she loves you less, Emmie.'

'He's not family.'

'No, but he's had a hard time and we need to be kind to him. You can do that, can't you?'

'I suppose so.'

'He thinks you're very pretty,' Rose added, smiling.

Emily shot her a sideways glance and shrugged, but Rose could see that she was pleased. The last thing Rose needed was squabbling between Emily and Jago. The next few days before the court case were going to be fraught enough from her point of view without her younger sister having tantrums. However, Emily seemed mollified by Jago's description of her and she went to sit close to them. She even joined in the conversation, which was a relief, and Rose left the room quietly, hoping to have a few words with her father before everyone gathered in the dining room for luncheon. She was about to go to her old room when she heard the key turn in the latch and her father walked into the entrance hall. He saw her immediately and his lined face crinkled into a smile.

'Rose, my dear. You've come home.'

'I'm staying at Longfleet for a while, Papa, but after that I will return home for good.'

Matthew took off his gloves, hat and greatcoat, and handed them to Winnie, who had appeared as if summoned by magic.

'Come into my study, Rose. We'll have a chat before luncheon.' Matthew turned to Winnie. 'I trust luncheon will be on time?'

Winnie bobbed a curtsey. 'Yes, sir.'

He nodded. 'Excellent.'

Rose followed him into his study, where he took his seat behind his cluttered desk. 'Now then, Rose. What have you got to tell me? How is Mr Rivers' effort to clear his name progressing?'

Rose sat down and launched into a full explanation of the events that had brought her back to Abbotsford and why she had chosen to stay at Longfleet Hall until after the court case. Matthew listened attentively.

'I think you've done the right thing, Rose. It's a bad business all round, but hopefully it will come to an end very soon.'

'We can only hope that Dalby doesn't find a way to evade justice, Papa. He is a bad man and will stop at nothing to achieve his ends.'

'You've done well. Rose. We can only hope that the case comes to a satisfactory conclusion.'

'And you don't mind if I stay at Longfleet for a while, Pa?'

'One day I will lose you, Rose, as I will all my daughters,' Matthew said with a wry smile. He glanced at the ornately carved wall clock. 'I think it is time for luncheon. Shall we go and rescue Jago from being cross-examined by your mama and Emily?' He stood up and walked slowly round the desk to open the door just as Winnie came hurrying along the hallway.

'Luncheon is served, Vicar.'

'Thank you, Winnie.' Matthew proffered his arm to Rose. 'I am as hungry as a hunter. Your exploits have sharpened my appetite.'

To Rose's surprise, her mother joined them for the meal although she retired to her room when they had finished eating, apparently exhausted by her efforts. Matthew went back to his study to write some urgent letters. Rose was about to suggest that she and Jago left for Longfleet when Tom and Marianne returned from their trip to Dorchester. There was no getting away early now, and they went to the drawing room where Winnie obliged with a tray of coffee and cake for Marianne, who said that travelling to town, together with trying on her bridal gown, had made her hungry.

When they were all seated, and at Marianne's request, Rose found herself relating the events of the past few days in even more detail. Tom was obviously horrified, and Marianne's cheeks paled as Rose told them of the kidnap, with additional details from Jago, which were rather exaggerated but created a sense of the fear they had endured.

'You don't think that Dalby and his men will try to abduct Jago again, do you, Rose?' Marianne clutched Tom's arm, her eyes wide with anxiety. 'They won't come here, will they?'

'That's why we are staying at Longfleet Hall,' Rose said stoutly. 'There are plenty of servants there to protect us.'

'Monty had better not try,' Jago added, fisting his hands. 'I won't stand for any more of his nonsense.'

'You didn't save Rose last time.' Emily eyed him suspiciously. 'I think you are all talk.'

'Emily, don't be rude.' Marianne frowned.

'But she's right in a way. You are just one, Jago. If Montague Dalby is as bad as you say, then he will have accomplices.'

'I agree with Marianne,' Tom said hastily. 'You do need to be very careful for the next few days especially, Rose. Particularly as you say that Dalby is involved in illegal dealings. No doubt he has accomplices or there might even be London gangs involved.'

'How did you get here today, Rose?' Marianne glanced out of the drawing-room window. 'I don't see a vehicle outside.'

'We rode,' Jago said proudly. 'Rose is a good horsewoman.'

Rose smiled. 'Thank you, Jago. That's praise indeed, coming from you. Yes, we borrowed horses from Rivers' stables at Longfleet.'

'When you come again I think you should travel by carriage with a burly coachman and a footman to protect you.' Tom looked from Rose to Jago. 'It might be best if you leave now while there is plenty of daylight.'

'Surely it's not as serious as that, is it, Tom?' Marianne asked anxiously.

'It's better to err on the safe side, my love.' Tom smiled at Rose. 'We need you to be our maid of honour, Rose.'

She laughed. 'Don't worry. Nothing will keep me away from your wedding. But you are probably right, Tom. We will leave now and I promise to come in a carriage with an armed guard next time.'

'And a military escort,' Jago added, grinning. 'I've given my witness statement so I doubt if I am of much interest to my mother's stepson now. We are not related in any way, so he doesn't need me.'

'Unrelated?' Emily said sharply. 'I thought Montague Dalby was your stepbrother, Jago.'

Marianne held her finger to her lips, glaring at Emily and shaking her head. 'It's none of our business, Emmie.'

Emily stared at Jago, open-mouthed. 'If Dalby is your mama's stepson, but he isn't related to you,' she frowned, 'does that mean that Mrs Dalby isn't your mama, Jago?'

'As Marianne said, it's none of our business.' Tom rose from his seat. 'Come along, you two. I'll help you tack up your horses and set you on the road to Longfleet. We don't want any more trouble.'

'I only asked,' Emily said sulkily. 'Why don't you tell me things, Rose? I'm not a baby.'

Jago laid his hand on her arm. 'My actual mama is a French lady who lives in a château, and my pa is a French villain, who is probably in prison as we speak.'

There was a moment of shocked silence. Marianne's hands flew to cover her mouth and Tom placed his arm around her shoulders as if to protect her from such shocking news. Rose gazed at Emily, who was staring at Jago as if he had said something amazing.

'No, really? How exciting, Jago. Have you met them?'

Jago puffed out his chest. 'Of course I have. But I must say that my real mother is the lady who brought me up from a baby. She is Monty's stepmother, although I dare say she wishes she had never set eyes on him.'

Tom moved to Jago's side and patted him on the back. 'Well said, Jago. You do her credit.'

'Will you tell me about the French lady and her château when you come next time?' Emily said excitedly.

'I might.' Jago gave her a condescending smile. 'She is very beautiful.'

'Oh!' Emily's lips quivered. 'I suppose she must be.'

'But you are quite pretty,' Jago added casually.

Rose exchanged amused glances with Marianne. 'It's time we left, Jago. Tom is right. We had better start off for home, but we'll come again soon.' She rose to her feet and kissed her sisters before following Tom and Jago from the room.

As they rode back to Longfleet, Rose realised that she had not given enough thought to the possible dangers that might beset them. Dalby was undoubtedly a criminal and quite possibly not acting on his own. She knew now why Rivers had been so keen to send her and Jago to the relative safety of his country house. She decided that she had better think of a way to keep Jago occupied closer to home. He was, after all, just a boy, even though he had experienced things that would have terrified a grown man. She glanced at him as he rode beside her and she realised how fond she had grown of him. He had not taken Felix's place, but he had begun to heal the scar left on her heart after Felix died. She knew she must protect him, no matter what.

They arrived safely at Longfleet and Lucy greeted them with obvious relief. She waited until Jago had left the drawing room before turning to Rose with a concerned frown.

'I know I cannot wrap Jago up in cotton wool, but I am afraid for him while Montague is at large. I know Montague is my stepson, but I sincerely hope that he gets a custodial sentence for all the wrongs he has done.'

Rose nodded. 'I agree. We'll keep Jago safe between us.'

'But he must not realise we are doing so.' Lucy walked over to a small escritoire set beneath the window and took out a sheet of writing paper.

'I received this letter today, Rose. It comes from the manager of the tea plantation I inherited from Leonard, my first husband. I have decided to sell and invest the money elsewhere. I know that Montague has his eye on my fortune, but I am not the foolish woman he took me for.'

'I can see that,' Rose said with a smile. 'I'm sure you're right to sell, unless you decide to move back to live in Ceylon.'

'No, that isn't my plan, Rose. I will buy a property and I will have enough to live on comfortably, as well as taking care of Jago. I know that Benedict is happy to have us living here, but there will come a time, fairly soon, I think, when he will want to marry and have a family of his own.'

Rose was suddenly alert. 'You think he has chosen a bride?'

'I can't be sure, of course, but I have my suspicions. Anyway, that isn't what I wanted to talk to you about. I can do so now that Jago is out of the room.'

'What is it, ma'am? You know you can tell me anything.'

'I have to return to Colombo to finalise the sale and sign the necessary documents. It's important that I do it in person or I am afraid I might not get the best price. I have to prove that I am the legal owner in order to finalise the deal.'

'It sounds a wonderfully romantic place. Wouldn't you like to live there again?'

Lucy shook her head. 'The plantation is high up in the hills. It's isolated and it always seemed to be raining, which is good for the crop, but not much fun if you are stuck on a remote hill station. I believe the tea export industry is rapidly gaining momentum, but I am not a businesswoman. I would rather take the profit now, however small, and at least I will be a free woman.'

'Didn't Montague's father make sure you were well provided for?'

'The estate has gone to Monty. My late husband thought I was well provided for with the money I inherited from my papa and from Leonard. My aim is to be independent and to keep what is mine for Jago and myself. I don't care about the Dalby estate. Montague can have that with my blessing.'

'So when will you leave for Ceylon?'

'I don't want to desert Benedict, but there is nothing I can do for him. I intend to book passages for myself and Jago on the next ship bound for Colombo. By the time we return I hope that Benedict will have cleared his name and that Montague will be in prison.'

'What do you think Jago will say when you tell him?'

'He is still a child and I am his guardian. He will accompany me.'

Rose glanced over her shoulder to see Jago standing in the doorway. She could tell from his expression that he had overheard all or part of the conversation.

'Why are you going to Ceylon, Mama?' Jago demanded angrily.

'I'm sorry, Jago. I was going to tell you.' Lucy turned to face him. 'I have to sign away ownership on the plantation and it must be done in person. I'm taking you with me for your own sake.'

'I don't want to go with you, Mama. You can't make me.'

'You are under age, and I am responsible for you. I love you, Jago, and I want what's best for you. Besides which, we will have a wonderful sea voyage. It will be an adventure for you.'

'I love you, Mama. But you are not my real mother

and you cannot force me to go with you. If I have to leave here then I will return to Provence and stay with Madame de Fontenay.'

Lucy collapsed onto the nearest chair, her hands clasped over her mouth. 'You are so cruel, Jago. I have loved you as if you were my own child and now you turn on me.'

'That's not true, Mama. You are treating me as if I were a possession. You should have asked me if I wanted to accompany you, but the truth is that I don't. I'm sorry if it hurts you, and it doesn't mean I don't love you, but I am fourteen now. I am almost a man and I know what I want.'

Rose laid her hand on Lucy's shoulder. 'He's right, ma'am. Think of everything he suffered when you allowed Montague to send him to sea on that dreadful ship. I think he ought to be given the choice.'

Lucy jumped to her feet. 'You are both against me. It's too much to bear.' She ran from the room and slammed the door behind her.

'I didn't mean to upset her,' Jago said gloomily. 'But I want to stay here and make sure that Cousin Benedict doesn't suffer on my account.'

'It's not your fault that Montague accused him of wrongdoing.'

'I know that, Rose. But Benedict only became involved because of me. I want to see Monty put away so that he cannot do any more harm. If Mama wishes to return to Ceylon, that is her choice and I think she has her own specific reasons.'

'Why do you say it like that?' Rose asked, eyeing him curiously.

'Because I think there is a gentleman there that she rather likes. I was very young when we lived in the plantation house, but I remember Mr Derwent, the man who used to take us both out for jaunts in his carriage. He taught me to ride a pony and he always seemed to be around. Then Pa died and Mama met Mr Dalby, who was visiting Colombo on business. They were married within weeks and we sailed back to England. It was in the school holidays that I first met Monty.'

Rose sighed. 'It seems she has a good reason for returning to Ceylon to complete the sale of her property. After all, it will be the income she needs to keep herself, and you, come to that. I think you should go upstairs and talk to her, Jago.'

'I'll let her calm down first. Then I'll try to explain how I feel, but whatever happens, Rose, I am not going with her. Will you stay here with me until Benedict comes home?'

'Yes, of course I will. My family don't seem to mind. They are too taken up with Marianne's wedding plans to worry about me. Besides which, I rather like Longfleet Hall. It's a wonderful old house and we've yet to explore the grounds properly.'

'We could have the horses saddled early tomorrow morning and go for a long ride,' Jago said eagerly. 'One of the grooms told me there is an ice house close to the lake. I wonder when it was last used.'

'We'll find out tomorrow,' Rose said, smiling. 'But perhaps I ought to go upstairs and talk to Lucy before you try to apologise.' She held up her hand as he was about to argue. 'No, I don't blame you, Jago. However, it's obvious that Lucy does think of you as her son, and she loves you.'

'I know she does and I love her, too.'

Rose linked her hands in the crook of his arm. 'Then I have a suggestion. Let's go upstairs together and make things right. Neither of us wants to see her upset. All you have to do is to say you're sorry and reassure her.'

'I won't change my mind, Rose.'

'No, I know that. You are a stubborn boy, Jago. You remind me of Felix and of myself, too. But sometimes you have to put other people first, especially when you are the only thing they have in the world.'

'Apart from Mr Derwent in Ceylon,' Jago said with a mischievous grin.

'If you mention his name I promise I will not be responsible for my actions.' Rose frowned but her lips twitched as she tried to control the desire to giggle. 'Come on, Jago. Best foot forward, as Mama used to say.'

Chapter Twenty-Four

Jago made peace with Lucy, although he still refused to consider accompanying her to Colombo. She in turn agreed to postpone leaving until after the trial, although Rose suspected that Lucy hoped that, given time, Jago might change his mind. However, the next few days passed off without incident and were more enjoyable than Rose had expected. She and Jago rode around the estate and explored the ancient ice house, although there was only an empty underground chamber and a suspicion of wet mud in the centre to prove that once it had been filled with frozen lake water.

The day after that, they roamed further and had luncheon at the King's Arms in Dorchester, after which they rode back to Abbotsford and stopped for a couple of hours at the vicarage. Jago and Emily went for a walk, leaving Rose alone with Marianne.

'Have you heard anything from Benedict?' Marianne put down the stocking she had been mending. 'When is the trial taking place?'

'It's tomorrow, at midday, I think. I haven't heard anything from Rivers. I've been putting all my efforts into keeping Jago occupied. It takes my mind off what might or might not happen.'

'Surely you don't think that Benedict will lose the case, Rose?'

'All I know is that Montague Dalby managed to evade capture by the French police. The fact that he committed crimes in France and escaped punishment really bothers me, Marianne. It seems that he is a slippery character.'

'Is he at liberty now?'

'I don't know. I wish I did, although I suppose he will have to attend the trial, as he's the plaintiff. I'd give anything to sit in the public gallery, but I have to stay at Longfleet. Lucy wants to return to Colombo in order to complete the sale of her property. She tried to persuade Jago to accompany her but he refused, so there's been some tension between them.'

'He's a young man now,' Marianne said seriously. 'I'm sure he has a mind of his own.'

'He has indeed and I think Lucy finds that hard to accept. Jago is devoted to Rivers, and he's quite capable of taking off for London so that he can act as a witness in court, even though he has made a statement. But that would put him in danger from

Dalby, who obviously still sees him as a threat. It could cause even more trouble for Rivers.'

'Maybe it would have been better if you had both stayed on until the trial is over. After all, it is just Dalby's word against Benedict's. At least that's how it seems.'

'I don't know. The law is so complicated. I wouldn't even try to understand the ins and outs of the matter. I just hope Rivers is exonerated and that he returns to Longfleet.'

Marianne gave her a searching look. 'Why do you always use his surname, Rose?'

'I don't know. I haven't thought about it.'

'Could it be that calling him Benedict might force you to acknowledge the truth?'

Rose looked away. 'I don't know what you mean.'

'Yes, you do. I know you so well, Rose. You have feelings for Benedict Rivers, only you won't admit it, even to yourself.'

'I wouldn't say feelings, exactly. I respect him and I like him – at least, sometimes I do. At other times I could cheerfully strangle him.' Rose pulled a face. 'On the other hand, I can't wait to see him again.'

'My point exactly,' Marianne said smugly.

'Is that love, Marianne? Do you feel like that about Tom?'

'I suppose so, in a way,' Marianne said, smiling. 'I know I am happier when I am with him than I am when he is not here. I want to spend the rest of my life with him and have his children. In fact, I can't wait until June when we get married. It's not too far off now, Rose.'

'Heavens, no. You're right it's only about two months away. Here I am, talking about me and my confused feelings and forgetting all about you and your wedding. I haven't chosen my gown yet.'

'I can help you there. It's been uppermost on my mind since I picked the design I like.' Marianne rose to her feet and went over to her sewing table. She produced a piece of paper, which she handed to Rose. 'I copied this from a ladies' magazine. I thought it would suit you. Miss Shackleton could run it up for you in a matter of days, so she said.'

Rose examined the drawing and smiled. 'Yes, it's very pretty. I'd better make an appointment with her. I suppose you've chosen the material?'

'I have. It's pink silk, the colour of the roses that grow round the front door. I thought that you and Emmie could carry posies of them as they will be out in time for the wedding.'

'Unless we get an icy blast of inclement weather and snow from the east,' Rose said, smiling.

'You know very well that is unlikely.' Marianne sighed. 'I know you are teasing me, Rose. But I am determined to keep calm. Nothing is going to spoil our wedding day. The sun will shine and everyone will be happy for us. All the horrid things that have been happening will be forgotten.'

'I'm sure you're right.' Rose folded the sheet of paper and tucked it into her reticule. 'From now on I command ill fate to leave us alone and then everything will be wonderful. Now I'd better go upstairs and sit with Mama for a while.'

'She's been a bit down recently, but I'm sure you can cheer her up. You know how it is, Rose. Sometimes we go on for weeks or even months when she is her old self, and then something happens to upset her.'

Rose nodded. 'I haven't forgotten. I'll show her the drawing you did and we can discuss my gown.'

'Perhaps you can persuade her to have a new outfit made for herself. At the moment she doesn't seem interested.'

'I will try.' Rose stood up and made a move to the door. 'It will take my mind off that wretched trial.'

Marianne picked up her mending. 'What will you do if Rivers loses the case against him, Rose?'

'I can't think about that now. It's just not possible.' Rose hurried from the room and headed upstairs.

That night Rose found it almost impossible to sleep. Despite her confident words, she was plagued with worry about the case against Rivers. She struggled with feelings that she had crushed and tried to ignore, but which had surfaced during her conversation with Marianne. The maelstrom of emotions had almost overcome her during a long conversation with her mother, who had shown a surprising amount of insight into the problems that beset Rose. Although her mother spent days, weeks and sometimes months isolated in her room, it amazed Rose to discover just how much Mama knew about what was going on downstairs. Her parting words had come as a shock and Rose found herself dwelling on them in the dark, cold early hours.

'Rose, take my advice, my dear,' Mama had said firmly. 'If you care deeply about that man, don't allow that chance to love and be loved slip away. Follow your heart.'

Eventually, after tossing and turning for an hour or more, Rose knew then what she must do. She threw off the coverlet and swung her legs over the side of the bed. Her bare feet touched the polished floorboards and made her shiver, but she stood up. If she dressed quickly and threw a few things into a valise she could leave the house while everyone slept. She checked to make sure she had money for the train fare. There was enough to get her to London – she would worry about the return fare later.

A quick look at the brass clock on the mantelshelf convinced her that she would be in time to catch the first train to London if she left now. It was a long walk, but if she stepped out briskly she could do it with time to spare.

It might be late spring but the nights were still chilly. However, Rose was oblivious to everything other than the need to reach the railway station. She walked quickly, ignoring the odd rustle in the hedgerows and the strangely human sound of cows coughing in the fields. An owl screeched as it flew overhead and somewhere in the distance the eerie howl of a dog fox made her shudder, but she kept going. Nothing was going to come between her and Rivers in his time of need. She might not be able to contribute anything to the defence, but at least she could sit in the public gallery and demonstrate her support for him.

Streaks of pale light in the east heralded the dawn as Rose climbed on board the London-bound train. At this early hour she was able to find an empty first-class compartment, although it was surprising how many passengers crowded into the third-class carriages. She recognised most of the travellers and acknowledged their astonished looks with smiles and nods, although she knew that word would fly round the town and reach the vicarage probably before Winnie had laid the table for breakfast. Marianne would understand and perhaps Mama also. It would be up to them to explain to Papa and Emily. As for Jago and Lucy, Rose had left a brief note on her dressing table. Jago might want to follow her but with luck he might even listen to his mother on this occasion. Lucy would most certainly put a stop to his desire to travel to London. For once Rose was not concerned about the feelings of others. All she could think of was seeing Rivers again and willing him to win in court.

The train was annoyingly slow, stopping at every station to drop off passengers and allow others to board. Rose was increasingly impatient and anxious. She did not want to arrive too late to watch the proceedings. However, when they arrived at Waterloo Bridge Station there was just enough time to take a cab to the law courts. The fare took most of Rose's money, but that was the least of her worries. Progress was so slow, due to heavy traffic. They were delayed even longer when an accident occurred and the cabby had to find another route. Rose could have cried with frustration but there was nothing she could do other than to sit and fume, willing all the carters, coachmen and cabbies to get out of the way.

By the time they drew up outside the law courts Rose knew she must have missed the trial. She ran into the building, but a clerk confirmed her fears, although he could not tell her the outcome. Rose stood in the middle of the marble hall, dazed and close to tears. Then, as she turned, she saw Rivers striding towards her.

'Rose! What are you doing here?'

She ran to him and he caught her in his arms, holding her so close that she could hardly breathe. However, he released her almost immediately.

'You're free, Rivers.'

He laughed, holding her at arm's length. 'You sound disappointed. Did you hope to see me marched off to the cells?'

'No, of course not. I wanted to sit in the public gallery and cheer you on. Well, not exactly cheer, but I needed you to know how much I cared.'

'You do?' Rivers gazed at her for a moment and then he glanced over her shoulder. 'Are you here on your own? Tell me you didn't travel to London by yourself, Rose?'

'I couldn't sleep for worrying. I had to do something.'

Rivers tightened his grip on her shoulders, but was prevented from saying anything when Will hurried up to them, his black gown flapping, and his wig slipping to one side. He smiled when he saw Rose.

'Has he told you the good news, Rose?'

Rose shot a sideways glance at Rivers, who had released her abruptly. 'No. I mean it's obvious that he won the case.'

'It was dismissed,' Rivers said, smiling grimly. 'A warrant for Dalby's arrest has been issued, as he didn't turn up in court.'

'I lost my chance to put forward a brilliant defence,' Will said, sighing. 'I could have made my name today, Rivers.'

'You'll make it defending someone more worthy than I.' Rivers took Rose by the hand. 'I should be very angry with you for placing yourself in jeopardy, but I suggest we go out and celebrate a successful end to this foolishness. Besides which, I'm starving. What about you, Rose?'

'I haven't had anything to eat since last night. I am very hungry now.'

'You'll accompany us, Will?' Rivers turned to him with a smile.

'I can't, unfortunately. I have to go back to the office to write up a report for the senior partners in my chambers. Maybe this evening?'

Rivers nodded. 'I see you've brought a case with you, Rose. I don't suppose that Mrs Pilbeam will mind if you stay in Doughty Street tonight. She seems to have taken a liking to you.'

'I think she is lovely,' Rose said enthusiastically. 'I think we should all go out to dinner this evening, including your aunt, Will.'

'I'm sure she would be delighted.' Will straightened his wig. 'I have to change before I leave, but I will look forward to seeing you both tonight.' He walked away and was immediately accosted by one of his colleagues.

'That leaves just you and me,' Rivers said, smiling. 'I suggest we get something to eat before we go to Doughty Street. We'll have the real celebration tonight.' He proffered his arm.

Rose frowned. 'Just a minute, Rivers. If there is a warrant for Dalby's arrest, that means he is still at large. Do you think he might yet go after Jago?'

'Where is Jago now?'

'He's at Longfleet Hall with Lucy, but she's talking about returning to Ceylon to finalise the sale of her property.'

'He should be safe enough there. Do you know when my aunt intends to leave?'

'She said she would wait until after the verdict, but she won't know the result yet. In any case, she has to make the necessary arrangements and I imagine that might take time.'

'Does she intend to take Jago with her?'

'She wanted to, but he refused.'

'That sounds like Jago. He has a mind of his own.'

'Would you allow him to stay with you?'

'Of course, but I will have to work hard to persuade my aunt to change her mind. Anyway, Rose, we'll travel back to Abbotsford tomorrow, but in the meantime we will enjoy ourselves. How does that sound to you?'

She slipped her hand through the crook of his arm. 'It sounds wonderful. Everything has been so topsy-turvy, especially for the last few days, and I've been so worried about the court case.'

'You were worried about me?'

Rose shrugged. 'Among other things. Did you say something about finding a place to eat, Rivers? I feel quite faint from lack of nourishment.'

'Of course. How thoughtless of me, but I'm glad to know that you were worried about me.'

'Only a little,' Rose said defensively.

Mrs Pilbeam was delighted to see Rose again and more than happy to have her old room made ready for one more night. Moreover, she was all of a-flutter when Rivers invited her to dine with them that evening. She accepted and then said she had nothing smart enough to wear, which was Rose's cue to accompany her upstairs and go through Mrs

Pilbeam's considerable wardrobe. Having two sisters who also suffered moments of panic when faced with an unexpected invitation, Rose was able to keep Mrs Pilbeam calm enough to choose a suitable outfit. That accomplished, Rose went downstairs to join Rivers in the parlour. He was seated by the fire reading a copy of *The Times*, but he looked up and his warm smile went straight to her heart. She realised that she would have been devastated had the case gone against him and he had been given a custodial sentence. What had started out in the magistrates' court as an accusation of deception and fraud had somehow escalated into a criminal trial, and then suddenly it was over.

Rose went to sit in a chair opposite him. 'You must be relieved, Rivers.'

'I am, although I had complete faith in Will. He's going far as a barrister.'

'I can't wait to go home and tell everyone. They will be so relieved and we can look forward to Marianne's wedding without any worries. I suppose the police will catch Dalby.'

'Yes, eventually. He is sly, but he's not very clever. He relies on using his fortune to bribe his way out of difficulties if he cannot get there by sheer intimidation. Much good will the money do him in prison.'

'You know that he has taken the money that his father left to Lucy, as well as the property?'

'Yes, and now that my case is settled I will suggest that she uses Will to act for her against Dalby.'

'If Dalby is caught and convicted it should be straightforward, shouldn't it?'

'One would think so, but as we've said before, the law is complicated. However, if Lucy clinches the sale of the tea plantation she will be financially independent, although perhaps not quite in the style to which she was accustomed.'

Rose smiled. 'One of the reasons that Jago doesn't wish to go to Ceylon is that he thinks his mother has a gentleman friend who might become important in her life. I don't think he relishes the idea of another stepfather.'

'Who can blame him? I'm more than happy to be his guardian, should his mother remarry, and there's Blanche de Fontenay. She would welcome him with open arms if he decides to return to Provence.'

'It's such a shame that Le Fleuve was razed to the ground in that awful fire. I really loved the old house. It would have been wonderful to be there in the summer and see the fields of lavender and the olive trees heavy with the fruit, not to mention the grapes ripe and ready to pick.'

Rivers folded the newspaper and set it aside. 'Actually, I am planning to return there very soon, Rose. I need to sort out the business and set everything straight as we left in such a hurry.'

Rose stared at him aghast. 'You're going away again? Will you be home in time for Marianne's wedding?'

'I hope so. I will certainly do my best, if it means so much to you.'

'It really does. But what about Jago? Will you leave him at Longfleet, or will you take him with you to Provence?'

'That's for him to decide. I think the boy is tired of other people making plans for him. He's quite capable of choosing his own destiny. He might change his mind and accompany his mother to Ceylon, or perhaps he would rather come to France with me. I'll leave it to him.'

It all happened so quickly. Lucy had been busy contacting people she knew from when she lived in Ceylon and she found a couple who were travelling to Colombo in less than a fortnight's time. She had been unsuccessful in persuading Jago to accompany her and so she booked her passage and had left alone. Rivers also wasted no time in making arrangements for himself and Jago to travel to Le Fleuve. They sailed on the *Sadie Lee* with Rose waving them off from the quay wall.

There was nothing left for her to do other than return home and throw herself into helping Marianne with her wedding plans. However, Lady Buckingham, as always, had taken it upon herself to organise everything. She had booked several marquees to be erected on the lawns at The Manor. She had ordered the invitations and had given Marianne a list of the guests whom she had selected to attend the wedding. It was left to Marianne and Rose to add their choice of guests as well as to write the invitations and take them to the village post office.

The one area where Lady Buckingham had no say at all was in the choice of the wedding gown, and the outfits for the maid of honour and the bridesmaid. Marianne did not wish to have any more attendants, although Winnie Banks's youngest sister was chosen to be the flower girl. Winnie was bubbling over with excitement at the honour bestowed on her family and she promised to stay up all night before the wedding, collecting rose petals and scented herbs for little Beth to strew in the newlyweds' path.

Rose, Marianne and Emily spent a good deal of time visiting Miss Shackleton, the dressmaker in Dorchester, although Grace accompanied them only once. She was so exhausted after the outing that she spent the next few days in bed. After that, Miss Shackleton was very obliging and she visited the vicarage for Grace's subsequent fittings.

Every morning after breakfast, Rose waited eagerly for the postman to arrive with replies to the invitations, although secretly she was hoping to receive a letter from Rivers, or a few words from Jago. However, none came and she had to fight off feelings of despondency. She had a sneaking suspicion that they had settled into life at Le Fleuve. Even if the old house was uninhabitable, there were cottages available, which used to house itinerant seasonal workers. Rose supposed they were too busy to think of keeping her up to date with their progress. She would surely have heard if Dalby had dared to show his face. She could only hope that he had gone into hiding and they would never hear of him again. Rose decided to concentrate on her family and the wedding. She would put all thoughts of Rivers, Jago and Le Fleuve out of her mind, since they had obviously forgotten her.

It might have been the sensible thing to do, but Rose was fully aware that being sensible like Marianne was not in her nature. She was impulsive, impatient and had it been in her power she would have packed her bags and travelled on her own to Provence. Rivers had led her to believe that he cared for her, but she was beginning to think that he had forgotten her existence. If that was the case, she was better off on her own. She forced herself to concentrate on the present, putting all that had happened in the past firmly behind her. She would not think of Rivers; she would not!

The only member of the family who seemed to understand Rose's problem was Marianne. Emily spent most of her time at The Manor, ostensibly helping Lady Buckingham with preparations as the wedding drew closer, but Rose knew that Emily had taken a fancy to Tom's cousin, Peter Buckingham, who was close to Emily in age. He was staying at The Manor while his parents were travelling on the Continent. Marianne thought it very amusing.

'Wouldn't it be funny if Emmie married Peter? Later on, of course, when she is much older.'

'I would be the odd one out,' Rose said smiling as she sorted through the acceptances. 'I think we have them all now, Marianne. Do you want to give the list to your future mother-in-law?'

Marianne pulled a face. 'Do you know how scary that sounds? I love Tom with all my heart, but I must confess I am rather nervous about living at The Manor, under the thumb of Lady Buckingham.'

Rose laughed. 'She won't live for ever. When she dies you will be lady of the manor.'

'Don't say things like that, Rose.' Marianne glanced over her shoulder as if expecting someone to be hovering in the background, ready to tell their father what Rose had said.

'I know, I'll go to hell for such wicked thoughts.' Rose put the pen down and flexed her fingers. 'I've no idea who half these people are, have you?'

'No, but I expect I will get to know them quite soon. I will be there behind Tom and his mother when receiving guests. You know how much Lady Buckingham likes to entertain. And please don't talk about her passing on again. I know I will burst into laughter next time I see her if I think of her early demise.' Marianne shook her head. 'You've put the wicked thought in my head and I'm afraid it will stay there.'

'Nonsense, Minnie. You will be the perfect daughter-in-law. It's just fortunate for Tom that he chose you instead of me. I would probably end up locked in the attic so that I didn't make some dreadful *faux pas*.'

'You are so silly, Rose. But you always make me laugh.' Marianne picked up the guest list and studied it. 'There's no mention of Benedict Rivers. Is he coming?'

'I don't know. I haven't heard from him or from Jago.'

'That's too bad of him, Rose. His feelings for you were so obvious.'

'He must have met someone else, or perhaps he has fallen in love with Blanche de Fontenay. She is really beautiful, and she's nice, too. A lethal combination, I fear.'

'I'm sure that's not true. You are worrying about nothing.'

'Am I? He promised to come home for the wedding and it's only two weeks away now, with not a word from him.'

'Then there must be a good reason for his silence. Perhaps he has written to you and the letters have gone astray. He might be on the way home as we speak.'

Rose shook her head. 'I walked to Longfleet Hall yesterday and no one there has heard from him. He would have sent word to them if he was due to return soon.'

'There, that proves my point. If no one has heard from him it means that something has gone awry. It isn't personal to you.'

Rose piled up the remaining replies to the invitations and tied them with a ribbon. 'There, you can keep these and stow them away until you are an old lady and wish to remember your special day.'

'Don't be sad, Rose. You'll have your special day, too.'

'Really? I'm finished with men, Marianne. I will remain a spinster and devote my life to good work.' Rose stood up, glaring at her sister. 'Don't you dare laugh. I am going for a long walk.'

She left the room, ignoring Marianne's protests. Suddenly the vicarage and the whole of Abbotsford seemed too small to hold her. Rose grabbed a shawl on the way out and set off for the village.

The noonday sun beat down on her bare head as she strode out, heading automatically for the quay. The whole village seemed to be slumbering in the summer heat and there were very few people about. Rose reached the quay and came to a sudden halt. There, at anchor in the bay, was the *Sadie Lee*, and a familiar figure leaped ashore from the rowing boat as it grated against the stone steps.

Chapter Twenty-Five

Jackson looked up, grinned and tipped his cap. 'Good afternoon, Miss Rose.'

'Good afternoon, Jackson. It's good to see you again.' Rose gazed at the *Sadie Lee* as she sat serenely at anchor. 'Is Mr Rivers on board?'

Jackson shook his head. 'No, miss. I've got orders to stand by ready to bring him and young Jago back to Abbotsford, but so far no word from him. Maybe he's decided to stay on in France for a while.'

'Have you got business ashore?'

'Just going to order supplies.'

'I see.' Rose tried hard to conceal her disappointment. 'Do you expect to receive orders soon?'

'Who can say, miss? We'll leave for Cherbourg tomorrow at the turn of the tide. Are you thinking of coming with us?'

He seemed to have read her thoughts. Rose hesitated before answering and then she nodded. 'I might. I haven't heard from Mr Rivers for a while. When did you last see him, Jackson?'

'About two weeks ago, miss. We landed some cargo that he had ordered, and hired carts to take it from the port to Le Fleuve. We'll be leaving tomorrow to collect a cargo from Cherbourg and deliver it to Rotterdam. The *Sadie Lee* has to earn her keep.'

'I understand.' Rose managed a smile. 'Well, it's good to see you, Jackson. I mustn't hold you up.'

'Thank you, miss. Any time you want to travel on board the *Sadie Lee*, just let me know. You're quite a favourite with the crew. If you change your mind we sail mid-morning tomorrow.'

'Thank you. I'll remember that.'

With one last glance at the ship bobbing gently on the calm waters, Rose turned away and started walking homewards. Jackson's invitation to her to sail with them on the *Sadie Lee* was as tempting as it was ridiculous. Marianne's wedding was taking place in less than three weeks. Everything was arranged, or at least everything over which they had any control was finalised. Rose could not speak for Lady Buckingham, but she did not doubt her ladyship's competence when it came to organising such an event. As Rose trudged up the hill to the vicarage, she found herself longing to get away, and part of the yearning was to see Rivers again. He had allowed her to think that he cared, but his actions were the opposite of those of a man in love. She was suddenly overcome with anger. He had toyed with her affection and then he had left the country. It was the action of a cad and a coward. She quickened her pace. It would serve him right if she travelled to Provence and faced him with the truth. But when she arrived home she put all such thoughts out of her mind. This was Marianne's time and neither she nor anyone else would be allowed to cast a shadow over the proceedings.

Rose went down to breakfast next morning wearing her travelling outfit. She had left a small valise in the entrance hall, packed with a few changes of clothes she might need for the coming days.

Marianne, who had taken to rising early, was already seated at the table. She looked up but her smile of welcome faded. 'Rose. Please tell me you aren't thinking of chasing after Rivers.'

'I have to settle this one way or another, Minnie. I can't allow him to let me think that he loves me and then disappear for weeks on end. I won't allow him to put a blight on your wedding day either.'

'You said that the *Sadie Lee* was at anchor, but I didn't think you would be mad enough to travel to Provence on your own. What will I do if you are not back in time to be my maid of honour?'

'Don't worry about that, Minnie. I wouldn't miss it for the world. I am going to Le Fleuve and nothing

438

is going to stop me. I want him to say it to my face if he has changed his mind. I know how much he loves that old house, even though it was razed to the ground. If I were jealous, which I am not, it would be of Le Fleuve.'

'I don't suppose there is anything I can say that will change your mind. I mean, never mind your good name, or the dangers you could face, are you sure that seeking him out is the best way to go about a matter of the heart?'

'I don't know, but it seems as if providence has stepped in with the *Sadie Lee* on hand. I met Jackson on the quay wall and he offered me free passage to Cherbourg. It won't be the first time I have made the journey.'

'But not on your own. It's a terrible risk, Rose.'

'I can't sit here and wait patiently for Rivers to make up his mind. If he is more in love with his property in France than with me, I can accept that, but I must know. If I wait until he returns I will never know whether he has come back to follow his heart or out of duty. I don't want that sort of relationship, Marianne. I need a man who loves me as much as I love him.'

'You love him?'

Rose snatched a piece of toast that lay untouched on Marianne's plate. 'Yes, for my sins I do. I love the wretched man and I need to know why he has deserted me when I need him to be here.' Rose took a bite of the buttered toast.

'I understand, or I think I do. But please sit down and have some breakfast before you leave. And what do I tell Mama? Are you going to speak to Papa before you go?'

Rose swallowed and shook her head. 'No. It's better coming from you for both of them. You will put it tactfully and without undue drama.'

'But, Rose, have you got enough money for the journey?' Marianne reached for her reticule and opened it. She took out a silk purse and laid it on the table. 'Take this. It's all that I have but it will make me feel better if you have it.'

'I can't take your money,' Rose said hastily. 'You will need this yourself.'

'Tom has more than enough for both of us. I have everything I want, Rose. You might be glad of a few extra pennies when you are travelling. Please take it.'

Reluctantly Rose picked up the purse. She opened it and tipped the gold sovereigns onto the palm of her hand. 'This is too much. Where did you get such a lot of money?'

'I've been saving for years. It was to be for my trousseau, but as I said, I have everything that I want. Take it and please don't argue. You can pay me back later, if you insist.'

'I do, and I will.' Rose slipped the purse into her own reticule. 'You are the best of sisters, Minnie, and I love you. But I really must go now and hope that Jackson is still ashore.'

Marianne rose to her feet and hurried round the

table to embrace Rose. 'Please be careful. Look after yourself, Rose.'

'I will and I'll be back in time for your big day, Minnie. That is a promise.' Rose gathered up her belongings and hurried from the room.

As luck would have it, Rose found Jackson in the baker's shop, filling a large basket with rolls and loaves of crusty bread. He smiled when he saw the valise.

'I thought you'd accept the invitation, miss. I told them to make a cabin ready for you.'

'Why were you so sure?' Rose asked in a low voice, hoping that Ned Guppy could not hear.

Jackson laid money on the counter and opened the shop door. 'After you, miss.'

Rose waited until they were heading towards the quay. 'How did you know, Jackson?'

'Call it intuition, miss. Some things are meant to be.'

On board ship Rose received a warm welcome from the crew. None of them seemed to think it odd that a young woman had chosen to travel alone, and that boosted her confidence. Any doubts she had about the journey began to dissipate the moment she felt a change in the movement of the ship. She knew then that they had raised the anchor and were on their way to Cherbourg. A little after mid-morning, driven by hunger, Rose made her way to the saloon where she found Jackson talking earnestly to one of the crew.

'You'd best bring him here, Smith,' Jackson said, dismissing the man with a wave of his hand.

'Aye, aye, sir.' The seaman shot a wary glance at Rose as he hurried from the saloon.

'We have another passenger, Miss Rose.' Jackson cleared his throat nervously. 'An unexpected one at that.'

'Do I know him? I assume it is a gentleman.'

'It is a male person, miss. I hesitate to call him a gentleman, although that's the title he gives himself. Apparently, he was rowed out to the ship last night while I was ashore. He convinced the bos'n that I had agreed to take him to Cherbourg.'

'Who is this person, Jackson?' Rose turned her head at the sound of the door opening and found herself face to face with none other than Montague Dalby.

'You?'

'It's too long since we last met, Rose.' Dalby's smile did not reach his eyes, which were cold as agates. 'You did not expect to see me again.'

Rose turned to Jackson. 'We should go back to Abbotsford at once, Jackson. This man is wanted by the police.'

'I can't do that, miss. We have to be in Cherbourg by tomorrow morning. We'll give him up to the French authorities.'

Dalby shook his head. 'I don't think you'll do that. I will take Miss Northwood with me and you

442

wouldn't want anything to happen to her. It will be like old times, Rose. Do you remember Paris?'

Rose faced him furiously. 'It is something I will never forget, but if you think I will allow you to use me in that way you are quite wrong.'

'We'll see about that. In the meantime, I'm hungry.' Dalby slumped down on a seat at the table. 'Bring food, Mr Mate. For the lady, too. We will have a civilised luncheon together.'

Jackson's expression was grim as he nodded and hurried from the saloon.

'Sit down, Rose. I don't wish to have neck ache from looking up at you.' Dalby sat back in his chair, grinning smugly. 'It will be easier if you go along with my plan, my dear. I am going to travel through France and buy a passage on a ship that will take me back to Ceylon. I intend to run my late father's plantation myself from now on. At least until the English authorities have lost interest in me.'

'You won't get away with this,' Rose said furiously. 'You deserve to be sentenced to a very long term in prison for what you've done.' Rose slammed out of the saloon, almost colliding with Jackson. 'That man is a criminal, Jackson. You must inform the French police the moment we land in Cherbourg.'

'Aye, miss. That's what I intend to do.'

'Good, and in the meantime I'll take all my meals in my cabin. I'll stay there until we land tomorrow. I refuse to have anything to do with that dreadful man.'

'I understand, miss. Believe me, I had nothing to do with allowing him to come on board. We'd set sail before his presence was drawn to my attention.'

Rose laid her hand on his sleeve. She could see that Jackson was distressed. 'It isn't your fault. He is calculating and utterly without conscience, as I discovered months ago. He is also dangerous, so handle him carefully. Don't risk your crew or the ship because of him.'

'Thank you, miss. I don't know what Mr Rivers will say when he finds out I've let him down.'

'He'll be delighted to learn that Dalby is in the hands of the French police, so please don't worry, Jackson.' Rose left him standing outside the saloon and she went straight to her cabin, locking the door behind her. It was the worst start to her journey that she could have imagined, but she was not going to allow Dalby to get the better of her. She could only hope that the French authorities would cooperate with the police at home and lock Dalby up so that he could not do any more harm.

Next morning she was awakened early by someone knocking on the door.

'Who's there?'

'It's the cook, miss. I brought your breakfast. We'll be landing in half an hour or so.'

Still drugged with sleep, Rose got up and opened the door, but before she had a chance to shout for help she was lifted off her feet and flung back on the bunk.

Dalby stood over her. 'Get dressed and pack your bag. We're leaving now.'

'We're still at sea,' Rose protested. 'I can feel the deck moving.'

'We're almost in port so we need to act quickly. You are coming with me.'

'No.' Rose shook her head. 'You can't make me.'

'Put your clothes on or I will throw you overboard in your nightgown and the French fishermen will think they've caught a mermaid.'

Rose knew him well enough to be convinced that he would carry out his threat. She pulled a travelling costume over her chemise and slipped her feet into her boots.

'You won't get away with this.'

'And you won't get across France without an escort. You must be crazed with love for Rivers to think you could do it alone.'

'Shut up. You don't know what you're talking about.'

Dalby reached down and grabbed her arm, twisting it painfully until she yelped.

'Now walk with me. Keep quiet or I will take pleasure in breaking a few of your bones. We haven't much time.'

Rose attempted to kick his shin but he jerked her arm and the pain was so intense that she felt faint. Almost before she knew it they were on deck and he lifted her over the side with surprising strength. Despite her past experiences of climbing down the rope ladder, her arm ached and she felt dizzy, but she managed to reach the waiting boat. Someone grabbed her and pushed her down on the seat while Dalby climbed down to join them. He clamped his hand over her mouth as she opened it to cry for help and he barked instructions in French at the man holding the oars. The boat slid away from the *Sadie Lee*, gliding over the water with barely a splash. It was still dark, with just a hint of light in the sky to the east.

After a while Rose gave up trying to free herself, and Dalby's tight grasp on her relaxed a little. She could see the lights from the port growing closer and Dalby bent his head so that his lips were close to her ear.

'Make a sound and I'll silence you for ever. Don't imagine that I am bluffing, Rose Northwood. From now on you and I are travelling together. A couple will attract less attention than a single man. Behave yourself, and by tomorrow evening you should be in Provence and I will be on my way to Marseilles.'

There was nothing that Rose could do other than give in. She could see that the crew member who was rowing them to shore had probably been paid for ignoring her plight, and she would have to wait for a chance to escape from Dalby once they were on dry land. She stopped struggling and sat quietly until they reached the quay wall, where Dalby grabbed her by the arm and propelled her up the slimy stone steps. He guided her through the busy dockyard, where he hailed a fiacre, bundling her unceremoniously in with a warning against attempting to escape while he gave the cabby instructions. He climbed in beside her and shut the door.

'Don't be scared, Rose. That was all an act to make people think I was abducting you, but now that little drama is ended I can speak easily.'

She clutched the side of the seat as the fiacre jerked into motion. 'What are you talking about, Dalby? You dragged me off the ship and threatened to kill me.'

'Had I tried to persuade you to come with me I knew it would have been a waste of time, but I need you as much as you have need of me.' Dalby leaned back in his seat. 'I know what you think of me, with complete justification, but in this instance I am attempting to atone in my own way. You cannot travel all the way to Le Fleuve on your own. It would be madness and asking for trouble. I, on the other hand, am a wanted man, but the gendarmerie will not be looking for a couple. This trip benefits both of us.'

'You manhandled and threatened me, and now you expect me to help you to evade the law?'

Dalby shrugged and smiled. 'Why not? What have you got to lose? You get to your destination safely, and so do I.'

Rose stared at him in disbelief. This was a completely different Dalby from the one she thought she knew. He was actually making sense and his whole personality seemed to have changed. However, it could just be an act. 'Why pick me? Couldn't you hire someone to accompany you?'

'Maybe I want you to know that I am not all bad. I've done many things of which I am not proud, but I like you, Rose. Had we met under different circumstances I think we might have been friends.'

'I could never forgive you for what you've done to Jago.'

'I agree. That was unforgivable, but I didn't know he was the Frenchwoman's offspring and that Guy Colbert was his father. Believe it or not, Guy was my friend. Perhaps he will join me one day in Ceylon.'

'Is that where you are going now?'

'It is, only I chose a roundabout route to put off the police. I won't be able to return to England or France, come to that. But it doesn't matter. I will be quite happy living in the plantation house. Help me now and you will never see me again.'

Rose thought quickly. 'Your stepmother is already on her way to Ceylon. She plans to sell the tea plantation she inherited from her first husband. Will you promise not to contact your stepmother or Jago in the future?'

He made a show of crossing his heart. 'I promise. Have we got a deal, Rose?'

'I can't believe I'm saying this, but yes, we have.'

The journey was long, involving several changes of train and finally a carriage ride. They travelled for the most part in silence, speaking to each other only when necessary, but Dalby kept to his word and he insisted on seeing Rose safely to Le Fleuve. They parted outside the gates and he bent down to brush her cheek with a hint of a kiss.

'Rivers doesn't know what a lucky man he is, Rose. If he doesn't make you happy there would be a warm welcome for you in Ceylon.'

'Thank you, Dalby, but I don't think that's likely. I never thought I'd say this, but I hope you get there safely.'

Rose left him standing outside the gates as she walked slowly towards the farmhouse. She could scarcely believe that she was here but she was suddenly nervous and unsure of her welcome. The house was hidden by trees and flowering shrubs and the air was heavy with the scent of lavender growing in the fields, together with the aroma of the wild herbs, crushed under foot as they tumbled from the verges. As Rose reached the curve of the gravel drive she steeled herself to see the blackened ruin, but the sound of running feet made her turn her head and Jago raced up to her. He gave her a clumsy hug, causing her to drop her valise.

'Rose, I can't believe it. What are you doing here?' He held her at arm's length. 'Why did you travel all this way on your own?'

Close behind him, Rose could see Rivers striding towards them and her heartbeat quickened. She was momentarily lost for words.

'Rose! What in heaven's name are you doing here?' Rivers pushed Jago aside. 'How did you get here?'

Her response was lost as he wrapped her in a warm embrace, kissing her until she was too breathless to speak. He released her at last and slipped his arm around her waist.

'Jago, bring Rose's valise. We'll show her what we've been doing all this time.' Rivers glanced at Rose, smiling. 'I can't believe that you made the journey here on your own. That was incredibly dangerous and foolish, but I am so glad to see you, Rose.'

Jago picked up the case and dusted it off. 'We were planning on coming home next week. Did you think we'd deserted you?'

Still dazed by their welcome, Rose shook her head. 'No, well, I wasn't sure if you had remembered Marianne's wedding.'

'Of course we did. More importantly, I have something to show you, Rose.' Rivers guided her along the curve in the gravel drive, which opened out suddenly, giving a full view of the old farmhouse. It looked as it must have done all those years ago when it was newly built. The walls were glowing with a blush of pink and the shutters were painted a luscious shade of green. Large terracotta pots had been placed at intervals filled with scarlet geraniums vying for attention with white moon daisies and trailing ivy.

'It's amazing,' Rose breathed softly. 'It looks as if there has never been a fire.'

Rivers beamed at her. 'That's exactly why we've worked so hard, my darling.'

The term of endearment was not lost on Rose and she gazed at him in surprise. 'You always loved this place, Rivers.'

'And so do you, which was why I wanted to have it rebuilt exactly as it was.'

Jago bounded on ahead, but the door opened and Blanche de Fontenay stepped out to greet them. Rose experienced a sudden sharp pang of what could only be jealousy. Had Rivers done all this with the beautiful Blanche in mind? He had known her for a very long time and they had made no secret of their friendship. However, Blanche obviously had no such reservations and she greeted Rose with a warm smile.

'What a lovely surprise, Rose.' She looked round, eyebrows raised. 'Where are the others? You surely didn't travel on your own?'

'You won't believe it when I tell you,' Rose said warily. She did not want to spoil the moment by mentioning Dalby's name, although she knew she would have to divulge it sooner or later.

'Never mind that now.' Blanche ushered them into the entrance hall. 'I've been helping Benedict with furnishing the farmhouse. I tried to remember exactly what was here, so I hope you approve, Rose.'

'I'm sure I will.' Rose gazed round, too stunned to take in all the small details that Blanche had included.

She seemed to have remembered more about the old house than Rose could bring to mind.

'I have some business to finalise,' Rivers said cheerfully. 'But I'll see you at dinner, Rose. Tomorrow I'll take you on a tour of the estate. It's all looking at its very best at this time of the year.'

Blanche headed for the staircase. 'Come with me, Rose. I'll show you to your room. The redecorations upstairs are not yet completed so it's not the room you had previously, but I think you'll like it. Jago, will you bring Rose's case?'

She ascended the stairs with such an air of confidence that Rose's heart sank. Perhaps Rivers had done all this for Blanche. Maybe it was a mistake to have arrived unannounced. She followed Blanche with a feeling of foreboding.

Chapter Twenty-Six

The room that Blanche showed Rose was situated at the front of the house. It was much larger than her old bedchamber, with three tall windows shedding light on the new carpet in pretty pastel shades. The huge four-poster bed was draped in white lace with a quilted pink satin coverlet and matching pillow shams. The rest of the furniture was in the Italian style, painted white with the ornate decorations picked out in gold.

'It's a room fit for a princess, is it not?' Blanche smiled as she stroked the coverlet.

'It's beautiful and far too grand for me,' Rose said nervously. 'Are you sure this is for me?'

'Of course it is. Rivers chose the furnishings himself. You would disappoint him if you wanted something different.'

Rose was not convinced, but she did not want to seem ungrateful. After all, she would only be staying for a couple of nights and then they would have to leave for home. Marianne's wedding was of the utmost importance.

'My sisters would be green with envy,' Rose said, smiling. 'It really is a delightful room.'

'I'm so glad you approve. Anyway, I'll go downstairs and tell Cook there will be two for dinner tonight. I'll take Jago home with me and then you and Benedict can dine alone.'

Blanche left the room before Rose had a chance to say anything. She turned her attention to unpacking the few belongings she had brought with her. However, she could not rid herself of a nagging feeling that there was something between Blanche and Rivers. His kiss had said otherwise, but on the other hand it could have been motivated by guilt. Perhaps his time at Le Fleuve, with Blanche helping to renovate the house, had brought back memories of their youthful involvement. It had never been acknowledged, but Rose suspected that Rivers had been fond of Blanche, although her affair with Colbert had put an end to that relationship.

Rose put her clothes away and went downstairs to find Blanche in the drawing room. There was no sign of Rivers.

'I've just sent for coffee,' Blanche said, smiling. 'Angeline has returned to work here.'

'Jago always got on well with her.'

'She's a good girl, but talks rather a lot.'

Rose glanced over her shoulder and greeted

Angeline with a smile as she entered carrying a tray of coffee. 'It's nice to see you again, Angeline.'

Angeline bobbed a curtsey. 'Thank you, Mademoiselle.'

'What happened to Madame Laurent?' Rose asked, knowing that Angeline would have the answer.

'She left the village, Mademoiselle. Gone to live with her sister, they say.'

'Thank you, Angeline,' Blanche said hastily. 'That will be all for now.'

Angeline took her time leaving the room, dragging her feet as if hoping to overhear something of interest.

Blanche shook her head. 'That girl is a terrible gossip, but she works reasonably hard and she gets on well with the new cook, who is proving her worth.'

'I'm surprised that Madame Laurent did not get arrested for setting fire to the place.'

'It was supposed to have been an accident, and she's far away now. She can't cause any more trouble for the family.' Blanche handed Rose a cup of coffee.

'Thank you.' Rose put the cup aside to cool down. 'Are you and Jago getting along well, Blanche? He's a lovely boy and he's had such a hard time.'

'He's everything I could wish for in a son, but I am only too well aware that Lucy raised him and he loves her. I can't get back the lost years, but I can be a good friend to him and he understands that. He's agreed to spend the rest of the summer with me, after your sister's wedding, of course.'

'That's wonderful. He certainly looks happy.'

'Jago told me that he would like to spend Christmas at Longfleet Hall so that he can visit your family at the vicarage. He said that your mama has taken a liking to him and he hoped his presence might comfort her at Christmas. I hope you don't mind that we discussed it.'

'Of course not. That's a lovely idea. Mama finds it so hard to cope at that time of year. Jago's presence might make all the difference and we could start celebrating Christmas again.'

'That's what he hoped might happen. I think the terrible treatment he suffered and the way you all looked after him during his illness has really left an impression on him and made him much more sensitive to other people's problems.'

'He is like one of the family. We all love him.'

'And Benedict?' Blanche sipped her coffee. 'How do you feel about him, if you don't mind me asking?'

'I, well, I . . . it's hard to explain.'

Blanche put her cup down and leaned forward, gazing at Rose. 'It's obvious that you two love each other. I say this as an old friend of the family.'

'I thought perhaps—' Rose broke off, once again at a loss for words.

'I've been helping Benedict to put the old place to rights, Rose, nothing more. And, of course, I've been here for Jago. Benedict has a special reason for everything he's done, but it's not my place to tell you.' Blanche looked up as Jago breezed into the drawing room.

'When do you want to leave, Ma?' Jago gave her a cheeky grin.

'We'll go as soon as you're ready,' Blanche said equably. 'Send for the carriage, please, Jago. We'll be home in time for dinner.'

'I'll do that right away, but I'll be back tomorrow, Rose. You can tell me everything that's been going on at home.' Jago left before Rose had a chance to respond.

'He is just the same,' Rose said, laughing. 'We've missed him at home.'

'I'm so proud of him.' Blanche sighed. 'I count myself very lucky that he accepts me without question.'

'You will come back to Abbotsford with us, won't you?' Rose asked eagerly. 'You did receive the wedding invitation?'

'I did, but I wasn't sure if it would embarrass Lucy. The poor woman has been through enough.'

'She left for Ceylon some time ago and she won't be back in time for Marianne's wedding, if at all. I think she has her eye set on husband number three. Lucy isn't the sort of woman who enjoys being on her own.'

'In that case, yes, I will come with you. I suppose I can stay at Longfleet Hall with Jago.'

'I'm sure you can. It's a huge house.'

'I look forward to seeing it.' Blanche rose to her feet. 'That sounds like my carriage outside. I'll see you again very soon.' She kissed Rose on the cheek. 'It was brave of you to come all this way. I hope Benedict takes good care of you.'

'Thank you, Blanche.' Rose stood up and went to the window to watch Jago open the carriage door for his mother. She was about to turn away when she saw Rivers stroll up and exchange a few words with Blanche. He waited until Jago had taken his seat before closing the door. He turned and headed into the house.

Rose was suddenly unsure of herself, but Blanche has assured her that there was nothing deeper than friendship between her and Benedict Rivers. It was all very confusing, but there was no doubting her own feelings as he walked into the drawing room. Rose had to restrain herself from rushing towards him and throwing her arms around his neck. However, his smile surrounded her in the warm glow, and the next moment she was in his arms. His kisses sent waves of happiness rippling throughout her whole body and she returned them with equal fervour. When eventually they sank down on the sofa, with his arms holding her close to his heart, she laid her head on his shoulder.

'I was afraid you might not want me, so I had to come here, if only to find out.'

'Didn't anyone at home try to prevent you from travelling alone?' Rivers shook his head and smiled. 'You don't have to answer that, my darling girl. I know nothing will stop you once you've made up your mind to something. But how did you get here?'

'You won't like this, Rivers,' Rose said warily. 'I asked Jackson to take me to Cherbourg, but Dalby was also on board the *Sadie Lee*.' She laid her finger on his lips as he was about to speak. 'He scared me at first, but he didn't hurt me.'

'If he had, I would hunt him down and make him pay,' Rivers said grimly. 'Where is he now?'

'He's on his way to Ceylon by some circuitous route so that the police can't trace him. He won't be coming back, Rivers, so good riddance, I say.'

'Rose, I love you more than life itself, but when are you going to stop calling me Rivers? My name is Benedict and I would dearly love to hear it on your lips.'

Rose turned her head to look into his eyes. 'I love you, too, Benedict.'

He kissed her again and she was lost in the warmth and comfort of his embrace. The world could stop now, for all Rose cared, just as long as she was in Benedict's arms. She murmured his name again and he covered her face with soft butterfly kisses.

'I'm never letting you out of my sight again, Rose. Tomorrow we set off for home. I have something very important to ask your papa.'

'You promised to show me round the estate tomorrow.'

'It will wait. The reason I've worked so hard to rebuild and renovate this old house is because it will be my wedding present to you, Rose.'

'Oh, Benedict. That's a lovely thought.'

He smiled. 'There's one condition, though.'

'And what is that?' Rose asked dreamily.

'That you say yes when I propose properly.'

'I promise to think about it,' Rose said laughing.

*   *   *

The *Sadie Lee* dropped anchor in the bay three days later. Marianne's wedding was only a few days away and Rose was eager to get home to help with the final preparations. Rivers insisted on accompanying her and he went straight to her father's study, leaving Rose to give Marianne and Emily a detailed account of her adventures. They were suitably impressed, although Emily admitted to being envious and flounced off upstairs to complain to her mother. Marianne smiled indulgently.

'She's such a child. Were we like that at her age, Rose?'

'Worse, I suspect. Anyway, I'd better go and tell Mama what really happened so that she doesn't get in a state because of what Emmie is probably telling her.'

'Has Benedict gone to ask Papa for your hand in marriage, Rose?'

'What put that into your head?' Rose stared at her sister in surprise. 'I never mentioned anything to give you that idea.'

Marianne laughed. 'Rose, you are as transparent as a glass of water. It's obvious that you two are in love, and I can't think of anything else that would make a man so eager to speak to Pa.'

'Well, as a matter of fact, yes,' Rose said reluctantly. 'You are right, as usual.'

'That's wonderful.' Marianne clapped her hands, her hazel eyes sparkling with pleasure. 'We can have a double wedding.'

'But you're getting married in a week's time.'

'Exactly so. All the arrangements are made and the guests invited. I expect there will be a few more added to the list, but I'm certain that Lady Buckingham will rise to the occasion. It will be so wonderful, Rose.'

'I suppose it would be convenient. But I would have to ask Benedict.'

'My goodness! Have I heard correctly? You just called him Benedict and you are prepared to ask for his opinion. That is what I call true love, Rose.'

'Now you're being silly, Marianne,' Rose said severely. 'I'm going upstairs to talk to Mama.'

However, she had just reached the door when it opened and Benedict hurried into the room, followed by Emily. He picked Rose up and swung her round.

'Your papa has no objections, my love. I am free to propose to you when I can find a suitably romantic moment.'

'I think we all know what her answer will be,' Marianne said, smiling. 'I think we should have a double wedding next week. What do you say, Benedict?'

'I think it is a wonderful idea. The sooner I make Rose Northwood my wife, the better, as far as I am concerned.' Rivers held Rose even more tightly. He kissed her on the lips. 'What do you say, my darling?'

Rose wriggled free from his grasp. 'I would have liked moonlight and the scent of roses to go with a beautiful diamond ring.'

Benedict released her and produced a small

shagreen-covered box from his breast pocket. He flicked it open and took out a gold ring set with a large diamond surrounded by sapphires. 'I had this made for you in Paris, where I stopped off on my way to Le Fleuve.' He went down on one knee. 'My dearest Rose, will you marry me?'

She nodded and smiled, suddenly finding it difficult to speak. 'Yes,' she murmured as he slipped the ring on her finger.

Benedict was on his feet in an instant and he kissed her tenderly. 'I can't bear to wait any longer, Rose. A double wedding it shall be. Unless you have any objections.'

Rose smiled dazedly. 'I think that sounds wonderful.'

Marianne frowned. 'I know it was my suggestion, but on second thoughts I doubt if Lady Buckingham will agree. You know how she loves to be in charge and this will upset her plans.'

'And there isn't time for the banns to be read,' Emily added hastily. 'But I do want to be maid of honour to both of you, and you haven't got a dress or a veil, Rose.'

Rivers had been listening to the conversation. 'First of all, you will be a wonderful maid of honour, Emily. Secondly, now that Mr Northwood has agreed to officiate at our nuptials I could go up to London to get a Special Licence. And I will buy you the most beautiful wedding gown and veil to be had, Rose.'

'I agree to the Special Licence, but I will wear the

gown made for me when I was to be Marianne's maid of honour. It's perfectly lovely and I'm sure someone will lend me a veil.' Rose smiled. 'If we don't do this now, it might take months to arrange our wedding. I don't want to wait.'

'Someone had better tell Lady Buckingham,' Emily said primly. 'You are all getting ahead of yourselves.'

'If it's all right with you, I'll accompany you to The Manor, Marianne.' Rivers held out his hand. 'It's the least I can do. I just hope that Lady Buckingham has forgotten about the court case and simply remembers my generous donation to the funds for the new church roof.'

'We'll find Tom and I'll speak to him first,' Marianne said eagerly. 'Tom can handle his mama.'

'Are you really sure you want to do this, Marianne?' Rose said earnestly. 'I don't want to spoil your big day.'

Marianne gave her a hug. 'It will be even more special. A double celebration, Rose. I love the idea.'

'Then I'll go upstairs and tell Mama. I don't want to upset her.' Rose sighed. 'She's been so much better recently.'

Marianne rose to her feet. 'I'm going to fetch my bonnet and shawl. Wait for me, Benedict. We'll go and brave the lioness in her den.'

'I'm coming, too.' Emily hurried after Marianne as she left the room.

Slightly dazed by the sudden turn of events, Rose made her way upstairs to her mother's bedroom.

Grace listened quietly while Rose explained the situation.

'Well, my dear,' Grace said calmly. 'You know that woman only too well. She won't agree, at least in the beginning.'

'It *is* her home, Mama.' Rose sighed. 'We are asking rather a lot of her. Perhaps it would be best to wait.'

Grace heaved herself from the chair. 'Hand me my cane, Rose. I am not going to allow Florence Buckingham to ruin my daughters' happiness.'

Alarmed, Rose reached for the ebony cane, but withheld it. 'No, really, Mama. We are grown women. There is no need for you to upset yourself.'

'Stop chattering, Rose. Give me my cane and find my best shawl for me, and my bonnet with the blue ribbons. I am going to call on Lady Buckingham. We will see who comes out best.'

There was nothing Rose could do or say that would prevent her mother from going downstairs, dressed for battle with her old adversary.

Marianne, Emily and Rivers had been about to leave the house, but they stood by helplessly.

'You, Mr Rivers,' Grace said in a commanding voice. 'Give me your arm, sir. We are going to The Manor.'

Rivers proffered his arm, smiling. 'Of course, ma'am. I can see where Rose gets her spirit and courage from.'

Grace shot him a sideways glance. 'Precisely so. But I warn you, Mr Rivers, if you do not treat my daughter properly you will have me to contend with. My husband is a saint – I am not.' She glanced at the rest of her family, who were apparently dumbstruck. 'Where is young Jago? I wish to see him soon.'

'Yes, Mama,' Marianne said faintly. 'Of course.'

'And tell Winnie to lay another place at table for dinner tonight. I think I might join you. We have a great deal to organise if you two girls are to be married in a week's time.'

There was nothing Rose could do other than to follow them.

The scene between Lady Buckingham and Grace Northwood left Rose open-mouthed. She had expected Mama to crumble beneath Lady Buckingham's scathing comments, but Grace was on the warpath. Rose began to realise that her mother was fearless and utterly ruthless where the welfare of her family was concerned. Without raising her voice, Grace started by putting Florence Buckingham firmly in her place. Having done that, Grace changed her tactics and took on a more persuasive stance, subtly underlining the advantages of having such a wealthy patron as landowner and successful businessman Mr Benedict Rivers linked to the Buckinghams by marriage.

'And, of course,' Grace said as a parting shot. 'Everyone of note will be invited to the wedding, plus a few other distinguished personages. Your reputation as the most celebrated hostess in the county will be confirmed by all who attend.'

'It would take a miracle to organise such an event in so short a space of time,' Lady Buckingham said doubtfully.

Grace smiled triumphantly. 'My husband deals in miracles all the time, Florence. I am certain we can work together to make this the double wedding of the century.' Grace glanced at a side table laden with cut-crystal decanters and glasses. 'Perhaps we should drink to our success? A small glass of sherry would be most welcome.'

'I think you've made the right decision, Mama,' Tom said firmly as he slipped Marianne's hand through the crook of his arm. 'It will be a day to go down in the history of Abbotsford, run by you two redoubtable ladies.'

'Hear, hear.' Rivers took Rose by the hand. 'I count myself to be the most fortunate man in the world.'

After a week of hectic activity, the morning of the wedding dawned fine with the promise of a beautiful midsummer day to follow. All the arrangements had been carried out with haste, but Rose had checked and checked again until she was satisfied that nothing could go wrong. Martha Huggins and Fanny Jones had decorated the church with beautiful arrangements of garden flowers, and the scent of roses, jasmine and lilies almost overcame the smell of musty hymnals. The invited guests were shown to their seats, and those who merely wanted to attend the service had to stand at the back of the nave, or wait outside in the shade of the yew trees. The whole village had turned out to watch the bridal procession and soon every pew in the church was filled to capacity.

Grace sat in the front pew, together with Blanche, who had arrived in Abbotsford two days before. Grace had taken an instant liking to Blanche and they were obviously at ease in each other's company. Rose had been worried that Mama might look upon Blanche as a fallen woman. However, she began to realise that her mother might have withdrawn from society temporarily after Felix's tragic death, but, for all that, she was a woman of many years' experience and understanding of the ways of the world. Rose knew that she herself still had a lot to learn about people.

Lady Buckingham and the rest of Tom's family sat on the opposite side of the aisle, and for once, Lady Buckingham seemed content to take second place. She smiled graciously at everyone and sat quietly beside her husband, who had managed to get home for the festivities.

When Rose and Marianne arrived at the church their bridegrooms were already at the altar. Looking incredibly handsome in their morning suits, Tom and Benedict stood on either side of the aisle. Jago was looking very grown up in his best suit, standing as Benedict's best man, and Tom had an old friend from medical school acting for him.

467

Rose and Marianne had opted to walk up the aisle together as their father was performing the double ceremony. Emily followed them as maid of honour and Winnie's little sister walked on ahead, strewing rose petals and herbs that had been freshly picked from the vicarage garden. Rose glanced round at the smiling faces as she and Marianne processed slowly to the sound of George Finch manfully attempting to play the 'Bridal Chorus' from *Lohengrin* on the organ. Marianne was a keen follower of fashion, and this piece had been played at the Princess Royal's wedding eighteen months previously. George was struggling a bit, but no one in the congregation seemed to notice as all eyes were on the two brides. If their father was anxious about officiating at his daughters' nuptials, he did not show any sign of nerves and the ceremony went smoothly, with a rustling of handkerchiefs and subdued sniffs from the ladies in the congregation.

Marianne and Tom spoke their vows first, and suddenly the nerves that had assailed Rose since earlier that day vanished as her father turned his attention to her and Benedict. She knew she would remember this day for the rest of her life. Everything was perfect, and within seconds she would be united in marriage with the man she adored, safe in the knowledge that her love was matched and returned. She laid her hand in Benedict's as he slipped the gold ring on her finger, and their eyes met in a smile that melted her heart.

Dilly Court

Discover more from
the nation's favourite author
of historical drama.

Sign up to Dilly Court's email
newsletter or follow her on Facebook
to hear about new books, exclusive
competitions and special offers

Join the community:
https://smarturl.it/DillyCourt

🌐 www.dillycourt.com   **f** dillycourtauthor

The Rockwood Chronicles

High upon the beautiful cliffs of the Devonshire coast, the once proud
Rockwood Castle is crumbling into ruin. Can the Carey family save
their home and their family before it's too late?

In this spellbinding six-book series, Dilly Court opens a door into Rockwood Castle -
chronicling the changing fortunes of the Carey family...

Book One: Fortune's Daughter

Abandoned by her parents, headstrong Rosalind must take
charge of the family. Until the appearance of dashing
Piers Blanchard threatens to ruin everything...

Book Two: Winter Wedding

Christmas is coming and Rockwood Castle has once again been thrown into
turmoil. As snowflakes fall, can Rosalind protect her beloved home?

Book Three: Runaway Widow

It is time for the youngest Carey sister, Patricia, to seek out her own
future. But without her family around her, will she lose her way?

Book Four: Sunday's Child

Taken in by the Carey family when she was a young girl,
Nancy Sunday has never known her true parentage.
Now eighteen years old, can she find out where she truly belongs?

Book Five: Snow Bride

The course of true love does not run straight for Nancy. Her life is filled with difficult
choices - but with Christmas around the corner, which path will she choose?

Book Six: Dolly's Dream

The eldest daughter at Rockwood, Dolly, dreams of a bigger life
beyond the castle walls. But with the family's future under threat,
will Dolly's heart lead her astray - or bring her home?

Turn the page for an exclusive Christmas Tree decoration pattern from *Quilts from the Country* by Stuart Hillard!

Stuart Hillard is one of the leading craft experts in the UK, Patron of the Quilters' Guild of the British Isles, fabric designer for The Craft Cotton Company, knitwear designer for Stylecraft Yarns and presenter on *Sewing Street TV* where his blend of expertise, fast, fun demos and achievable designs has made him a fan favourite. His career in crafting began over 30 years ago when he started making and designing quilts and teaching workshops, but it was his breakout appearance in the first series of Channel 4's *The Great British Sewing Bee* that really launched his career. Stuart has authored four bestselling sewing books: *Sew Fabulous; Use Scraps, Sew Blocks, Make 100 Quilts; Simple Shapes Stunning Quilts* and his fourth *Bags for Life* was voted best sewing book of 2021 in the Creative Book Awards.

For more information, visit:
www.stuarthillardmakes.com and www.pavilionbooks.com

Show off your homemade quilt by tagging:
@stuarthillardmakes and @pavilionbooks

Embroidered Tree Decorations

PROJECT SIZE
Finished decorations 4½" (11.4cm)
or 5" (12.7cm)

YOU WILL NEED
- 6 x 6" (15.2 x 15.2cm) white or cream solid fabric
- 6 x 12" (15.2 x 30.5cm) light fusible woven interfacing
- Red embroidery floss and needle
- 12–15" (30.5–38.1cm) red ric rac
- 6 x 13" (15.2 x 33cm) red print fabric
- Decorative button
- 9" (22.9cm) sisal string or fine ribbon
- 1 small sisal tassel
- Small quantity fibrefill or toy stuffing
- Glue stick
- Small wooden embroidery hoop (optional)

SKILLS USED
- Hand embroidery
- Faced appliqué
- Attaching buttons
- Making a pieced backing
- Closing a gap using a ladder stitch

Let's make the tree decorations!

1   Trace one of the snowflake designs onto your piece of white background fabric. It's easy to reduce or enlarge the design so it's a perfect fit. Each snowflake sits inside a corresponding circle. Don't mark or embroider that yet – you'll use it later for marking your backing.

2   Cut a 6 x 6" (15.2 x 15.2cm) piece of interfacing and iron to the wrong side of the background fabric.

3   Hoop the fabric if you wish, then work the snowflake design using a backstitch throughout and French knots for any dots.

4   Trace the circle from your chosen snowflake onto the remaining 6" x 6" (15.2 x 15.2cm) interfacing and then lay this on top of your embroidery.

Carefully sew around the circle, sewing directly on the drawn line and using a slightly smaller than normal stitch.

5   Cut a slit in the back of the interfacing and turn the embroidery through to the right side. Push the circular edge out very neatly and then iron in place to fuse the embroidery to the backing.

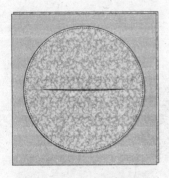

6   Use the glue stick to attach a piece of ric rac around the embroidery edge, tucking half the ric rac under the circle to create a wavy edge. The raw ends need to be tucked under neatly, but this is where you will sew a button so it doesn't have to be perfect! Baste your sisal tassel to the bottom of your embroidery.

7   Use a circle larger than your embroidery to cut out one piece of red print fabric. Pin your embroidery to the centre of this circle and topstitch the embroidery in place, sewing very close to the inner circle edge.

8   Fold the piece of sisal string in half and baste to the top of the embroidered front, with the loop hanging down.

9   Take the rest of the red print fabric and fold it in half, press, then cut through the fold to yield two rectangles. Sew the rectangles together again, leaving a 3" (7.6cm) gap in the centre (see next page). Layer this pieced backing with the embroidered front, right sides together, making sure that the loop and tassel are carefully tucked inside. Sew around the

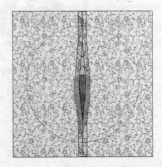

circle using a ¼" (6mm) seam allowance. Trim the backing fabric to within ¼" (6mm) of the seam and turn through to the right side. Press carefully.

10 Push a little stuffing or fibrefill inside the decoration to pad it out. Slip stitch the opening closed using small hand stitches.

11 Sew your button in place using small hand stitches.

12 Deck the halls!

If you prefer you can use backing fabric instead of interfacing to face the embroidery. Turn through and press, close the gap, and carefully glue then topstitch ric rac around the outer edge. Add a button or two for extra country charm!